It's not often that a historical romance so eloquently transports you to an earlier time period so precisely and allows the reader to be swept away in every detail without a second thought.

The tone of this beautifully written book, the pace of the adventurous story line, as well as the extremely lovable characters, were all perfectly in sync throughout the book. The reader can easily get lost in the story while truly feeling as if they are encapsulated in another time and place in history.

The language and dialogue fit the time period perfectly and the book is masterfully crafted, telling a rich tale of the beautiful and brave Amaryllis and her young siblings' travels while fleeing peril at their heels. It's easy to fall in love with each character introduced along the way, each telling their own story as well. Thoughtfully placed plot twists keep the reader guessing and the sweet love story of Reginald and Amaryllis will keep the reader rooting for them throughout the book.

Reginald's sister Selena is a particularly strong female character, while the young children and an adorable dog named Fate provide some light humor.

Each character, lovingly written, pulls the reader into the story, contributing to the elegance of this beautiful work of fiction. Love stories like this are timeless. If you are looking for a wonderful historical romance with a truly satisfying conclusion, I highly recommend Fate Takes A Hand.

**By Kristen Morgen, author of Behind The Glass,
Administrator of the FB group Behind the Book**

One of the prerequisites of the historical romance is the author's ability to nail historical references down in credible fashion. Even a cursory reading of *Fate Takes a Hand* reveals Martin put a great deal of research into shaping her fictional universe in a believable fashion and it adds a veneer of realism to *Fate Takes a Hand* that enhances the overall quality of the work.

Martin ascribes motivations to her characters that never stretch or snap the boundaries of disbelief. In many works of this type, characters often operate according to formula, but Martin avoids such traps through emotion and craft. Her characters are three-dimensional rather than serving as cardboard vehicles she employs for the express purpose of advancing plot and their responses are, at least in part, shaped by historical context rather than operating in a historical vacuum.

The novel moves at a good clip without ever rushing the action or plot development. Martin exercises consistent control over her prose throughout the entirety of the book and it is difficult to imagine any reader feeling cheated by the reading experience. Her descriptive powers are considerable without ever overwhelming the reader with self-indulgence. The ending of *Fate Takes a Hand* wraps up each strand of the plot in satisfying fashion and ends the book in conclusive fashion. Celia Martin's *Fate Takes a Hand* provides a reading experience any devotee of historical romantic fashion will enjoy and holds up under multiple readings.

REPROSPACE REVIEWS™

Fate Takes A Hand

To Andi —
Hope this is a
fun read for you.
Celia Martin

Celia Martin

KITSAP PUBLISHING

KITSAP
PUBLISHING

Fate Takes A Hand
First edition, published 2020

By Celia Martin

Book Layout: Tim Meikle, Reprospace

Copyright ©2020, Celia Martin

ISBN-13 Softcover: 978-1-952685-04-0

Published by Kitsap Publishing
P.O. Box 572
Poulsbo, WA 98370
www.KitsapPublishing.com

Also by Celia Martin

To Challenge Destiny

"Exquisite passion and breath-taking action! A historical romance feast!"
Curt Locklear - Laramie Award Winner

"Martin proves she has the vision and talent to make bygone times come alive for modern readers."
Anne Hollister, Professional Book Reviews

A Bewitching Dilemma

"A willful heroine cornered by a relentless foe and a dashing sea captain tormented by his past cast their lots against the tides of a history dark with treachery. A compelling read cover to cover."
Michael Donnelly - Author of False Harbor

With Every Breath I take
A love story laced with fun and surprises

Taking A Chance

"I've no hesitation to recommend this five-star read to new or old readers of historical fiction."
Trisha J. Kelly - multi-genre award-winning author of children and middle school books, and of cozy mysteries and crime thrillers.

"Celia Martin captures the complex landscape of people dealing with Puritanism which squelches the fun out of life for ordinary people. A great backdrop for the heroine to shine as she strives to marry the man she loves"
C.A. Asbrey - author of the 19th century murder mysteries, 'The Innocents' and of articles on history for magazines and periodicals.

Precarious Game of Hide and Seek

"Celia Martin's historical romance ranks as above average fare in the this genre.
REPROSPACE REVIEWS™

cmartinbooks.kitsappublishing.com

To all those with empathy in their hearts.
Where would we be without caring souls?

A Collection of Romantic Adventures

Follow the romantic adventures of the D'Arcy, Hayward, and Lotterby families, and their captivating friends in seventeenth century England and the American colonies. In Fate Takes A Hand, Amaryllis Bowdon, fearing her aunt means to kill her brother, two-year old Sir Charles, flees her home with her two young siblings. In her desperate flight, she never expected to be aided by Lady Selena D'Arcy and her much too handsome brother, Reginald D'Arcy. Be sure to watch for And The Ground Trembled when Lady Elizabeth D'Arcy goes to London to find a husband, but does William Hayward, the man she falls in love with, love her or is he just after her large dowry?

Excerpt from
And The Ground Trembled
At the end of the book.

Visit my web site at:
cmartinbooks.kitsappublishing.com

Chapter 1

England 1681

Amaryllis Bowdon set her portmanteau down and shifted her young brother to a better position on her hip. She lodged the canvas bag she carried on her shoulder more securely and squatted to retrieve the portmanteau. It was heavy, and she debated discarding some of the items she had stuffed into it but decided all the articles were needed.

A crackling noise in the woods to her left made her start and her heart jumped into her throat. A squirrel raced up a nearby tree then sat on a branch to chatter at her. "Irksome creature," she hissed when her heart resumed its proper pace in her chest.

"Ryllis, I am tired," came her six-year-old sister's plaintive little voice. "Can we not rest for a bit? This bag handle hurts my hand."

"No, Tabitha." She looked down at the sweet face turned up to hers. "We must reach the inn before they close their doors for the night. We must not bring undo attention to ourselves. They will be curious enough about us arriving at this hour of the night."

"Well, could you carry my bag for a while?"

"Oh, really Tabitha, how can I carry your bag. 'Tis all I can do to carry Charlie and his bag and this portmanteau. Now do start walking. We must hurry on."

Tabitha set off, her bag knocking against her leg. "They will not catch us will they?"

"No dear, they will not catch us. With the potion Cook gave Nurse Palmer, she will sleep into the morning. We will be on the stage bound for Leicester before we will e'er be missed."

Amaryllis looked down the moonlit path and prayed she was right. Did the children's nanny arise at her normal hour, the carefully laid

1

plans could go awry, and they must not go awry. Charlie's life depended on their clandestine escape.

※ ※ ※ ※

Reginald D'Arcy shifted on his saddle, arched his back, craned his neck, and waggled his shoulders. He was tired. He should not still be in the saddle this late in the evening. He glanced up at the full moon that brightened the night sky before he glared over his shoulder at his sister. She appeared as fresh as she had when they set out that morning. Yet the delay that kept them from reaching their evening's destination in a timely fashion was entirely her fault. He had known when they left on this journey that traveling with Selena would mean trouble, but the first two days had gone smoothly enough, despite being held up on their second day out by a brief but torrential downpour, which in all fairness, could not be blamed on Selena. Foolishly, he had dropped his guard. But today, naught but their third day out, her delaying tactics had begun. That Selena would do anything to postpone her arrival at her final destination was a given. But get her there he would, then the devil take her. He shook his head. Nay. She was his sister and he loved her. Besides, he doubted even the devil would be a match for Selena.

Spoiled, that was what she was, spoiled. 'Twas his father's fault. The Earl of Rygate doted on his only daughter. After their mother's accident that left her paralyzed from the hips down, Selena had had no one to curb her antics. Having four brothers, she copied them and expected to do whatever they did. Proud of Selena's prowess on horseback and her near preternatural way with animals, their father seldom attempted to discipline her. When she took to wearing her brother's clothes when she went riding, he condoned the action saying, "'Tis safer to ride astride. I cannot think the side-saddle, combined with the cumbersome riding costumes women are expected to wear, are at all practical." As long as Selena appeared appropriately gowned at the dinner table, or when they made occasional trips to London, he had no objections to her indecorous conduct within the confines of their estate or the nearby village.

To be honest, Reginald admitted, he had no objections to his sister's brazen behavior. Only two years separated them in age, and she had been a much more satisfactory playmate than had his older brother, Giles, heir to their father's earldom. No, he but wished he had not been the one selected to escort Selena to their Uncle Nathaniel's. Uncle Nathaniel's wife, their Aunt Rowena, was to turn Selena into a lady that Selena might find a husband. Reginald wished his aunt luck. In truth, he doubted the task could be accomplished.

"Master Reginald, I do think I see the lights of Albertine ahead."

Reginald's valet, Bernard Nye, brought Reginald's attention back to the present, and he peered into the darkness. Indeed, he did see the dim twinkling of lights, no doubt betokening a few townsmen not yet in their beds or tradesmen working late, and the inn where, God willing, they would reside for the night. The innkeeper should be expecting them. Word had been sent ahead to reserve accommodations, but they were arriving so late. Could be their lodging had been given to other travelers. Good inns were hard come by. In the village down the road where they stopped to refresh themselves, he had thought they might spend the night, but Selena's maid maintained in adamant terms, did they stay in that inn, they would all leave the next morning with a number of tiny vagabonds accompanying them.

"Sir, would you have me ride ahead and insure all is in readiness?" Nye asked.

"I think that a fine idea. How I might fare without you, I want never to discover." Reginald meant what he said. Ten years Reginald's senior, Nye had been with Reginald since he went off to Oxford. Nye had been his mainstay when he traveled through Europe on his grand tour, and now he was seeing to their comforts on their journey to Whimbrel, Uncle Nathaniel's estate in the north of Leicestershire. When possible they would stay the night with friends of the family, but the occasional stopover at an inn was unavoidable. This was one of those nights.

Riding up beside Reginald, Selena said, "Does Mister Nye go to secure us a meal? I am near to starving."

Reginald turned to his sister. She offered him a bright smile, her teeth gleaming in the moonlight. Her face devoid of embellishments, her near black hair tied behind her head, and her slim figure clothed in a man's apparel, she could easily pass for a youth. No one would suspect she was Lady Selena D'Arcy. Still angry at their long delay, Reginald did not return her smile.

"You deserve to be hungry," he snapped. "I yet cannot believe you have kept us from our supper and our beds for that mangy whelp."

Selena laughed, the sound tinkling out into the night air. "Fate is no longer mangy. You know well Esmeralda would never allow him to ride in the coach with her did he have so much as one flea left on his poor little body. Poor dear has been scrubbed until his skin looks pink beneath his hair. And that splint the surgeon put on his leg will keep him from being a nuisance."

"So you have named him have you? I suppose that means you are set on keeping him." Selena had found the small black-and-white dog by the roadside. His left hind leg broken, he looked as if he had been run over by a cart and left by the side of the road to die. Cold, hungry, and whimpering, the dog had wrung Selena's heart. Naught would do but she must take him up, find a doctor to set his leg, have him bathed, then deposit him on a blanket on the floor of the coach. Selena's maid, after years of service in the D'Arcy household, knew better than to complain. 'Twould do no good and would but delay their journey even longer.

"I shall keep him unless I find him a good home before we arrive at Whimbrel," Selena said. "We have several days travel ahead of us. Who knows what will transpire."

Who indeed could know, Reginald thought. With Selena, anything was possible. Setting his heels to his horse, he urged the animal into a trot. He could see the inn at the edge of the town. All would be bustling as the innkeeper and his minions prepared to greet their guests.

※　※　※　※

Smiling, Selena watched her brother ride off. She could not blame him for being irritated. They had spent a great deal of time finding a surgeon to set Fate's leg. At first the man had refused, saying, "I treat people not animals," but when Reginald poured a handful of coins into his palm, he readily complied. Even took great care not to cause undue pain to the little dog. Then of course Esmeralda insisted Fate be bathed.

The surgeon's wife supplied a tub and soap. To give Fate credit, though he seemed not to care much for the bath, after a few whines, he made no other protests. Finally, he had to be fed. Selena insisted he be given a broth with shreds of beef. "His stomach may be delicate. We know not how long he has been without food. Best we have a care, is he to ride in the coach."

Letting the coach catch up with her, Selena peered in the window, and raising her voice to be heard through the glass window, asked, "How does my friend? Not been a bother has he?"

"To my knowledge he does fine. Other than a couple of stretches, he has not moved since he curled up on that blanket," Esmeralda said, leaning forward that she might see Selena.

"Splendid. We near our night's destination. Has Mister Nye not done so, do please order our meals. I must see Brigantia is properly rubbed down," Selena said, patting her mare's neck. She had trained Brigantia herself and was proud of her mare's stamina and easy gait. Reginald's gelding, Sherard, might be faster and sturdier, but his gait was far from smooth. She could well imagine Reginald would tire of their journey long before it was ended.

She on the other hand dreaded the journey's end. She would be giving up her freedom, but she had no choice. She had promised her mother she would pay heed to her Aunt Rowena and would do as she was bid. What else could she have done but give her word when her beloved mother, tears welling in her sapphire blue eyes, had begged her compliance. "My dear daughter," her mother said, taking her hand, "a mother's greatest wish is to see her children live into their adult years. I have been blessed that my children are all hale and hearty. But a mother also wants her children to be happy and to love and be loved. To know a love like your father and I have known is God's most prized gift. We never let a day go by without offering a prayer of thanks to the Lord. I could wish no greater joy for you, Selena, than that you should know such love."

"I know how much you and Father love each other." Selena squeezed her mother's hand. "Anyone who sees the two of you together could never doubt your love. Nor do I doubt your love for me and my brothers. But Mother, I am happy now, happy here. I love my home." She shifted her gaze to the open window. "Am I meant to find love, might I not find it here?"

"I would be overjoyed, my dear, did you find love here in this shire and settle nearby that we might visit whenever we please. But you know every eligible man and boy within riding distance and none have caught your fancy. And I dare say," her mother raised her golden eyebrows, "nor have you caught theirs."

"But Mother …" Selena started to protest, but her mother held up a hand to stop her.

"I have heard all your excuses multiple times over, Selena, I need not hear them again. No man is going to take to wife a woman who behaves like a hoyden. A man needs a wife to be his helpmate, to see his home is comfortable and is run smoothly. To see their children are properly reared. He needs his wife to be a lady. That is what you must learn to do, dear child of my heart. You must learn to be a lady. And as, due to my injury, I have not been able to instill these virtues or skills in you, I have asked your Aunt Rowena to train and guide you.

"Now I must have your word that you will be biddable and follow Rowena's instructions. Promise me." Her mother's misty eyes sought hers, and Selena nodded and gave her word. She loved her mother too dearly to do otherwise. Like it or not, she must learn to be a lady.

🌼 🌼 🌼 🌼

Esmeralda Shadwell clucked her tongue. At forty-five, she was too old to be bouncing around in a coach for days on end, but when Lady Rygate had requested she accompany her daughter to Lord Rotherby's, she had assented. That Lady Selena was being allowed to make the journey on horseback, she found shocking but not surprising. Shaking her head, she recalled the argument that ensued when Lord Rygate attempted to insist his daughter ride inside the coach.

"I promised Mother I would go to Aunt Rowena's and when there, I would be biddable, but I will not go am I not allowed to ride Brigantia. I will not have someone else ride her, nor will I tie her to the back of the coach and have her eating dust day in and day out. 'Twould not be good for her. Plus, she needs to be properly exercised."

"Oh, Ranulf," Lady Rygate interposed, "this is your doing. Had you not sanctioned her behavior when she first started donning breeches and riding like a man, she would not now be such a hoyden." The lovely lady smiled at her husband and softened her words. "I cannot blame you my love. I also failed to curb her antics. But go to Rowena she will, and must we allow her to ride her horse, so must it be."

"As you say, Angelica. No doubt she will arrive in much better humor does she ride Brigantia." He turned to Selena. "But when you get to your Uncle Nate's, do you ride, you ride side saddle, like a lady. Do you understand me, daughter?"

Selena pouted, but nodded her head. "Yes, Father."

And so Selena had, as usual, gotten her way, and Esmeralda jostled around in the roomy coach by herself – except now for the dog. She found the days dreadfully dull. Naught to do but stare out the windows or nap. She had tried knitting but every time they hit a bump, which was often, she lost a stitch or pulled a strand lose. Traveling in broad daylight, she had no fear of highwaymen, but as night closed in around them, she was glad that besides the coachman, postilion, and two foot-men, two outriders and Reginald's valet, whom she knew to be an excellent shot, also accompanied them. Lord Rygate took every precaution to ensure his daughter had a safe journey. All the same Esmeralda was glad for the bright moon overhead. She guessed the footmen were, too. No doubt they preferred clinging to the back of the coach to running ahead of it with lanterns in hand to light what passed for a road.

Upon arriving at the inn, Esmeralda was helped from the coach by the footman, Norwood. A likeable youth with a big toothy grin, he always took the greatest of care when assisting her to alight, unlike the other footman, Handle, who was always reserved and seemed indifferent to the struggle it took her to get in and out of the high-wheeled coach. "I am to see to the dog, Mistress Shadwell," Norwood said. "Lady Selena says after he has done his mess, I am to hold him until I can settle him before a warm fire in either the parlor or her chamber."

"Very well, Norwood, scoop him up and do as you are bid with him." She should have known the dog would not be sleeping in the stable.

The innkeeper's chubby wife greeted her at the door. Bowing and nodding, she wheezed, "The bedchambers are readied with clean sheets as well as quilts, the table in the best parlor is laid, and at this very instant hot water is being taken up to the bedchambers."

Esmeralda acknowledged the woman's speech as Bernard Nye came out a door off the public room. "Ah, Mistress Shadwell, we are arrived at last. No doubt you are exhausted. Do you wish to go up to your room and refresh yourself, I will await Lady Selena and escort her up."

"What of supper?" Esmeralda asked.

"It has been bespoken. Should be ready by the time Lady Selena is done with her ablutions."

"Thank you, Mister Nye. Do you, please, have our portmanteaus brought up."

He nodded. "That I will do."

She answered his nod with one of her own then turned to a waiting chambermaid and followed her up the stairs. Esmeralda liked the valet. She knew him to be devoted to Reginald. He was deferential, efficient, and at times quite jovial – when his duties did not require his attention. But he was not a man who would stand out in a crowd. A plain dresser and of medium height and build, with no distinguishing facial characteristics, and with light-brown hair and hazel eyes, he might be passed on the street a dozen times a day and never be noticed. But Reginald, to his credit, recognized Nye's value.

Chapter 2

Surprised to find the inn all a-bustle, Amaryllis, with Tabitha at her heels, slipped in the door behind a woman of prodigious size who had descended from a magnificent coach. The coach was painted a burnished gold and had a coat of arms emblazoned on the door, but what amazed Amaryllis the most were the large glass windows. Her family coach had naught but blinds. Were they lifted, the weather and the dust blew in the open windows.

Once inside the inn, Amaryllis attempted to gain the attention of the innkeeper or his wife. The innkeeper's wife, engaged in fawningly accommodating the large woman's every wish, ignored her, and the innkeeper danced attendance on two well-dressed men at a table in the back corner of the public room. Waving their mugs in the air, the men boisterously demanded more ale. The innkeeper obliged them while informing them their room had been readied.

"About time," sang out the younger of the two men.

"Had we been expecting you, Mister Toms, we would have had your room ready," the innkeeper said, emptying the pitcher of ale into their mugs.

Amaryllis missed the man's answer as the innkeeper's wife tapped her on the shoulder and asked in an indifferent tone, "And what would you be wanting?"

"A room for the night, please," Amaryllis said, wishing her voice sounded firmer.

The woman looked at Charlie and Tabitha and narrowed her eyes. "Where's your husband?" she demanded.

Amaryllis had her story ready. "A wheel on our wagon broke. My husband said he dared not leave the wagon with all our belongings. He said the children and I must go ahead and spend the night at an inn. I am... I am to send help to him come morning, do you so please to give me directions to the blacksmith."

Her eyes still narrowed, the innkeeper's wife cocked her head. "You got the coin to pay?"

"Oh, indeed." Amaryllis shifted her brother in her arms. "Charlie, I must put you down that I may get to my purse." Setting the child on the floor next to his sister, she bade Tabitha hold his hand. Digging in her pocket, she pulled out a leather coin purse. "How much for the room?"

The woman eyed the purse. "I am thinking you will be wanting a private room, and I have but one left. 'Tis at the top of the stairs. 'Tis small, but one bed, but then you be not very big. You and your little ones should fit in the bed fine, though 'tis naught but a cot."

"I am certain it will do us fine." Amaryllis looked down at her young siblings. "We are quite tired. I wonder might we go to our room now?"

Holding out her hand, the innkeeper's wife wriggled her fingers. "That will be a shilling and two. And do you be wanting more than one candle, 'twill be extra."

Amaryllis believed she was being overcharged, but she had no choice. She pulled the required coins from her purse. "I do think one candle will suffice us for a small room," she said, stooping to pick up Charlie and her portmanteau.

The chambermaid who had taken the imposing woman up to her room, returned, took the portmanteau from Amaryllis, and with candle in hand, escorted Amaryllis and her siblings up to their room. "'Tis like to be a tad noisy, this room is," the girl said, setting down the portmanteau and handing over the candle. "What with everyone tromping up and down the stairs."

"We will not mind," Amaryllis said, letting Charlie slide from her arms to the bed. "We are that tired, I cannot think we will take note."

"Be sure you bolt the door. You would not want some drunkard barging in on you."

Amaryllis's heart sputtered at the thought. She thanked the girl for the advice and promised she would make certain to bolt the door. She had not liked the way the man the innkeeper had addressed as Toms had ogled her as she crossed the room. She had felt his eyes on her as she climbed the stairs, but she had not looked to see if he watched her enter her chamber.

"Well, now, here we are. All safe for the night." Amaryllis threw the bolt then turned to look about the small room. A narrow bed, a washstand with a heavy, chipped crockery bowl and pitcher, a straight rung-back chair, a small round table, and a couple of pegs on the wall for hanging clothes. She smiled at the pair staring expectantly up at her. "Tomorrow we take the stage to Leicester and then one to Derby. And before you know it, we will be with your Aunt Juliet. Your mother's own dear sister. Will that not be grand?"

"Are we through walking?" Tabitha asked.

Amaryllis gently tugged her sister's golden curls. "Yes, my little buttercup. On the morrow we board the stage. No more walking. Now, we must go to sleep that we can be up bright and early."

"But I am hungry," Tabitha said.

"I hungry, too," Charlie said, his previously drooping brown eyes framed in thick dark lashes now wide awake.

Amaryllis reached into her pocket and felt nothing but crumbs. "Oh, little ones, I am sorry, I have no biscuits left. You each had two."

"But I am still hungry. I am thirsty too," Tabitha complained, her lower lip quivering.

"Me, too," chimed in Charlie, bouncing on the bed and causing the ropes to squeak.

Amaryllis sighed. Of all nights for the children to have been punished by sending them to bed with no supper, why had it been this night. She had not dared change her plans. She had needed the full moon to light their way to Albertine. And they had to be in Albertine come morning were they to catch the stage going north. But most importantly, she had to get Charlie away from her father's brother's wife to the safety of his mother's family.

Well, she would have to feed them. She could hear Charlie's stomach rumbling. Poor babe. "Very well, but do settle down. Let me but straighten my hair, and then I will go down to the kitchen and see what I can find. No doubt this late there will not be much."

※ ※ ※ ※

Reginald followed his sister into the inn. Nye met them at the door.

"Your rooms are ready, and your portmanteaus are in your rooms." He bowed his head. "Lady Selena, I will escort you up."

"Where is Fate?" Selena asked.

"He is on a blanket before the fire in the parlor where your supper will be served. He has had a bowl of water, and is currently gnawing on a bone the inn's cook provided him." Nye then nodded toward a plump, moon-faced woman in a yellowed apron. "Mistress Morly, the innkeeper's wife, was not in favor of having a dog residing inside her inn, but I assured her he had been recently scrubbed, and she kindly agreed to let him stay indoors."

Reginald guessed Mistress Morly had acquiesced when a few coins had graced her palm. He found the look on her face amusing. Her eyes popping, she stared open-mouthed at Selena. His sister's appearance often had that effect on people. No one expected an Earl's daughter to be dressed in breeches and a coat like a man.

Selena nodded to Mistress Morly then looked back at Nye. "Thank you for seeing to poor little Fate. And I do suppose you thanked the cook for the bone?"

"I did, my lady."

"Splendid. Well, then, do lead on Mister Nye," she said. "I am starved, but I must need wash and change before I may eat. I promised Mother I would do so."

The innkeeper's wife belatedly bobbed a curtsy. "Do you need anything, my lady, you but need ask. Happy to oblige."

Ever gracious to people of all ranks, Selena smiled and warmly thanked Mistress Morly before following after Nye. Reginald followed her. He admired his sister's easy approach to people. To her, no one was beneath her notice. As they reached the top of the stairs, the door of a room abutting the landing opened, and a child's voice could be heard asking. "You are sure they will not catch us, are you not, Ryllis?"

A delicate white hand held the edge of the door, and a gentle voice answered the child. "Yes, Tabitha. I have told you half a dozen times, they will not catch us. Now I will find you and Charlie something to eat. You bolt this door after me and open it again only for me."

Selena halted. Reginald sighed. Selena had heard the exchange between the woman and the child. Not good. Did Selena think someone was in trouble, she would think she needed to help. What would she involve them in now? But when the door opened and an angel appeared, all he could do was gape and pray Selena would not disappoint him. She must interfere.

The angel looked startled when she saw Selena and him at her door. She started to back up, but Selena stretched out a hand to her and said, "Please, I heard you say you were after something to eat. Join my brother and me. We have ordered supper to be served in the private parlor below. Oh, I am Lady Selena D'Arcy," she added when the angel still looked concerned and ready to duck back into her room. She nodded to Reginald. "My brother, Mister Reginald D'Arcy. We would be honored by your company. That includes your children, of course."

When the angel continued to stare, Selena pulled the tie from her hair and shook her head. Her mane of straight, dark hair floated about her shoulders. "Do forgive my appearance. We have only just arrived, and Reggie and I needed to see to our horses before we could see to our own needs. I would never trust an inn's ostler with my Brigantia. Do say you will join us. After this dreadful long day, we could use some company other than each other."

Reginald held his breath while awaiting a reply. He could not think when he had seen a lovelier woman. Golden curls peeped from under a crisp lappet cap. On the darkened landing, with naught but an oil lamp casting a glow, he could not make out the color of her eyes, but they were lovely all the same. And she had the sweetest little nose, and the most kissable looking lips.

"Is aught the matter, Lady Selena?" Mistress Morly called up from the bottom step.

Selena waved a hand at the innkeeper's wife, "Nay, Mistress Morly, we have but stopped to have a word with Mistress …" Leaving the sentence unfinished, she waited expectantly for an answer from the young woman who looked poised for flight.

"Amaryllis… Norton," the angel at last answered. Reginald did not miss the pause before she gave her last name. He guessed Norton was not her true name. No matter, at least she had answered Selena. And Selena took full advantage of her answer.

"Mistress Morly," she said, "do set three more plates at our table.

Mistress Norton and her children will be joining us."

"Yes, milady," Mistress Morly answered though her face showed surprise.

The angel started to protest, but Selena gave her no opportunity to voice excuses. She interrupted her saying, "I am starving as you and your children must be. And I must need change as must Reggie, but he will return in but a few moments to escort you and the children down." Selena hurried off, leaving him to make a bow, and promise he would make haste.

❀　❀　❀　❀

"But, but …" Amaryllis tried to answer the handsome Mister D'Arcy, but he hurried away before she could say more. Overcome by the eccentrically dressed Lady Selena, Amaryllis knew not what to make of the situation she found herself in. She could not think how or why, but she was somehow committed to joining these strangers for supper. She could not now go down to the kitchen to get something for the children to eat when the innkeeper's wife was setting places for them at the D'Arcys' table. And though late as it was, the children had to be fed.

Stepping back into the room, she slowly closed the door, and leaning against it, said, "Tabitha, Charlie, I must make you presentable. We are to have supper with Lady Selena and her brother, Mister D'Arcy."

"Who are they?" Tabitha asked, her blue eyes large in her pale face.

Amaryllis shook her head. "I have no idea. I have only now met them. But for some reason I cannot fathom, Lady Selena insisted we join them. And so we must." She straightened. "So here now, let me get you cleaned up."

Pleased to find the water in the pitcher was still slightly warm, she poured some into the bowl and set the pitcher on the floor. She tended her own ablutions first, then scrubbed Charlie's and Tabitha's hands and faces, combed their hair, and brushed dirt and leaves from their shoes and clothes. She hoped they all looked presentable. In the dim light cast by the one candle, she could not be certain.

A tap at the door made her gasp then ask, "Who is it?"

"'Tis Reginald D'Arcy, Mistress Norton. Are you ready to go down to supper?"

For a moment she panicked. Could she get out of this? She looked down at Charlie and Tabitha. They stood expectantly waiting for her to open the door. Their trust in her calmed her. "Yes," she said, "we are ready." Throwing the bolt, she opened the door.

The man awaiting her was even more handsome than she had first thought. His smile, showing strong straight teeth, lit up his dark eyes. He had broad shoulders and narrow hips and his dark, shoulder-length hair gleamed in the dim landing light. He bowed slightly at the waist, and held out his arm. "May I?"

He expected her to take his arm, but she instead bent and scooped up Charlie. Blowing out the candle, she said, "Tabitha, Charlie, this is Mister D'Arcy. Say you are honored."

"I am honored," both children chimed, and Tabitha curtsied.

"Well, I am honored, too, Tabitha and Charlie. And most pleased to make your acquaintance."

Amaryllis liked the sound of his voice. Not too deep, not too high, and it had a merry ring to it, a joyfulness. Almost as if happy laughter might burst forth at any moment.

"Might I carry young Charlie?" he offered holding out his arms.

Charlie, seldom bashful, held out his arms, and surrendering him, Amaryllis took Tabitha's hand. Mister D'Arcy propped Charlie on one hip and again extended his arm to Amaryllis. "Ladies, let us go find us some supper."

This time she did take his arm, though not but for two steps. The staircase was too narrow for them to descend three abreast, so he stepped aside and allowed her and Tabitha to proceed him. At the bottom of the steps, he once more proffered his arm, and she placed her hand on his forearm. His eyes kind and gentle, he smiled down at her. "I cannot thank you enough for joining us this evening. You and the children will enliven our meal immensely. This has been a most trying day. At least for me."

"Why was it trying?" Tabitha asked.

"Oh, Tabitha, that is not polite," Amaryllis scolded, but the handsome man at her side laughed the joyful laugh she had known was hiding in his voice and said, "When we enter the parlor, you will see the cause of my grief."

Puzzlement clouded Tabitha's face, and she asked, "Your grief is in the parlor where we are going, Mister D'Arcy?"

Squatting with Charlie balanced on one knee, he took Tabitha's hand. "You must call me Reginald, or even better, Reggie. Mister D'Arcy makes me sound too old, does it not?" Tickling Tabitha under her chin, he added, "And have no fear of my grief that awaits us in the parlor. What is grief to me may well delight you and Charlie." He ruffled Charlie's neatly combed hair, making the light brown curls again stand on end, and then rose. "Let us meet our Fate, shall we?"

Chapter 3

The children looked both expectant and wary of Reginald D'Arcy's riddle, but they would soon see what grief he had deposited in the parlor. Amaryllis found she was as curious as her siblings, but as they were about to enter the parlor, the man the innkeeper had called Toms jerked up from his table to stumble over in front of them, blocking their entrance.

He swayed and squinted his eyes. "Hey now, I say, I saw you arrive." He looked at Amaryllis. "Thought mayhap you was a doxy, but then what with the children, I thought, not so. But now, here you are with this gent. I cry foul play. I saw you first."

Tabitha shrank back against Amaryllis's legs, but Reginald – Amaryllis liked his name – shifted Charlie to a different hip and asked, "What is this, man? What are you blathering about?"

Toms continued to sway but refocused his eyes on Reginald, though he pointed at Amaryllis. "The doxy there, I saw her first. By rights, I should be the one to bed her."

Amaryllis gasped at the drunken insult, but Reginald stiffened and thinned his lips, and had he not been holding Charlie, Amaryllis was certain he would have hit the insolent man. Instead, a tightly folded fan rapped Toms's shoulder with enough force that he spit out an, "Ow!," and reached up a hand to rub the assaulted area.

"Here, sir, why do you block my brother and our dear friend's entrance into the parlor?" came a crisp voice, and Amaryllis stared in wonder at the speaker. Lady Selena looked nothing like she had at the door to Amaryllis's room. She was striking. Mayhap not beautiful, but she looked every inch the lady, the daughter of an earl. Her dark hair was pulled starkly back from her face and wrapped in a bun atop her head. She wore no cap to conceal its shining glory. She was wearing a sapphire-blue gown over a cream-colored petticoat, and a lace chemise showed at her neckline and shoulder length sleeves. Though she wore no facial embellishments, her skin glowed with nature's own coloring – pink cheeks, rosy lips, and lightly-tanned skin that enhanced rather than detracted from her appearance. Her eyes, not dark like her brother's but a blue-green, danced in merriment, and a slight smile touched her lips.

Lightly tapping the fan in her hand, she seemed to be waiting for Toms to speak, to offer an excuse for his behavior. Behind her towered the woman from the luxurious coach. "Why do you but stand there man?" she demanded. "Be you deaf? Lady Selena has asked you a question."

For a moment Toms looked mystified, then he shook his head, his hair flying about his face. "Lady Selena, you say?" he managed before looking back at Amaryllis. "Then you are with her. Oh, Mistress, 'tis begging your pardon I am. I am overly tiddly, or I would not have made such a mistake. A friend of Lady Selena. Indeed, Mistress, do accept my apology." He tried to grasp Amaryllis's hand to bend over it, but she shrank back, and Reginald gave him a nudge that sent him staggering backwards. He caught himself on the edge of his table, straightened, and made an awkward bow. "Lady Selena. My pardon. Mister Morly did mention he was expecting a fine lady this evening. I am Richard Toms. If I at any time may be of service to you, please, you have but to ask, and I will respond with utmost urgency."

Lady Selena laughed, a tinkling laugh, and said, "Well, at the moment, Mister Toms, did you but step aside, you would be of great service to us. We would like to enter the parlor that we may have our supper."

"Dicky, Dicky," the older man at the table said, "do sit you down afore you get us thrown out. I have no mind to try to find another bed somewhere at this late hour." Rising from his seat enough to grasp Toms's sleeve, the man pulled his friend down onto a stool.

To Amaryllis's amazement, Lady Selena smiled sweetly at both men and actually thanked them for their courtesy. Courtesy! Still offended by Toms's remark, Amaryllis wondered if mayhap Lady Selena had not heard Toms insult her. Well, it mattered not, Reginald was shepherding her and Tabitha into the parlor. Lady Selena and the towering woman, followed after them, though at the door, Reginald stood aside and allowed the women to enter first.

No sooner were they in the room, and Tabitha demanded, "Where's your grief?"

Reginald pointed to the hearth. There before a warm fire upon a small blanket lay a little black-and-white dog. At the children's screeches he thumped his tail repeatedly, but he did not rise. "You may pet him," Lady Selena said, "but do be careful of him. He has a broken leg."

"Oh, poor doggie," Tabitha said, hurrying to the pup's side. Charlie, squirming in Reginald's arms, demanded, "Down, down."

No sooner was he on the floor than his stubby legs carried him over to the hearth to join his sister and the little dog that seemed not to know whether to be pleased or apprehensive with all the new attention he was receiving.

"Does he have a name?" Tabitha asked, running her hand along the dog from head to tail.

"Fate," Lady Selena said. "Again, I must ask you both to be very gentle with him."

"How was he hurt?" Tabitha asked.

"I cannot say," Lady Selena said. "We found him by the wayside and spent a good portion of the day finding a surgeon who could mend his leg, and then he needed to be bathed. He was a very dirty, and hungry, little dog."

"Yes," Reginald said, "and now you know my grief. My day was spent not in arriving at our destination at a goodly hour, but in finding care for that cur."

Tabitha stopped her petting and looked up in surprise. "Oh, Reggie, you cannot say you had no wish to aid this nice little doggie."

Despite the fact Reginald had requested he be called by his given name, or even his nickname, Amaryllis blushed at her sister's use of it. It somehow seemed disrespectful. Yet he responded as if Tabitha's address was precisely what he wished. "Indeed little miss, that is exactly what I mean. Do I not monitor my sister's antics, our coach will be filled with every stray dog and cat between here and Leicester. Why, there will be no room in the coach for Mistress Shadwell." He paused and turned to the large woman. "My manners are near as bad as Selena's. Forgive me. I have not introduced Mistress Shadwell, Selena's maid and traveling companion."

He nodded toward Mistress Shadwell and said, "May I present Mistress Amaryllis Norton and her children, Tabitha and Charlie." Mistress Shadwell and Amaryllis acknowledged the introduction, and the children looked up at the sound of their names. Tabitha rose, made a quick curtsy, then rejoined her brother beside Fate. What a strange name for a dog, Amaryllis thought, before turning her thoughts to the table laden with food. In the excitement of finding the dog, her siblings seemed to have forgotten their rumbling tummies.

The door opened and a neatly, but plainly, dressed man entered. "Master Reginald," he said, "the table is set but for the sallet and the mutton stew the cook has been keeping warm. Are you ready to be served?"

"Oh, yes, Nye," Reginald said. "I had near forgotten how hungry I am. Do bring on the stew, and have you not yet eaten, do please to join us." Reginald hastily introduced Mister Bernard Nye, his friend and valet, he termed him. These D'Arcys were unlike any aristocrats Amaryllis had ever known. Not that she had known any high-ranking peers, but she would swear none of them would be sitting down to supper at the same table with their serving staff. In Medieval days they might have all dined in the great hall together, but not at the same table.

Mister Nye declined supper. Being hungry, he had sat down to a substantial meal in the public room with the footmen and outriders. "How are our people being treated, Mister Nye?" Lady Selena asked. "Are the accommodations acceptable?"

"Aye, my lady," he answered. "The dormitory is quite adequate, but the coachman and postilion have chosen to sleep near the coach. Mister Pit says he will feel better is he at the ready do any thieves think to have easy pickings."

Reginald laughed. "And does he have that old fowling piece at his side?"

Bernard Nye smiled, "He does, sir."

"Let us hope then he has no disturbing dreams," Lady Selena said, her eyes twinkling. As Nye exited, Lady Selena, like Reginald, insisted she be addressed by her given name. Amaryllis, in turn, said they must call her by her given name. She had not liked lying to these kind people by giving them the fake surname of Norton.

By the time Amaryllis, with Selena's help, had Tabitha's and Charlie's hands washed at a bowl on a table near the hearth, and had Charlie seated on a high stool and Tabitha atop a thick cushion on a chair, Mister Nye returned with a huge tureen of stew. He was preceded by a serving maid who held the door for him, and another who carried the sallet. Amaryllis guessed the parlor to be the best the inn had to offer, but it was still quite plain. The table was sturdy and covered with a white table cloth, but the pewter dishes and knives and spoons were of a poor quality. Naught but a very poor tapestry decorated one wall, and other than the table and chairs, and the washbowl stand, the only other piece of furniture was a small sideboard with two candelabras atop it.

Amaryllis could not say the food was lacking, though. The table bulged with a variety of dishes from a boiled sallet of leeks, endive, onions, cauliflower, and dandelion leaves to three kinds of cheeses, two breads, a rye and a crusty wheat bran, butter, sliced chicken, pickled herring in a savory sauce, and the pottage of mutton, carrots, turnips, and parsnips. For sweets at the end of the meal, they had a choice of suet pudding, egg custard, or dried blackberry tarts.

Once they were all seated, Reginald dismissed his valet. "You have had a long day, Nye, you need not stay. The inn's maid can serve us. Go on to bed do you wish."

"As you say, sir." The valet nodded and left, but Esmeralda Shadwell joined them for supper. Seated at the end of the table, she spoke only when addressed. Yet Amaryllis did not believe the woman felt uncomfortable sitting with her mistress. She but seemed tired.

Everyone being hungry, at first no one spoke, but as appetites were satiated, Selena and Reginald enlivened the table with several tales that had the children in giggles – Selena's pet goat that chewed up her father's favorite hat, the cat that had her litter in her oldest brother's horse's stall. Afterward the horse would not be content did he not have the cats with him. "Poor Giles, does he wish to stay overnight anywhere, he must take a cat with him, or he cannot take Cirilo, his magnificent Spanish stallion," Selena stated then punctuated with her tinkling laugh.

The most amusing story though, concerned the baby ducks. Eyes glistening, Selena bent forward and looked at Tabitha and Charlie. "We have a large fish pond near the house. It is also home to a number of ducks." She frowned. "Well, this part is sad. One night, a fox came and killed a mother duck that was sitting on her eggs. Ten eggs there were, am I not right, Reggie?"

"Yes, ten, and Selena found the eggs and took them to her room, unbeknownst to Mother or Father. She kept them warm, and then one night they hatched. Well, those ducklings decided Selena was their mother."

"Oh, no," Tabitha gasped, her hands to her cheeks, "they thought you were their mother!"

Amaryllis smiled at her sister's obvious delight. She noted Charlie's eyes were also all a-sparkle. The D'Arcys were good with children.

"Well, those ducklings followed me everywhere," Selena said. "But the maids complained about the er … the er … mess they made, and Mother insisted they had to stay outside. The gardener built them a little hutch, and I put warm blankets in with them and that is where they slept at night. But during the day when I went outside, they followed me about. Did I go in the house, they waited by the door. But that worried me. I was afraid a hawk might swoop down and get them, so I asked Mother could a footman stay with them when I had to be indoors."

Reginald took up the tale. "You will not guess the amount of pleading that went on before Mother agreed that one of the kitchen scullions could be assigned to watch over the ducks. I cannot think the cook was pleased, but the scullion seemed to enjoy his assignment."

"The ducks reached an age when they needed to learn to swim." Selena ignored her brother's intrusion. "Since they would only follow me. I could think of naught to do but to lead them into the pond."

"And so she did," Reginald said. "Waded in up to her waist, and the ducklings followed right after her. They were all good little swimmers."

Amaryllis joined the children in laughing at the image presented. "Whatever did your mother think of that?" she asked.

"We thought it best not to tell her," Selena said, "and none of the servants would ever want to tell her either. No one wants to worry or upset Mother. She is too well loved."

"Selena escaped many a reprimand because no one wishes to cause Mother any grief," Reginald said. "Actually, I suppose we all had our share of escapes from various misdeeds."

Amaryllis wondered that the lady of the house would be so poorly informed, but she said nothing. These D'Arcys continued to amaze her.

"'Twas teaching the ducks to fly that caused the greatest problem," Selena said.

"You taught them to fly?" Tabitha asked, her eyes wide in amazement.

"She tried," Reginald said. "At least, we attempted to give them flying lessons."

"Reggie tied a rope 'round my waist," Selena said, "and the other end to a branch of a tree, then he and our younger brother, Artemas, took the birds up the tree in a basket. I was on a chair, and I kicked the chair away and was swinging by my waist and flapping my arms. Arty and Reggie took each duckling from the basket, had them look at me, then dropped them. They fluttered their little wings and made it safely to the ground. But once on the ground, none of them tried to fly up to me. They but flapped their wings and quacked and looked up at me."

Amaryllis was holding her sides, she was laughing so hard. She could not remember when she had laughed so much. The children looked happier than she had seen them since before their uncle and aunt had entered their lives. The strain was gone from their eyes.

"That is when Esmeralda came out," Reginald again interposed and looked at Esmeralda at the end of the table. "You were aghast, were you not?"

Esmeralda nodded. "Yes, never any knowing what these two will be up to. Still no knowing."

"Did the little duckies ever learn to fly?" Tabitha asked.

"Yes, they did, but I think they learned by instinct. 'Tis the natural thing ducks do," Selena said. "Now, enough about ducks. I am ready for dessert."

"Oh, me too," Charlie said, a grin spreading across his face to brighten his sleepy eyes.

"Well, then, let us have some," Reginald said, and he looked to the serving maid, who, with tears of mirth sparkling on her cheeks, was at the ready to serve the desserts.

"This is much better than what we get at home, is it not, Charlie?" Tabitha said, licking her lips after a spoonful of custard.

"Oh?" Selena said. "And what might you eat at home? Is your cook a poor cook?"

"Oh, no, Cook is a very good cook, but Aunt Elva says children our age should not eat rich foods," Tabitha said. "She says 'tis not healthy. We are to eat bread and water for breakfast and supper, and for dinner we get a warm pottage of oats or peas."

Selena's eyes widened, and she looked to Amaryllis for confirmation. Amaryllis flushed hotly. She had tried to stop her sister's indictment of her aunt, but had not been able to get Tabitha's attention. "Who is Aunt Elva that she makes such decisions?" Selena asked.

"My sister is impertinent," Reginald interrupted, glaring at Selena. "We mean not to pry."

Selena accepted her brother's reprimand with a smile and a nod, "Indeed, Amaryllis, please accept my apology. 'Twas but a shock to hear such sweet children are treated in such a fashion."

"There you go again," Reginald snapped. "Your apology is no better than your prying." His dark eyes brimming with kindness and not a little aggravation, he looked at Amaryllis. Oh, she liked his eyes. She had trouble not getting lost in them. "Do forgive Selena," he said. "She is spoiled and has never been taught to hold her tongue. 'Tis why we make this journey. We go to our uncle's estate in northern Leicestershire."

Selena's tinkling laugh made Charlie, despite his drooping eyelids, look up from his plate and laugh his childish chuckle. Selena acknowledged his accompaniment then said, "I am a shameless hoyden, or so says my mother. She sends me to my aunt's that I may learn to be a lady and mayhap in the process, I will learn to mind my tongue. I apologize. I mean not to be rude."

"You are not rude," spoke up Tabitha. "And you are very pretty, near as pretty as Ryllis."

"Tabitha, now you are the one being rude," Amaryllis said.

Tabitha looked confused. She looked from Amaryllis to Selena and back to Amaryllis. "What said I that was rude?"

Before Amaryllis could again rebuke her sister, Selena said, "You said nothing rude, Tabitha. You but spoke the truth as you see it, and I thank you for your defense and your honesty. We are, mayhap, two of a kind, but my brother thinks at my age I should know better." She nodded to Charlie. "Look there to your brother. He is falling asleep and may fall off that stool. Shall we have Reggie help him down, and you and he may say a short good night to Fate?"

Amaryllis looked at her brother as did Tabitha. The poor little fellow could scarce keep his face from dropping into his plate. His head would bob, and he would catch himself before he ended up with his nose in his custard. Amaryllis started to rise. "Oh, I must get him to bed."

Selena placed her hand on Amaryllis's wrist. "Let Reggie set him down. Charlie will want to say good night to the dog, as will Tabitha. Do you not?" she asked Tabitha, expectantly.

Tabitha looked up with pleading eyes. "May we please, Ryllis? Just a few pats."

Amaryllis sighed and nodded. "Very well, but only for a moment. We must get to bed are we to be up to catch the stage tomorrow. And I am tired."

Tabitha offered her a big grin and clambered down from her chair as Reginald swept Charlie off his stool and deposited him near the hearth. Amaryllis smiled as her brother curled up next to the dog, and her sister curled up next to Charlie and reached across his back to stroke the dog. Both children would soon be fast asleep and would have to be carried up to their bed, but she had no doubt Reginald would help her see to them.

Amaryllis started to thank the D'Arcys for their kindness, but Selena spoke first. She dismissed the serving maid, then with a sweet smile, she addressed her personal maid. "Esmeralda, you must be tired. Do you please go and ready our beds. I will be up shortly."

Mistress Shadwell showed no surprise at being dismissed. She but acknowledged the request. Rising, she bid Amaryllis and then Reginald good night, and with a rustle of skirts, left, closing the door softly behind her.

Selena looked over at the hearth then back at Amaryllis. "I do believe the children are asleep." She patted Amaryllis's hand and said, "'Tis time we talk. Now, if you please, I would know what you are running from and how we may help."

Chapter 4

Reginald knew he should not have been surprised by his sister's question, but he was. And certainly Amaryllis was taken by surprise. She blanched and shrank back in her chair. "What, what do you mean?" she stammered.

"I mean, you and the children are running from something. I know you are not their mother. First off, you are too young to be Tabitha's mother unless you married at some ridiculously young age. Second, they fail to call you Mother. They call you Ryllis. Third, you wear no ring." She looked pointedly down at the hand she had been patting. "And fourth, I heard Tabitha ask you if you would be caught. You assured her you would not, but I heard the trepidation in your voice. You need help, and we would like to help you."

Amaryllis was shaking her head as Selena spoke. Reginald read the fear in her eyes. His sister was right. She needed help, and he could not remember when he wanted more to be of service. He leaned forward. "Trust us, Amaryllis. Surely you see we mean you no harm."

She turned her lovely eyes on him, and he nearly drowned in their beauty. Sky blue were her eyes, a heavenly sky blue. How could he convince her she need not fear them? Fate! He glanced over his shoulder at the dog and the children all curled up together before the hearth. He looked back at Amaryllis. "Would someone who rescues dogs by the side of the road be any less caring for frightened children? Let us help you, for the children's sake."

Some of the fear seeped from her eyes. She gnawed her lovely lower lip. God, if he could hold her, kiss away her fears. Thanking God she was not married, at least she had not denied Selena's assertion concerning her married status, he held her gaze. Barely daring to breathe, he waited. Finally, she dropped her gaze, and in a voice so quiet Reginald had to lean forward to hear her, she said, "Tabitha and Charlie are my half-sister and brother. Their mother died a few days after Charlie was born. Father died in November. Father's brother, Uncle Irwin, and his wife and their two sons moved into our home. Uncle Irwin and the children's mother's father, their grandfather, are Tabitha and Charlie's guardians. Well, Sir Cyril is the legal guardian, but he lives in southern Cheshire, and wanting the children to be able to continue living in their own home, he was pleased to have Uncle Irwin and Aunt Elva take over the immediate custody of Charlie and Tabitha. He has no idea how the children are being treated. I have written him, but I have … I have had to guard what I may say. I dare not make accusations."

"So now you wish to take the children to Cheshire?" Selena asked.

Amaryllis shook her head. "Nay, 'tis not safe. We would be caught before we could reach their grandfather. As my uncle is their acting guardian, he would take Charlie back home." The fear again in her eyes, she hesitated then said, "I believe Aunt Elva means to kill Charlie."

Reginald huffed in amazement, and his sister, eyes narrowed, but stared. Then in a voice of controlled anger, Selena asked, "Why would she want to kill that sweet child?"

"Because she wants her husband then her elder son to inherit Churlwood and the baronetcy that now belong to Charlie. For years I was Father's only child. Uncle Irwin and Aunt Elva must have counted on the inheritance. The land is entailed you see, so that it remains with the title. It must go to the most direct male heir. But then Father married Beatrice Yardley. It surprised everyone. She was considerably younger than Father, but they were happy together." Amaryllis half-smiled. "Beatrice was shy, and a bit drab, but I do think Father made her feel special, even pretty. He was broken-hearted when she died."

"So where are you taking the children?" Selena asked.

Her eyes misty, Amaryllis pulled herself up. "I am taking them to Derbyshire. Their aunt, their mother's sister, has gone there with her husband to visit his sister. Aunt Elva should have no reason to think we would flee northeast. I know their aunt will help us. She is a dear person."

"Well, I see no reason we cannot take you there," Selena said, and Reginald widened his eyes. What had she said? They were not headed to Derbyshire. Or were they?

"You cannot think to take those children on the stage," Selena continued. "Have them exposed to all manner of rudeness. No, 'twill be but a little out of our way. And you and the children will be good company for Esmeralda. I know she is bored beyond words."

Amaryllis was again shaking her head. "Oh, we could not so impose on you."

"How would you be imposing?" Selena shrugged. "We are going northeast as well."

"Mayhap as you are journeying into Leicestershire, we could travel as far as Leicester with you." Amaryllis still looked doubtful. "Then we could take the stage from there to Derby, and you would not be terribly inconvenienced."

Selena smiled. Reginald knew that smile well. That was her 'I won' smile. But this time he was pleased to see it. He could think of nothing he would enjoy more than having this heavenly creature traveling with them. He knew, too, they would be going to Derbyshire.

"Splendid," Selena said. "'Tis time we all go to bed that we may be up on the morrow and be gone from here before your absence can be discovered." She cocked her head and eyed Amaryllis. "I am assuming you are not expecting to be discovered missing at an early hour."

Amaryllis blushed. "The cook put a potion in the children's nurse's ale to make her sleep more soundly and a bit longer."

Selena laughed. "Excellent! I will look forward to hearing more about your escape at a later date. Now 'tis off to bed. Reggie, do you get Tabitha. Amaryllis, can you carry Charlie?"

"Yes, I carried him half the way here tonight."

"Fine. I will get Fate."

❦ ❦ ❦ ❦

Amaryllis could scarce believe her good fortune. She was tempted to pinch herself to be certain she was not dreaming. She and the children would not have to endure the terrible ride atop the stage, which was all she could afford, not having the funds to buy inside seats. And with the money she would be saving from this leg of the trip, she might be able to purchase inside seating at least part way from Leicester to Derby.

Selena D'Arcy had offered to take them to Derbyshire, but Amaryllis would not feel right allowing the D'Arcys to go so far out of their way. They were already being so generous. The inn's chambermaid who had served their supper, met them at the door, and lighted them up to their rooms. She relit the candle in Amaryllis's room as Reginald deposited a sleeping Tabitha on the bed. Amaryllis put Charlie down beside his sister and turned to thank her new friends.

"Are you needing any help getting them to bed?" Selena asked with a nod to the children.

"Oh, no." Amaryllis shook her head. "I will but slip their gowns off and tuck them in. They may sleep in their day shifts tonight."

"Very well," Selena said, and she gave Amaryllis a brief one-armed embrace, the little dog resting in the crook of her other arm. "We will be off bright and early tomorrow. But do you need anything tonight, I am but two doors down."

"Thank you. I cannot begin to tell you how grateful I am for your kindnesses."

Reginald smiled at her, and her knees went weak. What was this effect he was having on her? "You are more than welcome," he said. "We will enjoy the children's and your company. Fact is, you will make this a much more enjoyable trip." He bowed. "Do bolt the door," he added as he and his sister exited.

After securing the door, Amaryllis looked fondly down at her siblings. How pleased they would be in the morning to learn they would be traveling in the D'Arcys' coach. Not that they had any idea how grueling traveling on the stage would be. Still, they liked the D'Arcys and would enjoy knowing they would be spending more time with them. Neither child did more than mumble as she removed their shoes and outer clothing. After tucking her siblings into the corner of the bed, which was little more than a cot, she hung their clothes up on the pegs. She spread her own gown and petticoats over the one chair in the room. The bodice, skirt, and petticoats would need service her for their entire journey as would the children's travel garments, but they had several shift and hose changes and fresh clothes to don when they reached their destination.

Feeling more hopeful than she had in months, she blew out the candle and crawled in beside her siblings. At first the room seemed incredibly dark, but after a few moments, her eyes adjusted, and the moonlight, seeping in through the tiny curtained window, cast a dim glow over the room. On the morrow they would head north. When their absence from Churlwood would be noted, she could not guess. Hopefully not before the dinner hour. The children's nurse would not want it known her charges had disappeared. She would at first search for them herself.

Eventually, though, Nurse Palmer would have to tell Aunt Elva the children were missing. The servants would be questioned. Nurse Palmer might accuse Cook of drugging her, but Cook would deny it. Uncle Irwin would side with Cook. Cook had once before threatened to leave when Aunt Elva had tried to interfere in her meal planning. Uncle Irwin had declared he would not lose her services. She was too good a cook. His rotund belly proclaiming his love of food, he ordered Aunt Elva to stay out of the kitchen.

Someone would discover clothing was missing. Aunt Elva would send servants to question neighbors, but at some point her aunt would realize Amaryllis had spirited the children away. Ultimately, Aunt Elva would decide they had to be on the way to Cheshire. How wrong she would be. Amaryllis grinned. Charlie was safe. He was out of Aunt Elva's clutches. In less than a week, they should be in Derbyshire, and she could turn Charlie's care over to his Aunt Juliet who would contact Charlie's grandfather.

Amaryllis sighed. For the first night in weeks, she could sleep in peace. Mayhap she would dream about the handsome Mister Reginald D'Arcy. The idea set her body a-tingle. She wondered if such dreams were a good idea. They would part in Leicester, and she would never see him again. The thought saddened her, but she pushed it away. Reginald was handsome and kind, and she meant to enjoy her time with him.

🌾 🌾 🌾 🌾

Bernard Nye wished Reginald a good night then blew out the candles. He settled onto his cot, stretching out his legs and wriggling his toes.

It had been a long day, a long evening, but one had to expect delays when traveling with the D'Arcys. Reginald blamed his sister for their late arrival, and in this case, the blame was justified. But when he accompanied Reginald on his grand tour of Europe, Nye could remember numerous occasions when Reginald had led them astray. In Reginald's case, a pretty face was usually the distraction, but in one instance, a horse being mistreated had raised his young master's ire. The resulting fray had nearly landed them in a French prison cell. Fortunately the gendarme was bribable, and the carter was willing to accept payment for the damage to his goods. Goods Reginald had thrown off the cart to lighten the load for the overburdened horse.

Smiling, Nye wondered what adventures this new development would add to their journey. That the young woman had some kind of problem was obvious – that the D'Arcys had decided to help her no matter the difficulties was a given. He had to admit Mistress Norton, was that her name, was a pretty thing, and the children were cute and precocious. Whatever the situation, it should make the tedious journey more bearable, at least from his point of view. He could not help but wonder how Esmeralda Shadwell would view the new circumstances. 'Twould mean company for her in the coach, but also more responsibilities.

Mistress Shadwell agreed to this journey because of her great affection for Lady Rygate. Jostling about in the coach was hard on the older woman, but a younger maid could have had no influence over Lady Selena. Lady Rygate had known well that a stable matron was needed to curb her daughter's antics. After Reginald's and his excursion on the continent, Nye would have preferred a respite with his family, but Reginald had been given the task of conducting his sister to Whimbrel, and of course, Nye was expected to accompany Reginald. Nye could not complain. He was well paid. The younger son of one of Lord Rygate's wealthier tenants, he had forsaken the land, having little chance of an inheritance, to enter into service with Lord Rygate. In time, he had been picked to act as personal servant to young Reginald. The two had formed a bond, and Nye guessed when Reginald one day assumed control of the estate he would inherit from his mother, Nye would be offered the position of steward.

He closed his eyes, happy in the knowledge his prospects were secure. What the immediate future would bring, he could not say, but he had no doubt it would be interesting.

Chapter 5

Wade Felton watched Mistress Bowdon and the two children climb into the stately coach after an imposing older woman. A footman then placed a small, black-and-white dog with a splint on its leg on a blanket on the floor of the coach. A handsome young man said something to the passengers of the coach and a youth patted the dog. Then the door was closed, and the footman swung up onto a foot stand at the back of the coach. The young man and the youth mounted their fine-looking horses, and the small cavalcade set off.

Felton ambled over to the inn's ostler, a heavy-set man with several days' stubble on his chin. Grinning, Felton said, "Was I not mistaken, that were Mistress Bowdon of Churlwood that did board that coach. Where might she be headed?"

The ostler eyed him malevolently. "What is it to you where the young miss be headed?"

Felton widened his grin, doffed his hat, and wiped his brow. "Bain't none of my business. But when I worked at the Churlwood, the lady were kind to me. I thought mayhap she had recently married, and I missed me chance to offer her felicitations."

"Well, you be mistaken. The young lady be Mistress Norton, not Bowdon."

Felton nodded. "Ah, guess I should have known 'twas not her. 'Twas some coach, though."

The ostler snorted. "Them D'Arcys is too fine to have the likes of me caring for their coach or their horses. Coachman says they will see to their horses themselves. Said all I need do is see the horses have clean stalls and fresh hay. Slept inside the coach the coachman did, and the postilion on a mat by the wheels. Coachman says he will tike no chance the D'Arcy belongings might be robbed. We run a respectable inn I tells him, but no matter."

34

Again snorting, he shook his head and started to turn away, but Felton stopped him, saying, "Some of them servants what works for them peers think they are a heap better'n the rest of us."

His disapproval obvious, the ostler nodded. "Aye. They come in late last night. Still expecting a fine supper. Kept me wife, she being the cook, up late preparing a meal." He cocked his head and his eyes softened a bit. "Must say though, that Lady D'Arcy, she is first rate. She and her brother seen to their own mounts, but the vail she pressed on me was as fine as if I had curried her horse meself. Wife said Mister D'Arcy's manservant gave her a fine gratuity, too."

Felton racked his brain. He could not remember seeing any young woman on horseback. He was certain the ostler could not be talking about the large woman who had been the first to board the coach. "I saw no lady on horseback," he finally said as the ostler started to walk away.

The ostler chuckled and looked back over his shoulder. "Well, now, you might not have noticed her, her being dressed like a gent and riding astraddle. Looks like a youth she does. That is what I took her for last night when she rode in. Mayhap them fine ladies can do whatever they please," he huffed, striding away.

Pushing aside the idea of a lady dressing and riding like a man, Felton hurried after the ostler. "I suppose the other ladies and the children were mighty weary," he said. "Arriving late like that."

"The young mistress and her children were not part of the D'Arcy party when they arrived. Seems they must haf been expecting to meet up with the D'Arcys. Wife says they joined the D'Arcys for supper. Guess they were old friends," the ostler threw back over his shoulder as he stalked back to the stables.

Felton slowly nodded his head. He knew he was not mistaken. The young woman going by the name of Norton was Mistress Bowdon. She was too beautiful for him to mistake her. 'Twas her beauty that got him fired. What was she up to? What was her connection to the D'Arcys? 'Twas his guess, the children with her were the Bowdon children by the late Baronet's second wife. That meant the boy was the new baronet, master of Churlwood. Could Mistress Bowdon be eloping? Possible, though why would she take the children? He decided he would meander over to Churlwood and see was anything untoward going on. He had learned over the years that whenever anything appeared baffling, there was a good chance he could come into a few coins. With the old baronet gone, should be safe to visit the estate. He rubbed his grizzled chin and looked down at his grubby coat and breeches. He would spruce himself up first. Best to make a good impression.

❀ ❀ ❀ ❀

Amaryllis smiled at her sister. The child, seated next to Mistress Shadwell in the forward-facing seat, was chatting gaily with the older woman. She was telling Mistress Shadwell the story Amaryllis had recently read her about a beautiful princess rescued from a vicious dragon by the valiant Sir Lancelot. Some of the plot got a little twisted, but Mistress Shadwell made no complaints. She but smiled and nodded and asked an occasional question.

Sitting on the coach floor with the dog, Charlie seemed to be enjoying the story as well. When Tabitha had Sir Lancelot draw his sword, Charlie drew a make-believe sword and slashed it around over his head until his little fist hit Amaryllis's knee. His mouth formed an o, and wide-eyed, he said, "Sorry, Ryllis."

"That is all right, Charlie, but be careful. You would not want to hit Mistress Shadwell."

Mistress Shadwell glanced down at Charlie. "Are you certain you are comfortable on the floor, young master?

He looked up and grinned. "Yes, Mistress. I like to pet the doggie."

"Well, as long as you are both content." She looked over at Amaryllis. "You are having no trouble riding backwards, Mistress Norton? You are not feeling ill?"

Amaryllis blushed. She had not yet told her kind benefactors their real surname. She would have to do that soon. Mayhap when they stopped for their noon meal and to rest the horses. "I am doing fine, thank you," she said. "I have always rather liked traveling despite the discomforts." As she spoke, the coach hit a particularly rough bump, and they were all jostled about on their seats. The thick padded cushions helped minimize the worst of the bumps and bounces. The children seemed to find the jostling amusing. They both giggled whenever a bump sent them flying up then back down on their bums. The coach's swaying and rocking from side to side as its large wheels rolled over the rutted road had almost a soothing quality. It certainly seemed to put the dog to sleep, and Charlie's head was starting to nod. He should be sleepy. He had had a very late night for a two-and-a half-year-old little boy. Did he drop into sleep, she would pull him up on the seat beside her and pillow his head in her lap.

In the past six months since his father's death and the arrival of his uncle and aunt and their two sons, the little guy had been through so much. She hoped he was young enough he would not remember the painful incidents. He was a resilient little fellow, cheerful and amiable, brimming with love and good will. Looking down at his sweet face, Amaryllis felt her heart swell with love. That Charlie and Tabitha would be at a safe haven in less than a fortnight lifted her spirits immensely. This time last week, she had been desperate. Then a letter arrived from the children's mother's sister. She and her husband would be visiting her husband's sister in Derby. Before returning to their home, they planned to visit Churlwood. Amaryllis's fears for Charlie mounting, she decided she could not wait for the visit. She had to act. Did she hesitate, Charlie might be dead by the time his aunt arrived.

Aunt Elva and Uncle Irwin had been in the house little more than a week when Charlie tumbled down the stairs in the main hall. Amaryllis had just entered the hall, and she screeched when she saw her brother come crashing down, head over heels. She fell to her knees beside him. He blinked his eyes and giggled. Crying his name, she clasped him to her breast. She looked up to the top of the staircase at her aunt. Her face bland, devoid of emotion, Aunt Elva asked, "Is he all right?"

"I think so," Amaryllis said. "I have told him not to go down the stairs without help."

"I started to help him, but he pushed my hand away," Aunt Elva said. "Where is his nanny that she was not with him?"

"This is Molly's afternoon off. She goes into town to visit her family."

Aunt Elva sniffed. "I am not certain I approve of such a young nurse. We may need to find a more experienced woman who has no need to run home to her family."

Rising with Charlie still in her arms, Amaryllis said, "Molly is a good nurse. She was Tabitha's nurse, and her mother was my nurse. The children love Molly."

"Well, we shall see," Aunt Elva said, and raising her chin, she stalked away.

That evening when Amaryllis came up to say goodnight to the children, Tabitha whispered, "Aunt Elva pushed Charlie."

Her arms around her little sister, Amaryllis pulled back enough to look into the child's eyes. "What did you say?"

Tabitha's eyes shifted from side to side then she again whispered, "Aunt Elva pushed him. I saw her do it. Charlie was scooting down on his bottom, and she pushed him with her foot."

"Surely you are mistaken."

The girl shook her head. "No. I saw her. She never smiles at us. Does she not like us?"

Amaryllis hugged Tabitha. "How could anyone not like you two sweethearts? She is but used to her rough and tumble sons. Give her time. She will come to love you as I do."

Tabitha looked doubtful and Amaryllis was also doubtful, but she could not believe their Aunt Elva had pushed the child down the stairs. That the boy had nothing more wrong with him than a scratch on his nose was a miracle. But not two weeks later, he had a horrible gash on his leg and bump on his head from a fall out of a tree.

"How was I to know he would climb up the ladder after me," said Dorian, Aunt Elva's younger son. At fourteen, he was surly, and with his blemished skin, dirty hair, and watery, near-sighted eyes, unappealing.

Amaryllis could believe Charlie might try to climb a ladder – she could not believe Charlie would follow Dorian. The boy had made no attempt to befriend either Tabitha or Charlie. He ogled Amaryllis in a most disturbing way and was constantly trying to brush up against her, but he ignored the children. Never went near the nursery. Fortunately, the following day, he was to return to his boarding school. But in the meantime, she wanted to know what truly happened. Having insisted her uncle send for the local physician, then being assured by the kindly

38

man that Charlie had no internal injuries, and the bump on his head was not serious, Amaryllis started asking questions.

Returning to the nursery after walking the physician to the door, Amaryllis asked, "Molly, why was Charlie not with you?"

Her large brown eyes red with crying, Molly said, "Oh, Mistress Bowdon, you must know how much I love Charlie and how upset I am that he should be injured."

"I know that Molly, but why did you leave him alone outside?"

Molly looked warily from side to side as Tabitha had done two weeks earlier. Her tone fearful, her round, freckled face apprehensive, she said, "I would never have done so, Mistress, but your aunt's maid said your aunt wanted to see me immediately. I started to get Tabitha and Charlie, but the maid said I was to hurry. She said she would mind the children. I told her they should come inside. They had been out in the cold long enough." She lowered her voice. "I cannot say I liked leaving them in her care. She is very haughty. But I did as I was bid. I was told your aunt awaited me in the parlor, but she was not there. I searched for her but never found her, then I heard all the commotion and hurried back outside."

"Was Dorian outside when you left the children with Aunt Elva's maid?"

"Nay, Mistress. I cannot say I saw him. But the ladder was there. Charlie never went near it, though. He was happy playing with his spinning top." She gave a half-smile. "Not that he could keep it going long. But he was persistent."

"Have you since seen my aunt to ask her what she wanted of you?"

Molly shook her head. "I tried to ask her, but she brushed past me." Molly's lip trembled. "She said I was … I was an untrustworthy nurse. Oh, you cannot think that, can you?"

Amaryllis looked into Molly's misty eyes. She patted her on the shoulder. "No, Molly. I think you are a fine nurse. Now, do please entertain Charlie. Mister Brighton says he should sit quietly for the rest of the day. And he says not to let him go to sleep before his regular bed time."

"Yes, Mistress. I will set up his horses for him. He likes to play with them."

Amaryllis smiled. "That will be good." She looked at Tabitha and Charlie sitting at their little table playing with their Jacob's ladder. Tabitha was so good at keeping her brother entertained. Soon though, they would need to seek a governess for Tabitha.

Tabitha, when later questioned, told Amaryllis she had not seen Charlie climb the ladder. "I would have stopped him," she declared. "But Aunt Elva's maid took me in the house. She did scold me – said I spoiled my gown and that I needed to change it." Tabitha shook her head. "Honest, Ryllis, 'twas but a few leaves on my gown. I tried to show her I could brush them off, but she would not listen."

"So she left Charlie alone?"

"No, Dorian was there. She asked Dorian to mind Charlie."

Being but two, Charlie had been too young to tell his side of the story, but the incident had started Amaryllis wondering if the two accidents had really been accidents. The third incident had been minor. Charlie had been scratched by Aunt Elva's cat. Aunt Elva, despite Amaryllis's protests, had used the happenstance to dismiss Molly and hire Nurse Palmer.

Another large jolt brought Amaryllis's thoughts back to the present. As she had formulated her plans, she could never have dreamed they would be traveling in such a luxurious coach, aided by such kind-hearted people. "Mistress Shadwell," she said, "are the D'Arcys always so kind and generous? I cannot think how I can thank them enough for inviting us to travel with them. What a blessing this is for the children."

Mistress Shadwell gave her a warm smile. "Indeed, they are ever generous. Some might say to a fault. I believe they inherited their loving natures from their mother. She is the sweetest, gentlest, and the loveliest person you could ever hope to know."

Amaryllis nodded. "Lady Selena and Mister D'Arcy do speak very lovingly of her."

Mistress Shadwell nodded. "They are devoted to her." Then her eyes saddened and her mouth drooped. "Eight years ago Lady Rygate was in a terrible accident," she said. "Her coach overturned. Four of her children were with her. Fortunately none of the children were seriously injured. Lady Rygate, however, was left paralyzed from the waist down."

Amaryllis's hands flew to her mouth, and she gasped, "Oh, how dreadful."

"Despite her encumbrance, Lady Rygate is ever cheerful, ever kind," Mistress Shadwell continued, her eyes softening and misting with unshed tears. "Consequently, we can none of us deny her any requests." She smiled again, a wry smile. "'Tis why I am here. At my age I had no desire to travel from Rygate to Whimbrel, but Lady Rygate did ask me." She sighed. "I could do naught but agree to her request."

Amaryllis could now understand why none of the D'Arcys or their staff informed Lady Rygate of the mischievous antics of her children. How unfortunate such a lovely person should have suffered such a terrible accident.

"What is paralyzed?" Tabitha asked.

Amaryllis looked at her sister. How to explain such a thing to a six-year-old child? She dared not remind the child of their father's last few days. Their father, having suffered the apoplexy, had been unable to move or talk or even eat. Amaryllis and her father's manservant had done their best to make his last days comfortable, bathing his forehead, giving him small sips of wine, chafing his cold hands. The local physician had suggested several treatments Amaryllis had rebuffed, considering them too vile to inflict on her beloved father. The Baronet's consciousness had been fleeting. Fearing her father might die without seeing his children, Amaryllis reluctantly brought Tabitha and Charlie in to say goodbye to their father.

Tabitha had been devastated by her father's appearance and lack of mobility, and Amaryllis believed she had erred in letting the child see her father one last time. "Tabitha, you must remember Father as he was before he became so ill. Remember how he used to tickle you, how he used to jiggle you on his knee, or carry you about on his back. Remember how much he loved you and Charlie. That is what you must never forget."

The little girl had solemnly promised she would always cherish the good memories, but Amaryllis knew the bedside horror had haunted Tabitha for many a night. She could not bring that frightful time back to the child. It was a memory best left in the recesses of the mind. She glanced down at Charlie and the little dog then looked back at her sister. "See how Fate, with the brace on his leg, cannot move his leg.

For now his leg is paralyzed. That is how Lady Rygate's legs are. She cannot move them. When the brace comes off Fate's leg, he will be able to move it again, but Lady Rygate will never move her legs again. Because of the accident, her legs are permanently paralyzed"

Tabitha's lower lip trembled, and she looked up at Mistress Shadwell. "I am sorry Lady Rygate was hurt. I wish she could get better soon. She sounds like a nice lady."

Mistress Shadwell looked down at Tabitha and smiled. "Thank you, Mistress Tabitha. You are a good girl. You have a kind heart."

"I sorry, too," Charlie said.

Mistress Shadwell nodded. "Well, indeed, you have a kind heart, too. And I am most pleased all of you have joined us in our travels. I was quite lonely here in this big coach all on my own."

"Shall I tell you another story?" Tabitha asked. "I know one about a knight and a mean giant. 'Tis Charlie's favorite."

"Yes, oh yes," Charlie said, bouncing on his knees. "Tell that one!"

"By all means, tell me about the knight and the mean giant," Mistress Shadwell said.

"Mayhap, you should wait on the story, Tabitha," Amaryllis said. "We have a long journey yet. You might want to save your stories for another day."

"Oh, no, I want it now," Charlie whined, and Tabitha's face fell.

"Very well," Amaryllis said, "does Mistress Shadwell not object."

Both children brightened, and Tabitha said, "Oh, but she likes the stories about knights, do you not, Mistress Shadwell?"

Inclining her head, Mistress Shadwell answered, "You are correct, Mistress Tabitha. Stories about knights are my favorite. Just like Master Charlie."

Tabitha looked at Amaryllis. "See Ryllis. I made certain they were her favorite."

"So be it," Amaryllis said with a smile, and Tabitha began her story. As the child's cheery voice bubbled on, Amaryllis closed her eyes and envisioned Reginald as the brave knight.

Chapter 6

Elva Bowdon paced back and forth across the parlor floor. Why had Amaryllis run away with the children? What did she know? Or suspect? Had she gone to the Yardleys'? Where else could she have gone but to the children's grandfather? Elva stopped her pacing and chewed a nail. Had she not encountered the maid returning to the kitchen with the children's uneaten breakfast, when might their disappearance have been noted? Their nurse had attempted to excuse her late sleeping, had tried to blame the cook.

"She must have drugged me," Nurse Palmer said. "I would ne'er otherwise oversleep."

Elva would not be at all surprised had the cook drugged Palmer, but she chastised the nurse all the same and demanded, "You had best find those children. And quickly!"

Employing every maid and footman, the search had begun. Every room in the house was searched. The grounds, the stable and other outbuildings, the estate woods, all were scoured. Elva sent Palmer to search the village church and to question the vicar. She insisted her husband take several men to search the village, and question the tenants. All was for naught. No sign of Amaryllis or the children. 'Twas Elva's personal maid who discovered Amaryllis's portmanteau was missing. Then Palmer declared she was certain a small satchel was not to be found.

Her heart thumping, Elva made a decision. "Irwin, you and Averil must chase down the stage headed to Aylesbury. I cannot but think Amaryllis is taking the children to their grandfather's."

"Why would she do that?" Averil asked.

Averil was Elva's older son, and she loved him dearly, but he could be dense. "Because she thinks I am being too strict with the children. 'Tis for their own good. They are too spoiled, but Amaryllis would not heed my wisdom. She would forever nag at me. Now she has run off with them, and you and your father must bring them back."

"Really, Elva, I cannot think she would attempt to take those children by stage all the way to Cheshire," Irwin Bowdon said. "Surely she must be hiding at a friend's. She but wants to scare us that you may relent in your strictness with young Charlie and Tabitha. Should we not first visit some of the local families?"

Elva glared at her husband. Was he also a dunce? She knew well he had no desire to go chasing after the stage. He was aging. His joints creaked, his knees ached, and his protruding stomach made any long-distance travel, especially on horseback, disagreeable. That he had once been a handsome man, handsome enough to win her love, now seemed incredible. His once thick, dark hair had thinned to near balding. At home he wore a comfortable turban, but did he go out, he was forced to wear his wig which he claimed gave him a headache. Sometimes when she looked at him with his sagging jowls and the deep pockets under his eyes, his yellowing teeth and pudgy hands, she felt revulsion.

She knew she was no longer the beauty she had once been, but she had kept her figure. And her skin, when properly powdered and painted, showed few wrinkles. Her maid was a wizard with her creams and oils, and Elva paid her a high wage to keep the woman at her side.

"I cannot but think Father is right," Averil said, his gray-blue eyes, so like his father's, showed he also had little desire to heed his mother's direction. He was not as handsome as his father had been in his youth, but when properly attired, he made an impressive enough figure. He would make a fine baronet one day – was Charlie out of the way. Having recently gained his majority, Averil was wanting more often of late to assert himself. At times she was willing to let him. This was not one of those times.

"Must I do all the thinking for this family? Does Amaryllis reach Charlie's grandfather and tell him her little lies about us, he could well attempt to have us put out of this house while he takes over Charlie's guardianship. Is that what you dunderheads want!"

Father and son shook their heads. "No, dear, I see your point," Irwin said. "We will head out right away."

She caught her husband's arm. "Irwin, you need bring back only the boy. Let Amaryllis and Tabitha go on to Yardleys'."

"But will not Amaryllis tell Sir Cyril all the lies you are concerned about?" Averil asked.

Elva smiled. "She can tell him all she wants. It matters not so long as we have Charlie. And does Sir Cyril come to see how Charlie fares. He will find all in order. Now go! The both of you!" She fluttered her hand at them and watched them hurry away. Still, she worried. What if she had guessed wrong? What if Amaryllis had some other plan?

"Mistress Bowdon." A footman tapped on the parlor door, and she bade him enter.

She looked at him hopefully. "What is it? Have the children been found?"

The footman shook his head. "Nay Mistress." He wrinkled his nose and curled his upper lip. "There is a man to see you. Says his name is *Mister* Felton, but I cannot think him a gentleman."

"Felton? I know no Felton. What does he want?"

"He will not say, Mistress. He but says he must speak with Mister Bowdon or you."

Curious, Elva said, "Very well. Show him in." Could be he knew something about the children.

The man entered, pulling off his cap as he came through the door. "Name is Felton, Mistress Bowdon, Wade Felton, at your service."

"What do you want Felton? I am very busy." She did not like the looks of the man even though she could tell he was newly shaven and had apparently donned clean or at least relatively clean clothing. She still picked up an offensive body odor when he drew closer.

Felton looked over his shoulder at the footman. "'Tis a private word I am needing with you, Mistress Bowdon."

Elva nodded to the footman. "That will be all, Dill. Close the door. I will ring do I need you." The footman inclined his head, backed out of the room, and softly shut the door.

Elva looked back at Felton. "Well?" she demanded.

Felton smirked. "Well, indeed. I did pass through the village and did hear the tenants saying you be looking for Mistress Amaryllis and for young Sir Charles and his sister."

Elva brightened. "You have seen them?"

"Aye, that I haf."

"Where, where did you see them?"

"Well now, Mistress Bowdon, I am not a rich man. Finding work can be hard and …"

"Yes, yes, you will receive adequate recompense do you truly know where they are."

He grinned. "They are a ways from here by now."

"Ah, ha! I knew it! You saw them board the stage to Aylesbury."

"Nay, Mistress Bowdon, they boarded no stage, and they were not headed to Aylesbury."

She narrowed her eyes. "You had best not be lying to me."

He shook his head. "Nay, I am telling no lie. They are headed northeast, but not by stage."

"So tell me what you saw, or so help me I will call the constable and have you arrested for withholding information about a possible abduction."

"You need not get nasty, Mistress Bowdon. I come here to tell you what I seen. Mistress Amaryllis and the two little ones are traveling in the D'Arcys' coach. And a fine coach it is."

"The D'Arcys'?" She narrowed her eyes. "Who are the D'Arcys? We know no D'Arcys."

"Well, Mistress Amaryllis must know 'em cause she popped right in the coach, and it set off along the road to Leicester."

Elva stared at the man. Was he lying? Amaryllis going northeast? It made no sense. And who were these D'Arcys she was traveling with? Then she remembered a letter Amaryllis had received from Charlie and Tabitha's Aunt Juliet. Their aunt was visiting her husband's sister in Derbyshire. Amaryllis must be taking the children to their aunt. But it was a long journey, and anything could happen. And should anything happen to the boy, Amaryllis would be blamed.

She had no idea who these D'Arcys were, but she felt certain she was right about where Amaryllis was headed. That was what mattered. She narrowed her eyes and studied Felton, looking him up and down from his rough work boots, coarse linen stockings, and worn woolen breeches to his dingy coat and vest and grimy shirt. Guessing him to be in his mid-thirties, she judged him a ne'er do well, but he did not seem lacking in intelligence. What might he do for the right amount of money?

Felton shifted on his feet. "About that recompense, Mistress Bowdon?"

"Tell me, Mister Felton, how would you like to make enough money so you would never need to work again? Never need be subservient to anyone? Say you had a nice yearly annuity."

Felton straightened, cocked his head, and narrowed his eyes. "You offering me an annuity? What is it then you are after me to do to get that kind of blunt?"

"You look like a man who has been in his fair share of scrapes. You also look like a man who has not always been given his fair due. You are smart, you know you are smart, but people misjudge you. You are not given the respect due a man of your wit and capability. Am I not right?" She watched Felton straighten his shoulders and puff out his chest.

Raising his chin, Felton squinted down his nose at her. "There be times I haf been slighted. But, you are right, I am smart. Did I not recognize Mistress Amaryllis? Did I not know something was cavey, her there with the children in Albertine like that?"

"Indeed, you were most astute, most wise. And you have told no one else, no one in the village what you saw?" As she suspected, Felton was susceptible to flattery, but she had to make certain no one would connect him to her.

He shook his head. "Nay, I but listened. Then I came here. So about this annuity? What is it you are a-wanting me to do?"

Chapter 7

When Reginald rode up beside the coach to tell Amaryllis their night's destination was in sight, she admitted to being ready for the day's journey to end. When they had stopped at an inn for a respite for the horses and for a noonday meal, Amaryllis, after apologizing for her earlier deception, told the D'Arcys her real surname.

"You have no need to apologize," Selena said. "You were wise not to reveal your name while still at the inn. What if we had slipped and had accidentally addressed you as Mistress Bowdon. We would have given you away. But I admit to being surprised you were not recognized by someone in Albertine."

"I doubt anyone would know me. Not at the inn anyway. We never stayed overnight there, home being not an hour away. And we never shopped there. Father preferred to go to Watford. He had friends he liked to visit there. It took us but a couple of hours to get to Watford, and the selection of goods was superior to those in Albertine. Our tenants shop in Albertine, and sometimes the steward has need to order goods from the smith or some other of the merchants, but the manor's village meets our smaller needs. It has a church, a carpenter, a potter, a thatcher, a barrel maker, a cobbler, and a growing cloth industry of weavers and dyers. And of course, we have a mill. Anyway, I had no choice. I had to chance no one would recognize me."

"Wise thinking," Reginald said, "but how did you get from your home to the inn? Surely you cannot say you walked all the way?"

Amaryllis shook her head. "Nay. Cook again helped me. For the past two years she has been courted by a widower, a wealthy tenant from a neighboring estate. She arranged to have him await me under a sheltering willow tree where he and his donkey cart would be shielded from prying eyes. He kindly carted us near to Albertine. To a path that cuts through a meadow and then a small wooded area. He would have brought us into town, but he might have been recognized, and I could not risk getting him in trouble. We had need to walk but a little less than a mile." She smiled at her sister. "Seemed a long walk to Tabitha I do think."

Tabitha, whose mouth was stuffed with a plum tart Reginald had insisted on ordering for her, could do little more than nod vigorously.

Selena laughed then asked, "What of your cook? Will she not get into trouble for drugging the children's nurse?"

"I cannot think so. First they could never prove it." Amaryllis dabbed at her mouth with her napkin before continuing. "Second, Cook, Mistress Bridger is her name, though I cannot think when she is ever called such, is an excellent cook, as Tabitha did mention. After my mother's death, she had complete control of the kitchen. I was too young to plan menus, and Beatrice, the children's mother," she glanced at Tabitha and Charlie, "was too shy and unassuming to even think of giving Cook any directions. Did we have guests, or was but the family dining, we ate what Cook served us. It was always delicious. However, Aunt Elva decided she wanted to plan the menus – Cook rebelled. She said she would marry her suitor, and Aunt Elva could find herself another cook." Amaryllis smiled. "Uncle Irwin is mild-mannered and usually lets Aunt Elva have her way in near everything, but not where Cook was concerned. He told Aunt Elva she was to stay clear of the kitchen. Did she do anything to cause Cook to leave, he would send her back to their house in Langley, which is where they lived before moving in at Churlwood. Uncle Irwin had a small law practice there, and they have some income from Aunt Elva's dowry."

Amaryllis rolled her eyes upward and arched her brows. "Where his stomach is concerned, Uncle Irwin can be quite adamant. Aunt Elva knew better than to thwart him." Waggling her head, Amaryllis concluded, "So again, to answer your question, Selena, I doubt Cook will even be questioned. She could well walk out the door and not look back."

Reginald chuckled. "Good for your Mistress Bridger. I cannot but think our cook at Rygate would applaud her. He rules our kitchen. Oh, he will consult with Mother, but never with the housekeeper. I do think he has a continual feud going with her."

"I am certain he does," Selena said. "They cannot abide one another. Did Esmeralda not intercede on a regular basis, I believe they might actually come to blows. Of course, Mother has no idea of the animosity between them. Is Mother present, they are naught but courteous and solicitous to each other."

"Mistress Shadwell told me of your mother's accident. I am so very sorry."

Selena gave her a soft smile. "Thank you. Mother is the dearest person, and despite being partially paralyzed, she is the most vibrant person. No one can help but love her." She shook her head. "But here now, is everyone finished eating, should we not get back on the road? I should think the horses rested. What say you Reggie?" She looked to her brother.

"I think it might be a bit soon yet, but we will see what Mister Pit says. Does he think they need a bit longer rest, we could take a stroll and stretch our legs. The day is lovely, and I saw a pond on the edge of town. And I think I saw baby ducks. Might be fun for the children."

"Oh, yes!" Tabitha said. "Might we go see the duckies."

"Duckies, duckies," Charlie sang out. "I want see duckies."

Selena laughed. "Now it would seem we have no choice, dear brother. We must take that stroll even does Mister Pit say the horses are ready."

"Oh, no, we mean not to hold you up," Amaryllis said. "Children, hush, we are guests, you must not carry on so."

"Nonsense," Reginald said. "A walk will do us all good." He turned to his valet. "Nye, do you please advise Pit we will be taking a stroll. Then join us do you wish."

Nye rose from his place at the end of the table next to Mistress Shadwell. "Thank you, Master Reginald, I could use a bit of a walk. I will join you after I have consulted with Pit."

"Oh, and Mister Nye," Selena said, "do please ask Norwood to come get Fate. After Fate has met his needs, Norwood can put him in the coach." She looked over her shoulder at the little dog thumping his tail on the hard plank flooring. Amaryllis was amazed the dog seemed to already have learned his name. And he seemed devoted to his savior.

"I will tell him, Lady Selena," Nye said before exiting the private parlor. The footmen, outriders, coachman, and postilion had dined in the public room. They had chores to attend before they could eat, but Selena and Reginald had seen to their own horses themselves before sitting down to their meal. Amaryllis smiled inwardly. The D'Arcys were a constant source of amazement.

The walk to the edge of the town was short, but Amaryllis enjoyed stretching her legs. Reginald carried Charlie piggy-back, and Charlie chuckled with glee when he bounced him a few times. Baby ducks were indeed in the pond, and both children cooed over them. The mother duck kept her ducklings at a distance, but a couple of male ducks came close and quacked at the children.

Selena, in very unladylike fashion, squatted down beside Tabitha. "Now what do you think those two are telling us?"

Tabitha giggled. "They are saying stay away from the duckies or we will peck you."

"Could be," Selena said, "or could be they are asking, did you used to be our mother?"

"Oh, do you think these might be your baby ducks?" Tabitha looked wide-eyed from Selena to the ducks and back to Selena.

"Well, I have no idea how far ducks might travel, but a couple of my males took off and never came back. And they were quite handsome. Just as these two fellows are."

Tabitha's grin was so wide it seemed ready to split her face. "Oh, I will bet these are your ducks, and they came to say hello. Might we pet them?"

"Yes, pet them," Charlie said.

"No time for petting," Reginald said, and relief flooded Amaryllis. She could well imagine Selena wading into the pond after the ducks. "Here comes Nye," Reginald added for emphasis. "I have no doubt 'tis time to get back on the road."

"All are ready when you are, sir," Nye said when he reached them.

The two ducks paddled away and Tabitha went, "Ahhh, they are leaving."

Selena laughed. "They said their greeting. Now wave goodbye, and let us be on our way. As we stay with friends of my father tonight, we cannot wish to arrive too late in the evening."

The children waved, then Reginald scooped Charlie up and headed off at a gallop that again had the little boy chuckling. Assured by both Selena and Reginald that the Hinghams would have no trouble accommodating her and the children, Amaryllis still felt slightly ill at ease at the prospect of imposing upon people who were not expecting her, though she knew such hospitality was the norm. Her father had always been ready to accommodate travelers, many who were but friends of friends.

For the next couple of hours, her mind drifted from one subject to another as the children and Mistress Shadwell napped. Her reverie came to an abrupt halt as the coach drew to a stop before an old manor house that looked to have seen few changes since it had been built. She guessed it to date from the fourteenth century. Its square crenelated tower, covered in ivy, was but two stories high. A multipaned window had been added above the ground-level arched doorway. A long, low building connected the tower to a two-story house with a sloping, tiled roof and two large chimneys.

A footman hurried to take the heads of the horses, and the other footman, Norwood Amaryllis believed was his name, opened the door to the coach and let down the steps. "You go ahead," Mistress Shadwell said. "It takes me awhile to climb out." Tired and bored after the day's travel, the children needed no additional invitation to exit. Tabitha bounced out and Charlie clambered down the steps. The footman held out his hand to help Amaryllis descend. She looked down to mind her steps, and upon looking up, found an aged man with kindly blue eyes had emerged from the tower. His bright blue coat and tan breeches looked fresh and unwrinkled as though but recently donned. His gray hair floated about his stooped shoulders. Holding out an age-spotted hand, he offered her a generous smile. "Welcome to you, Lady Selena. I am Jacob Hingham. 'Tis a pleasure to have you stopover with us."

Amaryllis blushed. "Oh, no sir. I am not Lady Selena, I am …"

She was interrupted by Selena. Selena had dismounted but still held her horse by its reins. "Mister Hingham, how kind of you to greet us. I am Selena D'Arcy." She held out a hand toward Amaryllis. "This is our dear friend, Mistress Amaryllis Bowdon. She and her sister, Mistress Tabitha, and brother, Sir Charles Bowdon, are traveling with us." She indicated the children, and as Mistress Shadwell was being helped from the coach by Norwood, Selena added, "And this is my maid and traveling companion, Mistress Shadwell."

Reginald had come up beside his sister, and sweeping off his hat, he said, "I am Reginald D'Arcy. We do most heartily thank you for providing us lodging, Mister Hingham."

Hingham stared in surprise at Selena, as well he might, Amaryllis thought. 'Twas hard to connect this woman dressed in male attire with the woman she had shared the supper table with the previous evening. Shaking his head as if to clear it, Hingham's genial smile reappeared. He bowed over Selena's hand. "Welcome to all of you. We have been looking forward to your visit, brief though it may be. My wife and I have a great fondness for both Lord and Lady Rygate, and we look forward to hearing how they fare. Do come in, come in. The air is beginning to chill. We have a fire going in the hearth in the house, and a mulled cider ready to warm your insides. My men will direct your men to the stables and show them where they will bed tonight."

"Thank you, Mister Hingham," Reginald said, "but Selena and I like to see to our horses ourselves. Do please take Mistress Bowdon and the children inside. We should not be long."

Hingham again looked surprised, but he managed to say, "Of course, of course." He turned to Amaryllis. "Mistress Bowdon, Mistress Shadwell, please step this way."

A footman held open the door to the tower and Amaryllis, followed by the children, Mistress Shadwell, and Hingham, entered the hall. It was easily as old as Amaryllis had suspected, mayhap older. The hall was a bustle. Servants were laying white cloths over trestle tables then placing trenchers and spoons, goblets and noggins, and linen napkins on the tables once the cloths were in place.

"Look," Tabitha said, tugging on her sister's skirt. "The hearth is in the middle of the floor."

"Indeed it is, young miss," Hingham said. "This keep dates from the thirteen hundreds – long before chimneys became prevalent in most homes. Other than adding the window above the door to allow for better lighting, we have chosen not to alter the hall. But you will find the rest of our home has all the modern comforts, though it dates from 1542." He looked with obvious pride around the hall then brought his focus back to Amaryllis. "'Tis not often we have guests of such distinction as the D'Arcys. We thought to honor them with a banquet. Several of the local gentry have been invited, and some of our more prominent tenants will be in attendance."

Extending an arm towards an open door, he directed them to a passageway leading from the hall to the main house. "But come, let me introduce you to my wife. She awaits us in the parlor. You may warm yourselves while your rooms are made ready."

Absently scooping up Charlie, Amaryllis wondered how the D'Arcys would feel about this *honor* after their long day on the road. Mistress Shadwell took Tabitha by the hand, and they followed after Hingham. Still feeling she was imposing on the Hinghams, Amaryllis hoped the D'Arcys would soon join them. The passageway to the house had several windows that let in the last rays of the day's sun. The flooring was slate, and the clip-clop of their heels resounded against yellow plastered walls.

Hingham passed through the door at the end of the passageway and stood aside for his guests to enter a well-appointed parlor aglow with a multitude of candles. A cheery fire in a cobblestone hearth added a warm comfort to the room. Green woven-rush matting covered the floor, and the sweet scent of dried lavender pervading the room mingled with the scent of warm cider. Two women standing at a sideboard turned when the entourage entered. The older one, obviously the lady of the house, had beautiful white hair piled artfully upon her head, and her gown, though not of the first fashion, was of a rich blue satin. It had a gold-embroidered stomacher, and the white lace collar and cuffs of her shift peeked out below the sleeves of her gown and at her neckline. The other woman, a servant or companion, was modestly dressed in a dark green gown with a white apron.

The older woman smiled sweetly, and advancing toward Amaryllis, held out her bejeweled fingers and cooed, "Welcome, Lady Selena."

Amaryllis again blushed, but Hingham quickly corrected his wife and introduced their unexpected guests. He then introduced the woman in the green gown as his cousin, Mistress Parr.

"Well, we must see another chamber is readied." Mistress Hingham turned to her husband's cousin. "Kate, do you tell Gertie to ready the chamber next to Lady Selena's. And I suppose we must need ready the nursery."

"Oh, please no, Mistress Hingham," Amaryllis said. "Tabitha and Charlie can sleep with me. You have no need to go to extra trouble for us."

"But the children will need a place to eat their supper, and someone must see them to bed. You my dear will be at the banquet," Mistress Hingham said, a sweet smile on her face.

Amaryllis returned the smile though she wished she could skip the banquet. She would prefer to go to bed early after their long day.

"The children can eat here in the parlor with me," Mistress Shadwell said. "And does Mistress Bowdon approve, afterwards I will see them to bed. I am that tired myself and think I must need retire early tonight. I am not so young, as you may well judge."

Amaryllis could do naught but approve the plan when Mistress Hingham clapped her hands and said, "Splendid. Kate do you see that supper is served in here to Mistress Shadwell and the children. Now do please serve her a cup of cider, then see Gertie gets that room readied. When you return, you may take Mistress Shadwell up to her room that she may refresh herself."

Kate nodded, handed Mistress Shadwell a cup of cider, and exited as a footman entered the room. "Mister Hingham, sir, we have put the luggage in the rooms, but for Mistress Bowdon's and the children's. We knew not where to put theirs."

"Leave them with Gertie" Hingham said. "She will take them up. You have seen to the D'Arcys' servants and their horses."

"Yes, but there is a dog."

"A dog?"

"Yes, sir, and one of Lady D'Arcy's footmen says she will want the dog fed and bedded in her room. Seems the little dog is injured."

"That is Fate," spoke up Tabitha. "His leg was broken. Somebody ran over him, but Selena rescued him. He is a dear little dog."

Amaryllis pulled her outspoken sister to her side. "Tabitha, be polite."

Tabitha frowned. "What did I do?"

"I have told you, children are not to enter adults' conversation unless you are spoken to."

"I forgot." Appearing but minimally contrite, she looked at Hingham. "I am sorry, sir."

Hingham chuckled. "I have a grandson who at your age was just as outspoken. And as you seem to know all about the dog, I can but thank you for telling us about him." He turned back to the footman. "Do as Lady Selena wishes. Feed the dog, then put him in her room."

The footman bowed himself out, and Mistress Hingham urged Amaryllis and her siblings to warm themselves by the fire. "I know 'tis spring, but the night air is chill yet. I like a comfy fire. Now let me give you some cider."

"Tabitha may have a half cup, and I will give Charlie a sip of mine," Amaryllis said. "He and Tabitha are both still milk drinkers."

"I will have Kate make sure they have milk with their suppers," Mistress Hingham said, ladling cider into silver cups. "Here is for you, little miss," she said, handing a cup to Tabitha.

Taking the cup in both hands, Tabitha thanked her hostess. Her eyes and Charlie's were big and round as they gazed about the room. Amaryllis thought it one of the most comfortable looking rooms she had ever seen. Lovely tapestries of outdoor scenes adorned three walls. Two candelabras with twenty candles ablaze hung from the cream-colored ceiling, and glowing candles in copper wall sconces on either side of the three doorways cast a luminous luster over the room. The polished sideboard, drop-leaf table, game tables, and washstand all gleamed. Patterned tufted footstools sat in front of two matching cushioned chairs before the hearth, and a day bed of red velvet with gold braid graced the wall opposite the one with the sideboard.

She guessed the rest of the Hinghams' home would be equally entrancing. She liked it, but it in no way resembled her own modern home. Her father had started building their new house the year King Charles returned to the throne. The old estate house, dating from the days of King James, had been demolished, and the sight used for new stables. She had little memory of the original house, but she liked the numerous windows and the clean burning chimneys due to superior draughts of the new house. She also liked her home's openness and its symmetrical design. It appealed to her sense of orderliness. She could not help but wonder when she would again see her beloved home. For a moment, the thought of the unknown future started her heart pumping, but she pushed the thought aside, and at Charlie's urging, gave him a sip of her cider.

Showing great interest in the new coach Lord Rygate had purchased for his daughter's trip to northern Leicestershire, Hingham broached several questions concerning it to Mistress Shadwell. Spared the need, at least for the moment, to answer any questions about her relationship to the D'Arcys, Amaryllis again wished they would soon make their appearance.

Chapter 8

Kate returned with Selena and Reginald in her wake. "They came in through the back entrance," Kate explained.

Hingham had not had time to tell his wife about Selena, and the woman stared at her guests in stunned silence. Even after introductions were made, she still seemed confused. At last she managed to extend her hands and move forward to greet Selena. "Welcome," she said in a faint voice. "'Tis a great pleasure to have you stay with us."

Mistress Shadwell set her cup down on the sideboard. "Lady Selena, I will go up and ready your clothes for this evening's festivities." She looked at the Hinghams. "I assure you, she will look perfectly presentable in a short time, but I do think a bath would improve her immensely."

Mistress Hingham still seemed at a loss as to how to react, so her husband said, "Kate, once you have seen Mistress Shadwell to her room, do see the tub is taken to Lady Selena's room, and have Cook start heating water for her bath."

"Yes, Jacob," Kate said. "This way Mistress Shadwell." She held out an arm and Mistress Shadwell preceded her out the door. Amaryllis guessed Hingham's cousin to be a poor relation who was happy to have a home. She also guessed the placid, middle-aged woman was acting as an unpaid housekeeper. Still, the options for women of no or minimal income were few. The Hinghams seemed like kind people. No doubt Kate's lot was better than it appeared. Amaryllis recognized her own good fortune. She was endowed with a generous dowry as well as the privilege of staying in her home for as long as she might wish – her lifetime, did she so choose.

Selena's tinkling laugh as she tickled Charlie and asked him if he would like a romp outside with Reginald before his supper seemed to put Mistress Hingham more at ease. Their hostess smiled and agreed with Charlie and Tabitha that a romp was a good idea. "Then so you shall have one," Selena said. "Right, Reggie?"

He agreed to the idea. "Once I have finished my cider," he added.

Hingham had taken over his wife's duty and provided Selena and Reginald with their drinks. He insisted Amaryllis take the cushioned chair next to his wife then pulled up chairs from the table for himself and Reginald. Unmindful of her unladylike appearance, Selena had grabbed a foot stool and positioned it next to Tabitha's. She plunked Charlie onto her lap, and wrapping him in a cuddly embrace, gazed up expectantly at Hingham.

With everyone settled, Hingham asked after the D'Arcys' parents. Assured they were doing well, he said, "We will forever be grateful to your father for saving our son's life at the battle at Worcester. We tried to dissuade Harry from going to fight what we feared 'twas a lost cause, but Harry would fight for his king. I shudder to think of the consequences had Ranulf, excuse me, Lord Rygate, not been at Harry's side to dispatch the roundhead who came up on his blindside."

He looked at Reginald. "Your father was like another son to us. He and Harry were at school together, first at Eton and then Oxford. Both schools being so near, and your father's home at Wealdburh being so distant, he was often here in our home."

"We have heard many of their stories," Reginald said, and turning to Amaryllis, added, "When King Charles returned from exile, Sir Harry was knighted for his bravery at the battle of Worcester."

Amaryllis appreciated the way Reginald included her in the conversation. And the way he looked at her, near left her breathless. She could get lost in the depth of his dark luminous eyes.

"Sir Harry is often a guest at Rygate," Reginald continued. "He and Father are still the best of friends. They go on many an outing or excursion together. I cannot think they have missed many a fall hunt at my Uncle Nate's."

His pride in his son apparent, Hingham's blue eyes sparkled. "Indeed, Harry has regaled us with many a tale about his hunts at Lord Rotherby's with your father. And 'tis always a pleasure to have your father visit when he stops by here on his way north."

"How does your dear mother?" Mistress Hingham asked. The poor woman still seemed bemused. Seeing a lady, the daughter of an earl, dressed in a man's attire was a tad daunting, Amaryllis thought.

"Mother is wonderful as always," Selena said. "No one could be more dear." She looked down and then back up. "She has great hopes for me, and I hope I may not disappoint her, but I fear the prospects are not good."

"What do you mean, dear?" Mistress Hingham asked.

Reginald laughed. "She means the odds of her becoming a lady and finding some man willing to marry her are not very likely. However, Mother is ever hopeful."

Amaryllis would have been angry had she been so insulted, but Selena joined in her brother's laughter, and as Selena's laughter was apt to do, it set Charlie to chuckling. Her eyes wide, Mistress Hingham looked from Reginald to Selena to Charlie. Mistress Hingham could well be wishing she had never planned the celebration to honor the D'Arcys, Amaryllis feared. Their hostess had no way of knowing Reginald and Selena, well Reginald anyway, could be perfectly well behaved. And both would look exemplary.

Hingham told the D'Arcys the plans for the evening, and Selena looked delighted. Reginald, however, looked at his sister with a frown in his eyes. That Selena was a trial to her brother was becoming more apparent all the time. Despite his wariness, he said, "Well, no doubt your guests will soon be arriving. I had best give Tabitha and Charlie that promised romp then get myself back to clean up."

"That might be best," Hingham said. "Guests should be arriving anytime now."

Reginald set down his cup and held out his hands. "Come my little troubadours, let us go chase down that squirrel I saw on the oak tree out back. He looks so fat, he could hardly scamper from one branch to another. I dost think he doth eat too many acorns."

Both children sprang up, ready for the adventure Reginald promised them. Amaryllis smiled and her gaze met Reginald's as he clasped the children's hands in his own finely shaped hands. His eyes seemed to delve into hers. She found herself mesmerized until he laughed and looked down at Charlie. "Yes, Sir Charles, stop your tugging. I am at your command. Let us go."

Amaryllis found her bedchamber enchanting. A canopied bed with gold quilted counterpane sat between two windows. A small coal fire glowing in the tiled hearth took the chill from the room, and colorful rag rugs brightened the flooring. A dressing table with a round, gilded-framed looking glass hung above it and a tufted stool occupied the wall opposite the bed. A pine chest at the foot of the bed was draped with soft woolen blankets. A wash stand with a china bowl and pitcher gracing it and clean towels hanging on its side bars stood near the hearth. She had finished washing and had donned her gown, and Gertie, the young freckle-faced maid, was combing out her hair when Tabitha and Charlie returned. They were brimming with tales of their adventure with Reginald. "We could not find that squirrel," Tabitha said, "so we went down to the pond behind the stables. We thought we might find some ducks, but no luck."

"No luck," piped up Charlie, shaking his head in such a way Amaryllis was hard pressed not to laugh. Unfortunately, Gertie did laugh, but she covered herself by making it sound like a cough. Charlie looked at the maid suspiciously before turning his attention back to Tabitha who was continuing her tale.

"Next we went to see the peacocks. Oh, they are so lovely. At least their tail feathers are. But Reggie says only the males have the pretty feathers. He says the mothers are dull so they can hide and protect their nests and their eggs."

"They have big eggs," Charlie said, his eyes large, round, and earnest.

Tabitha giggled. "I would not want to have to eat an egg that big." Then she too looked more serious. "I wonder we had no peacocks, Ryllis. Reggie says they have some."

"I cannot say why we had none. Mayhap they are a bother, or they eat too much."

"They screech," Charlie said. "I cover my ears." He put his hands to the side of his head to demonstrate his action.

"It sounds like you had a fun time with Mister D'Arcy," Amaryllis said, "but now you must need let me finish getting dressed. Tabitha wash your hands and face then help Charlie. You both look a fright. We will have to clean you up some before you can join Mistress Shadwell for your supper in the parlor."

Tabitha and Charlie did as bid, and Gertie began using the curling iron on Amaryllis's hair. The style might not be up to the quality of Amaryllis's own maid at Churlwood, but it framed her face prettily, and she was satisfied with it. Gertie had insisted on the tiniest touch of rouge to her cheeks. "You have had a long day, but you will not want to look wan," the maid said. "A bit of color to enhance your own beauty cannot be wrong."

"Oh, you look beautiful, Ryllis," Tabitha said in a breathless whisper.

Amaryllis stared at herself in the guilt-framed looking glass. She had to admit to being pleased with her appearance. Gertie stood back from her and cooed, "Mistress Tabitha is correct. You look beautiful. No doubt every gent at the banquet will want to dance with you."

"There is to be dancing besides the banquet?" Amaryllis turned to question the maid. She could not think it would be right for her to dance. Fact was, she was still in mourning for her father, him dead but six months. The beautiful gown, the banquet – she should have said no to both, but she had not wanted to seem ungrateful.

Gertie's brown eyes gleamed. "Oh, dancing indeed. The Hinghams are set on showing the D'Arcys a memorable evening." She made a circle with her finger. "Now, do please turn, Mistress Bowdon. I must need make certain my stitches are not showing. Good thing you and Lady Selena are near in height, and we had no need to adjust the hem. 'Twas naught to take a tuck here and there to make the gown fit your smaller waist."

Amaryllis turned slowly until she was again facing herself in the mirror. The gown was one of Selena's. Selena had brought it over herself, saying, "Oh, do please wear this. I hate myself in pink, but Mother will forever insist I can wear pink. Why I cannot imagine. But with your lovely golden hair and blue eyes, it will be perfect."

The gown was a shimmering pink satin with a silvery gauze overlay. The petticoat was a white satin with tiny pink roses embroidered on it. It was near the loveliest gown Amaryllis had ever seen. She had tried to refuse the offer, fearing she might do damage to the gown, but Selena had been insistent. "Surely you cannot have brought many things with you in naught but your satchel. Mother had three trunks packed for me. I cannot believe I shall ever have need of so many gowns." Her tinkling laugh punctuated her statement. "Now I must hurry. Esmeralda insists I must bathe. She says I smell of horses, and no doubt I do." Before Amaryllis could say anything else, Selena was out the door, and Gertie arrived to help her dress.

"I hungry, Ryllis," Charlie said, and Amaryllis turned her attention to him.

"Well, before you can join Mistress Shadwell, we must do something with your hair."

"You need not worry with the children," Gertie said. "I will see they are presentable then take them downstairs. You go ahead and join Mistress Hingham in the parlor. She said she would await you there."

Amaryllis looked at her young siblings. "Will you two promise to be on your good behavior?" she asked. "And do as Gertie and Mistress Shadwell bid you?"

"We will," they both promised.

"And you will not be afraid here on your own after Mistress Shadwell tucks you in later this evening?"

Tabitha jutted out her chin. "I am not a baby."

Amaryllis smiled. "Of course you are not. My apologies." Holding out her arms, she squatted and the gown puddled about her feet. "Both of you come here and give me a kiss."

The two scurried into her embrace and kisses were exchanged, then Amaryllis rose and patted her gown to smooth out the crumples. Hearing the sound of muted voices, she looked out the window and saw guests arriving. Brightly burning torches lined the drive up to the keep, and people walking, others on horseback, and some carriages were making their to the Hinghams' door. The moon had risen and its glowing light added a joyful brightness to the night sky. Feeling a bit shy and nervous, she gave Gertie and the children a little wave and hurried out the door. To her relief, Reginald emerged from his room at the same time.

"Ah, Amaryllis, you look ravishing." His generous smile and kind words calmed her.

She returned his smile. "Your sister was so gracious to loan me this gown."

"It becomes you far more than it ever would her. Selena looks poorly in frills and lace. 'Tis my guess she will be wearing a blue or a green gown of the plainest mode. Her hair will be piled in a bun atop her head with little in the way of adornment." He took Amaryllis's arm and directed her toward the stairs. "But by evening's end, she will have charmed, offended, or surprised every person in the room from the gentry to the servants. She treats everyone with the same courtesy, or lack thereof," he added with a chuckle.

"She has been naught but kind to me – and to Tabitha and Charlie. I cannot believe she would offend anyone."

"She never intentionally offends anyone. She simply cares not what she may say or do. Selena can dance, her manners at the table are appropriate, and she can even look attractive once Esmeralda has worked her magic. But she seldom attempts to control her tongue or her actions."

They reached the bottom of the staircase, and Reginald escorted Amaryllis to the parlor. She could not think what to say about Selena. Indeed, she had never met a woman like her before. A woman who rescued not only dogs by the side of the road but people in perilous situations. A woman who dressed like a man and rode astride. A woman who curried her own horse. A woman who had a warmth unlike anyone Amaryllis had ever known.

While Hingham greeted his guests in the keep, Amaryllis and Reginald chatted with Mistress Hingham. The table being set for Mistress Shadwell and the children reminded their hostess of suppers in the parlor with her son and Reginald's father. "What a lovely mannered boy was your father," she told Reginald. "We never had cause to call either boy to account."

"That would be Father," Reginald said with a chuckle. "'Twas my Uncle Nate who was ever in trouble, ever into mischief. I suppose you know of his escapades as a highwayman during Cromwell's rule. Robbing from the rich Puritans to send aid to Charles during his exile."

"Yes, we are aware of his larks. Truth is, he hid out in our stables once, though I had no knowledge of it for several years. When the roundheads came snooping around, I was insulted and quite honestly told them we had not harbored any highwaymen."

Reginald chuckled. "Now that is one story I had not heard. I will insist upon hearing it when we reach my uncle's."

Amaryllis stared openmouthed before she gasped, "Your uncle was a highwayman?"

Reginald turned to her and laughed. "One of the best. Quite notorious were he and his men. Brave and daring. They did it all for their King. They kept only enough of their gain to meet their basic needs. The rest went to Charles. When Charles returned to the throne, he made my uncle an earl, as he also did my father, and he knighted or in some way rewarded all the men in my uncle's gang. For the nine years after King Charles's loss at Worcester in fifty-one, until his return in sixty, my uncle and his band of men were on the run. But Uncle Nate lost nary a man during those nine years, though they did have a number of close calls."

Amaryllis was again at a loss for words. These D'Arcys were full of surprises. Fortunately she had no need to say anything for Selena entered the parlor. She wore the same blue gown she had worn the previous night at the inn, and she looked just as lovely. Mistress Hingham stared at her for a moment before her face split in a wide smile, and her eyes glowed with delight. She would not be shamed before her guests. Selena no longer looked the hoyden.

"Shall we join our guests in the keep," Mistress Hingham said, and Reginald, bowing slightly, offered their hostess his arm. With a nod, she placed her hand on his forearm, and they advanced down the passageway leading from the parlor to the keep. Selena fell in beside Amaryllis and whispered, "I was right. You look stunning in pink."

Amaryllis blushed and thanked Selena. "You look stunning yourself," she said.

Selena's merry, tinkling laugh floated down the passageway. "Thank you. And I have promised Reggie I will be on good behavior tonight. So do you see me do or say anything amiss, do tell me. The Hinghams are kind, and I wish not to offend."

Amaryllis nodded. "I will do my best." Not that she thought she would have any sway over Selena D'Arcy.

Chapter 9

Seated at the high table between Amaryllis and his sister, Reginald was thoroughly enjoying himself. Thus far, Selena had offended no one. Hingham was to her left, and she and their host had discussed horses at length, before switching their conversation to hunting dogs. Both subjects were safe, and Selena, being knowledgeable on both subjects, was behaving acceptably. That left Reginald free to direct his attention to Amaryllis.

He was looking forward to the dancing. He intended to claim as many dances with Amaryllis as he could manage. In glancing about the keep, he noted near every male at one time or another let his gaze rest on Amaryllis. Not that he blamed them. She was an extraordinarily beautiful woman. He had little wish to share her, though he knew he would not be able to monopolize her time, much as he might desire to do so.

Her voice soft and sweet, she questioned him about his home and his family. He readily answered her with a couple of tales of his boyhood as well as a description of his home. "Rygate is lovely," he concluded. "I wish I could live there always, but one of the reasons I was selected to escort Selena to Whimbrel is because I must need visit the estate I will inherit from my mother in Nottinghamshire. After delivering Selena, I am to acquaint myself with the manor, the tenants, and the steward, in preparation of becoming the master there. Sounds deadly dull to me, but there you have it." He shrugged. "My future."

She smiled that sweet, lovely smile that made her eyes sparkle, and his heart thud. "You are fortunate to have an estate, do you not think so? Many younger sons are given no lands to call their own. They are left to their own devices. They must go into law or the ministry."

"Too true," he answered. "I do count myself blessed. At the same time, I cannot relish hibernating in the country. I think I may need keep

66

an apartment in London as does my father."

"I have ne'er been to London. Is it very grand? I have heard such stories, but I can scarce believe some of them."

Surprised by her statement, Reginald said. "Your father never took you to London? You have never been presented at court?"

She shook her lovely head, making her earbobs dance. "Nay. Father said he could not care for London. Too crowded, too dirty and smelly, too expensive, and too far away."

Reginald laughed. "He was right on all accounts but the 'too far away'. Why I would say London is little more than a day and a half's journey by coach from Albertine."

"I know you to be right, but Father had the gout. Travel of any distance could be painful."

Reginald nodded. "Ah, I understand. We have a neighbor suffers from it something fierce. 'Tis sad. He used to so enjoy the hunt. Now he does little but hobble around." He smiled again. "All the same. You must someday see London. Besides its negatives, it has many positives. Lovely parks, excellent museums, shops where you can buy anything imaginable, all kinds of entertainments from plays or operas in the theaters, to puppet shows and animal acts in the parks. Beautiful houses abound, and balls and festivities of various sorts are never-ending."

"You make it sound entrancing. Hopefully someday I may journey to London. But now we go in the opposite direction. Charlie's safety is my priority."

"As it should be," he said, but he decided once Charlie was safe, he meant to see Amaryllis Bowdon experienced London. How he was to do that, he had no idea. He had responsibilities and obligations that could not be ignored, but already he was imagining having Amaryllis on his arm as he introduced her to the delights of London.

When at last the supper ended, the tables were cleared that the dancing might begin. Amaryllis protested, that still being in mourning, she should not be dancing, but Reginald convinced her that as she had not been wearing black, due to her fear of arousing suspicion at the inn the previous night, and as no one but he and Selena knew her to be in mourning, she should continue on as though she was not in mourning. 'Twas better than having to explain her situation to the Hinghams, and they in turn would have to explain it to their other guests. No, 'twas far too confusing. At last Amaryllis agreed, and Reginald led her onto the floor. He knew he was the envy of every man there, and he gloated shamelessly. He would have to relinquish her hand from time to time, but come the morrow, she would be leaving with him. How lucky could he be.

❉ ❉ ❉ ❉

Selena was not sorry when the evening's festivities ended, and she could go to her bed. Not that she had not enjoyed herself. She had had near as many men seeking her hand for a dance as had Amaryllis. She enjoyed the rollicking country dances, but the sedate bassadance bored her immensely. Reginald danced once with her and complimented her on her behavior. She laughed and teased, "We are now even for the delay I caused by rescuing Fate, are we not?"

Her brother had glanced at Amaryllis. "Aye, we are even."

That Reginald was attracted to Amaryllis was easy to see. And why not? Amaryllis was lovely and sweet and brave. Selena liked her and her young siblings. And she admired Amaryllis for striving to protect Charlie. He was such a cute little fellow, she could scarce believe anyone would want to do him any harm. Still, she had read enough to know that evil existed in the world, and some people would stoop to any level to achieve their goals. From what she could discern, money and power seemed to be the foremost driving forces. Had not Richard III imprisoned and probably killed his own nephews?

She had bid Esmeralda not wait up for her, and she tiptoed into her bed chamber so not to awaken her slumbering maid. This journey could not be easy on the older woman, and the poor dear would have to return to Rygate once she had seen Selena delivered to her aunt and uncle. At least with Amaryllis and the children joining them, Esmeralda had company in the coach.

For safety's sake, Esmeralda had snuffed out the candles, but she had left the drapes open, and the full moon shown in through the window giving Selena all the light she needed to prepare for bed. Hating the intricate lacing on the gown, she struggled out of it, then shed her petticoats, hose, and silken shift. Donning her comfortable cotton shift, she let out a soft sigh. How was she ever going to become a proper lady when she hated the clothing ladies were condemned to wear? Hated the idea of riding side-saddle, hated the idea of attending to household chores and seeing that servants were doing their duties.

She knew she was fortunate to have been born into a wealthy, aristocratic family. More importantly, she had been born into a loving family. She had never known hunger nor want of any kind. She had servants to do her bidding, not that she did not always strive to treat them with courtesy. All the same, she knew they had to work, and for most of her life, she had had to do naught but play. She wondered if the servants resented their station in life. She thought she would. But then she also resented being a woman, or rather, the way women were treated. Men had so much more freedom. She could not think it at all fair.

With a shrug, she closed the drapes and slipped into bed. Snuggling under her soft down quilt, she stared into the darkness. They would not be rising early on the morrow. She could not think they would reach their next scheduled destination by evening. That meant they most likely would end up staying at an inn. They would have to send word to the family expecting them. She hoped they had not planned a big event to honor them as had the Hinghams. Not that she minded the delay. The longer they took to get to Whimbrel, the better she liked it.

🌿 🌿 🌿 🌿

Amaryllis was surprised to find Gertie had returned to help her undress. "I am sorry I failed to tell you that I could attend myself," she said in a whisper.

Smiling, the maid started working on the stomacher pins. "I am pleased to help," she answered in a hushed voice. Her nimble fingers flew, and in a moment she had the stomacher resting on a chair, and she turned her attention to the overskirt and petticoat bindings. Straightening, she asked, "Did you enjoy the evening?"

Stepping out of the petticoats and gown, Amaryllis said, "Oh, aye, 'twas lovely. And the people were charming and so kind."

"Was I right? Did you dance near every dance?"

Amaryllis blushed. "I did, but I must say I am now quite tired. I am not looking forward to rising early in the morning."

"Worry not. Lady Selena left word not to expect her to breakfast before ten."

"You mean we are not setting out first thing in the morning?" For a moment Amaryllis was concerned that her uncle might catch up with them, but she pushed the thought from her head. Her aunt and uncle had no way of knowing where she and the children were. A couple of hours delay in departure was of no moment.

Smiling, she shook her head. "I will be rising before ten. The children will be up and in need of their breakfast."

"You are not to worry about the children. Mistress Shadwell told them when they awoke, they are not to wake you. They are to come down to the parlor and breakfast with her." Gertie giggled softly into her hand. "Oh, they did have a fine time with Mistress Shadwell. You best pay heed or she will have them spoiled in no time."

"Why, what did she do?" Amaryllis had a hard time imagining the staid, older woman as someone who would spoil children.

"She let them each have a second helping of the plum pudding, she took them up to Lady Selena's room to play with the dog for a time, and before she put them to bed, she slipped down the corridor with them and let them peek in at the dancers. Then when she put them to bed, she told them a story. It was about a heroic young prince, but I had other duties to attend so was not able to stay to hear the full tale."

The maid sounded disappointed that she had not been party to the children's bedtime story, and Amaryllis smiled at the youthful serving girl. She liked the girl and hoped she was treated well by the Hinghams. She wondered what would happen to her personal maid at Churlwood. When planning her escape with the children, Amaryllis had given the maid the night and following day off to visit her family. She would have returned to find her mistress missing. No doubt she would be let go, possibly without a reference.

Amaryllis could not worry about her now. The maid had a home to go to. She would not be turned out with no place to go. And once Charlie was safe, Amaryllis intended to return to Churlwood. She would then make any necessary amends.

Her thoughts back at Churlwood, Amaryllis let Gertie comb out her hair then help her into her nightshift. A soft good night, and the maid slipped out the door leaving Amaryllis to crawl into bed next to her siblings and put out the candle on the table beside the bed. As her eyes adjusted to the dark, she listened to the children's soft breathing. How dear they were to her. They knew they were running away from their mean aunt, but they could not know how desperate their situation had become. It was the slow poisoning of Charlie that had given Amaryllis the courage to act before her aunt made yet another attempt on his young life.

She shut her eyes. She must push such thoughts from her mind, or she would never get to sleep. She should think cheerful thoughts. She could think about Reginald. Thoughts of him quickened her pulse. Mayhap thinking of him was not a good idea either. Yet, she did not want to ban him from her thoughts – at least not until she had reviewed the evening with him. She loved his smile, his voice, the way he looked at her sometimes as though he could gobble her up. Those looks made her breath catch in her lungs and sent a feeling to her lower regions like she had never before experienced. A pleasant sensation, but a sensation that left her feeling unfulfilled.

He had monopolized her evening. At the dinner table, she barely said two sentences to the woman to her right. She had done naught but learn the woman was the wife of a local squire whose property bordered on the Hinghams'. Before supper, she had been introduced to several women, but she never had a chance to chat with them. She was constantly on the dance floor. Most of the time, she was dancing with Reginald. When the locals did manage a dance with her, Reginald asked one of the local women to dance. She wondered if every woman who danced with him that evening went home with the same unrequited sensation she was experiencing.

When Hingham called an end to the entertainment, Amaryllis and the D'Arcys joined the Hinghams at the door to bid the final guests a safe journey through the brisk spring night. Twinkling lights from torches and lanterns stretched out into the distance as the revelers made their way to their homes. Amaryllis had gazed up at the full moon that had lit her path the night before. Had it been but one night since she had fearfully crept from her home? It somehow seemed a lifetime ago. Tonight she had laughed and danced, and until she crawled into bed with Charlie and Tabitha, she had forgotten her fears. How good it was to feel safe.

Chapter 10

Wade Felton could not believe his eyes. That had to be the D'Arcy coach turning onto the highway from a country track. Burnished gold, glass windows, he could make it out even at a distance. But how could that be? They should be miles ahead of him. They had had near a full day's head start. True, coaches traveled much more slowly than did a man on horseback, but he had not expected to catch up to them before mid-afternoon, and this was but mid-morning.

He could see but one outrider. Where was the other one? He spotted the D'Arcys. The lady sat her horse well, but he could not approve of a woman dressing like a man and riding astride. Undignified, it was. Who was the third man riding beside D'Arcy? His personal servant most likely. They had a coachman, a postilion on the left lead horse, and two footmen hanging on to the back of the coach. Any highwayman would be a fool to take on such a force.

But a group of desperate armed bandits? Might they think such plum pickings worth the risk? Mayhap? The D'Arcys had to be traveling with a substantial amount of money. And no doubt the lady had her jewelry and fine clothing. The fine duds of the wealthy could bring a hefty sum at any market. She had a lot of clothes, too, if the trunks atop the coach were any indication. But how could he find such men as he would need? In Albertine and surrounding area, he could have drummed up any number of comrades. He would have to think on it. In the meantime, he would hang back, keep his distance. At some point, he would have to overtake and pass them or they would get suspicious. When they stopped to rest the coach horses, he would keep right on riding. With luck, they would not even notice him.

The thought of killing a child did not sit well with him, but the idea of a lifetime annuity overrode his qualms. With the annuity Mistress Bowdon guaranteed him, he would never have to work another day in his life. Yet he would always have coins in his pocket. He chuckled. That tavern wench who thought herself too good for him would sing a different tune when he jangled a couple of sixpence in his palm. She would spread her legs for him fast enough then.

Rising up in the stirrups, he rubbed his bottom. He hated horseback riding. Mistress Bowdon had furnished him with his mount and saddle. She told the butler he bought them. That was her excuse for why he had come to see her. Was he not successful, did he not kill the young baronet, he would need to return the horse. At least that was the deal they had made. What Mistress Bowdon would do did he not return the horse, he did not know. He did not think he wanted to find out. She was a strong, determined woman. He would not want to cross her.

Mistress Bowdon seemed certain the young Mistress Amaryllis Bowdon was taking the children to their aunt who was visiting in Derbyshire. 'Twas hoped he could kill the child before they reached the aunt so the blame could be put on his sister for taking the child away from his safe home without his guardian's permission. But if not, he would have to manage the deed while the child was in his aunt's care.

"I have no idea who these D'Arcys are," Mistress Bowdon said, "but I am guessing Amaryllis will be thinking herself and Charlie safe. Her guard will be down. That should be to your advantage."

Felton hoped Mistress Bowdon was right. As yet, he had come up with no plan other than a holdup, and that did not seem too feasible. Well, he had long hours to reflect. He would think of something. Mistress Bowdon had remarked he seemed a resourceful fellow. Well, he was.

※　※　※　※

Throughout the morning, Reginald paid little heed to the rutted road. Trusting his horse to mind his footing, he eased up on the reins to give his horse his head and let him pick his way around the various obstacles in the road. Thinking about Amaryllis was far preferable to guiding the gelding around the dips, ruts, and mounds that made traveling across England so wearisome. The more contact he had with Amaryllis, the more enamored of her he became. She was not only beautiful beyond description, she was kind and gentle, brave and resourceful, and she danced divinely. He would love to steal a kiss from her, but as she was basically under his protection, honor prevented him from taking any unfair advantage.

At the Hinghams' ball, he had decided not to discuss her plight, but he was curious what her aunt had done that made Amaryllis think the woman was trying to kill young Charlie. He knew Selena was curious too, and he was a bit surprised his sister had so far managed to curtail her curiosity. That Selena would question Amaryllis he had no doubt. But she would not question her in front of the children or any servants, that he well knew. Thus far, since the first night when they had learned of Amaryllis's desperate flight, they had had no other opportunity to talk in privacy. Most likely this evening they would learn more once the children went to bed. He hoped they would find an acceptable inn for the night. With their late start, they would not reach their scheduled stop at the Girouards' home. He had had no choice but to send one of his outriders ahead to inform their hosts of their delay. He hated being short one outrider. The roads were not safe. He would have to make sure they found an abode for the night before evening shadows darkened the road. Sighing, he imagined they would have more delays before their journey concluded.

Once they reached Leicester and turned northwest to Derbyshire, as he knew they would, Selena would have to post letters to their last scheduled hosts informing them they would not be stopping over with them. Their father had gone to great care to ascertain they had suitable stops on their trek to Whimbrel, but after Leicester they would be staying in at least one unknown inn before they reached Derby. So not to overtax the coach horses, they could travel little more than ten or twelve miles before they needed to rest the beasts. That had them averaging little more than twenty miles a day. But today's late start meant they would do little more than fifteen.

Selena would also need to write their aunt and uncle and explain their side trip. He hoped his Uncle Nathaniel would not write to his father. His father would not be pleased did he learn Selena was not being taken directly to Whimbrel. Reginald frowned. What could he do? Selena would do what Selena wanted to do, and his father should know that.

Bernard Nye rode up, and Reginald turned to his servant. "Have you any news to relieve me of this infernal boredom?" he asked.

"Aye," Nye answered with a laugh. "I see a village up ahead. Should I investigate and determine do they have an inn suitable to offer us our dinner?"

Reginald nodded. "Yes, please do. I can hear my stomach rumbling. I had little appetite this morning despite the spread the Hinghams laid out to tempt me. And no doubt you and Esmeralda and the children ate early and are most likely hungry by now."

"I could do with a bite," Nye said.

"Fine, ride ahead. I will inform the others of our plans."

🌱 🌱 🌱 🌱

Amaryllis laughed and patted her stomach. "Nay, I can eat not another bite. Tempt me not kind sir." The inn where they stopped to bait the horses and tend their own needs provided a feast for their dinner. It was a small inn, in a rural setting, and Amaryllis would not have expected such opulence. Apparently a Lord Flitwick passed through with his entourage on a regular basis, and he expected to meet with a sumptuous meal whenever he arrived. He paid well to have his expectations met, consequently, the inn could afford to retain a cook of some renown.

"Reggie is no kind sir," Selena said, glaring at her brother. "He is a fiend. He thinks do I have one more tart, I will be too full to sit my horse. I will be forced to ride in the coach like a proper lady. Well, his plan will not work." She rose from the table. "I will put distance between me and those custard-filled tarts, which he knows full well are my favorite."

"How can you say such, Selena?" Reginald said. "Did I not offer another tart to everyone at the table?"

"You were not waving them under their noses as you did under mine." She strode across the room, and looked back over her shoulder. "I will be in the stable. I intend to give Brigantia a sugar morsel."

"Is she angry with you?" Tabitha asked as Selena exited the room.

Reginald chuckled. "Nay, Tabitha, she but teases. 'Tis seldom you will ever see Selena angry. 'Tis not in her nature. To her, all life is fun."

"'Tis a good way to be," Amaryllis said. "I do think laughter is good for the soul."

Looking at Amaryllis in a way that made her blush, Reginald said, "As is beauty good for the soul. I hold in my memory your vision from last evening." He looked at Tabitha and Charlie. "Did not your sister look lovely last night?"

"Oh, yes she did," Tabitha said, and Charlie echoed his sister.

Amaryllis smiled at her young siblings. Looking at them helped her gain control of her emotions. Reginald had her head spinning. The look in his eyes sent her heart to thumping, and sent her wits skittering off to who knew where.

"Will there be another ball tonight?" Tabitha asked.

Reginald chuckled. "Nay, little one. Had we been able to get my sister out of her bed earlier, and were we able to reach our scheduled destination, we might have again been feted. But instead of a ball, we must make do with an inn. But fear not. I have no doubt we will find something to entertain us."

Mistress Shadwell, who had been sitting quietly at the end of the table, rose and said, "Children, do you wish to play with Fate before we set out again, you had best come with me." She pointed to the door where the footman, Norwood, stood awaiting them. He held the small dog in his arms.

"He has been fed and watered," Norwood said, "and I do believe he is ready for a little exercise. He is getting around quite well with his splinted leg now, but Lady Selena reminds you to be careful of him."

"Oh, we will," Tabitha said, jumping up and running over to Norwood. She held up her arms to take the dog, but Mistress Shadwell said, "Nay, Mistress Tabitha. We will let Norwood carry him back outside. He is not a big dog, but he may be a tad big for you to carry."

Tabitha looked disappointed, but acquiescing without complaint, she, followed by Charlie and Mistress Shadwell, exited the room. Amaryllis was pleased the children seemed to have taken so to Esmeralda Shadwell, and she to them. After the harsh treatment at the hands of their aunt and their nurse, to have an older woman befriend them seemed an unlooked-for-blessing. Mistress Shadwell was always perfectly proper with them, as she was with the D'Arcys, but she seemed to take a delight in the children's youth and exuberance.

Not until everyone left the room did Amaryllis realize she would be alone with Reginald. Her heart skipped a beat then began pummeling her chest as she turned back around to face him.

Moving his chair closer to hers, he took her hand between his. "Amaryllis, we spent last evening speaking of naught but me. I would know more of your life."

Her hand trembling in his warm clasp, she swallowed and tried to control her skittering heart. "There is... there is little to tell," she stuttered. "We... we led a quiet life at Churlwood. We associated mostly with local families. Other than my uncle and his family, on my father's side, we had no other close relatives. Of course, Charlie and Tabitha have their aunt and a couple of uncles and their grandfather, but they live in Cheshire and rarely visit." With Reginald's eyes holding hers, she swallowed again and tried unsuccessfully to withdraw her hand. His nearness, his touch had her confused and near faint. "Father... Father had several friends living in Watford. They and their families often visited, or... or we visited them."

Reginald interrupted her stuttering monologue. "Had you no special suitor?"

Heat spread up her neck to her cheeks. "No..., no special suitor."

He smiled that smile that left her weak-kneed. "Good," was all he said, and rising he pulled her up after him. "Let us stretch our legs a bit before we renew our journey."

She could do nothing more than nod. Tucking her hand in the crook of his arm, he escorted her out the door, through the public room, and out into the bright sunshiny day.

Chapter 11

Felton peered left and right, then slithered out from under the coach and sprang to his feet. Grinning, he tucked his whittling knife back into his pocket. The deed was done, and he had not been discovered. Catching sight of the two men he had hired to keep the coachman and postilion away from the coach, he gave them a nod. The two had earned their pay. He saw them break off their conversations and head for the portal of the enclosure that surrounded the inn. He would join them back at the alehouse where he had met them.

He knew the moment he spied the two men scoffing down their ales, he had found his co-conspirators. Were they other than ne'er-do wells, they would have been employed at their work, not in their cups in the middle of the day. Knowing it would make him welcome, he ordered a round and joined the men. "I am needing some company," he said. "Need to drown me anger."

The two thanked him for the ale, then the smaller one slanted his squinty eyes and asked, "What be it has you roiled?"

Felton snorted derisively. "I just spotted the fribble what used me only sister, got her with child, then left her to her own means with nary a backwards glance."

Both men sat up straight. "Where is the bullyhuff? Who is he what thinks he can treat a woman in such a fashion?" the larger man demanded.

"A rich 'un, he is. Name is D'Arcy. Got a big fancy coach. Traveling with his future bride and her entourage." He put a hand to his eye to wipe away an imaginary tear. "As I said, nary a thought to me poor sister."

The smaller man nodded. "That would be the way with them Janus-faced rapscallions. Think they are better'n than the rest of us and can do whate'er they like."

"That be D'Arcy, all right," Felton said, curling his lips down in a frown.

The larger man wiped ale from his untrimmed mustache and said, "Shame there is naught you can do to such as him. Him being rich and all, there is ne'er aught you can do to avenge them what has been wronged."

The smaller man agreed, "Aye, naught to do but get stinking drunk."

"Aye," Felton said and after taking another slug of ale, he introduced himself as Smith. He learned the smaller man called himself Fields, the larger one, like him, went by the name of Smith. Inwardly chuckling, he ordered another round. Slumping on the table, he groused, while the two men commiserated with him. "Naught I can do, naught I can do," he moaned, shaking his head. Suddenly he jerked up on his stool and hammered his fist down on the table. "Nay, there is something I can do. That is, be you two willing to help me."

At first startled, the two men eyed him warily, and he quickly added, "There would be sixpence a piece in it for you."

They brightened. "What is it you would be a-wanting us to do?" Fields asked.

"Talk," Felton said.

"What do mean... talk?" Fields said, a leery look on his face.

"I am thinking 'twould be a good payback was D'Arcy and his bride to be delayed enough they should be late for their own wedding."

Chewing on the hairs of his mustache, the larger man cocked his head then asked, "How you going to manage that?"

"I am thinking an accident to their coach. Say a wheel breaks."

"You got some way of making sure a wheel breaks?" Fields asked, squinting his eyes to naught but slits.

Felton pulled out his knife, and both men straightened and eyed him guardedly. Rubbing his thumb over the sharp edge, Felton said, "I use this for whittling." He was skilled in the simple art and earned a ha'penny here, a farthing there. Enough to keep a roof over his head. "Was I able to get under the D'Arcy coach, I could pare down several of the spokes enough that when they hit a big enough bump in the road, of which there be plenty, the wheel will break."

Both men nodded and chuckled, and Fields said, "That would be a prize to see. But how you going to manage whittling down them spokes."

"That is what I need you two for. I need you to keep the coachman and postilion busy. Tell 'em you are certain you know them. Suggest any number of places you might haf met 'em. Just keep 'em talking and away from the coach."

And so they had. All had gone as planned. The D'Arcy footmen and outrider were having their meal, the inn's ostler was seeing to the horses. No one had been near the coach when he crouched down and bellied under it. The only heart-stopping moment had been when the D'Arcy woman had gone striding past headed for the stables, but she had not even glanced at the coach. Walked like a man she did. She needed a man to put her in her place. Licking his lips, he thought he would not mind being that man. Her male attire accentuated her figure and exposed a small portion of her shapely thighs. Yes, he would not mind teaching her how to be a woman.

Continuing to whittle, he breathed easier when she disappeared into the stables. He had finished his whittling and was up beside the coach when the large woman emerged from the inn with the two children and a footman. The children, low to the ground as they were, would have spotted him for sure. Luck had been on his side.

Safely back at the alehouse, he shared another round with his conspirators, paid them, then excused himself. He needed to sell the horse Mistress Bowdon had given him and buy a new horse. He needed to change his coat, too. Could not have the D'Arcy footmen or outriders getting suspicious did they see the same man following them. Especially not when the wheel broke. He rather hoped the large woman would fall against the boy, maybe kill him. He truly did not relish killing the child himself. Not that he would not do it, he would just rather not.

He imagined the most he could hope for though was a delay. A delay would give him more time to come up with some idea of how to achieve his goal and earn his promised annuity.

❊ ❊ ❊ ❊

Esmeralda repositioned herself into the corner of the coach and again closed her eyes. The jostling about of the coach made sleeping difficult for adults, but the children seemed to have no trouble falling asleep. She smiled and fingered Tabitha's soft curls. The little girl was curled up on the seat, her head in Esmeralda's lap. Mistress Bowdon had young Charlie's head pillowed in her lap. What pretty, well-behaved children they were. With a sigh, Esmeralda decided she could not object to Selena's plan to take them to their aunt in Derbyshire. She could not consider letting these sweet, gently reared children travel by stage. No, she would simply have to let Selena's mother and father know they had had no choice but to see them safely to their destination.

That Selena had found a means of delaying her arrival at Whimbrel would not surprise her parents. That Esmeralda abetted her in her deviation would surprise them, but she had confidence they would trust her decision. Still, she was responsible for Selena. She would have to get her safely to her uncle's. With their late start, she worried about what caliber of inn they would find to house them since they could not make it to their arranged stopover with the Girouards. She hated staying in inns. Even the best were never completely satisfactory. The beds were lumpy, or the water was tepid, the food greasy, or the wine of poor quality, other travelers were noisy, or rude, or vulgar. And there was always the risk of bugs was a room not sufficiently cleaned.

At least the day was clear and bright. The wind had a bit of a chill to it, but she was snug and warm in the coach. She wondered that Selena could prefer riding her horse to riding in the coach. The only time Selena had spent any time in the coach was near the beginning of their journey during a brief downpour. Reginald had insisted Selena get into the coach, and he and Nye had joined her. The coachman found a tree to shelter the equipage under, and a tarp had been spread over some low hanging branches to provide some shelter for the footmen, outriders, and horses. When the storm burst ended, the road was a mire, and drizzling rain continued intermittently, but Reginald said they could not delay. They had to reach their night's destination. Not only was the Huntley family expecting them, but all the horses would need a good rub down after the rain, and the men would need to be able to dry their clothes.

Esmeralda believed that had been near the longest day of her life.

Go a little ways, get stuck in the mud. Get out of the coach while the footmen and outriders pushed and shoved and the poor coach horses strained until the coach was freed. Get back in the coach, go a little ways, get stuck again. The hems of her skirt and petticoats were thick with mud by the time they reached the Huntleys. Thankfully, the Huntleys had not planned a celebration in the D'Arcys' honor. They had had a hearty, warming supper for them, but nothing elaborate. According to Selena they had a barn full of sweet hay for the horses, and groomsmen to curry them so the D'Arcy staff could change out of their wet garments, have a lusty meal, and find warm beds in the men's dormitory above the stables. Two maids had helped her and Selena change and had seen to drying and cleaning their clothing while Selena joined the Huntleys for supper. Esmeralda had joined Mister Nye in the kitchen for their meal. She had slept well that night, and the following day had dawned bright and sunny. Fact was, they had had nothing but sunshine for three days now. What a blessing. She prayed it would continue.

She could feel herself at last drifting into sleep when a loud snap sounded, then a crack, and before she could even scream, the coach tilted sideways. Amaryllis did scream and slid across the coach seat, in the process pushing her brother down on top of the dog, which let out a yelp. Tabitha was balancing on her head for a moment before she too toppled down to land on her brother and the dog. The pile of them were on Esmeralda's feet.

"My God, my God!" Esmeralda heard Selena cry, and in the next instant, the girl was peering in the window of the other side – now top side – of the coach. Before Esmeralda could say anything, Reginald yanked open the door and called, "Are any of you badly hurt?"

"I think I am all right," Esmeralda said, "and I do believe the children are not harmed. I am not sure about Amaryllis or the dog."

Since the coach was balancing partially on its side and not lying flat, trying to move was proving difficult. "I am all right," Tabitha said, "and so is Fate. Neither Charlie nor I landed full on him." She giggled. "He is licking my face."

"What of you, Amaryllis?" Reginald asked, and Esmeralda could hear the concern in his voice, see it on his face.

"I am not sure," she answered slowly. "My wrist is hurting. I may

83

have injured it trying to catch myself so I would not fall on the children."

"Well the main thing now is to get you out. Try not to move around until we get the horses unhitched and the coach secured so it will not fall over any farther. I will be right back," Reginald said, ducking away.

"I need to check on the footmen," Selena said. "The coachman jumped clear, but I fear Handle may not have been so lucky." She gave them a half smile. "Have no fear, we will soon have you safe and sound." With that, she too disappeared.

Esmeralda sat very still, bracing herself as best she could to keep from slipping forward off her seat. She must not slide down on top of the children. Amaryllis looked white, whether from fear or pain, Esmeralda could not tell, but she said in her most soothing voice, "They will have the children and you out of here in no time. For me, it may take a bit more time," she added, patting her girth.

Amaryllis gave her a wan smile. "I am not worried. I know we will all be fine."

Esmeralda nodded. She knew they would be fine. What troubled her was why they should have toppled over in the first place. The Earl of Rygate had gone to great expense to provide the best built coach available for this trip. Its wheels should not crack, but she had definitely heard a crack, right after they had passed over a rather minor rut. They had experienced far worse roads earlier in the trip. Something was not right.

Chapter 12

In little more than a heartbeat, Reginald, with the help of the postilion, had the team horses unhitched and tethered to a nearby tree. The small, wiry postilion had done a remarkable job of holding the horses steady during the accident. They had whinnied, and the horses closest to the coach had shied, but all the horses had quickly settled. Naught but the flicking of their ears and tails indicated their agitation. Had they bolted, pulling the coach along on its side, the coach passengers could well have been seriously injured.

Pit had twisted his ankle when he jumped from his perch, so he could do little but sit and watch. The footman, Handle, appeared to have broken his leg. Selena was seeing to him, trying to make him comfortable. She and Norwood had pulled Handle away from the coach and deposited him next to the grizzled, irascible coachman. Reginald directed the outrider and Norwood to detach the trunks, teetering, but still fastened to the coach roof, and prop them under the coach to keep it from shifting and tilting more. Soon they had the luggage loosened and were jamming a couple of trunks under the side of the coach.

"Halloo! I say there. Is everyone all right? Might I be of assistance?" a voice called, and Reginald saw a farmer advancing across his field toward them. He had left his oxen and plow, and was tromping across rows of plowed earth.

Reginald beckoned to the man, and the farmer clambered over his rock wall and joined them on the road. "Everyone is mostly all right, but we have passengers in the coach we must get out. The children we can hoist out with the luggage ties, but one lady is more on the hefty side. If you had a really sturdy rope we could use, we would be most grateful."

The man pushed back his floppy-brimmed hat and nodded. Thinning his lips in his weathered face, he said, "Aye, I can get you a good rope.

You will be needing a place to bide the night, I am thinking. I will be telling me wife she should ready a room for your lady."

"Ladies," Reginald said, "and that is most kind of you." He needed time to contemplate what this mishap would mean to them. The coach would have to be repaired. Everyone would need to be housed and fed, the horses would need to be baited and sheltered. He would worry with those problems after he had Amaryllis, the children, and Esmeralda safely out of the coach.

As the farmer hurried off to get the rope and to inform his wife they had surprise guests, the outrider brought Reginald the luggage ties. Reginald wished he had both his outriders with him and had not needed to send one off with a message informing the Girouards they would not be stopping over with them. He hoped they had not planned any special event on his and Selena's behalf as had the Hinghams. It had been most kind of the old couple, and he had enjoyed getting to dance with Amaryllis. All the same, it had meant a late start for them that morning. He looked at the sky. The sun was on its downward slide. They would have but a few more hours of daylight.

He turned to his valet. "Nye, when that farmer comes back, I will ask him if the nearest village has a blacksmith and how far it is to the village. Is it not too distant, the postilion and I can ride there tonight. Mayhap take the wheels with us. Could have them repaired by noon on the morrow. What think you?"

"It will take some doing to get the wheels off," Nye said. "The rear one is cracked near in half. I doubt it can be repaired. But we will know better when we get the coach righted again."

"Right you are," Reginald said. "Well, let us get those children out, shall we?"

He swung back up onto his horse and returned to the open door. Peering down into the coach, he said, "All right, which one of you mites is first to come out of that rabbit hole?"

"Fate is," Tabitha said, attempting to rise to her knees.

"Fate?" Reginald was surprised by her answer.

"Yes, I think his leg is hurting, being cramped down here with Charlie and me."

"So be it." Reginald dropped a roof tie rope down. "Can you slip that under his front legs and tie it tight around his back?"

"Yes, I can," Tabitha answered and did as instructed.

Reginald had started pulling the little dog carefully up when Selena joined him. "Oh, thank goodness Fate appears unharmed. There is my good dog," she said, reaching for her wriggling pet and clasping him to her chest. "You are safe, you are safe," she crooned to the dog, petting him on his head.

"Charlie is next," Tabitha said when Reginald again dropped the rope into the coach.

"Can you tie the rope around him the same way you tied it around Fate?" he asked.

"Yes I can," Tabitha said, just as positively.

"Good girl," Reginald said, watching Tabitha's small hands work with the rope. "Amaryllis," he said, "I know your wrist is injured, but can you make sure that knot is secure. Charlie will be heavier to pull up than Fate. I would not want that knot slipping."

"Could I reach him," Esmeralda said, "I would check it, but it is taking all I can manage to stay on this seat and not topple over on the children."

"You are doing fine," Selena said. "Once we get the children and Amaryllis out, it should make it easier on you. I am so glad you are not hurt. Pit has a badly sprained ankle, and I fear Handle's leg is broken. Norwood seems to have suffered only minor scrapes. All the horses seem to be all right, too, though, Tor, the back horse on the left side has a cut on his fetlock. Coach may have clipped him when it went over."

Reginald shook his head. Trust Selena to know how every person and every animal faired. And trust her to know the names of every one of the coach horses.

"I do think the knot is secure," Amaryllis said, and Reginald started ed slowly drawing Charlie up. The boy was heavier than he looked, and as Reginald strained, Selena, having handed Fate off to Norwood, snagged a hold on the rope behind Reginald's hands and helped hoist Charlie up. With Charlie dangling below the lip of the door, Selena took hold of his gown, and tugged him upward until Reginald could grasp him under the arms and pull him free.

Reginald patted the boy on the bottom. "How is that my little man?

You were near flying. Did you like it?" He was trying his best to make the children view the accident as a minor or even a comical event. He wanted no nightmares. He was already feeling guilty that they had offered, nay forced Amaryllis to accept their protection, and here, because of this accident, they could have been badly injured or even killed.

Charlie gave out with his usual chuckle, spread out his arms, and said, "I fly!"

"You did indeed," Selena said, taking him from Reginald, and settling him in front of her on her saddle. "Now you and I must get out of the way and let Mister Nye in to help Reggie pull up your sisters. I think it will take both men to get her to flying. How about we go over and sit with Handle and Pit and play with Fate."

Charlie nodded his head vigorously. "Yes, play with Fate."

As Selena edged her mount away from the coach, Nye nudged his horse up next to Reginald's. Neither horse seemed happy about being in such close contact, and Reginald's gelding started to bob his head and chomp on his bit as if to say, I have had enough of butting up against this coach. "Easy Sherard. You can do this," Reginald said, patting his horse's neck. "'Tis the only way we can be high enough to see into the coach. Now settle down and I will see you get two lumps of sugar tonight." Whether the horse understood him or not, he stopped his antics for the moment, and Reginald dropped the rope down to Tabitha.

"Now Tabitha, you must position yourself where Mistress Shadwell can fit the rope around you and tie the knot, like you did for Charlie and Fate. Can you do that?"

"I think so," she said, taking the end of the rope and handing it to Esmeralda.

"Esmeralda, can you balance yourself and tie the rope secure around Tabitha? I worry that because of her injured wrist Amaryllis would not be able to get the knot tight enough."

"I will manage," Esmeralda said, a determined set to her lips.

Reginald could see her feet, one braced against the coach door, the other pressing hard against the coach floor. Balancing on the coach seat, she slipped the rope around Tabitha. He held his breath, watching her effort to secure the rope without losing her stability.

"Done," she said, again placing a hand against the door to steady herself.

"All right, Tabitha, your turn to fly," Reginald said. She giggled, and he and Nye started pulling. Soon the little girl was gripping the edge of the coach rim, and Nye was able to reach around Reginald and lithely pull her up and out.

"There you go, young lady," Nye said, settling her on the front of his saddle. "Now I will but take you over to join your brother and come back and help get your sister out."

Tabitha turned to Reginald. "Thank you, Reggie. I like flying. It was fun."

"That is my girl," he said, chucking her under the chin before looking back down at Amaryllis and Esmeralda. Getting the two adults out would not be as easy.

Hearing the clink of harnesses, he looked up to see the farmer returning. Another man was with him, and that man led a pair of draft horses. "Ho!" the farmer said. "My brother-in-law saw the accident from his field. He thinks mayhap 'twould be better do ye right the carriage afore ye try to be getting your ladies out." The farmer indicated the horses. "If we attach ropes to the carriage, these horses can easily right it. You have enough men here to push from the underside then balance it until you move those trunks under it." He glanced over at Selena. "The youth there can push 'em under, I would think."

Reginald controlled a chuckle as Selena hopped to her feet. "Indeed I can," she said then looked down at the children. "Stay here with Pit and Handle and mind Fate."

"Yes, Selena," Tabitha answered as the farmer then his brother-in-law each did a doubletake when Selena spoke. She might look like a youth in the clothing she wore, but her voice was the voice of an aristocratic lady.

"Sirs, my sister, Lady Selena D'Arcy. And yes, she is perfectly capable of helping us right the coach. Your idea is splendid," he said, looking at the farmer's brother-in-law. "Let us get the job done, and then we will do introductions all around."

The farmer, glanced again at Selena, then nodded. "Aye, to work."

Reginald explained to Amaryllis and Esmeralda what they intended to do. "All you need do is remain as still as you can." They both nodded. The horses were attached with strong ropes to the upper side of the coach. The men took up their positions at the lower side, and Selena stood ready to dart in and push the trunks under the flooring of the coach. Reginald was glad they were good quality trunks. He had no fear they would not bear the weight of the coach.

Righting the coach seemed an effortless maneuver for the draft horses. Fine animals Reginald thought. He knew a number of his father's more prosperous tenants were changing from oxen to horses. They were as good in the fields as were the oxen, but faster when hauling a wagonload of goods to market or taking the family to the nearest town for market day or church.

The coach creaked back upright. No sooner was it secure than Reginald was peering in the window and asking if the occupants were all right. Amaryllis gave him a glowing smile that set his heart to humming, and Esmeralda said, "So good to be upright again."

The draft horses were untied and the coach steps let down. Concerned about Amaryllis's wrist, Reginald was gingerly helping her out when a man riding a dun horse, stopped to ask if he could be of assistance. Giving the man but a cursory glance, Reginald said, "Nay, but thank you for asking."

The horseman, his face hidden beneath a large floppy-brimmed hat grunted and said, "Glad all is well." He rode on as Reginald helped Esmeralda down the steps. Taking Esmeralda's hand, Nye helped steady her, and Esmeralda, again on firm ground, gave a breathy sigh of relief.

Hugging both women, Selena proclaimed them to be true heroines. Both denied her praise, but Reginald did think they had behaved with utmost self-possession.

With everyone safe, Reginald set about introducing his party. The farmer then introduced himself as Abe Wirth, his brother-in-law was Herve Barlow. Seeing how large the D'Arcy party was, Barlow welcomed them to house some of their horses and their staff at his home.

"As long as you both allow us to pay you," Reginald insisted, knowing well they could put a strain on the household finances. "Were we staying at an inn, we would be paying. No reason you should not be reimbursed for accommodating us."

The two farmers exchanged a look, shrugged, and Barlow nodded. "Aye, we will tike your coin and thank you for it. Now, I will be off to tell me wife what's ado, then I need finish me plowing." He pointed toward a neat-looking croft in the distance. "Not a far piece. Stable whatever horses you want in my barn. It has had its spring shoveling out and fresh hay laid. We sup with the sunset, and 'tis off to bed we go when it gets dark. No need using up candles."

"Aye," Wirth said. "We are much the same, but we will do our best to accommodate your needs. Wife said she would send the serving girl out to the spring house for some fresh cheese and butter. Yesterday was baking day, so the bread is fresh, and wife says she will be having a couple of plump chickens stewing ere long. Then she will get your sleeping quarters red up."

"Oh, my," Selena said, "we should be helping her. What a lot of work we are putting on your poor wife." She looked to Reginald. "I will ride ahead and stable Brigantia then see can I assist Mistress Wirth. You and Esmeralda can manage here, can you not?"

Before Reginald could answer, Wirth said, "Here now, milady, you cannot be expecting to be helping me wife. 'Twould not be proper."

Reginald put his hand on the farmer's shoulder. "Best not try to dissuade her. You will be wasting your breath. As you can tell by the way my sister dresses, she does pretty well what suits her." He looked at Selena who was swinging into her saddle. "Try not to offend Mistress Wirth, will you? You may be more in her way. You know little of house work."

Selena ruefully twisted her mouth, turned from him, and rode off toward the farmhouse. Shrugging helplessly, Reginald turned to Esmeralda. "Do you tell Nye what all you may need for the night, and he and Norwood will get your luggage to the house." At her assent, he turned to Wirth. "I need a surgeon for Pit and for Handle, and a wheelwright for our coach wheels. Will I find either in the nearest village?"

"We have no wheelwright, but we have a good smith. No surgeon either, however, the barber, besides letting blood, has been known to set a break." He gave Reginald a wink before continuing. "He is not licensed, so he can charge no fee. Folk pay him on the sly."

Reginald nodded. "I understand. I intend to ride into the village ere nightfall. I fear 'tis too late to take the busted wheels with me. However, I do intend to bring the barber back with me to see to Handle and Pit." He indicated the two men now sitting with their backs propped against Wirth's stone fence. "That said, I need be off once I see all secured here."

"Aye, sir," Wirth said. "I will get me cart to tike the ladies to the house, then I will tike the two of them," he nodded to Pit and Handle, "to Herve's. His wife will have them eating a warming stew and drinking as good an ale as you will find anywhere in the county. She will see to them right and proper till you get back with Holder. He is the barber."

"I thank you," Reginald said.

The farmer bobbed his head and strode off to get his cart. Reginald blew a sigh out through his nose. This was not how he had intended to spend his evening. He looked at Amaryllis. She was engaged in entertaining Tabitha and Charlie. Even after all she had endured, even with her possibly injured wrist, and her tousled hair, she was still breathtakingly lovely. He should be sitting down to a peaceful supper with her in a private dining room at a respectable inn, not worrying about seeing her and her siblings comfortable in a farmer's abode.

Esmeralda drew his attention. "I have our portmanteaus, Master Reginald, and Mister Nye has yours. I see no reason Mistress Bowdon, the children, and I, as well as our luggage, cannot ride comfortably to the house in Goodman Wirth's cart. Do you wish to be on your way into the village, we will manage. You need have no concerns."

He smiled at the beloved family servant. "I am certain you and Nye can see to everything. And I thank you." He stopped to again assure himself that Amaryllis was all right. At her assurance that she would be fine, and that she had complete confidence in Esmeralda and Mister Nye, Reginald called to his outrider. "Billings, mount up. We are off."

Swinging up onto his saddle, he spoke to the postilion. "After you have seen to the team, and had yourself a bite, you will need spend the night here with the coach. Be certain you keep a lantern lit until the moon rises. We would not want any late-traveling coach or rider to run into us, sitting here in the road as we are."

"Aye, Master Reginald," the postilion answered.

"And ne'er fear," Reginald added. "Norwood or Billings will relieve you at some point during the night."

"I cannot see why I cannot stay with the coach," Pit said.

Reginald gave his devoted coachman a wan smile. "I need you well and rested for when we have the coach repaired, and we can resume our journey." With that, he gave his horse a nudge and off they went.

Chapter 13

Amaryllis thought Reginald D'Arcy the most competent man she had ever known. She could not imagine how anyone could handle the ruckus so calmly. From the moment he had looked down into the coach at her, his dark eyes filled with concern, yet confidence, her fear had vanished. She had had no doubt he would successfully rescue them, and he had. Now he was off to bring help for the injured, and on the morrow, he would no doubt see the wheel was fixed, and they would soon be on their way.

The thought of parting from Reginald, of never seeing him again, gave her pause. She had to admit, she was immensely attracted to the man. When he touched her, he set her to quivering, set her heart to racing and her breath coming in little puffs. She had not the slightest doubt that she was falling in love with Reginald D'Arcy. She almost relished this mishap that she might spend more time with him. Yet, once they reached Leicester, they would have to part.

The children would hate saying goodbye to Fate and to Lady Selena. What a fascinating character was Selena. Amaryllis wondered whether Selena was helping the farmer's wife, or whether she was being a hindrance. The farmer was returning with his cart, a cart not unlike the one she and the children had ridden in the night of their escape. But rather than a donkey, a small shaggy horse, still in the midst of shedding its winter hair, was attached to the lumbering cart.

Esmeralda and Mister Nye saw to the loading of the cart, and Wirth assured the injured Pit and Handle he would soon return for them. Norwood remained with them while the postilion set off with the coach horses for Goodman Barlow's barn. "I will be needing to rub 'em down good and see to Tor's cut afore I return," he told Norwood.

"Do what needs doing," Norwood answered. "I will be taking a look at the back wheel. See if I can determine how badly 'tis broken."

The postilion answered something, but Amaryllis failed to hear what he said as the cart started up with a loud creak. They jostled around a bit and Charlie chuckled as he swayed this way and that, but Tabitha warned him, "Be careful 'ere you rock over on top of Fate."

The boy sobered and looked at the dog in his sister's lap. He reached over to pat the dog on the head. "Poor Fate," he said. "Good dog."

Amaryllis thought few dogs could hope to be so fortunate. This little dog was being pampered like royalty. Selena might have some strange habits, but she certainly had a kind heart. Who else would have scooped a dog up off the road and seen to its injury? And who else would have insisted that she and Tabitha and Charlie join their party? She could think of no one she knew or had ever known.

The cart pulled to a stop at the front of the farmer's freestone farmhouse. The farmer's wife, wiping her hands on her apron, emerged from the house. A bit on the plump side, with straw-colored blond hair and bright blue eyes, she looked to be a woman of good cheer, if slightly frazzled, as indeed she should be with such a party landing on her doorstep. But she wore a bright smile and graciously greeted her guests. When everyone was out of the cart, the farmer proudly introduced his wife, and she bobbed a curtsey.

"No need to be curtseying to me," Esmeralda said. "And once I get Mistress Bowdon, the children, and Lady Selena's articles set to rights, you let me know how I may assist you."

Goody Wirth thanked Esmeralda but said, "Lady Selena has a'ready been a great help to me. She took over minding the children, and helped me move me husband's grandmother into a chair by the window so as I could red up her room." She looked at Esmeralda then Amaryllis. "You but follow me, and I will show you where you will be bedding for the night. I meant to be giving Lady Selena our bedchamber, but she would not have it. Said she would not be putting me and my husband from our bed. I am afraid your beds may not be what you are used to."

"I am certain we will manage fine," Esmeralda said. "'Tis most kind of you to be furnishing us with a roof over our heads."

Entering the hall behind Goody Wirth, Amaryllis was pleased to note Goodman Wirth appeared to be a prosperous yeoman. His home was of a goodly size and looked to be capable of accommodating the unexpected guests. A brisk fire was glowing in a huge stone fireplace, and the contents of a large black cauldron, hanging on a strong iron crane over the fire, bubbled and steamed. A long-handled tripod pot sat off to one side of the hearth, no doubt keeping its contents warm. A servant girl with bright pink cheeks and thick blond braids was busy setting a heavy oak table with pewter and wooden plates. The table had been laid with a white cloth, and a bowl of fresh butter and a platter of cheese adorned its center.

A hutch, currently devoid of much of its ware, the pewter being used on the table, set in a corner next to a narrow set of stairs. A large work table below three tiers of shelving was covered with the makings of the upcoming meal – a loaf of bread, a bowl of dried apples, a crock of pickled beets or mayhap cucumbers, Amaryllis could not be certain. Chairs and benches, yet to be pulled up to the table, lined one wall under a window sporting bright yellow curtains.

Hearing voices from a room off the hall, Amaryllis smiled as Selena, a baby on her hip and a little girl at her knees, appeared in the doorway of what appeared to be a small parlor. "Ah, you are here," Selena said with her usual bright smile. She looked at Charlie and Tabitha. "Come meet Annelise and Argus. And bring Fate. I have been telling them all about him, and they know they must be very careful of him."

Charlie and Tabitha shyly joined Selena. It was a strange house to them. They were meeting new children, and they had been through a hazardous accident. Amaryllis was not surprised they were wary, but Selena soon put them at ease. "Come, come, Tabitha. Annelise is near five. I have been telling her how brave you and Charlie were when the coach tipped over. She is eager for you to tell her about how you flew right up out of the tumped over coach."

Tabitha, immediately brightening, looked at the little red-haired, freckle-faced girl and said, "We were flying like Selena did when she tried to teach the ducks to fly. Did Selena tell you about her ducks?"

Annelise's gray-blue eyes grew round, and she shook her head.

"Well, I will tell you," Tabitha stated.

"Before you start telling about the ducks, Tabitha, you must also meet Goodman Wirth's grandmother. Do make your curtsey to Granny Tekla Wirth."

96

The children again looked wary, but Tabitha, still clutching Fate, did as instructed. Charlie wrapped his arms around Selena's legs and peered out at the old woman. The woman was seated in a wingback chair by a window with real glass that looked out on a garden of vegetables and flowers. The room was neat and prettily furnished with a canopied bed, a large decorative chest, two small chairs, a drop-leaf table, and a washstand with a white, glazed bowl and pitcher below a shiny, tin looking glass.

Having absently followed after the children instead of her hostess, Amaryllis blushed. Selena was like the pied piper. Resisting her call was a near impossibility. Already Selena had charmed Goody Wirth, her children, and the old grandmother. Smiling brightly, the old woman welcomed the children to her home. Her melodic voice and sparkling blue eyes soon had the children relaxing. "Might I see your pretty dog?" she asked Tabitha.

"He is not my dog, but I wish he was," Tabitha said, stepping close enough to Granny Wirth that the grandmother might reach out a gnarled hand to scratch Fate behind his ears. "Fate belongs to Selena. She rescued him," Tabitha stated.

"Ah, yes, Lady Selena told me the story," Granny Wirth said, "but now, I would meet your sister." She turned her intense blue eyes on Amaryllis, and Amaryllis thought she had never seen eyes of such a vivid blue before. The old woman's eyes danced with merriment, and yet Amaryllis thought she saw pain in them. Pain the old woman concealed from the children.

"I apologize, Granny Wirth," Selena said. "I had not noticed Amaryllis had entered the room. Do meet my friend, Mistress Bowdon. She and the children are making our journey so much more enjoyable. How bored my brother and Esmeralda and I were before they joined us."

How kind, Amaryllis thought. Selena made it sound like she and the children were doing her a favor instead of the other way around. Taking the old woman's hand in hers, she saw a gentleness in Tekla Wirth, yet a strength and a sense of humor lurked in her exceptional eyes.

"Granny Wirth has told me the children are named for her parents," Selena said, jiggling the baby on her hip. "This big boy's name is Argus, it means vigilant. Annelise means graceful light. Is that not beautiful?" Amaryllis nodded as Selena continued, "Both Granny Wirth's parents' families go back to before the Conqueror. Back to when the Danes ruled this area." She turned to Amaryllis. "Is your wrist well enough for you to mind the baby? I best have a look at Fate." Nodding, Amaryllis settled the baby on her hip and watched Selena, still in her riding breeches, squat next to Tabitha. "I do thank you for taking such good care of Fate." Holding the dog in one arm, she pointed with her other arm to a splotch of sunlight on the floor. "Look, Annelise has her dollies out. She thought you and Charlie might like to play with them."

Two rag dolls in colorful gowns, and one small, carved doll in breeches and shirt lay on a small, braided rug. "Oh," Tabitha said. "Look at the pretty dollies. May we play?" She scampered over to the dolls, and plopping down on the floor, picked up a doll with blue-stitched eyes, a sunny mouth, and a yellow dress, the same yellow as the hall window curtains.

Joining Tabitha on the floor, Annelise said, "That one is mine." She picked up a second doll with a brown dress. "You can play with this one."

Tabitha eyed Annelise for a moment. Her lower lip in a pout, she clutched the yellow-dressed doll to her chest. Amaryllis was about to tell her to give the doll to Annelise when Charlie joined them and picked up the wooden doll. Seeing the look of joy on her little brother's face, Tabitha dropped her pout, and handing Annelise's doll to her said, "Oh, see how he likes the doll. He misses his horses. He has a whole set of wooden horses at home."

Amaryllis was always touched by how much Tabitha loved her brother. The siblings had a close and caring relationship that she hoped would last throughout their lives.

Annelise took the yellow-dressed doll and thrust the other doll at Tabitha. "Here, this one is for you." She looked at Charlie. "He can play with that doll, but that is Argus's dolly. For when he is older. Uncle Herve carved it for him and Aunt Jane made his clothes. It was a gift to Argus when he was born. Mother made my two dollies."

Tabitha had started rocking her doll during Annelise's speech, and Charlie, ignoring Annelise completely, was lightly thumping his doll on the floor. "I have dolls at home," Tabitha said, "and lots of other toys, but Ryllis said we had no room for them in our satchels."

"Who is Ryllis?" Annelise asked.

Tabitha pointed to Amaryllis. "My sister."

Annelise said, "Oh," and changing the subject, proclaimed, "My doll's name is Mary. Your doll's name is Bess."

Tilting her head to one side, Tabitha said, "I think I shall call her Lady Selena."

Amaryllis smiled and wondered if Selena had heard the exchange. She had been examining the small dog which set about licking her hands and trying to lick her face. At the dog's antics, Selena's tinkling laugh erupted, and the baby Amaryllis held on her hip turned his head sharply to see where the delightful sound had come from. "What a cute little fellow you are," Amaryllis said, "and so alert."

"He is a bright one. Six months old, he is," Granny Wirth said, her smile widening to show a number of gaping holes in her gum line. "And sturdy. Made it through the winter when many a child succumbs to the cold." Her eyes glazed over a little. "I lost four babes to the cold. Such little mites they were, trying hard to survive. But then the house I had then was not as solid and warm as this house. 'Twas wattle and daub with a thatched roof, not slate, and the wind crept in through the cracks." She shivered as if she could still feel the cold. Brightening, she said, "My son built this house. Married well, he did. Had a number of good crop years, and not but one sister needing a dowry. So he had the wherewithal to afford the laborers to build this nice stone house." She shook her head. "Died two year ago this spring. Almost a year to the day of his wife's dying. Fever going 'round. Came home from the village not feeling well, took to his bed, and two days later he were dead."

"Oh, Granny Wirth, I am so sorry to hear that," Selena said, rising with Fate in her arms.

Granny Wirth again shook her head from side to side. "Had we knowed he were so sick, we would have had him bled. Might have helped restore his humor. Abe offered to fetch the barber, but my son said he had no wish to spend the coin." She snorted. "Always watching the pennies. Now he is gone, but we still got the coin."

"I lost my father to the apoplexy," Amaryllis said. "No matter how they go, 'tis hard to lose someone we love."

Granny Wirth nodded. "Aye, aye."

"Well, here now," Selena said. "Are we not being morose. Let us move on to happier subjects. First, I will say, Fate seems to be well and hale. Second, I smell lovely scents coming from the hearth. Third, the children are happy at play. And most importantly, we and the horses are all alive and well-housed for the night. We could scarce be any more fortunate."

Amaryllis laughed. "Indeed, you are right. However, I do think Argus may be in need of a napkin change. He has been working rather hard for the last little bit, and I believe the aromas I am scenting are not coming from the hearth."

Selena's tinkling laugh again filled the room, and not just the baby turned to look at her. The children stopped their play, and Charlie's delighted chuckle followed Selena's laughter. Smiling, Selena said, "Let me leave Fate in Tabitha's care, and I will take Argus to his mother. She will see he gets changed. And does a pot need stirring or bread cutting, I can see to that. You, dear friend," she put a hand on Amaryllis's shoulder, "need to go upstairs and freshen up. Have Esmeralda bind your wrist, then rest a bit do you wish. I can mind the children."

"What of you? Are you not tired?"

Setting Fate down next to Tabitha and giving the dog a pat on the head, Selena straightened and said, "Goody Wirth had a warm bowl of water ready for me to wash up and a hot mug of ale awaiting when I came in from brushing down Brigantia. So I have been refreshed. Now 'tis your turn. Go ahead. You will feel better."

Amaryllis protested that she could also be of assistance, but Esmeralda appeared in the doorway and said, "Here you be, Mistress Bowdon. I have the room readied. Warm water in the pitcher and fresh towels laid out. You refresh yourself, then let me see to your wrist. Goody Wirth mixed up a compost and has given me some nice clean linen. After you have rested, I will bring up the children and get them readied for their supper." Turning to Selena, she added, "I have your gown laid out as well, my lady. We will be sharing the room with Mistress Bowdon and the children. Master Reginald and Mister Nye will be bunking in with Goodman Wirth's laborers, but the cots have good mattresses and clean sheets. I am certain they will do fine."

Selena had frowned when Esmeralda told her she had a gown laid out for her, but she brightened when her maid told her Reginald would be bunking with the farm laborers. "I am certain you are correct, Esmeralda. Reggie will survive. 'Tis most gracious of the Wirths to be providing us with food and beds. We will all manage quite comfortably. Now, I will hand Argus over to his mother and go up with Amaryllis to change my clothes."

Goody Wirth chuckled and took her baby. "I best go up and change him and feed him." Turning to her servant girl, she said, "Orpah, can you keep things from burning until I can feed Argus and put him down in his crib?"

Before the servant could answer, Selena stated, "Esmeralda can help, too, once she has tended Amaryllis's wrist." Looking to Esmeralda, she added, "Do I need any help getting into my dress, Amaryllis can help me."

"Well, follow me," Esmeralda said, "and I will show you to our room."

Amaryllis fell in behind Selena. What an interesting night this was going to be. She hoped Reginald would soon return. Somehow he made her feel all would be well.

Chapter 14

Felton took a long swig of his ale. So the boy was still alive. Looked not to have been injured even the least wee bit. Felton shrugged. Well, at least he had bought himself more time. He had kept his hat brim low so his face was hidden, but he had been able to see all that had happened. Not only were the D'Arcys shy one outrider, but it looked like a footman and the coachman had been injured. That could be helpful. Too bad the wreck had occurred in front of the home of an obliging farmer instead of away from any form of refuge.

He fingered the purse in his pocket. Mistress Bowdon had given him a fair amount of coin for his travel. He could take the money and the horse and disappear. But at some point, the money would be gone, he would have to sell the horse, and he would not even have his home to return to. He had little doubt but what Mistress Bowdon could twist things so he would need be hiding from the law as well. His tale would have little merit against hers. Plus he would not have the lifetime annuity she had guaranteed him. And that haughty tavern wench would not be warming his bed. No, he had to somehow kill the boy, but he needed to watch his coin carefully. Would not do to run out of money before the deed was done.

He would have to trade horses again. The dun was too recognizable. He hated to give it up, though. The horse was old, but it had a smooth gait. Easy on his backside. He was not used to so much riding. Gads but he wished the big woman had landed on the boy. Well, he could not live on wishes. At least he would have a day of rest. A day to consider his next plan of action. When emerging from the stable where he left the dun, he had seen D'Arcy and his outrider come riding into the village. They had headed straight to the blacksmith shop. He watched them for a moment, then fearing he might be noticed, he ducked into the alehouse. Later he would dawdle around to the smithy. See if he could determine how long it would take the smith to fix the wheel. Assuming he could fix it. If a whole new wheel had to be made, that would really cause a delay. The longer the delay, the more chance he had to come up with another scheme. Something was bound to present itself.

※ ※ ※ ※

Reginald was pleased with both the smith and the barber. He judged the barber, Holder, to be in his mid-forties. Graying at his temples, bit of a bulge around his waistline, but a cheerful soul, he was most willing to accompany Reginald to the Wirths. The smith, named Smith, was younger, but he seemed competent. He had been apprenticed to the previous smith, and had married his master's daughter, inheriting the business in the process. His large, work-worn hands and bare forearms were covered in burn scars. A hazard of the trade. But his blue eyes were bright, his smile quick, and his palm eager to grasp the gratuity Reginald offered him to ride back with him to collect the coach wheels that he might start on them first thing in the morning.

The ride back to the Wirths' took longer than Reginald had anticipated due to the smith's rumbling cart needed to transport the wheels to the village. They found Nye and the postilion awaiting them at the coach. With the sun resting on the horizon, the smith, with the postilion's help, removed the wheels. Nye led the barber off to Barlow's house to attend Pit and Handle, and Billings took Reginald's and his horses to the Wirths' barn to give them a feed and a rub down.

Once the wheels were off and loaded onto the cart, the smith said, "The larger wheel looks beyond my capability to fix, but I will not know for certain until I examine it in the light come morning. Could be ye will haf to tike it to the wheelwright in Northampton."

"Northampton! How far is that?" Reginald could not see them biding day after day at the Wirths, kind as the yeoman family might be.

Scratching his chin, Smith said, "Near twenty miles I would say."

"Twenty miles! None closer?"

"None I would be wanting to trust my family with."

"Gads!" Reginald thunked his palm against his head.

"Well, I will know better in the morning. Right now, I had best be getting back before it gets too much darker."

"You will ne'er make it afore dark," Goodman Wirth said. He had joined them as they discussed the wheel. "Best you come have supper with us, and head back when the moon is full up. Lot safer than trying to make your way in the dark."

Smith nodded. "Aye. Right you are, and I thank you for the offer of supper. I will admit, my belly is starting to rumble."

"Mills, we need light those lanterns," Reginald said to the postilion. "I will send Norwood with some blankets, and you two can take turns keeping watch on the coach tonight."

"Aye, Master Reginald, we will see the coach comes to no harm."

Reginald thanked his postilion then joined Smith and Wirth as they headed toward the farmer's house. He saw a lantern bobbing across the field from Barlow's croft, and heard Nye call to him. "Ho, Master Reginald, I have a report from the barber."

"I will wait for my man and join you soon," Reginald said, and Wirth and Smith proceeded on to the house.

"Handle's leg is broken, but not badly so," Nye said when he joined Reginald. "A minor fracture of the fibula. Holder put a splint on it, and he said Handle will need be careful. Might need have a proper surgeon look at it when we get to Northampton. He said the apothecary could give him a drug for the pain, but Goody Barlow had already given him something mixed in his ale, and he said he was feeling no pain whatsoever. Same for Pit. No pain. His ankle is but sprained. Goody Barlow had him soak it, then she rubbed some castor oil on it, then wrapped it up. Holder said it was as good a job as he could have done, mayhap better."

"Have they been fed?" Reginald asked.

"Just sitting down to supper now. The Barlows invited me to join them, but I said I had best check in with you."

"What of Norwood?"

"He is sitting down to supper with them as is the barber. Norwood says when he is finished, he will take a bowl of stew and some bread and ale out to Mills."

"Sounds as if all is well. We will have our supper with the Wirths. Ah, there comes Billings." He raised a hand in salute as the outrider

104

made his way through the gathering dark to join them. "The horses are bedded down to your satisfaction?"

"Aye, Master Reginald. Goodman Wirth keeps a clean barn. Had some oats set out in a bucket for our horses. A fine fellow, he is."

"Glad to hear all is in order. I have had enough disorder today. You go on to the Barlow's and have your supper. Tell Norwood he will be staying the night with Mills at the coach. Tell him to see can he borrow a couple of blankets from the Barlows."

Squaring his broad shoulders, and pulling on his thin, pointed beard, Billings asked, "Shall I take a turn at watching the coach?"

"Nay, are we here more than a day, you will be taking your turn tomorrow night. Now hurry on to your supper, and here," he took the lantern from Nye, "you take the lantern. Oh, and tell the barber to come by the Wirths when the moon is up, I will see he is paid, and he and Smith can ride back to town together."

"Aye, Master Reginald," Billings said with a bob of his head before striding away.

Reginald clamped a hand on Nye's shoulder. "Let us go get us some supper."

"I am ready," Nye answered.

❉ ❉ ❉ ❉

Reginald was pleased to find a basin of water awaited him and Nye. They quickly washed then joined the crowded table. Besides the Wirths, the D'Arcy party, and the smith, Goodman Wirth's two laborers and an apprentice, rescued from the poorhouse and bound to Wirth until he came of age, were also seated at the table. The youth could do little more than gawk at Amaryllis and Selena until Goodman Wirth threatened did he not mind his manners, he would be sent from the table. The boy, he must have been in his early teens, blushed under his freckles, mumbled an apology, and looked down at his food.

Reginald could not blame the boy. He had been equally bewitched at his first glimpse of Amaryllis. And when would the youth, or the laborers, or the Wirths for that matter, again be sitting down to sup with a lady of the realm, the daughter of an earl. He could well imagine the tales they would be telling.

Goody Wirth had given the four hard-backed chairs to Selena, Amaryllis, himself, and her husband's elderly grandmother. The rest, including Goodman Wirth, sat on benches or stools. Selena expressed surprise at the size of the table, but Goodman Wirth laughed and said, "Come harvest, we have cottagers and some villagers bed and sup with us until all the crops are in. That is why we have so many beds as well. Some can go home at night, but a number travel the countryside, going from farm to farm as needed."

"You seem to have a rather large holding here, Goodman Wirth. Must keep you powerful busy," Nye observed.

"Aye, 'tis true. Today I was finishing up plowing my last field while Ben culled the buds on the fruit trees. Too many buds, and the fruit will be too small. Ben has been with me long enough, I can trust him to know what to cull, what to leave. George was sowing the rye, and young Dirk there," he nodded at the youth he had scolded, "he is finishing the manure spreading. Hope to get the wheat sowed on the morrow and new poles readied for the hop vines. There is a good profit in hops. Anyhow, there is ne'er any end to what needs doing. But then idleness ne'er put bread on the table, huh?"

"Aye," Reginald said, "by the looks of your land and croft no one could ever accuse you of idleness. Is this a freehold?"

"Me croft and two hundred acres are mine free and clear, but I have a leasehold on another two hundred acres, plus I have rights to the village common, and the right, do I choose, for me pigs to feed on acorns in the manor woodlands. When Mister Toms's father started consolidating champion fields and enclosing them, I lost some prime strips. Still, I would say I am better off. I have no worry that a slovenly farmer's weeds will creep into my fields or that my fields will be flooded does he not keep his ditches cleared." He vigorously shook his head. "There are some as can complain, cottagers mostly, but me wife's brother, Herve, and I both agree, we have done better since the enclosure."

Pausing to take a sip of ale, he cocked his head. "Not that young Toms's father was not above taking more than his due from the common for his home farm, but overall, he played fair."

Toms, Reginald thought. Where had he heard that name? But he

106

brought his attention back to Wirth as the famer continued, "We have prospered and so has Toms. We have built a new stone milkhouse, and two daughters of a neighboring cottager do the milking and churn the butter. They live close enough, we have no need to house 'em. Now Herve, he built a fine new malthouse. His wife makes as good an ale as you will find in this county." He raised his mug. "'Tis what we are drinking now."

"Indeed, 'tis most tasty," Selena said, raising her mug and looking at Wirth. "I meant to compliment your wife, but I find my compliments go to her sister-in-law. But this meal is equal to the ale, and for that I know we must compliment Goody Wirth." Turning to Wirth's wife, Selena saluted Goody Wirth with her mug.

Goody Wirth blushed. "I know 'tis not the kind of meal you be used to having. And I know 'tis rare to haf the likes of the gentry sitting down to a meal with the likes of us, but ye did proclaim ye would be no special bother to us, and ye meant to sit with us, so here ye be."

"Indeed, and I can find no fault with anything you have prepared. The chicken is tender and delightfully seasoned. I do think this sausage pudding is the best I have ever tasted." Selena looked at Esmeralda. "Do you not think 'tis better than Mistress Craddick's?" She turned back to Goody Wirth. "She is the vicar's wife. Lives in the village near my home. She prides herself on her puddings, but yours is better."

Esmeralda agreed with Selena that it was indeed a fine pudding.

Reginald was pleased Selena refrained from mentioning the fact that the laborers had not been served any of the chicken. That would have embarrassed the Wirths, for obviously the chicken had been reserved for the Wirths' guests, including the smith, and themselves. But there was no lack of food. Besides the pudding, Goody Wirth served hunks of cheese, thick chunks of bread with a bowl of fresh butter, and a mutton pie with a crispy-crust and brimming with onions. Large crockery pitchers of ale set at either end of the table.

"Where are Tabitha and Charlie?" Reginald asked, and looking around the room, added, "And that cur of yours, Selena?"

"The children had their supper earlier," Selena answered, "with the Wirths' daughter, Annelise. They are now playing in the parlor. When we have finished our supper, then 'tis off to bed for them. Fate is with them. Tabitha is minding him." She looked to Nye. "I will ask you, please, Mister Nye, to take Fate out to do his duty before we settle him for the night."

"Oh, I would be happy to see to your wee dog," the youth said before Nye could answer. "No reason to trouble the gentleman here." He looked at Nye.

Reginald restrained a chuckle. The boy must think Nye, by the way Selena addressed him, and by the way he was dressed in quality riding boots, waistcoat, white shirt, and plain, yet stylish coat, that he was a member of the gentry. Fact was, Reginald wondered if the other laborers, or even the Wirths, had an inkling that Nye was his valet.

With nary a hint that the boy was mistaken about Nye, Selena graciously thanked him, then looking to Reginald, said, "Now that your hunger has been abated, do tell all. What of the wheel, and do you know how Pit and Handle fair?"

Reginald told her what he had learned of Pit's and Handle's conditions before telling her the wheel might be beyond the smith's ability to fix. The smith, shaking his head, corroborated Reginald's tidings, adding, "I will not know for certain 'til morn when I examine it."

When he finished speaking, Amaryllis asked, "You mean we might not be able to travel on for several days?"

Reginald heard the worry in her voice. "We may be delayed a day or two, but are you worried about the children's aunt not being in Derby when you arrive, why not write to her. Tell her the situation. Tell her you are coming with the children. 'Tis certain she will wait for you."

"Reggie is right," Selena said. "Write the letter tonight, and we can post it in the village on the morrow." She turned to Goodman Wirth. "Have you paper and ink?"

"Happens we do. I count myself a fair to middling businessman. I keep good records of what is bought and sold and what I pays out." He looked at Amaryllis. "After supper, I will set you up with what you need."

Amaryllis thanked him and Reginald, and both beamed at her. With the worried crease gone from her forehead, and a smile lighting her eyes, Reginald thought she looked like a fairy princess. She had not changed from her travel gown, but she had combed out her glorious hair and donned a fresh cap. Selena had changed from her male riding attire to her plainest walking dress. Its quality could be noted, but she had not overdressed for her simple surroundings. He guessed Esmeralda had insisted she change, otherwise, Selena most likely would not even have given her raiment a thought and would have sat down to supper wearing her breeches.

Reginald was pleased he had thought to have Amaryllis write to the children's aunt. Luckily it was her left wrist that had been injured, so she would have no trouble writing the letter. When he asked about her wrist, she said it no longer hurt, and she expected it to be much better by morning. Once the letter was posted, they would then be under no time constraint. What matter did the wheel need be sent to Northampton? That would give him more time with Amaryllis. And certainly Selena would not care how long it took her to reach Whimbrel. No, maybe this breakdown would not be so bad after all.

※ ※ ※ ※

Amaryllis lay awake listening to the soft breathing of the other occupants of the bedchamber. Exhausted, Tabitha and Charlie had fallen to sleep before Selena finished their bedtime story, or so Selena reported when she came back downstairs to see if Amaryllis had completed her letter to the children's aunt.

After sealing the letter with wax from a candle, Amaryllis handed it to Selena. "It will be posted first thing when we reach the village tomorrow," Selena promised.

Amaryllis thanked Goodman Wirth for supplying her with paper, pen, and ink, and then, professing weariness, said she would retire.

"Best we join you," Selena said. "I know the Wirths will be up before the dawn, and I have no wish to keep them from their bed." She looked at Reginald. "I plan to ride into the village with you tomorrow, so wake me. Do you leave without me, I will ride in on my own."

Reginald, having paid off the barber and wished him and the smith a safe trip home, frowned at his sister. "I will see you are awakened, but I plan to leave at first dawn, so be ready."

Selena nodded. "I will be ready."

Amaryllis wondered that Selena had so readily fallen asleep upon her cot. She doubted Selena had ever slept on anything so rustic. Certainly the small cot Esmeralda stretched out on barely accommodated her large frame. But Esmeralda, too, was soon lightly snoring. Before retiring, the Wirths had again offered their bedchamber to Selena, but she had again adamantly refused it, saying, "Good heavens, you cannot think I would take your bed when you are already being such gracious hosts. Nay, I am happy to share a chamber with Amaryllis and the children, as is Esmeralda. We will be quite comfortable."

Amaryllis had learned the chamber they were sharing was normally closed off when not in use by the harvesters. So Orpah, besides killing and hastily plucking the chickens Goody Wirth wanted for the evening's supper, had opened up the chamber, aired it out, and put fresh sheets on the cots. She had also had to make up two extra cots in the men's bedchamber. The girl had then helped cook the meal, set the table, and when everyone else sat down to eat, she saw everyone was served before she herself quietly squeezed in at the table. Amaryllis wondered if a romance might be developing between the girl and the laborer, Ben, a well-favored man with twinkling blue eyes. A couple of times, she had seen the two exchanging glances.

She knew that married life for laborers was not easy. Her father had always seen that his laborers, were they married, had a cottage and at least four acres on which to raise vegetables, rye for bread, and perhaps some barley to sell to local alehouses. Could be they would have some fruit trees that they might make cider and jam for themselves. They might also have a pig or a goat or mayhap some chickens, but on little more than two pounds a year in wages, they lived a meager life. Fortunately, their children were often able to find work in the Churlwood village, or nearby Albertine. If lucky, they might be apprenticed to an artisan. Some families earned extra money spinning or weaving wool, others might obtain extra work in the winter catching vermin or hewing wood. But no matter, those who were land poor had a hard lot.

Until meeting Selena, Amaryllis had given but slight thought to the plight of the lower classes. Having been raised with servants to do her bidding, she had never thought them her equal. She had simply accepted her status and theirs. But Selena, though recognizing her place in society, never indicated she thought that made her a superior human being. As Reginald had said, Selena was as gracious or as unintentionally insulting to people of all classes. Selena's willingness to pitch in to help Goody Wirth or Orpah was made even more evident when supper ended and Selena attempted to help clear the table.

"No, oh no, Lady Selena, good heavens, ye must not bother yerself. 'Twould not be right. No, you go have a seat in the parlor with Granny. Orpah and I will see to the cleaning while the men have their smokes." Goodman Wirth, after setting up the leaf table in the parlor and getting writing supplies for Amaryllis, had rejoined his two laborers at the table. Taking clay pipes from the mantle, they lit up. They had offered a pipe to Reginald and to Mister Nye, but both had refused, saying they would but relax with another mug of Goody Barlow's fine ale.

"Well, then," Selena said, taking Granny Wirth's arm to help her back to her chair in the parlor, "the least I can do is ready the children for bed." She looked to the youth. "Dirk if you would but take Fate for his walk, I will be obliged."

Jumping up, the youth said, "Aye, milady. I will directly," and he followed her into the parlor. Fate was given over to him, and the children were told to pick up their toys.

"Must we?" Tabitha cried. "Look at this fine castle we have built for the dollies." The children had stacked varying sizes of wooden blocks against a wall to form their doll house. Amaryllis guessed Goodman Wirth must have carefully cut and sanded the blocks before giving them to his children. "May we not play a while longer?" Tabitha begged.

"Nay, Tabitha," Amaryllis said. "You do as Lady Selena directs you. You have had a long day. You need your rest. You may set your castle up again tomorrow. Most likely you will have all day tomorrow to play with Annelise."

Kneeling to help the children put their toys into a colorful chest in the corner of the parlor, Selena said, "When you are all tucked in, I shall tell you a story. A story about a beautiful princess and a handsome knight." She tweaked Charlie under the chin, and he chuckled.

"A brave knight?" he asked.

"A very brave knight. Now tell Granny Wirth goodnight and kiss your sister. She will be busy for a bit writing a letter."

"What of Annelise? Might she hear your story?" Tabitha asked.

"Does her mother allow her to cuddle in with you until the story is finished, then of course, she may hear the story. Now say your good-nights as I bid you, then go ask Annelise's mother if she may bide with you long enough to hear the story."

The request had been granted, and Esmeralda and Selena had disappeared up the stairs with the children. The Wirth children slept in their parents' bedchamber. The babe, presently asleep in his crib would no doubt awake soon for another feeding, but by that time, the house would be settling down for the night. The servant, Orpah, slept on a trundle bed in the parlor to be near Granny Wirth should the old woman need aid during the night.

Amaryllis was beginning to have a new appreciation of the various classes she was coming into closer contact with. She did not think she had ever been unkind to her servants, yet she had never before considered how tired they might be. When she retired to bed, she had always had her maid there to assist her, to put away her raiment, to comb out her hair. And the maid had always been up before her in the morning, ready to help her dress and prepare for the day. The maid had to be ready at her beck and call, and when not needed by Amaryllis, she busied herself with washing delicates, mending rents, ironing, or numerous other little odd jobs that Amaryllis never gave a thought to. In the future, she decided she would give more thought to the treatment and needs of her servants.

Chapter 15

Reginald stared at the coach wheel. It would indeed need be sent to Northampton for repair. But that was not what surprised him. It was the spokes. "You see here," Smith said, pointing to three badly broken spokes. "It 'pears to me like they been whittled down. Then, when ye hit a bump wrong, these spokes were not strong enough. They busted, and that busted the wheel. When it went, the smaller front wheel broke off the axle, and down ye tumped."

"Are you telling me these spokes were deliberately whittled down?" Reginald fingered the sharp, broken ends of each spoke.

"'Pears that way to me. Though, I cannot think why a body would do such."

"I can," Selena said, and both Reginald and the smith looked up at her. "Someone meant to slow us down, mayhap even meant to cause injury, mayhap injury to a certain little boy."

"What?" Smith said, but Reginald's eyes met Selena's, and he gave the slightest shake to his head. No reason to give the smith any tales to tell. Yet, he feared Selena might be right. Had someone learned Charlie was traveling in their coach? Had that someone meant to maim or kill him? But who? And when had the whittling been done? Mills and Pit seldom left the coach unattended. Yet those spokes were not that way when they left Rygate.

"Pay my sister no heed," he said. "She is ever consumed with stories of daring knights and fearless damsels. I am guessing we somehow offended someone. Been known to happen."

"Aye," Smith agreed. "There be those what resent those who are moneyed. Once John Burke, a cottager what is as lazy as the day is long, fell into some coin. Did he use it to buy his poor wife and children shoes or a decent meal? Nay, he got himself falling down drunk and when he saw Mister Adkins – he is a wool broker what has a nice home up the road a piece. Anyway, Adkins come by on a new horse, and Burke, stumbling out of the tavern, saw him and attacked him and his horse. Said 'twere not right Adkins should have such a fine horse when he could not afford a new coat and with winter a-coming on."

Smith shook his head. "Fortunately, neither Adkins nor his horse were bad injured. Mister Toms would have tossed Burke out of his cottage, but Goody Burke pleaded so … where would they go, how would they live, she and the children? Mister Toms let 'em stay but with a firm warning that did any such incidents happen agin, Burke was out. There be plenty of laborers what would do a better job than Burke does. So, anyhow, I can see someone resenting your fine coach. For 'tis certain, I have ne'er seen its likes."

Having patiently listened to Smith's recital, Reginald said, "Well, 'tis done, and now the main thing is to get the wheel to Northampton."

"I will send me boy to fetch Jonas Hawke," Smith said. "He has a good-size cart. He can transport the wheel to Northampton for ye." Smith called to his son. A boy of no more than ten who was the image of his father bounded into the shop.

Reginald turned to his outrider. "Billings, go with the boy. Tell Hawke what we need and have him bring round his cart. The sooner he gets started the better."

"Aye, sir," Billings said, and he and the boy set off on their mission.

"You can fix the smaller wheel?" Reginald asked.

"Oh, aye," Smith said. "Might need to do a bit of work on the axle, too. Figure when I have the wheel readied, I will take me tools and head out to Wirth's. Most likely, not 'til the morrow. It being no use to have the little wheel readied too much afore the big one."

Reginald agreed, and once Hawke arrived with the cart, and the wheel was loaded onto it, Reginald decided there was naught else he could do for the moment. Best to return to the Wirths'. Amaryllis was awaiting news. And he wanted to have some time with her. He had asked her how she slept, and she told him fine, but he thought she looked heavy-eyed. Was her cot no wider nor softer than his, he could imagine she had not had a restful night. Esmeralda looked tired, too, but Selena and the children seemed none the worse for a night spent on such primitive cots. The thought of spending a couple more nights on said cots was not appealing. Nor did he like the imposition on the Wirths. They had a farm to run.

Deciding Billings should accompany Hawke to and from Northampton, Reginald gave him a hefty coin purse to cover the cost of the repair and to house him and Hawke until they could return with the wheel. Then with the wheel on its way, he, Selena, and Nye headed back to the Wirths'. They arrived to find Barlow, Wirth and his two laborers, and Norwood, Mills, and Pit engaged in an animated discussion.

"We mean to move the coach off the road," Pit explained. "Goodman Barlow and I came up with the plan last evening." He pointed out two strong poles resting on the ground. "Once we have the team hitched up, we slip them poles under the carriage. Between Barlow, Wirth and his two men, and Norwood, they can hold the wagon up while we slip Lady Selena's trunks out. Then Mills slowly has the horses pull the coach off the road and into Goodman Wirth's field. The men holding the poles walk alongside taking the place of the missing wheels." He pointed to a spot the other side of Wirth's rock wall where two low barrels sat. "We rest the axles on those barrels, and there the coach stays, safe and sound, until we have its wheels back on."

"Brilliant!" Selena said, clapping her hands. "And Pit, 'tis good to see you up and about. How does your ankle?"

"Pains but a wee bit, milady. Goody Barlow is a miracle worker, I am thinking."

"That is wonderful. I must make a point of meeting her and thanking her for taking such good care of you and Handle. How does Handle?"

"Not as well." Pit held up a hand to ward off her frown. "Oh, not that he is in any major pain. But to get around, he will need crutches."

"I could make him a pair," Barlow said, "but there is a carpenter in town could make him a better pair. Do a better job of padding 'em so's they are easier on the underarms."

"I will see we measure him for the length he needs, and after dinner, Nye can ride back into the village and order them," Reginald said. "Now that is settled, your plan is approved Pit. So get those horses hitched. Nye and I can help with the poles. Selena can pull her trunks out."

Mills quickly hitched the horses, and Barlow and Norwood picked up the poles, but Pit called, "Hold off. Coach coming and at a good clip. Best we not try moving the coach with another vehicle on the road. Do they try to pass us while we are a-struggling with holding the coach up, might give the horses a fright."

"Right you are," Barlow said, and they all looked at the coach barreling toward them.

"Ho, ho!" the coachman cried, pulling on the reins and bringing the coach to an abrupt halt that caused the coach to sway side to side, and the two lead horses to rear. Reginald noted the coach, pulled by four horses and with naught but a coachman and no postilion, was well-made, and under the layer of dust coating it, he could see a high gleam. The horses, if not as well matched as his father's team, were a good, sturdy breed.

No sooner did the coach stop swaying than a door popped open, and a slender gentleman in mustard-colored breeches and green coat, a white, ruffled shirt and side-cocked hat with a large, white feather plume, hopped out. A footman leaped off his perch at the rear of the coach, but he was too late to assist the gentleman.

"What goes here?" the gentleman asked. "Had an accident? Happy to assist if we can."

Reginald, instantly recognizing the man, knotted his fists. Selena must have recognized him, too, for she stepped between him and the gentleman. "Mister Toms, is it not?" she asked. "How nice to see you again. Goodman Wirth was just speaking kindly of you last evening."

Nice indeed, Reginald thought. Now he would have the chance to land a facer to the man who had so insulted Amaryllis at the inn where they had first met her and the children. He cared not that Toms was Wirth's landlord. "Selena, step aside," he demanded.

Ignoring him Selena said, "Mayhap you fail to remember me. I am Lady Selena D'Arcy. We met at the inn in Albertine." Not allowing Reginald a clear shot at Toms's nose, she added, "This is my brother, Mister Reginald D'Arcy. And yes, we have had an accident." She smiled. "Are you but patient, we have a plan to move our coach off the road, and you will not have to risk scraping past us."

His eyes popping out, the man surveyed Selena. She looked nothing like the lady he had encountered at the inn, but this day he was not

116

drunk, and he quickly found his manners. "Lady Selena." Taking her extended hand, he bowed over it. "Would that I could make amends for my hideous behavior at the inn." His gaze shifted to Reginald. "I know I was most offensive to your lovely lady, sir, and for that I humbly apologize." Reginald found he liked having Amaryllis referred to as 'his lovely lady'.

His pointed nose quivering, Toms added, "I was in my cups, but hear my excuse. 'Twas due to a quarrel with my betrothed. She broke off our betrothal. My uncle was attempting to console me, and because our room was not ready, we had a few too many ales. 'Tis not a good excuse, but I assure you, I am not in the habit of accosting women."

Sweeping off his hat, and half bowing, he said, "Now please, tell me how I might be of service to you. Might you need help moving the coach? A ride somewhere? My coach is at your service." He glanced around. "And what of accommodations while your coach is being repaired? I fear our village inn is hardly fit to accommodate you, my lady. Have you friends in the area?"

"We stayed here with the Wirths last night," Selena said, swinging her arm to indicate the Wirths' solidly built stone farmhouse. "Goodman Wirth and his wife, and Goodman Barlow and his wife kindly took us and our servants in, providing us with bed and board."

"Ah, good day to you, Goodman Wirth, Goodman Barlow," Toms nodded to the two farmers who doffed their hats and nodded to him. "Good men, both, never late with their rents. Wish all my leaseholders were so dependable. But that said, my lady, and kind as the Wirths and Barlows may be, quarters must be cramped. Would you not allow me to offer my home to you and your family and servants until such time as your repairs are completed? 'Twould help take the stain off my good name. I assure you, do you ask anyone around here am I an honorable man, they will say I am indeed, as was my father before me and his father before him."

His gaze again shifted to Reginald. "Mere Manse is just up the road the other side of the village. I have good stables for your horses as well. I can take the ladies there in my coach."

Reginald could not decide whether he was ready to forgive Toms, but the thought of more comfortable beds, mayhap a garden where he might walk alone with Amaryllis, and some evening entertainment other than a few yarns being told around the table while heavy pipe smoke hung in the air, all sprang to mind. Before he could make a decision, a querulous voice sounded from Toms's coach. "Dicky, Dicky, I declare, whatever is the delay? I demand you tell me what is happening. You know I am eager to get to the house."

"Oh, dear," Toms said, looking back at his coach. "My aunt. Give me but a moment." Hurrying back to the coach he looked in the door. "Dear Auntie Jane, there has been an accident. We must wait for them to clear their coach off the road before we can go on. And we may be having guests."

"Guests?" the voice queried, "what kind of guests?"

"Lady Selena D'Arcy, her brother, and their friends. 'Tis their coach had the accident."

"Well, help me out, I want to meet this lady."

"Now, Auntie, I think 'twould be best you remain seated, the road is dusty and would coat your shoes. You know you have on naught but your soft pumps."

"Oh, so I do, well then have the lady come to me," she imperiously snapped.

"Auntie, we cannot order Lady Selena around."

"Oh, I am happy to oblige," Selena said, and in an instant she was peeking in at the woman in the coach. Curious, Reginald followed after her and looked over her shoulder at the regal woman sitting against plush cushions in the well-appointed coach interior.

Fumbling over his words, Toms said, "La...la...dy Selena, may I pre...present my...my aunt, Mistress Jane Sermon of Watford. She will be on an extended visit with me while her home is being repaired from some fire damages. Careless cook, I am afraid."

The woman looked to be in her mid-to-late-fifties, Reginald thought. Her dark hair, streaked with gray, was pulled back in a stark bun, much the way Selena at times wore her hair. A small, white cap atop her head, a shawl of dark maroon resting on her shoulders, and her gown of a rich brown with gold trim spoke of wealth. Her gray eyes, not unlike Toms's in color, were quick and bright. She had the same long, slender nose and thin lips, but somehow on her the features looked august, not

118

foxlike as they did on Toms.

Opposite her sat a young woman with demure face, and hands folded in her lap. Reginald took her to be Toms's aunt's personal maid. Her raiment was plain, as was her appearance, but when she raised her eyes to look at him and Selena, he observed a definite twinkle in them.

"Let me look at you," Mistress Sermon demanded of Selena. "Be you wearing breeches?"

"Auntie Jane…." Toms moaned, but Selena merely laughed her infectious, tinkling laugh, and answered, "I am indeed, Mistress Sermon. To my mother's chagrin, I must admit to being a complete hoyden."

To Reginald's surprise, Toms's aunt burst out laughing. "Oh, my but you remind me of myself when I was young. At least while you are at the manor, even if for but a night or two, I can expect some spirited conversation. Splendid."

Looking over Selena's head at Reginald, she said, "And I suppose this handsome young blood is your brother."

Selena glanced back at Reginald and smiled. "I am proud to say he is."

"Good, good." Shifting her intense gaze to Toms, she said, "So get the carriage off the road that we may collect Lady Selena's trunks and be on our way. I am weary and I look forward to a nice hot bath." She looked back at Selena. "I am a believer in cleanliness. I have no fear of water or of complete immersion in a tub of water."

Laughing, Selena said, "I agree, Mistress Sermon, a bath does sound delightful, but before you invite us to Mister Toms's home," she glanced at Toms, "you must know Mistress Bowdon and her two siblings are traveling with us. I have my maid, who is more a companion, and Reggie has his valet. There is the coachman, two footmen, an outrider, and the postilion. We have a team of six horses, and we have four riding horses. Oh, and a small dog with a splint on his leg. Are you certain you wish such an assault on Mere Manse?"

The woman chuckled. "Of course, he does. He thinks 'twill keep me from harping on all his faults."

"Also, Mistress Bowdon must be willing to forgive you, Mister Toms," Selena said, turning to Toms. "You did cause her a great distress at our last meeting."

"What did you do!" Mistress Sermon demanded, but then she swiped her arm in the air. "Oh, never mind. Once the drive to the farmer's house is cleared, Dicky, you shall have the coach drive up to the door. I shall make your apologies to the lady."

When Toms started to protest she snapped, "No arguing, Dicky. Get moving."

Reginald hoped Amaryllis would be willing to forgive Toms. He was not sure he had forgiven him, but he found his aunt delightful. He would enjoy watching Toms being browbeaten by his imperious aunt. He would also enjoy the comforts of a manor house.

Giving the order to set the coach in motion, he and Nye prepared to take hold of the poles, but Toms had ordered his two footmen to help, so Reginald had naught to do but pull out Selena's trunks then follow in the coach's wake as it was moved slowly off the road to be safely propped on the barrels.

The horses were unhitched, Selena's trunks were deposited on top of Toms's coach, and the entire party proceeded to the Wirths' house to drink a toast to the success of their endeavor.

Chapter 16

As the procession advanced to the Wirths', Goody Wirth came out of the door, a look of consternation on her face. She must be wondering what now, Selena thought. Swinging off her horse, she hurried to her hostess's side. "Goody Wirth, I am sure you recognize Mister Toms." She pointed to Toms, striding along between Wirth and Barlow. The three men seemed to be having an animated conversation. "That is his coach," she added, nodding to the coach that was lumbering slowly over the rutted track leading to the house. "Mister Toms is escorting his aunt to his home, but Mistress Sermon, his aunt, insists upon having a word with Mistress Bowdon concerning an incident that occurred earlier on our trip. Oh, and Mister Toms has kindly offered to house us until our coach is repaired. That way you can get your life back to some semblance of order. I know well this is a busy time of year for you and your household."

Her brow creased, Goody Wirth gave but a brief nod then asked, "Will they be staying to dinner? If so, I will need more chairs. I will haf to send Herve to fetch some from his house."

Selena shook her head. "I know not," she answered. "I but know the men said they wished to toast the successful moving of the coach." She had given no thought to dinner, or that Goody Wirth would again be attempting to prepare a meal she thought suitable to place before gentry. What an intrusion they were on the Wirths' everyday life.

Joining them at the door, Esmeralda, and Amaryllis with baby Argus on her hip, peered out at the gathering crowd. "What is happening?" Amaryllis asked.

Selena decided not to answer Amaryllis until she had a chance to introduce Mistress Sermon. She hoped Amaryllis would forgive Toms. She wanted a chance to become better acquainted with Toms's outspoken aunt. That would mean staying at Toms's home.

The coach pulled up before the Wirths' home, a footman jumped down, opened the door, lowered the steps, and raising a hand, assisted Mistress Sermon from the coach. She stood tall, her backbone straight, her eyes direct.

"Mistress Sermon," Selena said, "allow me to present Goody Wirth, our dear friend, Mistress Bowdon, and my personal maid and companion, Mistress Shadwell."

Each woman dropped a curtsy to Mistress Sermon, but the woman waved her hand and shook her head. "Nay, nay, I am neither elderly nor noble, no need for curtseys." She looked at Goody Wirth. "Goodwife, I know I am inconveniencing you, but might I come in. I would like to have a word with Mistress Bowdon."

Surprise flashed across Amaryllis's face at Mistress Sermon's request, but Goody Wirth, blushing, immediately stepped aside. "Do come in. You may speak with her in the parlor. Do you wish privacy, I will need but a moment to help Granny Wirth into the hall."

"Nay, nay, 'tis nothing that private."

"Well, let me take Argus." She reached out to take her baby from Amaryllis, but Selena said, "Oh, let me, you have much to do with all the men coming here wanting ale."

"No, I wish for you to be present, Lady Selena," Mistress Sermon said. She looked over her shoulder. "Betty, gel, pop down here and take this little lambkin from Mistress Bowdon."

The young maid did bounce out of the coach with no help from the footman. She looked to be in her early twenties. She was a plain girl, her features neither ugly nor attractive, but her large round blue eyes danced with merriment. "Oh, do let me hold him. Indeed what a lamb he is. My, if he does not look like me brother's little one." She reached out her arms to the baby. "Will you come to me you little sugar lump? I could gobble you up."

Argus at first did naught but stare at the woman making overtures to him. He wrapped his arms around Amaryllis's neck and turned from the maid before peeking back around. Betty continued to hold out her arms, and after another moment, the baby went to her. She took him carefully, saying, "Now are you not the fine young fellow? Feel how sturdy you are. I will bet it will not be long ere you are walking. And

122

then will you be getting into things." Still talking to the babe, she entered the Wirths' home behind Mistress Sermon.

Goody Wirth led Mistress Sermon into the parlor and introduced her to Granny Wirth. Tabitha, Annelise, and Charlie, looked up from their play to stare at the newcomer. "My siblings, and Goody Wirth's daughter," Amaryllis said, having warily followed after Mistress Sermon.

Selena asked Esmeralda to help Goody Wirth serve the men, then she too entered the parlor. Mistress Sermon was remarking to Granny Wirth that she had an outstanding view from her window. "You can see your lovely garden and keep a watchful eye on the help as well."

Granny Wirth chuckled and gave a wink. "I see more than some folk think."

"I bet you do," Mistress Sermon said.

"Mistress Sermon," Amaryllis nervously interrupted. "I cannot think that I know you, so I cannot imagine why it is you wish to speak with me."

"You have never met me, child, though I knew your father. No, I am here to beg your abject pardon on behalf of my nephew."

"What?" Her brow wrinkling, Amaryllis shook her head.

"Though I have no details of what transpired, I understand my nephew was unforgivably rude to you, and yet I am here asking for you to forgive him. He says he was in his cups. Reason being the silly boy had a quarrel with his betrothed. Thanks to the overtures of his uncle, my younger brother, they have made up, and the plans for their wedding have been resumed. Marriage is just the thing Dicky needs to settle him down. Fine young gel he chose, good dowry. His father, rest his soul, would be proud of him."

Amaryllis was shaking her head. "I still cannot understand what this has to do with me."

Selena stepped forward. "Her nephew is Richard Toms. The man who accosted you at the inn in Albertine."

Amaryllis's eyes widened. "You cannot say he followed us here to have his aunt apologize for him?"

"Nay, his home is up the road, the other side of the village. He is taking Mistress Sermon to stay with him while fire damage repairs are done on her home in Watford. They came upon us as we were preparing to move the coach off the road. Mister Toms offered to help. Of course, I recognized him, and he in turn has offered us the hospitality of his home until the coach wheel can be repaired. Indeed, as feared, it does need be sent to Northampton."

Cocking her head, Selena peered at Amaryllis. How would her friend react to her explanation? She glanced at Mistress Sermon. That woman too was intently watching Amaryllis's face.

"Mistress Bowdon," Mistress Sermon broke the silence. "Dicky is not a bad boy. Really, I have never known him to do any misdeed without being abjectly sorry for it in the morn. I do hope you will let him make amends. I selfishly hope you will agree to stay with us the brief spell until your coach wheel is repaired that I might enjoy Lady Selena's and your company. 'Twill be frightfully dull at Mere Manse with just me and Dicky rambling about."

Amaryllis slowly nodded her head. "I have to say I was deeply offended by Mister Toms's remarks, but I realize we are a great burden to the Wirths. I have been feeling guilty all morning. Goody Wirth and her serving girl prepared us breakfast and had no sooner finished their clean up than they started preparations for our dinner. Such a lot of work goes into our stay here. And when we do leave, they will have all the extra sheets to wash and dry, the blankets to air. They are using up dried fruit that 'twas meant to hold them until the first berries ripen. They have killed chickens that now will not be laying eggs. So, yes, are we to be an imposition to anyone for the next few days, I would prefer we be an imposition on Mister Toms."

"Splendidly maintained," Mistress Sermon said. "And I shall make certain Dicky pays you every courtesy. I know you must wish to be back on your journey as soon as possible, but I intend to enjoy your company for as long as I may. We need let Dicky know." She turned to Granny Wirth. "I hope you will not mind too much that I am stealing these delightful young women away from you."

Granny Wirth's twinkling blue eyes met Mistress Sermon's direct gaze. "I have enjoyed their visit. Enjoyed watching the children at play. But Mistress Bowdon is correct, 'tis a mighty burden on Eda, me grandson's wife, and she has her second garden to get in yet. I know we will ne'er have the likes of you," she looked first at Selena and then

Amaryllis, "a-setting down to our table e'er agin, but you be right, we are not set up to house quality folk for any extended period."

Selena stepped over and gave Granny Wirth a hug. "I will not say good-bye at this time for I will return when we come to get the coach. But now I must see if I can lend Goody Wirth a hand." She turned to Mistress Sermon. "Do you stay to dinner?"

"So you are not too grand to sit down with the village farmers," Mistress Sermon said. "I like that. Well, I am not too proud either. Can Goody Wirth find room for us, I would be proud to sit at her table."

Selena was impressed with Mistress Sermon. She knew not many of the gentry would be willing to sit down with people they considered inferior to them. She looked forward to getting to know Toms's aunt better. "I will let Goody Wirth know."

"Yes, and tell Dicky he best send a footman to inform his house steward that he will be returning with a number of unexpected guests. In the meantime, I will sit here and enjoy a chat with Granny Wirth do one of you gels pull me up a chair."

Amaryllis hastened to pull a chair from the drop-leaf table over beside Granny Wirth. Mistress Sermon fluffed her skirts, and seating herself, indicated she was satisfied.

Selena checked that the children would not be a nuisance, and when both women said they enjoyed the children's giggles and babble, she and Amaryllis went to help Goody Wirth prepare for the number of people she would be serving.

❈ ❈ ❈ ❈

Amaryllis leaned back against the plush cushions of Richard Toms's coach and shut her eyes. The last two days had been draining. The fright she experienced when the coach turned over. Her growing recognition of the hardships and hard work the farmers and laborers endured had her mind in a swirl. Her feelings for Reginald had her emotionally confused. And to top everything off, she had not slept well on the hard, little cot the Wirths provided, though she knew they had done their best to make their unexpected guests comfortable. She realized that all her life, she had been spoiled. She was used to soft beds and soft sheets, fluffy pillows and warm blankets, sweet smelling candles, and wine or sherry, not ale, with her dinner and supper. She was used to playing the harpsichord, or reading, or engaging in a backgammon game in the evenings rather than retiring as soon as supper was ended. Nor was she used to being up before the crack of dawn. Or to getting up before a fire had been stoked in her bedchamber hearth.

She had never been responsible for seeing to Tabitha or Charlie's everyday needs. She had never done anything but play with them or read to them. Now she had to help them with everything from relieving themselves to getting dressed in the morning and readied for bed at night. She thanked God for Esmeralda. The dear woman helped her see their clothes were cleaned, their teeth brushed, their hair combed, and their hands washed before they sat down to eat. Thankfully, both children were biddable, and their manners were good.

The coach swayed and rocked as it went over some ruts, and Amaryllis quelled a gasp that wanted to escape. The memory of the coach wheel breaking was still too fresh. Opening her eyes, she saw that no one else showed any concern. Esmeralda was circumspectly answering questions about Selena that Mistress Sermon was putting to her, the maid Betty was playing a thumb game with Tabitha, and Charlie was curled up on the flooring next to Fate – both fast asleep.

Grateful Toms's footman had returned with a horse for him, and that she was not having to endure Toms's presence in the coach, she was yet amazed they would be staying in his home. The man had thought her a light skirt. Just thinking of his words and actions made her blush. He had most humbly apologized, but the insult still rankled, still hurt. However, she knew they would all be more comfortable at Toms's house. They really had upset the Wirths' routine, the orderliness of their lives. She knew Reginald compensated the Wirths and the Barlows royally for their hospitality, but she imagined they were more than happy to be rid of their quality guests.

Goody Wirth, after enlisting the aid of Goody Barlow, had set out a dinner to be proud of – mutton stew, broiled chicken, pigeon pasties, a sausage and currant pudding, rye bread with fresh churned butter and marmalade, stewed dandelion greens in a vinegar sauce, and for dessert, dried figs, cheese, and apple cider. The weather being nice, trestle tables had been set up outside for the laborers and the D'Arcy and Toms servants, excepting Esmeralda and Bernard Nye. They had been seated at the Wirths' table along with the D'Arcys, Mistress Sermon, Mister Toms, the Wirths, the Barlows, and herself. The Wirths' two milk maids were pressed into service to help Orpah. They served the outdoor diners at the trestle table, and Orpah served in the hall. Orpah and the milk maids were to have their meal after the others had eaten.

The children were fed early on bread and stew then put down for their naps. Betty, Mistress Sermon's personal maid, chose to eat early with the children, that she might keep an eye on them while everyone else had their dinner.

"This is a treat for me," Betty declared. "Having grown up with numerous siblings, and now having several nephews and nieces, I find I miss all the noise and bustle of children. Mistress Sermon and I live a sedate life."

"I never realized Betty had such a knack with children," Mistress Sermon said. "I must ponder this. But now, I cannot thank you enough Goody Wirth for inviting us to dinner."

Amaryllis doubted Goody Wirth had much choice. She could not have refused to invite Toms and his aunt to join them. Toms's manor lands formed a large portion of their farmland. They would want to stay on good terms with their landlord. And indeed, they did seem on jovial terms with Toms. To her surprise, Toms seemed to know a great deal about his tenants and his land. At least so it seemed from the snippets of conversation she heard.

She and Selena had both offered to help Goody Wirth, but shaking her head, Goody Wirth insisted 'twould not be dignified. "Lady Selena, ye cannot think I could hold up me head should I let you do work unsuitable to your station."

Selena's tinkling laughter floated over the hall. "Nay, you but know I am no hand at cooking and would be more in your way than I would be help. You cannot fool me. Come Amaryllis, we will go pack that we will be ready to leave when Mistress Sermon is ready."

And so, when the dinner and numerous toasts concluded, Toms's coach was readied, portmanteaus and satchels were loaded, and grateful good-byes were exchanged. Tabitha hugged Annelise and thanked

127

her for letting her play with her dolls and other toys. Charlie, following his sister's example, also thanked his young hostess. Then the caval-cade set off for Mere Manse, so named, Toms told them, because of the nearby lake.

The coachman and postilion had been left at the Wirths'. The coach being so near the road, Reginald wanted it guarded at night. The glass windows alone were of considerable value, and the plush interior was superior to seating found in most village homes. He wanted the coach in tact when the wheels were repaired, and they could resume their journey.

Again shutting her eyes, Amaryllis contemplated her feelings for Reginald. He had insisted upon sitting beside her on the narrow bench at the dinner table. From time to time, their shoulders or elbows touched, or their knees touched, and each time a scorching heat rose to her bosom. The physical contacts had a tendency to leave her breath-less, but when Reginald leaned in close, his eyes capturing hers, her whole being catapulted skyward. She had never experienced such feel-ings. They both thrilled and confused her, often leaving her tongue-tied and giddy.

She was glad she would have a couple more days with Reginald be-fore they resumed their journey. She knew they would have to part once they reached Leicester, the D'Arcys to continue on to their des-tination, and she and the children to board the stage bound for Derby. She wondered if she would ever see Reginald again. Once he delivered Selena to their aunt and uncle, what then? He said he had to go to his estate in Nottinghamshire. Might that be close enough to Derby that he would make a side trip to visit her? But then, by that time, she could well be on her way home. She would turn Tabitha and Charlie over to their Aunt Juliet. Their aunt would see the children were protected and taken to their grandfather. But where did that leave her? She really had nowhere to go but home. And she would have no money left after buying the stage passes to Derby. She would have to borrow from the children's aunt. How she dreaded the thought of returning home and facing Aunt Elva.

She firmed her lips. Churlwood belonged to Charlie, not to Aunt Elva. With the children no longer living in the house, their uncle no longer had any reason to continue living there as their guardian. She would tell them they must leave. Her shoulders sagged. She doubted she would be able to get them to leave. Perhaps the children's grandfather could be prevailed upon to press them to leave. If not, she supposed she would be stuck with them until Charlie came of age and could order them from his home.

These thoughts were doing nothing for her mood. Better to concentrate on the next couple of days. Better to think of this brief interlude she would have with Reginald. A smile tugged at her lips. She wondered if Toms had a harpsichord. 'Twould be fun to have some music in the evening after supper. She believed her wrist was well enough to allow her to play more simple tunes, and she would enjoy showing off her skill to Reginald. She imagined the light in his eyes as he complimented her. She wanted as many memories as she could accumulate. Then when she returned to Churlwood, she would be able to pull out the memories, and they would help her wile away the lonely days. Yes, best to think happy thoughts.

Chapter 17

Reginald was impressed with Toms's Mere Manse. The grounds were neat and well-maintained. A garden with a pond and fountain graced the grounds behind the house, a lush bowling green was on the south side of the house, and a wide circular drive led up to the house. The stables, like the house, were of stone and were clean and roomy. A woodland park near a small lake could be seen in the distance, and Reginald could imagine taking a nice ride with Amaryllis out to the lake. The house was roomy, having a total of ten bedchambers, four with servant anti-chambers off them. Ten years earlier, shortly before his death, Toms's father had added a third floor and an additional wing to the house.

"Father was not above usury," Toms said. "He made an outstanding profit on investments in a London bank. That profit paid for the remodeling. They now keep my head above water. I like my visits to London and tend to overspend," he admitted. "Auntie Jane thinks once I am married, I will settle down. I do hope she is right. Certainly, if anyone can settle me down, 'tis Clotilda. She is a sensible girl. Quite lovely, and soft-spoken, but she has an iron will. Despite that, I cannot help but adore her."

Reginald chuckled as he leaned back in his chair and took another sip of brandy. He would ever be grateful to the Wirths' for their generosity and kindness, but he far preferred the comfort of Toms's house. He had his own room with a good size closet for Nye. Toms's house steward had sent to the village to arrange for extra help for the unexpected visitors. Rooms had been aired, beds made, and a light, but sumptuous supper of barley soup, onion pie, mushrooms in wine sauce, fried eel, pheasant with dried apricots, mutton chops, a beef steak and kidney pudding, and a baked custard for dessert had been prepared. The women had been served a strawberry wine, and he and Toms had enjoyed a dark claret.

The commodious dining chamber was comfortably furnished. After the ladies adjourned to the parlor, and the tablecloth was removed to reveal the highly polished white oak table, the footman set out the brandy decanter and glasses and quietly left the room. The elegant sideboard was equally gleaming, and the chairs nicely cushioned. Normally, Reginald would have been happy to sit around with Toms and learn more about his manor. Despite Toms's admission that he was a spendthrift, his manor was well-ordered, and he seemed to have a good relationship with his tenants. Reginald thought he could learn a thing or two about estate management, but he found his thoughts kept turning to Amaryllis. She looked so lovely in another of Selena's gowns. Though less elaborate than the pink gown she had worn at the Hingham's, the blue skirt hitched up to expose a yellow petticoat and the close-fitting blue bodice trimmed in yellow over the cream-colored chemise was very flattering. He was eager to join her in the parlor. She, having learned from Toms that he had a harpsichord, had offered to play for them that evening.

"What do you think?" Toms's question brought Reginald's thoughts back to his present company.

"I must beg your pardon, Toms. I fear my thoughts had wandered. What did you ask?"

Toms chuckled. "No doubt your thoughts were on a certain lovely lady who awaits us in the parlor. A lady who has most kindly forgiven me for being so unforgivably rude. I asked if you thought we had delayed over our brandy long enough, and if we might now join the ladies."

Pushing back his chair, Reginald rose. "Indeed. I think 'tis time we joined the ladies."

�花 🌸 🌼 🌺

Delighted with how well Amaryllis played the harpsichord despite her bandaged wrist, Selena vigorously applauded each number. Though she had never had the patience to learn an instrument herself – it took too much practice, and she had always preferred being outdoors – Selena enjoyed singing. She was considered to have a good voice, and she and Reginald sang a couple of duets that brought them a round of applause from Toms and his aunt.

The cozy parlor, off the grand hall, was elegantly but not elaborately decorated. The gold brocaded couch was well cushioned as were the walnut armchairs. The pinewood floor was partially covered by two colorful hand-woven carpets. A third smaller, intricately woven carpet was displayed on a decorative chest. Green and gold floral patterned wallpaper graced the upper half of the walls above the wainscoting, and a white cornice mantelpiece over the flagstone fireplace added a brightness to the hearth with its glowing coals. A delicate, gold candelabra hung above the harpsichord providing a soft illumination over the harpsichord keys.

The evening progressed enjoyably until Amaryllis, unable to suppress a yawn, blushed fiercely and said, "I am sorry. I fear I slept poorly last night. I know I am dreadfully spoiled, but I could not get comfortable on that cot."

Selena laughed. "Esmeralda said the same thing, poor dear. I told her to go right on to bed this evening. Thankfully, Betty is so good with the children. She was happy to see to them."

Amaryllis looked at Mistress Sermon. "Dear, ma'am, I cannot thank you enough for allowing Betty to mind the children. They have taken so to her. 'Tis most kind of you."

Mistress Sermon's bright eyes looked down her long slender nose and her thin lips curved in a smile. "I had no idea Betty was so enamored of children. I think mayhap she has missed her calling. Her aunt was my personal maid from the time I was a young miss. When her hands became too arthritic to do the fine sewing and the hairdressing," she waved her own hands, "oh, all the numerous things a lady's maid is required to do, she suggested I let her train her niece, Betty, to take her place. Much as I hated to lose Nancy, I gave her an annuity that will keep her in comfort, and I took Betty as my maid. Betty is a good girl. She learns fast, and she is ever cheerful, even when I am at my worst, which Dicky can tell you is nigh too often. That said, I wonder if Betty would not be happier in a home filled with children. In the meantime, I am happy to have her help with Tabitha and Charlie. They are lovely, well-behaved children."

"Thank you, Mistress Sermon. I will say, I am proud of how well-mannered they are."

"Well, you trot on off to bed," Mistress Sermon told Amaryllis. "I think you will find your bed most comfortable. I told Mister Haines, the house steward, to assign a girl to you. Not that the girl will know aught about your needs, but she will see you have a warm bed and a cozy fire in the hearth."

"Thank you, and you, too, Mister Toms," Amaryllis said, looking from Mistress Sermon to Toms. "Emily, the girl Mister Haines assigned me, is quite sweet, and she did a fine job helping me dress for supper. I am certain she will be most helpful. And now I will bid you all a good night." With a smile and a nod, she looked to Selena and then to Reginald.

Reginald, already on his feet, was immediately at her side. "Have you a candle? Shall I see you to your room?"

Amaryllis smiled. "Mister Haines said he would leave candles at the foot of the stairs. And I know my way to my room. But thank you, Reggie."

Despite her protestations, Reginald accompanied her to the staircase where a footman awaited Toms's guests with a light for their candles. "Want to make sure all is in order," Reginald declared.

When he returned, Mistress Sermon said, "Dicky, do you show Mister D'Arcy your library. Your father's collection of books was his greatest pride, I do believe."

"Aye, Father was proud of his books," Toms admitted. "I cannot say I find many of the books of much interest myself, but there are a goodly number of them." He beckoned to Reginald. "'Tis my belief Auntie Jane is wishing to get rid of us, so come D'Arcy, I will show you the collection. The room itself is worth seeing. 'Tis a massive anti-chamber off the master bedchamber which I now occupy. The hearth is marble, the paneling is intricately designed, the shelving is of solid oak, and …," his voice tapered off as he and Reginald started up the stairs.

Cocking her head to one side and raising her brows, Selena turned to Mistress Sermon. "Is your nephew correct? Do you have something you wish to address, Mistress Sermon?"

Chuckling, Mistress Sermon, nodded. "I have ne'er been one to beat about the bush, Lady Selena. And think not to gull me, for I know something is amiss with Mistress Bowdon and her siblings. For one thing, her father could not be dead more than half a year, and yet she is not in mourning apparel. I have also noted she has but one satchel. Not much for a long trip. My guess is, the gown she wore this evening is one of yours. I would have the truth."

Pursing her lips, Selena met the older woman's bright gaze. "I am not certain I am at liberty to acquaint you with circumstances surrounding Amaryllis's situation."

"Nonsense," Mistress Sermon snapped. "I want to be of assistance if I can. Why is she traveling without a nurse maid for those children? And why is she traveling with you? Mistress Shadwell is most circumspect, all the same, I learned enough on our ride here this afternoon to know that you are newly acquainted with Mistress Bowdon. That you are headed to your uncle's estate near Rotherby, now by way of Derby. I learned about your dog, and that you collect strays. That is your way. I admire it. I do believe Mistress Bowdon is one of your strays."

Not giving Selena a chance to answer, Mistress Sermon charged ahead. "I, too, have been known from time to time to lend a helping hand to those in dire circumstances." She raised her chin. "I am a proud woman, but I am not too proud to sit down to sup with the hardworking yeoman, as you did witness today. And did I not see your need and extend a hand to you? You must admit, you will be far more comfortable here than at the Wirths' or at that abominable inn in the village. Now, I will have the truth. What is Mistress Bowdon running from? And has that brother of yours fallen in love with her?"

Selena had been trying to decide whether she should confide in the imperious woman, but the last question took her by surprise. Tilting her head to one side, she said, "I cannot answer for my brother, but if he has, 'tis fine with me. Then, too, I know not how Amaryllis may feel about Reggie. He is a dear, but he can be exasperating at times."

"Well, I want to tell you about the gel. I knew her father. Came near to marrying him."

Selena raised her brows and mouthed, "Oh."

"Our fathers were friends from their school days and had hopes Abner and I might suit. And we might have had Abner not met Amaryllis's mother." Mistress Sermon's gaze shifted and a small smile touched her lips. "Oh, she was a beauty, just as lovely as Mistress Amaryllis. Her father, being naught but a rector to a small estate, could provide her with but a meager dowry. But she being an only child, it was, in the end, enough to satisfy Abner's parents."

Her direct gaze shifted to Selena. "I will return to that later. Let me first tell you, I was pleased Abner chose to marry Clare. I had my eye on Jerome Sermon." She smiled wistfully. "My, he was a handsome man. From the moment I first saw him, my heart started going thumpty- thump. That he chose to marry me still amazes me."

Selena thought Mistress Sermon could well have been, if not a great beauty, a most attractive woman in her youth, but before she could voice her thoughts, Mistress Sermon continued, "My husband was a prosperous wine merchant, as was his father, his grandfather, and his ancestry on back for many generations. He and I were happy together, though we were never blessed with children. That said, though much of our estate will someday go to Jerome's brothers and their children, Dicky and his sister will inherit a sizeable portion from me when I pass on."

"Let us hope they will have a long wait," Selena interrupted her.

Mistress Sermon smiled and nodded. "Yes, I have every intention of making them wait. But back to Mistress Amaryllis. Though gentry, she has no peerage in her ancestry. Abner Bowdon's ancestors were merchants from Chester. Wool, salt, spices? I know not what. But a not-too-distant ancestor during the reign of King James purchased his baronetcy from James. The ancestor then bought the Churlwood Manor from an over-extended baron needing ready cash."

Selena started to protest, "Mistress Sermon, you need not tell ..."

Mistress Sermon held up a hand saying, "Please, do allow me to continue. I have my reason for imparting this information."

Acquiescing, Selena nodded, and Mistress Sermon, resettling on the couch, continued, "As I have already said, I was pleased to see you were not too proud to sit down to sup with the Wirths. They are good, hardworking people. The people of the land were here long before the Conqueror. The land was theirs before William usurped it and gave it to his barons."

Selena laughed. "Mistress Sermon, think you that I am in need of a history lesson?"

"No, my dear, I but wish to apprise you of Mistress Amaryllis's ancestry. Yes, her grandfather was a clergyman, but his father was naught but a wealthy yeoman. Wealthy enough to send his younger son to University, and that son, as a clergyman moved into the gentry class.

"You, Lady Selena, and your brother are children of a peer of the realm. Your direct ancestry dates back to the Conqueror. No recent yeomen or merchants besmirch your heritage."

"Well, perhaps not recent," Selena interrupted, "but on my mother's side we do have some merchants. Wool merchants, dating back to Edward IV. My guess is before they were merchants, they might well have been farmers. Whatever the case, they prospered, bought estates, sent their sons to university, and worked their way into the aristocracy. Fact is, the manor Reggie will inherit belonged to Absalom Wolcott, son of a wool merchant."

Mistress Sermon's raspy chuckle radiated out of her throat. "Glad to hear it. Truth be told, I suppose few of the peers today have not some yeoman or merchant in their ancestry. Makes them true English, and proud they should be of their English blood." She bobbed her head. "I know I am."

"Rightfully so, but what has my ancestry to do with Amaryllis?"

Mistress Sermon's eyes bore into Selena's. "The gel's grandfather was a dear friend to my father. They remained friends until they passed on. God rest their souls." Her gaze shifted to the doorway. "Through the years, I seldom saw Amaryllis's father. Occasionally he might attend a social gathering in Watford, but it was rare, and when we met, we did little more than nod in recognition of each other. Cannot say I ever saw his daughter until today."

Her gaze jerked back to Selena. "The child has lost her mother and her father. She has no one to look out for her. Because of the love my father bore her grandfather, I would not see her harmed. I would know if your brother's attentions to Mistress Bowdon are honorable."

Selena nodded in understanding. "I can assure you, Mistress Sermon, my brother would never do anything to dishonor Amaryllis. That

136

I will guarantee you."

"Yes, but she could be hurt does she think he is falling in love with her when he is but amusing himself. If he thinks her too far below his class for him to think of marrying ..." She left her sentence unfinished.

Shaking her head and twisting her mouth to one side, Selena regarded the older woman. "Nay," she finally said. "I cannot say whether Reggie is falling in love with Amaryllis, but her ancestry would have naught to do with his decision to wed does he in truth fall in love. You may rest easy on that score."

"Splendid. Now I would know why Mistress Bowdon is with you and why she is not in mourning. Think not that you can put me off."

Deciding she would trust Mistress Sermon, Selena said, "Very well, I will tell you what I know of the situation, and what has transpired thus far."

In short order, Selena acquainted Mistress Sermon with why Amaryllis was fleeing her home with her siblings and with all that had happened since they had met Amaryllis, including the damage to the wheel. "Reggie and I have not told Amaryllis about the wheel," Selena admitted. "We have not wanted to worry her."

Pursing her lower lip and rubbing her chin, Mistress Sermon said, "You must have been followed. The gel failed to deceive them about her plans. That being the case, we must take extra precaution to insure the boy's safety. I shall tell Betty she is not to let the boy out of her sight unless she leaves him with you or his sister. Fact is, I do believe when you depart, 'twould be best does Betty accompany you. Those children need a nursemaid."

"But what will you do for a maid?" Selena protested.

"I am old. I wear my hair in a simple bun as do you. I no longer bother with powder and paint. My needs are simple. I shall manage with one of the maids here until Betty can return. If she returns. Is she asked, and does she wish to continue on as a nursemaid to those two children, I would not ask her to do otherwise."

Selena rose from her chair and moved over to sit beside Mistress Sermon on the couch. Taking the older woman's hands in hers she said, "You are indeed a woman I could readily grow very fond of. I would count myself privileged if I might take up a correspondence with you.

You seem as ready to pick up strays as Esmeralda thinks I do."

Tears formed in Mistress Sermon's eyes. "You remind me of myself when I was young," she said. "I could never pass a beggar on the street without tossing him a coin. My husband once said I would give away his entire fortune did he not keep a tight fist on it." She gave her head a slight shake. "Not that I am not fond of my comforts, or that I would give any of them away, but can I give the occasional helping hand to those less fortunate, then so will I do. I have been blessed. 'Tis right I share at least a small portion of those blessings."

An, "Ahem," at the door drew Selena's and Mistress Sermon's attention. "Begging your pardon, milady," Norwood, Selena's footman, said. He held Fate in his arms. "I have taken the wee dog out to do his duty. What would you have me do with him?"

Selena rose. "Do give the dear to me. I am headed up to bed. And you do go to your bed. Your accommodations are acceptable?"

"Oh, yes, milady. Perfect."

"Handle is comfortable, not in pain after his ride over here atop the coach?"

"He is comfortable, my lady. The cook gave him a dram of something that eased his pain and put him right to sleep after he supped."

"Good. Then off with you," she said, taking Fate into her arms. "Esmeralda will bring Fate down to you come morning."

"Yes, milady," Norwood said with a slight bow.

Turning with her dog in her arms, Selena said, "Do you breakfast at any set time, Mistress Sermon. I fear I am not always an early riser."

"Nay, Lady Selena. Cook will make you some toast or eggs, whatever you may wish at whatever time you rise." Using the arm of the coach to push herself up, Mistress Sermon added, "I seldom eat much breakfast. I have little appetite in the mornings. Betty brings me some hot cider and dried prunes, and that generally does me until later in the morning when I may have some biscuits. You tell Mistress Shadwell to send one of the maids to the kitchen whenever you are ready to break your fast.

"Now, here comes my nephew. And about time," she scolded. "Did you think I would need no assistance climbing these stairs?"

"Nay, Auntie Jane, I made sure you would want my arm, and so I have returned after impressing Mister D'Arcy with Father's library."

138

"You were correct, Mistress Sermon, a fine library it is," Reginald said. "As good as any I have seen." He looked at Selena. "Are you headed for your room? I will accompany you."

Selena nodded. "Thank you. You may carry the candle for me as I have Fate."

After a round of goodnights, they all headed up the stairs, Mistress Sermon and Toms more slowly. Selena noticed the older woman, though her wit was quick and her back straight, seemed to have a little trouble with her knees. She hoped it was only from her long journey from Watford and not a permanent ailment. She liked the woman, and she was pleased to have an ally in her suspicion concerning the tampering of the coach wheel. She would have to tell Reginald about her discussion with Mistress Sermon, and their decision to make certain Charlie was never left unattended.

Chapter 18

Felton stretched out on the lumpy pallet Goody Burke had provided him. He would have preferred to continue to stay at the inn, though there was little enough to recommend it; poor food, poor ale, dirty bedding crawling with various small critters to add to his own current collection. Problem was twofold, the bill ate up the money Mistress Bowdon had given him, and he had no accountable reason to hang around the village. It would not do for him to be making people suspicious.

He had seen the D'Arcys ride into the village that morning to check on their wheels. Seen the larger wheel being carted off with the lone outrider attending it. After the D'Arcys left, he sauntered over to the smith's to find out what had transpired. "Got a horse I mean to trade," he said. "Good horse. Smooth gait, but getting old. I am a-feared he will drop dead on me afore I reach my destination. Thought mayhap you might know where I could make a fair trade."

"How far you headed?" the smith asked.

"Going to York. Got a brother there what has been ailing. Needs some help with his farm."

"That would be right kind of you."

Felton chuckled. "Nay, cannot stand me brother nor him me, but he is kin, and truth be told, I got naught to keep me 'round these parts."

The smith stopped his hammering and tilted his head. "What is it you are a-doing 'round here? Cannot say I have seen you afore."

"Nay, but stopping to visit with a friend for a day or two. Name of Burke."

Squinting his eyes, the smith said, "Not John Burke?"

"Aye, are ye a-knowing him?"

The smith harrumphed. "Ever'one knows Burke. How is it you are friends with him? Cannot say he has many a friend anywhere in these parts."

140

Felton had met John Burke at an alehouse the previous afternoon. Thinking the man might be the sort he could bamboozle into giving him a hand should he need it, he bought him a couple of rounds, listened to his complaints about the villagers and his landlord, a man named Toms, and learned he had a cottage not far from the village with a small shed attached where Felton could stable his horse and not have to pay its keep at the inn's stable.

Ready with his story, he said, "Met him some years back when we were both younger. I had been set upon by ruffians and left in a ditch. Likely would have died, but Burke found me, took me home, his good wife cared for me wounds, and I be alive today thanks to him."

Continuing his hammering, the smith harrumphed again. "Burke's wife is a good woman. Too good for the likes of him. Surprises me he helped you, but mayhap when he was younger and not so apt to drink so much ...." His sentence tapered off as he concentrated on his work.

Felton saw he was working on the D'Arcys' smaller coach wheel. "Peers you got a wheel to mend there. That belong to the couple of fellas I saw in here right before I came in?"

The smith glanced up at him but issued no answer.

"Looked like a couple of swells to me." He wondered if the smith might tell him that one of the fellas was Lady Selena, not a fella at all, but the smith remained mum. Not one to prattle about his customers, Felton decided. Trying another tactic, he said "Thought that wheel might be off the coach I saw broke down a ways back. I offered to help, but they said they had no need, having secured the coach and rescued the passengers, so I rode on into town."

Again stopping his work, the smith straightened and set down his hammer. He beckoned to a young apprentice to pump the bellows to renew the heat in his forge. "Aye, the wheel is off the coach you passed. Had to send the big wheel to Northampton. 'Spect they will be waiting a couple of days afore they can resume their journey. Now, you were asking 'bout a horse trade?"

Felton nodded his head vigorously even though he had already traded his horse. He knew he had gotten the lesser of the bargain, but his dun horse might have been recognized by D'Arcy or one of his men. Now he had but an old ginger-colored nag which he was stabling at Burke's.

He had had to trade his hat, too. Too recognizable. That, he really regretted. Did the weather change, and it start to rain, he would sorely miss the big, floppy-brimmed hat.

"Haf ye heard of anyone what is in need of a gentle horse? As I said, I am at needing one what can make it all the way to York."

Pursing his lips and wrinkling his brow, the smith said, "Ye might try Ezra Hacker. Lives but a ways outside the village. Small, stone cottage with a low, rock fence round it. He carts butter and eggs to Northampton once a week. He might be on the lookout for a gentle horse."

With that statement, the smith resumed his work. Felton thanked him and sauntered off down the road in the direction the smith had indicated. He wished he had thought to ask around before trading his horse with another customer at the inn. The man had been ready to depart, and fearing he might not find another person willing to evenly swap horses, he had jumped at the chance. Having nothing better to do, he continued his walk to the edge of the village. Spying a large maple, newly leafed out in brilliant green, he hopped the ditch that ran beside the road, and settled down under the tree to contemplate his next move.

Nothing came to mind, and eventually he wandered back to the inn to have his dinner. Again, not wanting to attract attention, he left the inn and went to the alehouse where he had met Burke the day before. His eyes adjusting to the dark interior, he was not surprised to find Burke already there and already with a mug in his fist. The man should be out plowing his meager field or sowing his crops, but there he sat, his face brightening at the sight of Felton.

"Well now, I made certain I would find ye here," Burke said, a spill of ale dribbling down his unshaven chin. Blinking his watery eyes, he said, "Haf a seat. I haf good news."

Felton pulled up a stool and beckoned to the alehouse keeper, a buxom woman with a jaundiced eye, to bring him a mug. He had had better ale, but this ale was cheap, and since he was not only buying for himself but for Burke, he could not complain.

"What is your good news?" he asked Burke.

"Me wife says 'tis fine do ye wish to tike supper with us and to spend the night. Says she will make ye up a nice clean pallet." He shook his head, making his dark, dirty locks swish about his grimy face. "She says a tu'pence should cover the cost."

"Most reasonable," Felton said. "But now, tell me, haf ye heard any news on that coach I saw overturned on me way into the village yesterday? As you know, I was concerned that no one should haf been injured. I do think I saw a young woman and a couple of children by the road."

Burke bobbed his head. "Oh, aye. According to Holder, he be the barber, he was called upon to set a footman's broke leg. 'Twere no other bad injuries. Coachman got a sprain. Ye can rest easy. Ever'one else was fine. The coach belongs to a swell name of D'Arcy. Wheels broke right in front of Goodman Wirth's croft." Burke scowled. "Wirth and his brother-in-law, Barlow, think they be bettern than the rest of us. Just cause they each got themselves a big piece of property. Turn their noses up at me they do." He waggled his shoulders. "Anyhow, seems the D'Arcy party put up with the Wirths last night. Now Wirth will really be putting on airs. Having quality folk sitting down to sup at their table and bed down in their house." Wrinkling his nose, he spat a big glob of spittle onto the straw-covered, roughhewn flooring.

Felton had waited up the previous night, thinking the D'Arcys would have to find some mode of transport, if only a farmer's cart, to bring them to the inn. It had never occurred to him they might stay at the yeoman's home. But then, considering the meanness of the village inn, he imagined they had had better accommodations than he had enjoyed.

The alehouse being situated right on the road, the clomping of horses' hooves, and the barking of village dogs grabbed his attention. Hurrying to the door, he saw the D'Arcys riding past. They were followed by a coach. Through the open window he could see Amaryllis's profile. He saw Lady Selena bend down toward one of the dogs yapping at her horse's heels and give the cur a light pat on the head. Surprisingly, the dog stopped his yapping and started prancing along beside her, his tail wagging wildly. He might have followed her out of the village had a young urchin not whistled to him. The dog stopped, looked after the disappearing rider, then back at his master. He seemed torn as to what he should do, but with another longing glance toward Lady Selena, he trotted back to the boy calling him.

Burke, who had joined Felton at the door and was peeking over

Felton's shoulder, said, "That would be Mister Toms's equipage. He is my landlord what I told you about. Never giving a body a fair shake. Always favoring the likes of the Wirths."

"His house far from here?" Felton asked, watching the party disappear around a curve.

"Nay, not more than a couple miles by the road. Closer as the crow flies. Why from my croft' tis but a jaunt acrost the common."

Turning, Felton urged Burke back to their table. "Close to hand, is it?"

"Aye, the common backs up on the village."

"Nay, man, I mean the house."

"Oh, aye, lack I said, just acrost the common. Got me a cow I let graze on the common. Toms's father, when he started fencing things in, took part of the common as his own demesne. Typical of those what got a lot to be a-wanting more, even if 'tis not their due."

Felton had to agree with Burke on that. That was why he cared not what he had to do to get his annuity. Turning families off the land they had farmed for generations meant nothing to the swells, even if it meant the families might starve to death. Their deaths were nothing on their consciences. So why should one small boy's death be on his. Still, he did wish the boy had been killed when the coach turned over. Seems the D'Arcys, though, had landed on their feet. They would now be staying at the local manor house. That would make getting to the boy a bit tougher. Would have been so much easier if they had had to put up at the inn.

He had spent the rest of the afternoon drinking with Burke, trying to figure how he could get to the boy, but as it grew time for supper, the two headed to Burke's home. A boy with a sack slung across his shoulder was coming from a field that adjoined the hovel Burke called home. The boy who looked to be no more than ten piped up, "Got the barley sowed, Father."

Weaving a little, Burke patted the boy on the shoulder. "Good, good. Someday you will make a fine farmer. Now where is yer sister, Bess? She bringing the cow in?"

"Nay. Nellie is bringing Maudie in. Bess is over to Mere Manse. Got work in the kitchen, helping the scullery maid. Seems Master Toms has

144

big important guests staying for a few days."

Paying no heed to the news about Toms's guests, Burke frowned and said, "Nellie is bringing the cow! Why she is not old enough. Yer mother should haf got the cow."

"All'st I know is, Mother said as how she had a meal to fix, and 'twas time Nellie started to do more chores," the boy answered his father, but his eyes were on Felton. Nodding at Felton, he said, "He the cove what has his horse in Maudie's shed and will be supping with us?"

"Aye. This is Mister Farr," Burke said, and turning to Felton, he said, "Me boy, Robby. He saw yer horse had plenty hay to eat last night."

"I thank ye for that," Felton said. He had chosen to use the name Farr rather than his real name. Better if no one knew his true identity.

The boy shrugged. "You are paying fer the nag's keep. Not that she be much to look at."

Felton chuckled. So the boy knew horses. "Nay, she is not, but she will be getting me where I need to go. So's all the same, I thank ye."

"Ah, here comes Nellie with Maudie. I will go help her," Robby said, handing the empty grain-seed sack to his father.

Felton saw a small child who could not have been much older than five, if that, trying to force an indisposed cow to cross a narrow ditch that ran around Burke's croft.

"Watch ye keep Maudie out of yer mother's garden or she will haf yer hide," Burke hollered after his son, then turned to invite Felton into his home.

Felton was surprised by the inside of the Burke abode. On the outside, the two-bay wattle and daub cottage looked near ready to collapse, but inside, it was neat and orderly. The clay floor had been swept and strewn with fresh herbs and spring flowers. He guessed the smell could have been overwhelming otherwise, what with the animals housed on the premises, but instead the smell was almost pleasant. And if the scent rising from a black cauldron sitting on a trivet over a raised hearth in the center of the room was any indication of his promised supper, he was in for a treat. Smoke from the low fire curled lazily upward to find its way out through a small slat in the thatched roof, at least what smoke was not hanging about the room making a slight haze.

Goody Burke, straightening from her stoop over the cauldron, turned bloodshot eyes on him. "Welcome, Mister Farr." No smile accompanied her greeting. She held out her palm. "You have the coin agreed upon?"

He nodded and reached into the pocket of the worn coat he had bought to disguise himself from the D'Arcys. Pulling out the leather pouch Mistress Bowdon had given him, he dumped two pence into his palm and started to hand them to Goody Burke.

"Here now," Burke said. "Give me them coins."

"Nay," Goody Burke said, "does he give 'em to you, he will not be sitting down to eat at my table, nor sleeping on my floor. I did the work, I get the pence."

Felton looked from Burke to his wife and back at Burke. He knew did he give the coins to Burke, he would use them for drink. Did he give them to Goody Burke, she would use them for food or some other necessity for her family. His thoughts went back to his mother. While she lived, she tried hard to see he had food in his belly, but his father was as apt to take whatever wages his mother earned working as a laundry maid and use it for drink, as would Burke did he give him the pence.

His mother had died when he was but six or seven. He could not remember. He could not really remember his mother except for her rough, red, cracked hands. He thought maybe he cried when she died, but that he could not remember either. After his mother's death, his father had left him to the not so gentle mercies of the cottager who had let him and his parents, for a meager rent, sleep in what had once been his chicken coop. He never saw his father again, and good riddance, but as soon as he was old enough to fend for himself, he left his guardian behind as well. Having felt the branch across his back one too many times, he had drifted from town to town, village to village, picking up what odd jobs he could. One old man, who needed help on his tenement, had taken him in. Had promised him he would leave him the tenement when he died, but turned out the old man had a daughter. She and her husband claimed the land, and he was chased off it. Eventually, he ended up in Albertine and found work as a groomsman at the Churlwood Manor. Had he not angered Sir Abner by casting his roving eye on Mistress Amaryllis, he supposed he might still be there, instead of here in Burke's dilapidated hovel, feeling sorry for a woman he did not know, and looking for a chance to kill a child.

Plopping the coins into Goody Burke's hand, he said, "What you got cooking smells too good for me to pass up. The pence goes to you." He turned back to Burke. "Worry not friend, I will buy ye a round of ale on the morrow."

Goody Burke tucked the coins into her pocket and said, "Soon as I feed the baby, we will eat. Bess is not joining us. She has work up to Mere Manse. I 'spect long as Master Toms has his company, she will have work there. 'Tis a blessing," she added, turning away. Going to a corner of the room, she picked a baby up out of a small, woven basket. The baby had not cried, but Goody Burke settled herself onto a low stool in the same corner, pulled out her breast and began suckling the babe.

To Felton's thinking, Goody Burke was too fine a woman to be married to a man like John Burke. Her speech was almost refined, and he guessed she might once have been quite pretty. He wondered how such a woman could have chosen Burke. But then, maybe she had had no choice. No way of knowing what might have befallen her or her family that she should have sunk so low in life.

"Here now," Burke said. "Pull up a stool at the table. I see the wife's got it all set. I will get ye some cider. Wife makes it herself. We got us a good apple orchard," he bragged, pulling out a barrel from under what looked to be Goody Burke's work bench and pantry set under the only window in the cottage. Burke found a ladle, and dipping it into the barrel, filled two wooden noggins. He handed one to Felton and raised his own in salute then threw back his head and guzzled down the light amber liquid. Smacking his lips, he refilled his noggin and joined Felton at the table.

Felton noted the trenchers on the table were stale bread, made of barley and bean flour, he guessed. Wooden spoons were at each place, as were yellowed, but clean napkins. He knew this kind of poverty, had lived it, but God willing, like it or not, he would complete his mission, and he would never have to live in such squalor again.

"Got me a good little tenement here," Burke was saying. "Got me an acre of barley, acre of beans, got me a middling to good cow. Me wife has got a good garden of herbs and peas and onions, and we are near 'nough to the manor forest for it to provide us with all the wood we need. I got me four children that haf lived through the winter, including that babe there." He nodded at his wife. "Got me a good and loving wife. Not much else a man could ask for, I am thinking."

Felton guessed Burke's wife could be asking for a whole lot more, including a man who would do some work. Well, at least the boy, Robby, showed promise. He hoped the lad would not disappoint his mother.

Goody Burke had finished feeding her baby and put it back in its basket when Robby and his little sister came in, each carrying a wooden pail. "Maudie gave good milk tonight," the boy said, "and we brung in your water for washing up."

"Good boy," Goody Burke said, absently tousling her son's hair. Using the same ladle Burke had used, she ladled milk into two wooden noggins and gave them to her daughter to set on the table. The little girl's brown hair, no doubt neatly braided in the morning, was now scraggly and falling about her small, round face. Large, brown eyes looked curiously up at Felton, and a tentative smile showed a missing front tooth.

He smiled back at her, displaying a couple of gaps of his own. He felt lucky those missing teeth were not his front teeth so his smile was not grotesque. "I petted your horse," the girl said, "and gave her grass from the common. She is nice."

Felton chuckled. "Your brother thinks she is a nag, and she is, but she is nice, I agree."

The girl looked at her brother who had poured some water from the pail into a large wooden bowl. Having pulled a small bowl of soap from a corner of his mother's work table, he was washing his hands, arms, and face. "He likes Master Toms's horse. Sometimes Master Toms rides acrost the common. I think his horse be too big and scary."

"Eh, Nellie, what do ye know. Come here and wash. Ye look a sight," Robby said, straightening and drying off with a thin towel his mother handed him.

Nellie stuck her tongue out at her brother, but she did go to the bowl to wash. With both children done with their toilets, Goody Burke hefted the heavy cauldron from the fire, set it on the table, and ladled a thick pea porridge onto each plate. Burke smacked his lips. "Got us

148

a piece of bacon in the porridge tonight on account of having ye for a guest," he told Felton. "It do give the porridge a right fine flavoring, it do."

With each trencher, filled, Goody Burke set the cauldron back on the fire. Felton guessed they would be having the remainder of porridge for their dinner come the morrow.

"Now what is this ye were saying 'bout, Bess, working up to the manor house?" Burke asked after mumbling a quick thanks to the Lord for their meal.

"Bess was in the village – like she does most every day, she took last night's cream to Goodman Hacker for his wife to churn into butter– when she learned Master Toms was to have unexpected guests. Real quality folk whose coach had an accident. One member of the party is even a real Lady." Her brown eyes softened and an almost wistful look came over her face. "I expect she will have silk gowns with frilly lace cuffs and a maid that does up her hair in some new wondrous fashion." She stopped and looking around the table, shook her head and said, "Such an imagination I have. Go ahead now and eat up afore the porridge cools."

So she had been a lady's maid, Felton thought. Now look at her. Bending his head over his porridge, he began shoveling it into his mouth, but glancing up, he noticed how Goody Burke sat with her back straight and brought the spoon up to mouth. Dainty she was. The others at the table were no better than he was, slurping at their trenchers. He had never sat down to sup with anyone of Goody Burke's status before. Someone who had once been a member of the upper servant hierarchy. Well, he decided he would let her hold on to her dream about Lady Selena. He would not tell her the lady rode her horse astride and marched about in men's clothing. She could not be any further from the image Goody Burke had conjured up.

"Mighty fine porridge," Burke said smacking his lips. "I will have some more, wife."

Goody Burke rose, retrieved the cauldron from the fire and ladled another scoop onto her husband's trencher. She looked at Felton. "And you, Mister Farr?"

He nodded. "Indeed, I will have more. 'Tis a sight better than what they serve at the inn. I thank ye again, Goody Burke, for providing me with this fine meal and a bed for the night."

She but nodded, ladled more porridge out, set the cauldron back on the fire, and resumed her seat. The children got no second helpings. He wondered how often they might go hungry. He had certainly gone hungry often enough in his youth.

No sooner was the meal finished than Goody Burke had the table cleared and the fire in the center hearth banked. Burke and his son set aside the trestle table, and Goody Burke spread out pallets on the floor. "We go to bed as soon as it is dark," she said. "We cannot afford to burn candles nor to waste wood keeping the fire ablaze. I have made you up a fresh pallet, Mister Farr. Hay is not as fresh as you might wish, but 'tis sprinkled with fresh herbs and daisies, so should smell clean. I washed the linen ticking ere I stuffed it, and the blanket was aired out all morning. Mind you, John snores a bit, but I will do my best to keep him on his side. Oh, and my daughter, Bess, will be coming in later. She will be working up to the house scrubbing pots until late. Not to worry, though. I told her where you would be sleeping, so she will not step on you."

And as quickly as that, the cottage went quiet except for the scuffling noises of clothing being shed. He had barely shed his shoes and coat and tucked his coin purse under his mattress before he heard Burke snoring. He heard Goody Burke smack him, heard a stifled snarl, then naught but heavy breathing.

The mattress might be lumpy, but it did smell fresh, and he had slept in worse places. His own small room in the back of old man Juff's brewery had room for naught but his pallet, two pegs to hang his clothes on, and a small table with a cracked water pitcher on it. He paid for the room by doing whatever chores Juff gave him to do. He then had to find what jobs he could to pay for his board. But soon his loathsome life would be changing. Soon he would think of a way to kill the little baronet, and he would be set for life. After all, Toms's house was just across the common. Something was bound to present itself. With that pleasing thought, he slept.

Chapter 19

Another glorious day with no rain and all was right in his world. Felton could not be happier. Burke's older daughter, Bess, had given him the best news he had had since starting out on his journey. Bess was a pretty girl of twelve or thirteen. She had large, round, blue eyes, dimples that popped in an out when she smiled or frowned, thick, blond eyelashes, the same shade as her thick, curly, blond hair, and a budding figure that would soon be putting the village boys on alert. Fact was, she made his mouth water. The odd thing about the girl was, unlike the younger children, she looked like neither of her dark-haired, dark-eyed parents. His guess – Bess was a by-blow, and that was how Goody Burke lost her position as a lady's maid, and ended up having to marry the likes of Burke.

Well, none of that was his concern. He learned from Bess that the man digging a new latrine had brought the pick down on his foot, causing a serious enough injury he could not continue digging. Felton saw no reason he and Burke could not apply for the job. He but needed to convince Burke they should ask for the job. Goody Burke thought it a grand idea, and it was the first time he had seen her smile. Indeed, with a smile, she was still a fair-looking woman. He doubted she would be for many more years, though. Not with Burke as her husband. He gave some thought to doing her a favor and ridding her of Burke, but then she might lose the tenement and have no roof over her head. Bad as Burke was, at least he provided them a place to live.

He had heard Bess come in during the night and make her way to her bed. She had been up early, as was her mother. "Bess, dear, do you impress the cook, mayhap they will keep you on once the guests leave," Goody Burke said, working to braid her daughter's unruly hair by the dim morning light coming through the window.

"Oh, I hope they may, Mother. 'Tis too bad I am not a boy, or that

Robby is not a boy grown. They need someone to dig a new latrine." She explained to her mother the problem, and Goody Burke had agreed 'twas too bad Robby was not yet old enough to take on the job.

Hearing the conversation, Felton had known it was his lucky day. No sooner was Bess sent scurrying back to the house, than he was up and presenting his plan to Goody Burke. With her help, they got Burke roused and dressed, but getting him to agree to the plan was not proving easy. Finally, Goody Burke said, "John, do you not go with Mister Farr to apply for that job, the next time you are passed out drunk, I will take a stick and beat you from head to toe. Beat you so bad you will not be able to get out of bed. And I will serve you naught but milk to drink, no ale, no cider. Now you know I mean it."

His blood-shot eyes widening, Burke stared at his wife. Felton had the feeling Goody Burke had used that threat before. "All right, I will go, but ye best fill me a jug of yer cider. Man can get mighty parched doing that kind of work."

Goody Burke clapped her hands. "Indeed, indeed, you and Mister Farr have your bread and cheese while I fill up a jug." Pulling out the cider barrel, she ladled some into mugs for them before filling the jug. "And have no fear. When you come home for supper tonight, I will have more bacon in the porridge for you," she promised, a bright smile on her face.

"What about dinner?" Burke asked.

"Oh, they are bound to feed you dinner at the manor house," Goody Burke said. "Probably plenty of fine ale to go with it."

Burke smiled at that. "Yea, I am at guessing they got quality ale, all right."

And so Burke, with cider jug in hand, followed Felton out the door. It was a pleasant walk across the common. The Burke's cow grazed contentedly alongside several other cows, a number of sheep, and a sad-looking horse which had definitely seen better days. Soon the house that had been hidden behind a clump of oak trees came into view. Barns, stables, carriage house, numerous other outbuildings, and well-kept grounds were a testament to the manor's well-being. Certainly Mere Manse, as Burke had called it, was as prosperous-looking and well-maintained as Churlwood.

Deciding they should ask the first person they saw where they might find the grounds' steward, Felton headed to the stables, but he stopped abruptly when he saw D'Arcy with Mistress Amaryllis by his side heading for the stables. "Let us go this way," he said. "I do think I saw a gardener out back. He should know who we should ask about the job."

Leading Burke away from the stables, he glanced over his shoulder. The lady was in riding costume. That meant she would not be around to mind her brother. At some point the children were bound to come out to play on this lovely spring day. He but had to be alert. Had to watch for his chance.

❀ ❀ ❀ ❀

Reginald was ecstatic. He was to have Amaryllis all to himself for the entire morning. Betty, after seeing to Mistress Sermon's breakfast and toilet, was taking care of Tabitha and Charlie. Selena was off with Toms on a morning ride around his estate. Esmeralda, having altered Selena's side-saddle riding costume, which Selena never wore, to fit Amaryllis, was having a well-deserved day of rest. His valet, Bernard Nye, was taking letters Selena had written to their parents and aunt and uncle into the village to be posted before going to the Wirths' to insure the postilion and coachman were not in need. Mistress Sermon planned to take a leisurely walk in the gardens then write a few letters and perhaps start a book. Norwood and Handle had been given a day of leisure, and Norwood had helped Handle out to a spot in the sun. Settling a table between them, he brought out a deck of cards, and when Reginald passed them on his way to the stable, he thought they could hardly look more contented. With all that had transpired over the past couple of days, this time of rest was good for all of them.

When he and Amaryllis entered the stables, Reginald found Toms's groomsmen had his horse saddled and one of Toms's more gentle mares saddled for Amaryllis. They led the horses outside, and Reginald handed Amaryllis up onto her saddle. She felt so light, her waist was so small, yet the feel of her hips stirred him in ways he knew he needed to guard against. He had known several women intimately, and when on the grand tour, had learned some enticing ways to pleasure a mate from a lovely French woman, but he had never felt the kind of stirrings, longings that moved him every time he came near Amaryllis.

Her beauty, her gentleness, her courage, all aspects of her enchanted him. The way she blushed when he complimented her or held her hand, the way she lit up when he entered a room, her joyful playfulness with her siblings, her concern for them, their love for her, all combined to fill him with delight and admiration. Yet her nearness almost drove him to distraction. He longed to taste her sweetness, her innocence, to feel her body pressed against his, to caress her lips with his. Oh, God, he needed to get such thoughts out of his head, or he would be unable to dismount when they reached the lake.

Holding his mount to a gentle lope, even though he knew Sherard was ready for an all-out run, he attempted to turn his thoughts and his conversation to mundane items. He commented on the fresh greenness of the meadow, the shimmering blue of the lake ahead that matched the blue of the sky, and the good fortune that Toms had come along and offered to house them until the carriage could be repaired.

"Yes, 'twas most fortunate Mister Toms happened upon us," Amaryllis agreed. "I have quite forgiven him for his rudeness to me. His hospitality could not be more pleasing, and his aunt is most entertaining."

"I am glad he has a harpsicord," Reginald said. "I truly enjoyed hearing you play last evening. I hope your wrist is not the worse for it."

She smiled brightly. "Oh, no. I have not even needed to keep it bandaged today." She held up her wrist. "I think 'twas but the merest sprain."

"I am awfully glad. I cannot tell you how devastated I am that we should invite you to travel with us and then to have such an accident befall the carriage." Neither he nor Selena had mentioned to Amaryllis Selena's suspicion that the wheel had been tampered with in an attempt to cause injury to Charlie.

"Oh, such accidents will happen. And you must not in any way believe I would think you could have managed anything differently. You were so brave. Your calmness kept us from panicking. You even had the children thinking 'twas a game. Oh, dear, now I am gushing on." Blushing, she lowered her gaze and turned her pretty profile to him.

Oh, my, he thought. I am lost. I have fallen hopelessly in love.

When they reached a grove of trees bordering the lake, Reginald dismounted, tethered Sherard to a tree, then helped Amaryllis down from her mount. He doubted the gentle mare would wander off, but he secured her reins before taking Amaryllis's hand and leading her down to a bench perfectly situated to enjoy the shade of the trees yet have a perfect view of the lake.

"How lovely it is here," Amaryllis said, settling on the bench. She pulled her skirt aside that Reginald might join her. "Your sister is so kind to loan me so many outfits. I do feel ashamed that I am so enjoying being out of black, yet my year of mourning is not near up."

"You should feel no shame," Reginald said, taking her hand in his. "Your father would be proud of you. You have saved his son and heir. He would in no way think you are insufficiently honoring him."

She gave him a soft smile. "I know what you say is true. Father was such a good man, and he was so glad he had a son. He would have hated to have Churlwood go to his brother and then his brother's sons. He feared they had not the love for Churlwood that he had. He worried they would not be fair to the tenants."

"That is something I must learn," Reginald said, turning to look out over the lake, yet keeping a loose hold on Amaryllis's hand. "I must learn to care for my manor. And for the people, the tenants that make it prosper. The manor has had a steward for years, but he is growing old and my parents decided I must learn what I can from him before he is given his annuity and retires from his office."

He chuckled deprecatingly, "I fear I have ne'er done anything that was not for my own amusement. I have ne'er had responsibilities. Ne'er had people's lives dependent upon my decisions. I must admit, I have great respect for Toms. He knows his tenants. Knows their worth. Knows what will make his manor profitable." He looked back at Amaryllis. "I realize I have much to learn."

"You have already proven yourself most capable, Reggie," Amaryllis said, a pink blush brightening her cheeks. "I know you will prove a very capable manager of your estate."

"Think you so? I wish I could feel more confident. Yes, I went to Oxford, and I spent the obligatory year at Gray's Inn so I have some knowledge of the law. I had a wonderful six months on the continent. But my dear Amaryllis, at no time was I ever responsible for the well-being of anyone but myself." He tightened his grip on her hand and captured her eyes with his. "Could I but be certain I could meet these obligations now being thrust upon me, I would feel in a better position to take on more pleasant obligations."

Amaryllis blushed an even brighter pink and blinked her eyes. "Oh, I do think you will be an exceptional manager of your estate. I cannot believe your fears are based on anything but your desire to make certain the people entrusted to your care and management have no cause to regret your assumption of your position of master of your estate. I have already seen how wise you are. I have seen how you care about the people who must look to you for instructions." Her eyes wide, she smiled softly. "You are most capable and need have no fears, especially as you have time to learn from your long-time steward. What you may question, he will answer."

Her praise elated Reginald, and she looked so lovely, her eyes brimming with admiration, her lips curving in a sweet smile. Without thinking he bent forward and lightly kissed her. So soft were her lips. At first they trembled, but quickly firmed and responded to his gentle pressure. Thrilling to the sweetness of her kiss, he came close to grasping her and pulling her into a tight embrace, but his sense of propriety returned, and he drew back. His heart pounded against his ribs, and his breath, ragged and shallow, had his head spinning. Naught but a simple little kiss, yet he could scarce maintain his composure.

Finally drawing in a breath, he managed to blurt out, "Oh, my dear Amaryllis, can you forgive me for being so bold? I hope you would not think I have anything but respect for you."

Her eyes wide and dreamy, she gazed up at him. "That is my first kiss. I have often wondered what a kiss would be like. It is most pleasant, is it not?"

Reginald considered pleasant to be a vast understatement, but all the same, he nodded in agreement. "Indeed, most pleasant, but do say you forgive me for being so bold."

"Why, there is naught to forgive. You did me no harm. I enjoyed the kiss."

Grasping both her hands, he said, "Dear, sweet girl. Could you but know the way you make me feel. From the moment I first saw you, I knew I could not bear to be parted from you. You are so very lovely, so very sweet. I realize we have known each other but a few short days, but I believe I have seen into your gentle soul. I would bear my soul to you, did you wish it. I am unpracticed in the art of love, but I would offer you my heart did it not offend you."

"Oh, Reggie, how could you ever offend me. Do you offer me your heart, indeed, I would take it and treasure it and treat it with the greatest of care."

Swallowing, he drew her hands to his lips and kissed her fingertips. "Can you mean you would consider marrying me? I have not but my manor in Nottinghamshire to offer you. And as I have said, I have no experience in estate management. I could bungle everything. I would understand do you wish time to see if I merit your love."

Freeing her hands, she captured one of his hands between hers. "Have I not just finished telling you how capable I think you are? How you can so doubt yourself is what I cannot understand. I, however, have no such doubts concerning your competence. When I am with you I feel safe and happy. So you see, if you are offering me your hand, then yes, I accept it."

A thundering in his ears and the drumming of his heart near overcame him, but grasping Amaryllis to his chest, he planted kisses on her brow, her cheeks, and finally her lips. That this angel who had suddenly appeared in his life would actually commit herself to his keeping left him feeling humbled and blessed. Her lips parted under pressure from his, and he sought her tongue and explored her mouth with a reverence he could only consider sublime. She responded to his kisses with an innocence and yet an eagerness that would soon become his undoing did he not release her and bring them both back down to earth.

Forcing himself to end the kiss and pull away from her enough to plant a kiss on the tip of her nose, he cleared his throat and rasped huskily, "My dear Amaryllis, you have made me the happiest man on earth. I cannot believe any man could be as lucky as I am. That you would consent to be my wife has enriched me beyond all my expectations."

Looking up at him out of dreamy eyes, she said, "I feel I am the lucky one. I knew I had fallen in love with you. Knew I dreaded the day we must part. But I never dared hope you might fall in love with me. I but hoped I might spend as much time as possible in your company before we would be parted. I could not even mind that we were delayed because it meant I would have more time with you."

"I had the same thoughts," Reginald exuberantly admitted. "'Tis Fate that has brought us together. And I mean that literally. Had Selena not stopped to attend that ragged cur, we would never have met."

Amaryllis giggled. "Who would have thought such a little dog could so change our lives. I must say, Fate now seems a most appropriate name for the little guy." Sobering, she added, "But the reason we met was my need to rescue Charlie from my aunt. I still have that obligation. I cannot think of or commit to my own future until Charlie is safe with his aunt."

Reginald nodded. "Of course. Charlie's safety is still our priority. Perhaps it is best do we say nothing of our betrothal until Charlie is no longer in any danger."

"Yes, yes, I do think that might be best. Tabitha and Charlie need no extra distractions. So much is topsy turvy in their young lives. Such an announcement might unsettle them. They are so young, and they depend on me."

"So be it," Reginald said, and rising, he pulled Amaryllis up with him. "Let us have a stroll about the lake before we must return for dinner. The path along the shore seems well-maintained, do you care for a walk?"

Allowing Reginald to tuck her hand in the crook of his arm, Amaryllis looked up at him with shining eyes. "Yes, I would enjoy meandering along the shore. The day is lovely, and so many flowers are in bloom. 'Tis a perfect day for a walk in the sunshine."

Noting that the path wandered in and out of the woods, Reginald thought it was also a perfect day for a few stolen kisses as well. He knew every time he kissed Amaryllis, every time he took her in his arms, he would be torturing himself. Ahhh, but it would be such sweet torture, he had no doubt he would consider it worth the pain.

Chapter 20

Selena had enjoyed her tour around Toms's manor. She had enjoyed a good race across a clover-strewn meadow – she and Brigantia winning, of course. She had complimented Toms on his manor and had learned it was larger than she had at first suspected, stretching into the next parish. That he knew all his tenants by name, she found admirable and could not help but wonder if her brother would someday be as competent a squire.

When they returned to the house, she found Esmeralda had laid out her blue gown for her, and after indulging in a quick hip bath, she descended to the parlor to find Amaryllis and Reginald had yet to make an appearance. She enjoyed a chat with Mistress Sermon, but was beginning to feel her stomach rumble when at last her brother and then Amaryllis arrived. With everyone assembled, they adjourned to the dining chamber. The meal was elaborate, the conversation lively, but Selena noticed something was different between Amaryllis and Reginald. The glances they exchanged, the smiles, a type of communication was flashing between them. She wondered what had transpired. What had happened on their visit to the lake? She knew better than to ask her brother anything. He would clam up. But mayhap Amaryllis might let something slip. She smiled, she could be patient.

After dinner, Mistress Sermon professed her need for a nap, but Toms led Reginald, Amaryllis, and Selena into the parlor. A card table had been set up, and the four of them sat down for a game of whist. Examining his hand, Reginald said, "Nye returned from the Wirths'. All is well there. Pit and Mills are fine, well fed by the Wirths, but bored."

"Oh, I can imagine," Selena said, shaking her head. "Night and day, naught to do but watch over the coach. I do hope Billings will soon be returning with the wheel." Glancing up from her own cards, she asked, "When do you think Crouch may be returning?" Their other outrider had been sent with a message to the Girouards telling them they would not be stopping with them due to their late departure. He had been told to then meet up with them again on the road to Leicester, but he, of course, could have no idea of their delay.

"I would guess when Billings returns," Reginald answered. "I told Billings did he meet up with Crouch, he should take Crouch with him to Northampton. In any case, I would not expect Billings and our coach wheel back for at least another day, mayhap two did the wheelwright have other jobs ahead of ours."

"Humph," Selena said. "Do I know Billings, he will make certain that wheelwright makes our wheel a priority, does he have to use bribes or threats."

Reginald chuckled. "Most likely you are right. Billings has not a lot of patience." He looked at Amaryllis and explained, "Billings is not a happy man is he not seated on his horse."

"Then what does he do when you are not traveling?" Amaryllis asked.

"Follow Selena around. Father would not allow her to ride off the manor unaccompanied, so Billings was most likely to be found following after Selena."

Selena frowned at her brother. "That is not all he does. Father often has messages that need be sent various places. Father has his fingers in various pies. With Mother's four major manors and a smattering of smaller manors, he has much to watch over." She looked at Amaryllis then Toms. "Each of us, with the exception of our youngest brother, Thayer, will inherit one of Mother's major manors. Thayer will inherit a small manor in Buckinghamshire. My oldest brother, Giles, as Father's heir to the Earldom, besides the manor from Mother, he inherits Rygate and the other smaller manors, as well as the house in Bath. Reggie will be visiting his estate after he deliveries me to Whimbrel."

"Yes," Toms said, "so he has mentioned." He turned to Reginald. "Do you wish, on the morrow, I could give you a tour of Mere Manse. Answer any questions you might have."

"Splendid idea," Reginald said, but Selena did not think he looked thrilled with the plan. He first glanced at Amaryllis, and after the slightest nod of her head, he responded in the positive to Toms's suggestion. Well, Selena thought, that would give her a chance to stroll about the grounds with Amaryllis and mayhap learn what secret she and Reginald shared.

"Begging your pardon, Mistress Bowdon," Betty said from the doorway. Clasping the hands of Tabitha and Charlie, she bobbed a brief curtsy. "The children have had their nap, and I wonder might I take them out into the garden again. They saw a pond from their window and were eager to see if any ducks might be living near it."

Amaryllis smiled. "Yes, of course. They have become attached to ducks lately." She glanced at Selena, and Selena returned her smile. "Please be careful they are not allowed too near the pond. Mishaps can happen."

"You need not worry about that pond," Toms said. "You would have to get far out into the middle of it before it would be over Charlie's head. It is more a reflective pond, and I doubt you will find any ducks."

Amaryllis nodded but said, "All the same, Betty, do be careful."

"We will." They started to leave, but Betty looked back over her shoulder. "By the by, we will have the little dog with us."

"Oh, good," Selena said. "He needs time outside." She knew Fate was still very attached to her, yet at the same time, the dog seemed happiest when with the children. She had already decided when they reached the children's aunt, she would offer to let the children keep Fate. Turning back to the game, she found her brother had trumped her king. Oh, bother, she thought, she and Toms were going to lose the hand. Well, such was fate.

※ ※ ※ ※

Felton believed his day to be wasted. He had worked as hard as ever in his life digging the latrine pit, hauling the dirt to the location the gardener had indicated. Burke had been near useless yet had received the same wage. Eight pence each for their day's labor plus their dinner and ale. Felton had only seen the little baronet at a distance and had come up with no plan on how to get closer to him. With the work done, he could do naught but trudge back across the commons to Burke's cottage for another meal of porridge then bed on the lumpy mattress.

Suddenly childish laughter drew his attention to a pond with a statue at the far end. He spotted the children and the maid minding them. Looking closely about in all directions, he saw no one else was near them. The D'Arcy footmen had gone inside the men's dormitory, the gardener and his two assistants were nowhere in sight. No stablemen bustled about. The only person near to hand was Burke. Clapping a hand on Burke's shoulder, Felton said, "You start on home. I am going to find the steward and see does he need anything else doing on the morrow. Pick up a few more pence ere I leave for me brother's."

Burke began vigorously shaking his head. "Nay, nay," he held out his hands. "I already have blisters. I cannot work another day."

Felton saw no blisters on Burke's hand, but he said, "'Tis but work for me I seek. You go on. I will catch up to you."

Eager to escape the possibility of more work being given him, Burke nodded and hurried his steps away from Felton. No doubt he would go home by way of the alehouse. Felton doubted Goody Burke would see more than a pence of her husband's wages, if that. He watched Burke long enough to be certain the man would not look back at him, then he turned his attention to the lively little scene by the pond. Perhaps his day had not been wasted after all.

The baronet was sitting on the ground and using a stick to play a sort of tug of war with the small dog with a splint on its leg. The maid appeared to be fashioning a sort of doll out of rags for the little girl. They were both chattering and laughing. None of the three had noticed him. Could he creep close enough, he could land a blow to the maid then toss the boy into the pond and be on his way before anyone could be the wiser. Blessing the blossoming shrubs that partially concealed him, he worked his way closer and closer.

Drawing in a deep breath, he sprang forward, sprinting across the short space between him and the nursemaid. The little girl glanced up as he neared, but not in time to warn the maid. Grabbing the maid by the shoulder, he turned her just enough to shove his fist into her jaw. He but needed to momentarily knock her out. He had no desire to cause her any real harm.

Falling over backwards, the woman landed on the little girl who let out a muffled screech. Felton turned from them to scoop up the wide-eyed boy. To his dismay, his dash to the pond with the boy was hindered. The dog grabbed hold of his ankle, sinking his small sharp teeth clear through to the bone. Yelping, he attempted to shake the dog lose, but the cur's teeth were caught in his stocking. Stumbling forward and still shaking his leg, he got close enough to the pond to heave the boy into it. As the boy splashed into the water, Felton stooped and jerked the dog off his ankle, a piece of his stocking ripping loose with the damned cur. Tossing the dog aside, he sprinted toward the stand of oaks that would hide him from view.

Glancing over his shoulder, he saw the little girl wading into the pond, heard her calling, "Ryllis, Ryllis." Heard that mangy, interfering cur barking. Damn that dog! Had it kept him from throwing the boy deep enough into the pond? Might the baronet's sister rescue him? He could not wait around to see. He had to get out of the village before anyone could come searching for him. Damn, damn, damn! How was he to learn whether the baronet had drowned or not. Damn!

Drawing close to the Burke's cottage, he slowed his pace, and drew in slow, deep breaths. Would not do to make Goody Burke suspicious. He crumpled his stocking down around his ankle, hoping it hid the blood and the rent. Opening the door, he saw the woman at her work table busily chopping onions. She looked up when he entered and looked around him as if expecting to see her husband. "Where is John?" she asked.

"I thought he would be here afore me," Felton answered. "I meant to ask did they have more work for me on the morrow, but finding no one to ask, I started back. Burke left afore me."

Goody Burke shook her head. "No doubt he went off to the alehouse. I should have known I could not count on seeing any coin from his labors. How much were you paid?"

"Eight pence." He reached into his purse. "Here be two for the board of my horse. Having no work for the morrow, I will be on my way."

"You are not staying the night?" Goody Burke looked and sounded surprised.

"Nay, I will get on up the road a ways. No reason to lolly-gag around. Farther on a piece, I may find me a job or two to pay me way. I thank ye for the bed and the fine meals. Now I will get me horse."

She nodded. "Safe journey to you, Mister Farr." She then turned back to her chopping, and he went to claim his horse. He quickly had the animal saddled and was soon trotting off up the narrow path leading into the village. He would go north. Find someplace to hide out and watch for the D'Arcy coach. 'Twas the only way he could learn whether the baronet lived or died. He would have to find new hose. His ripped stocking would give him away in an instant. Damn that cur. Damn him!

Chapter 21

Gnawing her lower lip, Selena watched Amaryllis rock her brother in her arms. Tabitha was cuddled in Esmeralda's arms, and Betty was stretched out on Mistress Sermon's bed with a cold, spring-water compress on her jaw. Mistress Sermon had insisted they all gather in her bedchamber once the children were dried off, their clothing changed, and their fears calmed. The well-appointed bedchamber offered two cushioned wingback chairs before the hearth, a tufted stool before a looking glass table, and a day couch at the foot of the bed. Selena sat on the couch.

Pacing the room, Mistress Sermon said, "I cannot believe such an incident should happen right here on Dicky's manor. 'Tis monstrous!"

Selena scratched behind Fate's ears. Curled up on her lap, the little dog seemed not to realize he was a hero. He but seemed happy to be receiving numerous pats and caresses. "The man is bold," Selena said. "I will give him that. But I cannot help but think after the incident with the coach wheel, we should have been more vigilant."

Amaryllis turned to look at Selena. "What do you mean? What has the coach wheel to do with this attack on Charlie?"

Selena shook her head. "We meant not to worry you. We could not be sure the wheel had been deliberately tampered with in an attempt to harm Charlie. You see, the spokes had been whittled down so when they hit a bump just right, they would break and the coach would do what it did. Turn over."

Amaryllis put a hand to her mouth. "You mean 'twas not an accident?"

"I am afraid not. But we could not be certain, so we thought it best not to frighten you. At least not until we might learn more. Never did we think the perpetrator would be so bold as to make his way onto Mere Manse. We thought having Betty watch over Charlie was sufficient. I

165

am sorry. From now on we will have an armed guard near to hand at all times."

Clutching Charlie closer to her, her eyes wide, Amaryllis said, "You mean by taking us up into your coach, we are responsible for the accident."

"Nay. The man, whomever he may be, who is bent on harming Charlie, he is responsible for the wheel breaking. Had you not joined our party ... Were you alone with the children on a stage. What might this villain have managed?"

"Dear God, let us not think such thoughts," interrupted Mistress Sermon. She stepped behind Amaryllis's chair and put a hand on her shoulder. "'Tis fate that you should have been placed in the D'Arcys's care. In memory of the great love and friendship between my father and your grandfather, I pledge to do all I can to help you in any way I can."

"Thank you, Mistress Sermon. You and Mister Toms have both been most kind."

"Speaking of Dicky, where can he be? Surely they have questioned all the staff by now." She looked at the door as if she expected her nephew to appear, but instead a young girl with unruly curls plaited into two braids appeared in the doorway.

Holding a heavy wooden bucket in one hand, the girl bobbed a curtsey. "Begging your pardon, Mistress Sermon. Cook sent me up with some fresh cold water for Mistress Betty's jaw."

"Oh, aye, that's a good gel. Bring it in," Mistress Sermon said.

Setting Fate on the couch, Selena stood and took the bucket from the child. She set the bucket down next to the bed, took the compress from Betty's face, and dipped the rag into the chilled water. Squeezing out the excess water, she reapplied the compress. "Poor Betty. Your jaw is all red and swollen, but I do hope 'tis paining you less."

"Indeed, I am much better, Lady Selena," Betty answered, wincing a bit. "I am but so sorry I can give you no description of the man. It happened so fast."

"You have no need to try to talk. 'Tis not your fault. But after what has happened to you, are you certain you still wish to accompany us to Derbyshire?"

166

Turning her large, blue eyes on Selena, she said, "Even more determined to go with you. I intend to make certain no more harm comes to those children do I have to scratch the man's eyes out." Her gaze darted to Mistress Sermon. "I am but worried that Mistress Sermon will have no one to tend her needs."

Mistress Sermon waved her hand. "Nonsense. My needs are minimal."

Standing near the doorway, waiting to retrieve the bucket, the young girl spoke up, "Begging your pardon, Mistress Sermon, but my mother could be your maid. She was once a maid for a fine lady."

"Was she now?" Mistress Sermon looked down her long nose at the child. "And who might be your mother? For that matter, who might you be? I cannot say I have seen you before."

"Nay Mistress, 'tis my first time to work at Mere Manse. I have been working in the scullery. My name is Elizabeth Burke." She smiled and dimples dotted each cheek. "I am called Bess. My mother is Elsa Burke. Before she married my father, she was a lady's maid."

"Indeed. Well, when you go home tonight, you tell your mother I expect to see her by mid-morning. I will interview her and see does she really have experience as a lady's maid."

The girl beamed. "Oh, yes, Mistress. I will tell her."

Handing the girl the bucket, Selena noted Bess's gown was shabby, but neatly patched. The girl's mother knew how to proficiently wield a needle. She hoped Elsa Burke would be a good substitute for Betty, and Mistress Sermon need not make do with an inexperienced maid.

Soon after the girl departed, Toms and Reginald entered the room. "Ah, 'tis about time," Mistress Sermon said. "I could not imagine what could take you so long unless you did indeed apprehend the murdering scoundrel."

"We had many to question, Auntie Jane," Toms said, "but we think we now have a lead on the man as well as a description of him."

"Have you!" Selena cried. Neither of the children had been able to describe the man. They had but called him the mean ugly man. That Charlie was alive was a near miracle. "Fate saved him," Tabitha had declared. "He bit the man on the leg and would not let go until the man dropped Charlie. I then had to get Charlie out of the pond. I am glad

Norwood came to help me."

Having spent the morning entertaining Handle, then enjoying a nap after dinner, Norwood had decided he needed to take a walk. He emerged from the men's dormitory in time to see Tabitha splashing into the pond. Realizing something was amiss he ran to her aid. Only after he had Charlie safely out of the pond, did he notice Betty lying on the ground. She had started to moan and struggle to sit up. His calls for help brought the stablemen running, and one had gone to fetch Toms. Chaos had ensued, but eventually some sense had been made of the situation, and once assured the children had not been seriously harmed, Toms and Reginald had turned to questioning the staff.

"So tell us what you have learned," Selena demanded.

"If this man is truly the perpetrator of this crime," Reginald said, "he is going by the name of Farr. The steward hired him and a cottager by the name of John Burke to finish digging a new latrine pit. The man originally engaged to do the project having injured himself. The steward said the two did a good job. He paid them their wages and thought they left the grounds. The steward says he was surprised Burke would be interested in doing the job. Apparently the man is a ne'er-do-well. A cottager, according to Toms, he only lets stay on because of his wife and family."

"That is right," Toms said. "Burke is worthless, but his wife is a good woman, and his son, though young, is hard-working and manages to pay the rent."

"Burke? Burke?" Mistress Sermon said. "I just told a young scullery maid to have her mother come see me on the morrow. Girl claimed her mother had been a lady's maid. She said her name was Burke."

Toms shrugged. "I know not whether Goody Burke was e'er a lady's maid, but it would not surprise me. She is neat and clean in her appearance and is well-spoken."

"Hmmm," Mistress Sermon said, moving from behind Amaryllis's chair to sit beside Selena on the day couch.

"Anyway," Toms continued. "After learning the man, Farr, was the only stranger on the grounds, we went to talk to Goody Burke. She told us all she could about the man, gave us a good description of him and his horse. She seemed puzzled by his villainy. She said he had been courteous to her and paid well for his and his horse's keep. She said she had been surprised that he had decided to leave so abruptly but had not questioned him."

"I sent Nye and Norwood into the village to find out anything else they could about the man," Reginald said. "Goody Burke said her husband met Farr in an alehouse in the village. Anything we can learn about Farr will be to our benefit."

"I cannot believe Aunt Elva would actually hire a man to … to." Amaryllis stopped and looked at Tabitha and then down at Charlie. She could not say 'hire a man to kill Charlie' in front of the children. They had been frightened enough by the episode.

Selena broke in, "Yes, so bold to hire a man to try to steal Charlie from you. Well, we will not let them steal you, Charlie." She rose and stepped over to ruffle the boy's hair. "We are going to keep you with us. Right?"

Charlie nodded, and looking up at Selena, stated in his piping little voice, "Right."

Selena laughed and that made Charlie laugh and soon everyone was laughing. The mood had lightened, but Selena knew their tribulations were not at an end.

✿ ✿ ✿ ✿

Amaryllis sat with Charlie and Tabitha while they ate their supper. She kept a bright smile on her face and joked and laughed with them, but her innards were in turmoil. She still could not believe her aunt had hired a man to follow them and to try to kill Charlie. How could her aunt possibly expect to get away with such a thing? But then, why should she not? Amaryllis had, in effect, abducted the children, taken them from their supposedly safe home, made them vulnerable to the attack of a depraved lunatic. Or so her aunt could claim. Had the man succeeded in drowning Charlie, Amaryllis realized, she would have been the one found guilty of aiding in her brother's death. God, she was frightened.

"Now look how well you two have cleaned your plates," Selena said, interrupting Amaryllis's morbid thoughts. "Now you may each have your honey cake."

"Might Fate also have a honey cake?" Tabitha asked as Selena placed a small plate with two cakes on it before the children.

"Indeed he may if you so wish it," Selena said. "Before Norwood takes him out tonight, he can stop by the kitchen and get Fate a cake."

"Fate was very brave," Tabitha said. "I was scared of the man, but Fate was not."

Selena reached down to pet the dog curled up at her feet. "Yes, he is a very brave dog and a very loyal dog. He has grown to love you and Charlie very much. Would you like to have him sleep here with you tonight instead of with me?"

Both children beamed. "Might he?" Tabitha cried before frowning and asking, "Oh, but will he not miss you?"

"I think he will be as happy with you two as with me. Now finish your cakes, and we will get you tucked into your beds, and I will tell you a story."

"A story about knights?" Charlie demanded.

"And princesses?" Tabitha added.

"Yes, a story about brave knights and princesses and their very brave dogs."

Charlie clapped his hands, then cramming the last of his cake into his mouth, he proclaimed, "I am ready."

"Me, too," Tabitha declared.

Amaryllis was grateful to Selena. Did the children have any fears before going to sleep, Selena would banish them.

Their faces and hands washed, their little teeth scrubbed, Tabitha and Charlie readily allowed Amaryllis to tuck them into bed. Giving each child a kiss, she hugged them close to her heart and tried not to let them feel her fear. "Now Selena will tell you a story, and Esmeralda will stay with you until I return. I will be sleeping up here with you tonight."

"Is Mistress Betty feeling better?" Tabitha asked.

"Yes, she is," Esmeralda said, entering the room in time to hear the question. "She managed some tasty gruel Cook made for her, and she is now resting peacefully. But she told me to tell you she will be ready to finish making the rag doll for you tomorrow, Tabitha. And she said to tell you, Sir Charlie, that she procured a bag of marbles for you from Mister Toms."

"She did!"

"Indeed she did. Now you lie back down in bed so Lady Selena can tell you a story. I will sit over here in this comfy chair and enjoy the story along with you." She looked at Amaryllis. "Mistress Bowdon, Master Reginald is awaiting you in the parlor. Supper will not be served until Lady Selena is finished up here."

"Thank you, Esmeralda," Amaryllis said, "I will freshen up and go right down. And thank you for staying with the children until I return."

Esmeralda gave her a soft smile. "No thanks are needed for such a task, Mistress Bowdon. I am only too happy to sit with them."

Her heart thumping heavily in her chest, Amaryllis, with the help of the maid assigned to her, hurried her toilet then descended the stairs to the parlor. She thought Toms and his aunt might be there, but only Reginald awaited her. Taking her into his arms, he held her tight against his chest and gently stroked her back.

"Oh, my dear love, I cannot express to you my sorrow that I failed to keep a closer watch over Charlie. But I do promise you, this Farr, or whatever his name may be; he will never again get anywhere near your brother, or you, or your sister. I promise you that."

Pulling away from him a little, she said, "Reggie, why did you not tell me about the coach wheel? Why did you let me think 'twas an ordinary accident?"

Shaking his head and shifting his eyes thoughtfully, he said, "I think because I could not credit the act was done to harm or kill Charlie. I thought it but the work of some envious, mean-spirited cullion who resented the fineness of our coach. How could your aunt have known you traveled with us? How could she have found and hired someone so quickly who would be willing to kill a child? None of this makes sense, and yet it would seem not only does your aunt know where you are headed, she has employed someone to kill Charlie." He cupped her chin in his hand and raised her face so her eyes looked directly into his. "That will not happen, Amaryllis. Again, I promise you, no harm will come to Charlie."

His eyes intent, he continued, "I know you thought you would be leaving us at Leicester and taking the stage to Derby, but I must tell you, Selena and I never intended to let you board that stage. Even before this incident, before the coach wheel broke, Selena wrote to our aunt and uncle that we would be making a side trip into Derbyshire. Selena is stubborn that way. When she makes her mind up to something, there is small chance of changing her direction."

"So I am learning," Amaryllis said with a weak smile.

"Besides," Reginald said, placing a light kiss on the tip of her nose, "now we are betrothed, I have even more reason to see you safely to your destination."

Hearing voices, the two stepped apart before Mistress Sermon, escorted by Toms, entered the parlor. "Ah, here you two are," Mistress Sermon said and informed Reginald, "Dicky has told Haines to have a cot set up for your man Norwood outside the nursery." At Reginald's thanks, she turned her bright eyes on Amaryllis. "I understand you are insisting upon sleeping in the nursery with the children."

"I am," Amaryllis said with a nod of her head.

"I cannot think anyone would be able climb up three stories then sneak in through a window to get to Charlie," Toms said. "All the same, I have ordered a man to stand guard outside, and the dogs are to be let loose after everyone has settled in for the night. That such an incident should happen here on my estate to my guests has me furious. I have talked with the constable, and he has alerted the village aldermen. Does Farr show his face anywhere, we will nab him."

"Thank you," Amaryllis said. She knew she would not feel Charlie was truly safe until the man was apprehended. Thank goodness she had Reginald to look after them.

"Have you all been waiting for me?" Selena asked from the doorway.

"Lady Selena," Mistress Sermon said. "The children are settled?"

"Settled and asleep. It was a big day for them. I trust they will have no nightmares, but Amaryllis will be near them as will Fate. I think they will be fine."

"Splendid." Mistress Sermon turned to her nephew. "Dicky, do ring for our supper."

"Yes, Auntie Jane," Toms said, picking up a large bell and giving it a jingle.

"Did Nye and Norwood learn anything in the village," Selena asked.

"They learned from the blacksmith that a man answering to Farr's description came around asking questions about our coach" Reginald said. "The man said he was headed north to visit his brother. They also found out a man of the same description, but going by the name of Hood, stayed one night at the inn. The same night we stayed with the Wirths. They found John Burke in an alehouse. The woman running the house said she had seen Burke with a man two days running, but she took no note of him. The man paid in coin. That was all she cared about. Burke could not believe his friend could have tried to kill anyone. Said we had to be mistaken."

"I think Burke is the one mistaken," Selena said.

"Aye," Toms said. "Burke would like anyone who buys him a drink."

The steward, Haines, appeared in the doorway. "Mister Toms, your supper is ready to be set out. Shall I have it served?"

Toms nodded. "Yes, there's a good man, Haines. Have them bring the dishes right up." He turned to Selena and offered his arm. "Lady Selena."

Selena accepted his arm, and as they headed for the dining chamber, Mistress Sermon fell in behind them. Reginald, extending his arm to Amaryllis, gave her a warming smile, patted her hand when she placed it on his arm, and escorted her out the door and down the corridor to the well-appointed dining chamber.

Though Toms's cook had prepared a substantial supper, Amaryllis had little appetite and only picked at her food. Nibbling on a piece of bread, she vaguely listened to the conversations buzzing about her. Her attention returned to those at the table when Selena touched her arm.

"Amaryllis, did you not hear me? I asked the name of the family that is hosting the children's aunt. I think 'twould be best did I let my uncle know where we are headed that he can keep my aunt from worrying."

"Oh, I am sorry. My mind is all aflutter. I still cannot believe what has happened. The children's Aunt Juliet is married to David Stoke. His sister, Mary, is married to a Mister Godwin Crossly. I believe he has a small estate outside Derby. I think Mister Crossly is an attorney."

Amaryllis cocked her head and looked first at Selena then at Reginald. They were both staring at her so strangely. "What?" she asked.

"You are certain the name is Godwin Crossly?" Selena asked.

"Yes. Is aught wrong?"

Selena started laughing and Reginald joined her. Amaryllis saw Toms and his aunt were also looking strangely at the D'Arcys.

Reginald found his voice first. "'Tis such a coincidence. Godwin Crossly is near a cousin to us. We know him well. He is our Aunt Rowena's second son by her first husband. This piece of news should make our aunt and uncle feel much better about our escapade. They will be greatly relieved. Selena must write them tonight."

"That I will. I cannot believe I failed to note the name on the letter you wrote at the Wirths'. I was weary and did but hand the letter over to Billings to post come the morning. No matter, we will be most pleased to see Godwin and his brother, Sir Milo, who lives near to Godwin," Selena said. "We have not seen either since near three years ago when we had a family gathering at Uncle Kenrick's estate in Oxfordshire. 'Tis always a grand affair. We are a large family. At that time, Godwin was less than two years married, but he already had a lovely daughter about six months old. Fact is, last I heard, a second child was on the way."

"That is correct," Amaryllis said, still trying to assimilate the surprising development. "They now have a son. That is why Tabitha and Charlie's Aunt Juliet and her husband went to visit them. To see the new baby."

"Oh, this is grand," Selena said. "We will be delivering Tabitha and Charlie to safety, and we will have a fine reunion with Godwin and Milo and their families before continuing on to Whimbrel."

"No doubt Selena will try to make it a long reunion," Reginald said with a smirk and a sidelong glance at his sister. "She will attempt to avoid the inevitable as long as possible."

"'Tis indeed a world of coincidences," Mistress Sermon interposed. "I will expect a detailed account from you, Lady Selena, when you have safely reached your destination. I cannot but feel that fellow, Farr, may yet attempt some mischief before all is said and done."

"I believe you to be right on that, Auntie Jane," Toms agreed, and turning to Reginald said, "That is why I have decided to ride as far as

Leicester with you. I will take two outriders. Could be, does the man see such a show of strength, he will give up the quest."

"That is most kind of you, and I thank you," Reginald said. "If Farr is but one man alone …, and he knows we are now wise to him …, he could well decide his schemes are useless."

"No thanks necessary," Toms said. "Least I can do. Besides, I know of a passable inn we can put up at in Northampton and a more than reputable inn in Leicester. I will send a man off to both inns on the morrow to tell them to prepare for our arrival in the next few days." He looked apologetically at Amaryllis. "As you know, when I am expecting a room, and it has not been readied for me, I can behave most foolishly."

Amaryllis blushed. She still recalled too vividly the insult Toms had inflicted on her, but his kindnesses had more than made up for his impudence. She managed a smile and said, "I trust these inns will be most accommodating."

"I would not have thought we could travel between Northampton and Leicester without stopping somewhere for the night," Reginald said. "According to information my father gave me, it is close to forty miles. We are averaging but twenty a day on a good day. Have to sufficiently rest the horses. They have a ways to go before we get to Whimbrel, then a long return trip."

"I thought of that," Toms said. "I have a hunting lodge, not two miles off the road, near midpoint between Northampton and Leicester. 'Tis rustic, but the beds are sound. I keep but a minimal staff there, but I can send additional help on ahead to ready it and lay in supplies if you think 'twould suffice."

"That will more than suffice, Mister Toms," Selena said. "I cannot think how we are going to repay all Mistress Sermon's and your many kindnesses, but we will contrive at some point to find a means of expressing our gratitude."

"Indeed, we must," Amaryllis said.

"Nonsense," Mistress Sermon said. "I but wish my old bones would allow me to join in your adventure. However, the trip here was all I can endure at this time. You can repay me by giving me a nice, long, newsy letter. As for Dicky, he is but happy he has found a way to escape me for a few days."

"Auntie Jane! How can you say such?"

"I say it, and I mean it. I know I am far from the easiest guest. Like to have things my own way. But now, is everyone through with supper, let us women adjourn to the parlor. This chair gives no comfort to my old bones."

Amaryllis rose with Selena and Mistress Sermon, but she excused herself. She wanted to be with the children. And 'twas only right Esmeralda should be excused from her watch. Selena gave her a brief hug and said she would have Norwood take Fate out before he should settle onto his cot outside her door.

In leaving the room, Amaryllis looked over her shoulder at Reginald. His eyes glowed with his love for her. She could see it, could feel it. She gave him a bright smile and hoped he could see her love for him in her eyes. So much had happened. It seemed like days had passed since she and Reginald had expressed their love for one another, and yet it had been but that morning. Her joyous mood had been doused by the near murder of her brother. Had Tabitha not reached him in time and pulled him to shallower water, he might have drowned. Dear God, she prayed as she climbed the stairs to the nursery, please let nothing else happen to Charlie. Please protect him.

Chapter 22

Sitting quietly in a tufted chair in the parlor, Selena observed the exchange between Mistress Sermon and Goody Burke. She had liked the woman the moment she saw her. She guessed Elsa Burke to be in her late thirties, though the worry lines about her eyes could give the impression she was older. Round, brown eyes that might once have glowed softly had a hard, bitter light to them. She had once been a pretty woman, Selena thought, pouty mouth with a full, lower lip, thin straight nose, arched brows and thick lashes. She carried herself well, shoulders back, chin up, gaze clear and straight forward. Her cap was clean, if yellowed by age, her dark gown patched, but like her daughter's, flawlessly mended. And she spoke clearly and distinctly, thoughtfully answering the questions Mistress Sermon put to her.

"You can read and write?" Mistress Sermon asked.

"Yes, Mistress. I went to petty school until I was seven. I then received additional training from the vicar's wife. She is the one who taught me to sew, to make and mend clothing and hose, to mix herbs for healing, to iron delicate clothing, and to clean stains away. When I was twelve, I entered service in the Wilton household in Northampton as an upstairs maid and an assistant to Mistress Wilton's personal attendant. I worked in that capacity for two years then was made personal maid to the Wilton's eldest daughter. She was fifteen at that time. I continued as her maid for three more years when Mistress Wilton made me her personal maid, her former maid having had a bad accident with an iron and being unable to continue as her maid."

"And why did you leave Mistress Wilton's service?"

For the first time Elsa Burke hesitated and her gaze shifted before returning to Mistress Sermon. "I married John Burke," she finally said.

Mistress Sermon nodded. "I see. Did Mistress Wilton give you a reference?"

"That was many years ago. I have no reference from her at this point."

"No matter. Do I decide I need a reference, I can always contact her. Tell me, how did you meet Mister Burke? I cannot say from what Dicky has told me of your husband, that you seem well-suited."

Selena shook her head. Mistress Sermon was nothing if not direct.

"My parents arranged the marriage," Elsa Burke said, her gaze unwavering.

"Um hmmm. Poor choice I would say."

Goody Burke blushed but she said nothing. She but waited for the next question.

"How many children have you?"

"Four. Bess is thirteen. She is at present working in the scullery here at Mere Manse. Robby is ten. Nellie is four, and my baby, Gunther, is near a year."

"Who would care for your baby if I decide to hire you?"

"Do you decide to hire me, Mistress Sermon, I must sleep at home. I can feed my babe in the morning before I come here to work. I can feed him at night when I go home. The rest of the time, he will be fine with pap. During the day, for a small fee, my neighbor, Goody Manton, will watch him."

"What of your other two children?"

"They have their chores. Robby has much to do in the fields. Nellie will help him."

"Should they not be in school?"

A choking laugh broke from Elsa's throat. "They have work to do. I teach them at night."

"What will your husband be doing?"

"John? Sleeping or drinking I would hazard."

Mistress Sermon snorted and Selena thought, oh, my, Goody Burke is honest.

"Goody Burke, Elsa, I like you," Mistress Sermon said. "I like your mettle. I shall give you a try."

"Thank you," Elsa answered and for the first time lowered her eyes.

Picking up a bell and ringing it, Mistress Sermon said, "I will have Haines take you to my room. My maid Betty is there attempting to set my things to right. Work with her. Does she approve of your skills
178

and knowledge, I will accept you on a trial basis. Because you must go home at night and may not be here when I wish to go to bed – and that means I will need have one of the house maids help me with my toilet, I will not pay you a full wage. I will instead pay you three shillings a month, plus your meals, for as long as I am residing here, or until Betty returns. I will advance you enough coin that you may make yourself a suitable gown and an apron to wear when serving me. You are agreeable to those terms?"

For the first time Goody Burke smiled. "Yes, Mistress Sermon. I accept your offer."

"Good. Now here is Haines." She looked to the steward. "Haines, escort Goody Burke up to my bedchamber and inform Betty she is to work with her, show her what I expect of my personal attendant."

"Yes, Mistress Sermon." Haines bowed slightly at the waist. "This way, Goody Burke."

"Well, what think you?" Mistress Sermon asked Selena after Elsa Burke had followed Haines from the room.

"I think you made a wise choice," Selena answered. "I like the woman. Though I cannot for the life of me imagine why her parents would have married her to a man like Burke."

"Humph! That is because you are yet an innocent. My guess is someone in the Wilton household got Elsa with child. She had to go home to her parents. They had to marry her off to someone. Most likely they had little to no dowry for her. Their choices were limited."

"Oh," Selena said, thinking what a sad thing to have happen.

"More than likely your mother and your aunt would not approve of my being so frank with you. But you are a sensible gel. More sensible than most. You are not apt to go all squeamish on me. Or to act like you think Elsa is now an unforgivable sinner."

"Nay, I would never think such."

"Exactly so. Now, where is Mistress Bowdon?"

"She, Esmeralda, and Norwood are out in the garden. Reggie made certain Norwood was armed before setting off on a tour of Mere Manse with your nephew."

"I would not mind a stroll in the garden myself. We have been blessed with more days of sunshine this spring than I can e'er remember."

"A stroll does sound delightful, but I have had a thought."

Mistress Sermon narrowed her eyes as she rose. "And what is that?"

"Elsa Burke's daughter – she seems a bright girl."

"I will give you that. She does."

"I am thinking she is meant for more than working in the scullery. I am thinking I would like to take her along with us to help Betty with the children and to act as Amaryllis's maid. Then, when Esmeralda must return, the girl, what was her name, Bess? Bess can be companion to her, at least back to here."

"Picking up another stray are you? I agree with you. The gel shows promise. We will stop by the kitchen and have Cook send the girl out to you. You can speak with her in the garden."

❈ ❈ ❈ ❈

Bess's large, blue eyes grew even larger and rounder and the dimples in her cheeks darted in and out as her lips went from smile to open-mouthed wonder to broader smile. "You want me to go with you to act as a maid to Mistress Bowdon? You mean this, Lady Selena?"

Selena chuckled. "I do indeed. You can read and write, can you not?"

"Oh, yes, I can. My mother says I have a very nice, neat hand. And I have been learning to sew since I was seven. Mother has been training me. Oh, Mother will be so excited!"

"This offer is dependent upon your mother's permission."

"Oh, she will say yes. I know she will. She will think this a grand opportunity for me. And, of course, it is. When do we leave?"

"When our coach is repaired. We received word this morning that the repaired wheel should be here sometime this afternoon. The blacksmith will then have to get it onto the coach. So hopefully, we will leave on the morrow."

The girl clasped her hands together and bounced on her toes. "Oh, I can hardly contain myself." Then she looked down at her splattered apron and worn gown. She looked back up, her expressive eyes having lost some of their joy. "But what shall I wear? I have one other dress, but 'tis not much better than this one."

Selena looked her up and down. "Well, you are a good bit shorter than I am. Still, your mother is a good seamstress, and you say you are good. I shall give your mother one of my gowns to take home when she leaves tonight. Together, the two of you should be able to alter it enough to fit you. Cut it up in any way you need and use the excess to make an extra bodice or even a gown for your younger sister."

"Oh, Lady Selena, you are too kind. You are certain you would not miss your gown?"

"I guarantee you, I will not miss the gown. I will ask Mistress Shadwell, my attendant, to pick something out for you. She will know what will work best. Now, you had best get back to work. I would not want your wage to be docked."

"No, milady, and thank you. Thank you!"

Selena smiled as the girl darted away. She had no doubt she had made a wise decision. This would be a grand adventure for the girl, and Selena meant to give her a glowing reference to help her secure work beyond that of scullery maid.

"You made that young poppy happy," Mistress Sermon said, linking her arm with Selena. "Between the two of us, we are setting the Burke women on new and hopefully brighter paths."

Selena smiled at the older woman. "Mistress Sermon, I cannot tell you how glad I am our paths have crossed. I feel we are kindred spirits."

"So we are, my dear, but I hope you will never become as belligerent as I am. I bully people. Especially my nephew. Cannot seem to help it. You on the other hand, are so gracious in your bullying, no one, other than perhaps your brother, even knows they are being bullied."

Selena laughed. "I do my best not to offend, but too often my best is not good enough. Mayhap my Aunt Rowena will teach me to overcome my impetuosity."

Mistress Sermon shook her head. "I do hope not. I hate to think of anything changing you. Continue to be true to what you know in your heart is right, and you will be happy. Ah, now I hear the children laughing. Let us see what they are about."

Strolling toward the sound of laughter, Selena thought about Mistress Sermon's words. If she allowed her Aunt Rowena to make her into a lady, would she be happy? But if she did not, would she continue to be a disappointment to her mother? What a dilemma. Could she be blamed that she wanted to put off getting to Whimbrel as long as possible? No matter what the outcome, either she or her mother would end up unhappy.

⚜ ⚜ ⚜ ⚜

Reginald had enjoyed his tour of Mere Manse, but he enjoyed even more being back with Amaryllis. Seated next to him at the dinner table, she looked rested, less frightened, and her bright greeting had set his head to spinning. Amaryllis, the children, and the numerous adults accompanying the children in their various activities all delighted in the bright, sunny morning and had taken advantage of another day of rest to explore the more extensive gardens extending out toward the lake.

"'Twas a lovely walk," Amaryllis said, "and the children had the opportunity to run and stretch their legs. I feel certain they will have no trouble settling down to their naps this afternoon."

"Who is with them now?" Reginald asked. He wanted no more incidents. The children must be safely guarded at all times – even in the house.

"Betty and Esmeralda and Norwood. They are having their dinner in the nursery, then Betty will put the children down for their naps. Esmeralda is to stay with them with Norwood outside the door. Betty is training Goody Burke to act as Mistress Sermon's maid while Betty is away with us. Oh, and your sister has hired Goody Burke's daughter, Bess, to come with us to act as my maid and to help Betty with the children."

Reginald glanced at his sister. She was involved in a conversation with Toms about the basic qualities of coach horses. So she had hired Burke's daughter to go with them. He wondered what had caused her to do that. Between Betty and Esmeralda, he doubted they needed any additional help, but no doubt something about the girl had stirred Selena's sympathy. It meant one more mouth to feed, and a more crowded coach, but he would not try to thwart Selena. It would do no good. She would have her way in the end. At least they would not be having to feed Handle. As Handle's leg seemed to be mending nicely, and a more competent surgeon was not needed to reset it, Toms had recommended they leave Handle at Mere Manse. Esmeralda could pick him up on her return trip to Rygate.

Reginald was beginning to think once they reached Derby, he would not be able to continue on to Whimbrel until his father sent him additional funds. He was not at this point running low, but he knew he still had a number of expenditures ahead of them. He could not be more pleased they would be staying with the Crosslys. Not only would they not have to put up in a costly inn, they could delay as long as they needed until his father sent him the funds.

He turned back to Amaryllis. "What of Betty? How does she fare?"

"Her jaw is a tad swollen, but she says she feels fine. She is still very angry. I do believe did she encounter Farr again, and did she have a gun, she would shoot him on the spot."

"And so he would deserve it," Mistress Sermon said, joining their conversation. "I would do the same, except neither Betty nor I know what the man looks like."

"At least we have a good description of him," Reginald said.

"True. But men can change their appearance. Still, I know you will have your guard up."

"That we will," Reginald stated adamantly. "That we will."

Amaryllis switched the conversation to a lighter subject, the flowering shrubs and bushes she had seen on their walk, and Reginald was pleased she chose not to dwell on Charlie's brush with death. When dinner ended and the women adjourned to the parlor, Reginald leaned back in his chair, took a sip of brandy and again thanked Toms for his generosity in accompanying them to Leicester.

"Wish I could go all the way to Derby with you. Just to be sure. But unfortunately, I have obligations I cannot ignore."

"Nay, please no apologies. You are doing so much. When we leave Leicester, we will be but two days on the road without your additional support. Selena has already written to our aunt and uncle and to the Crosslys so they know we are coming. We will be cautious and will stay alert, but I cannot think the man will make another attempt. Not when he knows we are wary."

"Most likely you are right. One has to wonder what kind of man would try to kill a child. But then, one must wonder what kind of woman would hire such a man."

"Yes, I will be glad when Charlie is safely with his grandfather."

"Mister Toms." Haines said from the doorway.

"Yes, Haines."

"Sir, a messenger has arrived for Mister D'Arcy. The man awaits him in the hall."

Reginald was immediately on his feet. "Ah ha, mayhap the wheel has arrived."

He and Toms both hurried to the hall to find the D'Arcy outrider, Crouch, waiting. "Crouch!" Reginald said. "Good to see you again. I trust you met up with Billings?"

"Yes, Master D'Arcy. I delivered your message to the Girouards. Most disappointed they were. Said they had been looking forward to hearing news of your family. But they were understanding. Anyway, I was headed back when my horse went lame. Horseshoe nail went right into the tender part of his hoof. Naught I could do but walk him to the nearest smith. Night fell, and I had to await the morning before I could get the smith to open his shop. Smith pulled out the nail and put on a new shoe. By that time I feared you would be worrying, but my horse was still a bit sore so I dared not press him. Then who should I see coming down the road but Billings. He told me all, and said you thought 'twould be best did I stay with him until the wheel was mended, in case we ran into any difficulties, and I was needed to take a message to you. So anyway, here I am, and Billings said to tell you he and the smith are even now on their way to put the wheel back on the coach."

"Splendid. Good work, Crouch. You ride on back to the coach and tell Billings I am on my way. I will get my horse saddled and be there in no time."

"I will go with you," Toms said.

Reginald frowned. "I suppose I best tell Selena. She will want to go. Want to thank the Wirths again. We will have to wait for her to change."

"You go ahead," Toms said. "I will tell Lady Selena and wait to escort her."

"Ah, Toms, you are indeed a good man," Reginald said, clapping his host on the shoulder before hurrying off to the stables.

184

Chapter 23

Amaryllis gave Mistress Sermon a warm embrace before turning and allowing Reginald to hand her up into the coach. They were finally to be on their way. The lovely coach was scratched on one side, but the coachman had cleaned the inside until it gleamed and not a speck of dust appeared on the plushly cushioned seats. Amaryllis took her place on the seat next to Esmeralda with Charlie in between them. Betty, Bess, and Tabitha sat across from them. Fate was situated on Bess's lap, there being little room on the flooring for him with two more pairs of feet taking up room.

Goody Burke looked in the door at her daughter. "Now you be a good girl, Bess. Do all that Mistress Bowdon and Lady Selena tell you to do."

"I will, Mother," the girl promised, her blue eyes glowing with excitement. Her riotous hair tucked under a crisp new cap, and her pale blue gown with neat bodice over a clean but slightly yellowed shift set off her clear complexion and bright, pink cheeks. Amaryllis guessed mother and daughter had stayed up most of the night remaking one of Selena's gown to fit the girl's smaller and more youthful figure, but both had been back at the house at the crack of dawn, Bess ready for the journey, her mother to help Mistress Sermon with her toilet and to see to her breakfast. Betty had confided to Amaryllis that she thought Goody Burke to be most competent and was certain Mistress Sermon would be satisfied with her work.

Goody Burke stepped back and Norwood closed the door to the coach. Handle, leaning on his crutches, stood to the side. He looked disappointed he would not be accompanying them. Amaryllis felt bad that his injury was due to the horrid man's attempt to kill Charlie – due to her dreadful aunt's hateful ambitions. How they would ever prove their suspicions against her aunt, she could not hazard, but that would not matter once Charlie was safe with his grandfather.

Looking out the window, she saw Selena give Mistress Sermon a long embrace. The older woman clung to Selena for another moment, then giving her a tearful smile, said, "Oh, mount up, gel, mount up. You lit up my life with your brief stay. Write to me."

Swinging up onto her saddle as easily as any male, Selena bent over to take Mistress Sermon's hand. "I will write soon. And our visit with you will always be a cherished memory."

Mistress Sermon nodded and stepped back. The coachman whistled to the horses, and with a slight jerk, the coach started to roll. "Oh my," Bess said. "Never did I dream I would e'er be riding in such a fine coach." She looked at Betty, then at Amaryllis. "Fact is, I have ne'er even ridden in so much as a cart." She then clapped a hand over her mouth, and her blue eyes grew round. "Mayhap I am not supposed to speak."

Amaryllis laughed. "Nay, Bess, you may speak. However, you are in training to be a lady's maid, so you need mind how you speak. Be careful not to blather or be loose-tongued."

"Yes, Mistress Bowdon," the girl said.

"Pay heed to Betty and to Mistress Shadwell. They will give you good directions."

Betty patted the younger girl on the shoulder. "You are among friends here. You need have no fears. Relax and enjoy your grand adventure."

Bess turned to Betty and smiled. "Thank you. I will do my best to learn all I can from you and from Mistress Shadwell."

"You will do fine, Bess," Esmeralda said. "I can tell you have been properly raised. And luck was with you the day you caught Lady Selena's eye. She is a good judge of character. She will see you have a promising future. Now, as Betty says, enjoy yourself, but do you start to feel ill, do let us know. The rocking of the coach, especially when you are riding backwards, has been known to make some people ill. Better we stop before any accidents happen."

"Oh, yes, Mistress Shadwell. I will do as you bid."

The girl was so eager to please, Amaryllis thought. Young to be leaving home, only thirteen, but many children were apprenticed at even younger ages. At least Bess would be with gentle, caring people. And did the child prove a fast learner, Amaryllis thought she might decide to keep her on as her maid once she and Reggie were married. The thought of Reginald brought a smile to her lips. They had had no time alone since he returned from the Wirths with the coach, but his eyes had spoken volumes. The way he looked at her, the way his eyes sought her lips. She could almost feel his lips on hers. Thinking of his kiss, she started to put her fingertips to her mouth, but at the last moment, controlled herself. As of yet, no one knew of their betrothal. Until Charlie was safe, she wanted all attention concentrated on him.

※ ※ ※ ※

Reginald was glad to be on the road. He had enjoyed their sojourn at Toms's manor. It had given him the chance to express his love to Amaryllis. He was still amazed that such an adorable, sweet, and beguiling creature as Amaryllis could have fallen in love with him, but he meant not to question it. That she stirred longings in him he had never before experienced, that her kisses left him breathless and befuddled, that her smile set his heart to thumping wildly leaving him near mad with desire was a thrilling new experience.

He wanted nothing so much as to get Charlie safely to the boy's aunt. Then his betrothal to Amaryllis could be announced. He meant to marry her as soon as arrangements could be made. He had no intention of waiting six months until her mourning period was over. No, he could not live that long without making her his own. They could have a quiet ceremony at the Crosslys', she could go with him to Whimbrel to deliver Selena, then they could go to his estate and set up housekeeping. To think, he had thought having to spend time at his estate would be tantamount to being thrown into debtor's prison, when now, the idea of having Amaryllis all to himself with no interference from family or friends seemed like a dream come true.

Reining in Sherard's prancing about – the horse was making it known he was eager for a good run – Reginald wondered if the man known to him as Farr had given up, or would he try again to kill Charlie. Having Toms and his two outriders with them, along with Crouch and Billings, gave Reginald a secure feeling. What could one man do against such a force? All the same, the man was shrewd and imaginative. He had managed to whittle down the spokes on the coach wheel. He had worked his way onto the manor grounds. If he was still out there, Reginald had no doubt he was hatching another scheme.

Selena rode up beside him and, breaking into his reverie, said, "I suppose you reimbursed the Wirths and Barlows for their care of Pit and Mills, our coach, and our horses. What we would have done without them I cannot imagine. And so I told Goody Wirth."

"Yes. I meant to tell you last night, but with all the arrangements to make for us to be ready to leave this morning, it slipped my mind. I pressed as much on Goodman Wirth and Goodman Barlow as I could. I believe because Toms was with us, they were hesitant about accepting more than what they believed covered their expenses. They would not want their landlord to think they were taking advantage of us despite my effort to express our gratitude."

"I thought as much. I tried to give Goody Wirth a sovereign. Tried to tell her it was my own special thanks for all the extra work we put her to, but she would not have it. So when I said goodbye to Granny Wirth, I slipped it into her pocket. I think she knew what I had done, but she said naught. Hopefully when she makes a show of finding it, the Wirths will not be offended, but will use it to give themselves a treat. Buy something they might not otherwise buy."

Reginald chuckled. "That's my Selena. Never one to be thwarted."

"What are you two consorting about?" Toms asked, riding up beside them.

"We were discussing your tenants, the Wirths and the Barlows," Reginald answered. "They are fine people. Cannot think how we would have fared had they not come to our aid."

"Aye, were all my tenants as hardworking and forward-thinking, I would not be considering enclosing the common and running a few more head of cattle on it."

Reginald looked at him in surprise and Selena said, "Enclose the common? What would your tenants and the villagers and cottagers who depend on the common to graze their animals do? How would they manage?"

Toms thinned his lips. "That is an issue. I know well it would wreck hardship on many. At the same time, the income from the manor has gone steadily down the past five years, and I will soon be taking on a wife and at some point, we will be starting a nursery. I will have children I must provide for. Was it not for the income from my father's financial investments, I would be operating at a loss. The most profitable industry in Northamptonshire is the manufacture of shoes and boots. Hides are profitable. I have no wish to turn any of my tenants off their land or to unfairly increase their rents as their leases come up for renewal. That would be worse than enclosing the common." He shrugged. "Ten of my tenants are in the arrears.

"When my father did away with the open-field farming …"

"Do you mean the three or four large fields with parallel strips of land belonging to individual tenants, and with certain strips or fields left fallow for grazing?" Selena asked.

Reginald understood her need for clarification. Her only knowledge, his, too, for that matter, of such field systems came from what they gleaned in listening to their father talk of their mother's estates that he had been managing over the years. Their home, Rygate, had never had open field farming. Surrey soils and landscape had never been conducive to open-field farming. It was better suited to sheep farming, forest management, and fruit and vegetable gardening made profitable by supplying the ever-growing London market. Their father had also invested in a local paper mill and a gunpowder mill to augment the family income. Rygate had far fewer tenants than Toms's Mere Manse, but Reginald had no idea whether any tenants were in arrears. His interest in the day-to-day running of the estate had been minimal at best.

"Yes, Lady Selena," Toms answered. "You described open-field farming perfectly. It is uneconomical, not to mention wasteful, what with the ditches and footpaths between the strips using up arable land. To improve production, Father consolidated each tenant's acreage into single farms, compact holdings, so the farming would be more efficient, no time wasted going from a strip in one field to a strip in another. He left it up to each tenant whether he wanted to build fences or grow hedges around his acreage, or whether he wanted to continue to farm or perhaps switch to pasturing sheep or cattle. Father divided the acreage up mostly by a lottery system, but the thing is, some tenants got better land than others.

"Still, farmers like the Wirths and Barlows have worked hard and made changes where necessary. The Wirths started growing more clover and grazing more dairy cows on their less productive acreage. They planted turnips and other root crops to feed the cattle over the winter. Now they have a thriving, and I do believe, growing dairy production. Where their land is more arable, they have continued to plant wheat and other grains, and Wirth and Barlow are both experimenting with hops. Fact is, I am thinking of putting some of my demesne land into hops.

"The Barlows' land is good wheat-growing land. Not the best for malt, but Goody Barlow makes as good an ale as can be found in these parts, and the inn in the village, as well as a number of tenants, are ever ready to purchase her overstock."

"You are saying your tenants in arrears are not adapting as well?" Reginald asked.

Toms nodded. "Aye, Asa Holder, he is the barber's older brother — being the elder son, he inherited the land tenure. He will not change his ways. He has good land, his wheat does well, his peas, oats, barley do well, but he will ever leave a section fallow rather than planting it in clover. I have yet to convince him the merits of growing turnips and overwintering more of his cattle. I have others near as stubborn. They still want to farm as their fathers farmed. Then if they need to reroof their home, or build a new barn, they go into debt and cannot pay their rent."

He shook his head. "Well, I will not be making a decision on the common today. Let us speak of cheerier subjects."

"Yes," Selena said. "Tell me about that new mare you bought. What are your plans for her? She has good lines, and a nice, small head."

With Toms and Selena engaged in horse talk, Reginald dropped back to concentrate on the previous discussion. The more he learned about the intricacies of estate management, the more he realized he needed to learn. He would soon be taking a wife, and he had no idea what the income from his estate would be. He had no idea what the estate house was like. He had been there only once, and that was in his early youth. He had near no memory of it. It had seemed large and dark and cold. He had no memory of the grounds. Was there a garden for Amaryllis to enjoy? What of the stables? And what would he do for a coach? The staff? Surely it had but a skeleton staff since only the steward lived there. They would need to hire servants. He hoped Amaryllis would know how to go about interviewing the needed help. Hoped she would know what servants they would need. Surely she would know that. She had run her father's household for a number of years after the death of her mother and then that of her stepmother.

He also had no idea what Amaryllis might bring to the marriage. What was her dowry? Not that it mattered. He loved her and would not care if she had not a penny to her name. His parents would care, but once they met Amaryllis, they would understand his love for her, understand why he had no intention of delaying his marriage to her. Her nearness drove him mad with desire, but his love for her was not just physical. He had fallen in love with her inner soul. Other than his mother, he had never known such a sweet, unselfish, unpretentious person. The women he had met at court, and even the daughters of the local gentry, were so full of themselves, so grasping. But Amaryllis. She was so unspoiled, so unselfconscious, and so lovely, though he believed she was unaware of her great beauty.

He dropped back to peer in the window of the coach and to ask Amaryllis if all was well. Her smile was near his undoing. He almost lost control of Sherard. The horse needed a good run. Laughing at himself, he glanced over his shoulder at Crouch and Billings. They both looked alert, and he could see they had their pistols at the ready. Toms's two outriders were leading the procession. They, too, looked as though they could handle themselves well if the need arose. Well, did all go as planned, and did they encounter no more delays, counting this day, they should be but five more days on the road, four nights. The last two days, without Toms's additional escort, could be worrisome, but he was determined to take the utmost precautions. Farr would not get another chance at killing Charlie.

Chapter 24

His eyes narrowed, his face hidden beneath his new low-crown, boater-shaped hat that he had helped himself to off a sleeping drunk the previous night, Felton watched the D'Arcy coach pass into Northampton. He had no immediate need to follow it. That coach would be easy enough to find. The D'Arcys would be staying at one of the best inns. That would narrow his search. What bothered him was the number of outriders guarding the coach, two in front, two in the rear. Plus, it looked like the squire from Mere Manse had joined them. They now had but one footman, though. Still, he had not planned on such a force. And those outriders were armed.

He knew his only chance now to get at the boy was to attack the coach. For that he would need a goodly number of men, the right locale, and some kind of surprise. Where to get the men was his biggest dilemma. He had to find the right element. Desperate men. Men with naught to lose. Hard-riding highwaymen would be best, but he would be unlikely to encounter such men. Yes, they were desperate. But they were men of some property. At least, they had horses. Some were ex-cavalrymen, but with no war to fight, they had no means of support. Some were quality folk who had lost their homes during the war and had never been able to recoup their losses. Those men would not be hanging about places where the law might become suspicious of them.

No, what he needed were footpads. No more than he would, they would not have guns. Men of his ilk could not afford guns or ammunition. But knives and heavy cudgels could be as deadly when properly used. An attack at dusk or in a forested area with six to ten men could well do the trick. Did the men keep the outriders busy, all he had to do was get the boy out of the coach and slit his throat. He had no wish to harm any of the others, but the boy had to die. He had to complete his task. He had spent too much of Mistress Bowdon's coin. He had sold her horse. Sold the horses he had traded for. And was soon to sell the saddle. He planned to use the money for the saddle to buy a stage ticket to Derby. That city should be large enough to enable him to find some men ready and willing to seek their fortune by attacking the D'Arcy coach.

He doubted any of the D'Arcy party would recognize him. He had his new hat, he had bought new clothes from a second-hand shop, had changed his stockings, and had paid for a shave and a haircut. He would guess he could walk right in amongst them, and they would never be the wiser. But then, none of them had really seen him. The day before, he had ridden right past the two outriders taking the wheel back to the D'Arcy coach, and even before he had changed his appearance, they had not recognized him. Well, he meant to learn what he could of their plans, but on the morrow, he would be boarding the stage for Derby. Let them think he had given up. Let them think they had nothing to worry about. The longer he delayed the attack, the more likely they were to let their guard down.

❦ ❦ ❦ ❦

Esmeralda sat staring at the pen and paper before her. She needed to write Lord and Lady Rygate, yet she was not sure how she should phrase things. She decided part of her problem was her weariness. The day had been long. Though roomier than most coaches, with so many people occupying it, even the D'Arcy coach had become stuffy and stifling. The stop for dinner had been brief. Toms had notified the tavern in advance that they would be stopping there, and a meal had been ready and waiting for them. It had been plentiful if not particularly savory. After dinner, they had managed but a short walk to stretch their legs before Reginald had them back in the coach. He was determined they would not be on the road after dark. No sooner did the coachman, Pit, inform him the horses were baited, and he was ushering them back into the coach.

Fortunately, the children drifted into their naps, and soon Bess and then Betty were nodding. Esmeralda had closed her eyes and hoped to drop off to sleep, but the memory of the coach overturning kept recurring, and she had been unable to doze. Amaryllis sat with her eyes closed, but whether she slept, Esmeralda could not tell. She suspected a relationship was developing between the girl and Reginald. Certainly Reginald had been smitten with Amaryllis from their first meeting. Esmeralda could understand why. Amaryllis was lovely, well-mannered, gentle, and modest. All admirable characteristics. Still, Esmeralda hesitated to write anything to Lord and Lady Rygate that might hint Reginald had formed an attachment. If he had, that would be his duty to inform his parents. She did need to inform them the girl was unexceptional, and they should have no fear Lady Selena was succoring a maid of questionable virtue.

Had she known any physical risk to Lady Selena or Reginald might come from their assisting Amaryllis and her siblings, she would have done her best to dissuade them from offering their aid. However, she doubted she could have convinced either Selena or Reginald to forego their plans. Whether to tell Lord and Lady Rygate about the possible danger to her charges was a different question. She knew Selena had written to tell them of the trouble with the coach wheel, but she doubted Selena had mentioned the suspected cause of the wheel breakage.

In the end, she decided she would write one letter to Lord Rygate telling him all that had transpired, including the fact that at present, they had a substantial escort. She would write a second letter to Lady Rygate. In that letter, she would praise Selena. She would tell Lady Rygate that Selena's behavior from manners to dress had been most pleasing. That would make Lady Rygate happy, and hopefully would keep her from worrying. 'Twould not do to have the dear lady upset. For a moment she thought about putting off writing the letters until the following evening when they were at Toms's hunting lodge, but then, posting the letters would be delayed. Better to write them and post them on the morrow. Then off to bed.

She was grateful she was not having to see to the children or to Amaryllis. Betty and Bess were quite capable of seeing to their needs. She had needed but to lay out Selena's dress, have water ready for her to wash, then arrange her hair, and send her off to enjoy supper with Toms, Reginald, and Amaryllis. She had then been able to enjoy a quiet supper by herself before settling down to write her letters. Well, the sooner she finished them, the sooner she could settle onto her cot. Selena insisted she not wait up for her. Selena was a considerate girl. But goodness, how trouble of one sort or another seemed to follow her about.

Amaryllis sat across the table from Reginald and tried to concentrate on the conversation that buzzed around her, but her thoughts kept darting back to the kiss Reginald had managed to give her before Toms and then Selena arrived in the private dining chamber. Reginald had been waiting outside her door to escort her down stairs to supper. The Blue Cow Inn was far superior to the inn in Albertine. Her room, which the D'Arcys were paying for, was most comfortable. The bed was large enough for her and the children, and Bess and Betty each had their own cots. She was pleased Reginald had promised to have one of the outriders stationed outside their door all night. They would work in shifts. Every precaution was being taken to keep Charlie safe.

"Now you relax," Reginald said when he escorted her down the stairs. "No one can get to Charlie. He is safe and secure. We have had a long day. Let us enjoy what we can of the evening before we must retire that we may be up early on the morrow."

Upon opening the door to the dining chamber and finding it empty, Reginald had swept her into his arms and gently kissed her. Hearing footsteps, they broke apart as Toms opened the door. "Ah, I see Lady Selena is not yet here," he said. "Thought I might be holding up supper. Not having my valet with me, I found I was all thumbs when I tried to change my waistcoat."

"Happy to have Nye help you," Reginald offered. "Not sure how I would manage without him. He makes certain I am presentable."

Like Toms, Reginald had changed coat and waistcoat, and had donned a clean shirt before coming down to supper. Amaryllis had changed into the same blue skirt hitched up to expose a yellow petticoat and the close-fitting, blue bodice trimmed in yellow over the cream-colored, chemise gown she had worn both nights at Mere Manse. Selena was certainly generous with the number of gowns she had given her, and she had offered to give her yet another one this evening, but Amaryllis had refused the offer.

"Nay, Selena, you have given me too many already. I have more than enough to last me until we reach the Crosslys' home."

Selena had laughed. "Oh, the more I can give to you, the fewer I have to sort through once I get to Aunt Rowena's. Mother would insist I have an entirely new wardrobe. I cannot say I find the new gowns particularly comfortable. Fortunately, I managed to pack several of my favorite gowns, including two sturdy gowns for walking. And I have my walking shoes as well."

Amaryllis wondered how Selena's aunt was ever going to change Selena. She also wondered if she would like Selena to change. Selena was such a caring, loving person. So she was not always ladylike, did it matter so much?

Selena arrived shortly after Toms, and soon the meal was begun. Toms and Selena chatted about the day, the horses, the condition of the road, and the food they were enjoying. Supper was much more tasty than their dinner. But Amaryllis kept wanting to put her fingertips to her lips. She wanted to feel Reginald's kiss. She had never dreamed a kiss could set her spine to tingling, her stomach to churning, and her pulse to racing. She loved looking at Reginald. He was so handsome. She could get lost in his dark eyes that looked at her with a longing she well understood, for she felt the same. He had said fate had brought them together, and she could not help but believe he was right.

She had not met a great number of men in her twenty years of life, but of those she had known, none had stirred even the faintest passion in her. But from the first moment she saw Reginald D'Arcy, she had been drawn to him. His concern for her and her siblings added to the attraction. She also enjoyed his merry humor, loved his deep-throated chuckle. She even liked the relationship he had with his sister, the gentle bantering between them. Fact was, she could not think of a single thing about Reginald D'Arcy that she did not find estimable.

"Do you not agree, Amaryllis?"

Realizing Selena had asked her a question, Amaryllis turned to her and said, "I do beg your pardon, Selena, I fear I was wool-gathering. What did you ask me?"

Selena laughed and repeated her question. "I said do you not think we are very lucky to have Betty and Bess with us? They are both so good with Tabitha and Charlie, and with Fate."

"Oh, yes. Betty is so competent, and Bess is so eager to learn. The children are already fond of both of them. And Bess is very good with your little Fate. She kept him on her lap almost the entire day. He just curled up and seemed most content. Slept when the children slept, but was ready to play and be petted when they gave him any attention."

"He is quite the little dear," Selena said. "I dread to think what might have happened had he not attacked Farr. I am so relieved his leg was not reinjured in the struggle."

"Amazes me," Toms interposed, "how well he gets around with that splint on his hind leg. He trots along like it is his normal leg."

Her eyes soft, Selena smiled. "Yes, he has adapted to the splint very well. If you could have seen the poor little guy when we found him by the roadside. Skin and bones, covered in mud, eyes full of pain. Near broke my heart. Now that he is getting enough to eat, he is filling out, his eyes are bright, and his tail is always ready with a wag." She looked at her brother. "Even Reggie has learned to like him. Have you not?"

"I never disliked him. I disliked the delay." He looked at Amaryllis. "But now I must say, I cannot be more happy about the delay."

Toms chuckled. "I have to say I am also happy you were delayed. Otherwise, we might never have met. That would not only be my loss, but Auntie Jane would have been deprived of one of the greatest pleasures she has had in many a year. For so she has told me."

"Your aunt is a true delight, Mister Toms," Selena said with a broad smile. "Meeting her has been a highlight for me as well. And so I told her."

"Much as I would like to continue our evening with a game of whist or some such," Reginald interrupted, "but are we to be up and off with the dawn tomorrow, I think 'tis best we all go to bed. Selena is not one for early rising."

Selena nodded. "Aye, Reggie is right. Once I am up, I am quickly ready. 'Tis the getting up I cannot care for. So, off to bed. I hope those clouds that were gathering this afternoon are not an indication of rain. All the same, I mean to have my waxed woolen cape handy."

"Best have your canvas leggings at the ready, also," Reginald said. "'Twould be even better would you ride in the coach does it rain."

Selena made a face at him. "Nay, it will be miserable enough in the coach if it rains, what with only one window to see out, the other one needing to be shuttered. Wish we could have replaced the broken glass in the other window. A curse on Farr."

Amaryllis, too, wished they could have had the window pane replaced. She hated that Farr had been able to damage the wheel and cause the coach to turn over thereby breaking the glass window. 'Twas but luck no one had been terribly injured, no one had died. At least the weather had been pleasant, and the road hard packed enough the dust had been minimal, so they had been able to leave the window shutters open. But did it rain on the morrow, the window would have to be shuttered. It would make the interior terribly dark. She had often traveled in the dark in her father's coach. Such travel often led to a queasy stomach. She decided she could easily become spoiled by the D'Arcys' coach with its glass windows.

She wondered if she and Reginald might be able to afford such a coach once they were married. Married. She was to marry Reginald D'Arcy. Her heart doing another little flip, she took Reginald's proffered arm as he turned to escort her up the stairs to her room. Toms and Selena both said good night as they entered their rooms. She wished Reginald could linger with her outside her door, but the outrider, Billings, was there on his watch. Reginald could do naught but wish her sweet dreams and stride away to his room.

Amaryllis was surprised when she opened her door to find both Betty and Bess had waited up for her. "Oh, you should be sleeping. You have had a tiring day."

"No more so than you," Betty said. "And this seems the perfect time to give Bess lessons in helping you prepare for bed."

"I suppose you are right. I could use help getting out of this gown."

"Yes, then when you are in your robe, I would show Bess about combing out your hair and braiding it for the night."

Amaryllis was happy to let the two young women minister to her. She was tired, and she wanted to let her thoughts linger on Reginald. She wondered when they would again have private time together. She had much to tell him. And oh, how she longed to feel his arms about her, to feel his lips on hers. She let Bess and Betty tuck her into bed next to her sleeping brother and sister. Betty then blew out the candles, and the room went dark. Time for those sweet dreams Reginald had wished her.

Chapter 25

Having enjoyed a sound night's sleep at the Northampton's Blue Cow Inn, Reginald was up and getting his party moving early. Selena had complained as usual at the early hour, but she had been ready on time, and they had set out with nary a hitch. They reached Toms's hunting lodge none too soon to Reginald's thinking. The day had been miserable, nothing but a light rain from morning till evening – thankfully, not heavy enough rain to cause the coach to bog down, but vexing all the same. Their halt for dinner had given them a brief respite, but despite his waxed woolen cape, he felt damp. However, upon arriving at the lodge, his spirits revived. He saw a chance to finally be alone with Amaryllis. After Selena's day in the rain, Esmeralda was insisting she have a long soak in a hot bath. Let the postilion see to Brigantia.

"If Mills cannot properly see to your horse," Esmeralda said, "I cannot see why your father keeps him on his staff. He should hire someone who knows something about horses."

Selena's light laughter floated out over the courtyard. "You win, Esmeralda. A tub of hot water it is." She looked at Toms. "You may have to delay supper."

"Enjoy your soak," Toms said. "I need to have a look at my horse. I do think he was favoring his back left a bit. A later supper is for the best."

Reginald smiled. With Toms busy in the stable, Selena in the tub, and the children being cared for by Betty, he could have Amaryllis to himself. Bidding Nye see to Sherard, he hurried after Amaryllis. Whispering to her that she should join him once she was changed, he hurried his own ablutions that he might be at hand when she emerged from her room. Pacing restlessly outside her bedchamber, he pivoted when he heard the door open and Amaryllis emerged.

Gads, she was lovely. She took his breath away. She was wearing a plain, peach-colored gown with few frills. The close-fitting bodice was open to the waist to reveal cream-colored, laced stays. The skirt was gathered onto the bodice in close pleats, and the full sleeves, ending at the elbows, were trimmed with a matching lace. Her golden curls peeped out from under a lacy cornet with lappets falling behind her shoulders. Her heavenly, blue eyes, glistening in the dim light cast by the flickering candles stuck on spikes set on protrusions sticking out from the cold stone walls, lit up upon seeing him, and a vibrant smile swept across her face.

Stepping forward, he clasped her hands in his. "You look glorious," he said.

She looked down and back up. "I am not dressed too plainly? This is the only gown I brought with me. I have no other but my travel wear. And of course, the two gowns and the riding costume Selena gave me, but the pink is too dressy, and I have worn the blue gown three nights in a row. I thought perhaps a change was in order."

"Have no fear, you look divine. Besides, this is a hunting lodge. I think we will find little formality here. But come, let us find the parlor."

Taking her arm, he steered her down the stairs and into the hall. A low fire burned in a grate in the center of the room, the smoke wafting upward into the high beamed ceiling. The walls were hung with painted canvases, and cushioned benches lined the walls of the room. A servant hurrying past with an armload of linen directed them to a door that opened into the solar.

"I have to ask Toms how old this lodge is," Reginald said. "I would guess it is as old as the Hinghams' keep, if not older."

"May well have an interesting history," Amaryllis said.

Nodding in agreement as they entered the solar, Reginald was pleased by the coziness of the room. A small table had been set for four. A serving woman finished placing napkins on the table, bobbed a curtsey and asked if they might like something to drink.

He looked at Amaryllis and said, "Mulled wine for Mistress Bowdon." When she smiled, agreeing to his choice for her, he added, "and a brandy for me, do you have it."

"Aye, I will see to them," the woman said, and bobbing another curtsey, left to do as bid.

"Alone at last," Reginald said, sweeping Amaryllis into his arms. He kissed her gently, his lips lingering softly on her sweet lower lip. As she eagerly responded to his ardor, he tightened his embrace and deepened the kiss. His heart hammering in his chest, his head in a swirl, he let his need for Amaryllis overrule his senses. His hand went to her breast, so soft and supple. His desire mounting, he loosened his embrace of her enough that his lips could travel down her neck to kiss the sweet mounds exposed above her bodice. Her squeak and sudden inhalation stirred him even more. He ached for her, but the sudden crack of a log in the hearth jarred him enough that common sense returned. He must do nothing to besmirch Amaryllis's reputation. A servant, or anyone, could walk in at any moment. With extreme effort, he reined in his desire and slowly loosened his hold.

Looking up at him, her eyes large and dreamy, Amaryllis said, "Oh, my, I never dreamed a kiss, and an embrace could be so thrilling."

"To be honest," he said, "neither did I. You, my dear sweet love, do things to me nobody else has ever done. Naught but looking at you sets my heart to hammering and my head to spinning. Gads, but I cannot wait until we are wed." Seeing her shiver, he wanted to again take her into his arms to warm her up. Instead, he led her over to the hearth.

"Your room is comfortable?" he asked, taking a poker to stir up the fire. His effort caused a log to drop with a little flutter of sparks into the flames.

"Yes, quite comfortable. This seems rather a large lodge, does it not."

"Been added onto, I do think." He frowned. "I wish I could give you some idea of what to expect at my estate house, but I fear I cannot."

Taking his hand, she said, "I am certain should anything be amiss, we can set it to rights. We have made no mention of my marriage portion." She waved her hand in front of him when he started to protest that her portion was unimportant to him. "Nay, it should be discussed. It is quite substantial I believe. At least I have always thought it so, but I have naught to compare it to. My father's man of business, not my uncle, is in charge of dispensing it when I marry. At the time of my marriage, I receive five thousand pounds, and I am to receive three hundred pounds a year until Charlie reaches his majority and then it drops to one hundred a year for ten years."

Reginald gave a soft whistle then kissed the tip of her nose. "My dear, I ne'er expected such a liberal settlement. I love you, have loved you from the first moment I saw you, and did you have no dowry, it would matter not to me. However, it could well matter to my parents."

Smiling sweetly, she said, "I would expect it to matter to them. You are the son of an Earl. Rightfully, your parents will want to know you are not marrying a penniless waif."

"Oh, how I long to scoop you into my arms and smother you in kisses, you adorable angel, but no doubt the maid will return with our drinks at any moment." Even as he spoke, the door opened, and the house steward entered with their drinks.

"Mister D'Arcy, Mister Toms asked me to inform you he will be down shortly. In the meantime, he says do you wish for anything, you are to let me know."

"For the moment," Reginald said, "these drinks are all we need. Thank you."

"Yes, sir," the steward said and withdrew from the room.

"To your health, my love," Reginald said, raising his glass.

"And to yours," Amaryllis answered before taking a sip from the amber-colored goblet.

They had not downed even half of their drinks before Toms arrived. Looking refreshed and in good spirits, he declared his horse had suffered nothing more than a pebble in the hoof. The pebble had been removed, and his horse would be ready to continue the journey on the morrow. "You will appreciate the Haycock Inn in Leicester," he said, accepting a goblet from his steward who had entered the solar almost on his master's heels. "Best inn I have ever stayed in other than ones in London."

"Give us a history of this lodge," Reginald said once the three of them had settled down at the table to await Selena.

Pursing his lips for a moment while rocking back and forth, he finally said, "Ah, this place does have the history. Originally, it was naught but the hall. William Rufus had it built. He liked to come to this area to hunt. He was mad for hunting. Seems to me, near all the Kings have been until Charles."

"Yes," Reginald said, "Charles likes his sports and his ladies, but hunting is not a priority with him. Ever so often he summons my father to join him. Usually to go to the races."

"Have you met the King?" Amaryllis asked.

"Oh, yes. Father was with him on the continent during his exile. They became very close. Fact is, my father often risked his life to pick up the bounty my Uncle Nate and his highwaymen collected to give to the King. Every time Father made a trip over here, he risked being caught and hanged for his participation in the fifty-one attempt to win back the throne for Charles."

"My father managed to remain neutral during the revolution and the Puritans' Commonwealth," Toms said. "He secretly sided with the Royalists, but he had no great love for Charles's father, though he was greatly distressed when Cromwell had him beheaded. Still, he believed the King often overstepped his rights."

"Indeed, a lot of people thought that way, but our family has always been loyal to the King. Over the centuries, the D'Arcy family has managed to be on the winning side repeatedly, and it has benefited us, I do admit.

"But do tell us more about this lodge. Someone added on to it."

"Should we not wait for Selena," Amaryllis said. "I believe she would find the history of the lodge interesting."

"Right you are," Toms said. "I told my steward to be on the watch for her and to have supper sent in as soon she arrives. In the meantime, I will regale you with a tale of the first time my father brought me here. Before the more comfortable changes were added." He shook his head and rolled his eyes. "I can tell you, this was a cold ..." He gave an exaggerated shiver. "Frigidly cold place. I was about twelve, I do think, and had been begging Father to take me hunting with him. Lord, how I wished he had not relented." Chuckling almost to himself, Toms described his first hunt on a frosty, autumn morning. His fall to the bone-chilling ground when his horse balked at a fence. His over-excited spotting of a prime buck that sent the deer racing away before anyone could get a good shot at him.

Reginald enjoyed watching Amaryllis laugh as Toms recounted his adventure. She was so beautiful, and yet her happy smile made her even more beautiful. How that was possible, he could not fathom, but there it was. He liked that she was such a caring person. Wanting to wait for Selena that Selena might learn the history of the lodge was one more example of her kind heart. Beauty and a sweet and generous nature – what else could a man want in a woman?

The steward opened the door, and Selena swept past him saying, "Have I kept you waiting an exorbitant time? Esmeralda would not let me out of the tub until I started to shrivel like a prune. I am near starved."

Toms rose when she entered and pulled out her chair. "Ah, dear lady, I have been torturing the lovely Mistress Bowdon and your brother with silly tales of my youth. I am certain they are pleased you have arrived to put an end to my sallies." Selena laughed and took her seat as Reginald and Amaryllis denied Toms's self-deprecating gibe.

"He has been telling us of his first hunting experience," Amaryllis said. "He means to impart the history of this lodge. We waited for you, thinking you might find it of interest."

"Indeed I shall," Selena said. "By the looks of the stone wall around the keep and the keep itself, I am thinking this lodge is much older than even the Hinghams' keep."

"You would be right there," Reginald said. "Toms tells us the hall was built by William Rufus. Now you know as much as we know."

"Your supper, Mister Toms," the steward announced from the door. He stepped aside and two maids entered with large trays laden with serving vessels.

Looking around, Toms said, "Splendid, splendid, set all on the table, and pour the wine. I feel certain Lady Selena must be dying of thirst."

Selena smiled. "I had a glass of wine while in the tub, but I am quite ready for another. 'Twill help me fall asleep tonight. I have no doubt Reggie will have us up early on the morrow."

"Hopefully, not so early as today," Toms said. "We have naught but fifteen or so miles to go tomorrow to reach Leicester, and the road from here to there is well-maintained."

"That is good news," Reginald said. "Now, if we could have no more rain."

"Aye, I am for that," Toms agreed before sweeping his hand over the table. "I think we may serve ourselves," he added, dismissing the servers. "Always informal here at Turnershure."

"Lovely," Selena said. "And as this heavenly smelling pottage is in front of me, might I ladle some up for each of you?" She peered into the vessel. "Looks to be a rabbit pottage."

"Dish away, sister," Reginald said, taking Amaryllis's plate and holding it next to the tureen. The meal was substantial; bread and cheese, halves of small chickens swimming in some kind of a gravy, fried cucumbers on a bed of wilted lettuce, a mincemeat pie, and the rabbit and parsnip pottage Selena was dishing onto the plates. Once everyone had been served and initial appetites satiated, Reginald asked Toms to tell them more about the lodge.

Toms took a sip of wine, set his goblet down, and with a nod, began. "Well, as I said, William the second, a most unpopular king, I might add, built this stone keep primarily for his hunting pleasure. 'Twas naught but the hall. I am guessing, as 'twas oft the case, the kitchen was a separate wooden building. Must have had barracks for the servants as well as stables. William's knights would have slept here in the keep with him. Ever ready to protect him.

"To my knowledge, it remained unchanged through several Kings. Then John decided to add on to it. My understanding is, he liked his comfort. He added this room that he might have a private place to retire with whichever mistress he had accompanying him. He added the kitchen that his food might be hot when it arrived at his table. And he added a small chapel. No idea why. He could not have been called religious. He often quarreled with the church."

"I have read King John was sly and cruel and devious," Selena said, "but I think initially he was more unpopular with the lords than with the common folk. A strong king is good for the people because he keeps his barons from abusing the serfs, but John's need for money to fight his wars in France, which he constantly lost, meant he had to keep raising taxes. That made the barons unhappy. And it made the people unhappy because the barons put more pressure on them to raise the needed funds. He had few of the capabilities of his father or grandfather."

"Very good," Toms said. "You know your history."

"Aye, she does," Reginald said. "She had the same tutor I had, and after I went away to school, she continued her education with our younger brothers' tutor."

"The history of England, and the world for that matter, has always been by far my favorite subject," Selena admitted. "But now, please, do go on with your tale of the lodge. I have interrupted you enough."

"No need to apologize, Lady Selena. Thanks to my Aunt Jane, I have learned to appreciate women's mental astuteness. Admire it, I would say. I am pleased to state my dear Clotilda has not only a quick wit, but she is well read and well versed in events of the day."

"She sounds delightful," Selena said. "I am sorry we had not the chance to meet her."

Reginald decided once he and Amaryllis were married and settled into their home, they would invite Toms and his future bride, Clotilda, to visit them. They owed Toms much for all his hospitality, not to mention his escort.

"I am afraid my education was rather more limited, Mister Toms," Amaryllis said, "but I do find the history of this lodge most interesting. Pray do continue."

Giving Amaryllis an admiring glance, Reginald said, "Yes, do continue."

Toms swallowed a bite of mincemeat pie before stating, "Let me see. We left off with King John. After John, little was done to improve the lodge. It was used so seldom, I suppose the other Kings found no need to add to it. 'Twas Henry VIII who finally decided to make the lodge more livable. He enjoyed his hunting, but also his dalliances. He added the upper bedchambers. He also expanded the kitchen, chapel, and this parlor. My great-grandfather bought it from King James who for some reason had no liking for it. My father is the one who added the hearths, which, believe me, make this old lodge far more comfortable than when I came here in my youth. Father also added the wainscoting in this room and bought all new furnishings for all the rooms but the chapel." He slowly shook his head. "Father, like King John, was not particularly religious. I cannot think he ever had a service held here. For that matter, nor have I."

"Well, I do say I appreciate the hearths," Reginald said, "especially after our day in the rain. 'Twas so nice to arrive in my chamber and find a warm fire glowing. And in here, the wood fire is so much more pleasant than coal."

Toms looked over at the fire. "Yes, but I do think I had best ring for my steward. The wood looks like it needs replenishing." He looked to Amaryllis and then Selena. "I hope neither of you are getting cold."

Both Selena and Amaryllis protested they were fine, but all the same, Toms rang for the steward who had a servant build up the fire. With the crackling of the fire and the soft glow of the candles, the wine began to give Reginald a feeling of complete contentment. He could not remember any time in his life he had ever felt so in harmony with the world. Amaryllis made him feel he could conquer the world. With her at his side, he knew he could turn Ardenstrath into a warm and friendly house. A prosperous, well-managed estate with happy tenants. Yes, Amaryllis would help him make his parents proud.

"You look like a contented cat," Selena said, interrupting his ruminating.

He patted his stomach. "Here I sit, well fed, and well wined. At peace with the world." He looked over at Amaryllis and smiled. "However, I can see by your eyes, Mistress Bowdon, that you are ready for your bed and some needed sleep. I suppose after this long day, we should all retire. We may not have as far to go tomorrow, but does it rain, it could be a tedious day."

"I agree with you," Toms said. "I admit to being relaxed but tired. Do we get a good night's sleep, we will all feel better in the morning. Tomorrow in Leicester at the Haycock Inn, we will be well feted. I admit, I shall miss your companionship when the following day, I must return to Mere Manse and prepare for the quarter session. I would prefer to see you safely to your final destination."

"You have done much to see to our safety and our comfort, Mister Toms," Selena said, rising as she spoke. "We could ask no more of you. But now, I admit to being ready for my bed."

Soon they were all traipsing up the stairs to their rooms. Reginald would have liked to give Amaryllis a good night kiss, but that was not possible. Sitting relaxing around the table, he had almost decided to tell Selena and Toms of his betrothal to Amaryllis, but he feared Amaryllis might think he had gone back on his word to wait until Charlie was safe to make their announcement. She wanted nothing to distract them from that goal. All the same, not being able to openly express his feelings for her was a distraction in itself. Only three more days to get through. He could do it. For Amaryllis, he could do anything.

Chapter 26

Letting his glance flick around the table, Felton took a sip of ale and surveyed the five men his new friend, Brody, had rounded up. Rough-looking men. The kind of men he had hoped to find. He had been wise to sell his horse and saddle and take the stage. Sitting atop the stage, clinging to his hat, he had entered into conversation with fellow passenger, Brody. He and Brody had quickly realized they had much in common, and Brody had convinced him to stop off in Loughborough rather than travel on to Derby. In Loughborough, Brody knew men who could help Felton with his enterprise.

The door to the alehouse being open, Felton had a perfect view of all the people and vehicles passing by. Almost directly across the road was the Star and Ball Inn. The only inn suitable to the gentry, Brody assured him. Sooner or later the D'Arcy coach would pass by the alehouse and turn in at the inn's courtyard. He but needed his henchmen to see the richness of the coach, the bounty they could glean, and they would be ready to help him ambush the coach.

Brody knew the perfect spot for the ambush. He and a cohort or two had ambushed other travelers in the same place. Midpoint between Loughborough and Derby the woods thickened and the road narrowed and dipped down into a gully. No place to turn around, no way to escape. Felton was certain Toms and his added outriders would no longer be accompanying the D'Arcys. Two days earlier, he located the D'Arcy party at the Blue Cow Inn in Northampton and had fearlessly gone right up to Toms's outriders. Neither had recognized him, and both had been chatty. They were only accompanying the D'Arcys as far as Leicester, then they would be turning back. Toms had to attend a quarter session and give testimony for one of his neighbors in a boundary dispute.

As long as he continued buying ale for his new cohorts, Felton had no worry they would grow restive. Knowing he would eventually be rewarded, he kept his mind on his goal. With each clop of hooves on the muddy road, he straightened, only to sink back down when some farmer passed or some local youths showing off their mounts cantered by. Shortly after ordering a fourth round of drinks, his patience paid off. Recognizing the D'Arcys' advance outrider, he gave a low whistle. "Here we go, me loggerheads. Turn and tike a look at that equipage and at those trunks piled on the top." Looking bedraggled and with heads drooping, the six matched bays pulling the coach plodded by. As Brody had predicted, they turned in at the Star and Ball Inn. Though splattered with mud, the richness of the D'Arcy coach could not be mistaken.

Smiling, he strode outside. Brody and his cohorts followed after him to stand gawking at the coach and then its passengers as they emerged and stepped gingerly onto the straw that had been strewn about the courtyard to save the guests' shoes from the mud and dung. "Gaa," uttered one of the men as Amaryllis Bowdon stepped down. "Would you be looking at that dainty morsel? I would not mind a tumble with her."

Felton did not yet remember all the men's names, but smirking, he cocked his head and said, "Nor would any of us. Could be an added treat when we tike the coach." He watched the man smack his lips. Yes, it would not hurt to give them a bit more incentive to do the job well.

Both the innkeeper and his wife were out to greet their illustrious guests. Bowing and gesturing, they welcomed the D'Arcy party into the inn. Felton saw the boy. The little baronet bounced out of the coach clutching the hand of the nursemaid Felton had knocked unconscious at Toms's garden. Next the large woman was handed down by the footman. As the wee dog that had caused him such grief was handed out to the footman, a nudge to Felton's ribs caused him to look questioningly at Brody.

"I noted the laidy you mentioned riding astraddle like a man," Brody said. "A woman like that needs a real man to teach 'er 'ow a laidy ought to behave."

"Bain't that the truth," the man beside Brody said, and Felton joined them in a chuckle.

Retuning his attention to the coach, he watched the portmanteaus being carried inside, then the coach was drawn away to the rear of the inn where the horses would be unhitched, rubbed down, and fed. His gaze was caught by a young girl standing in the middle of the inn's courtyard. She seemed to be staring at him. She seemed familiar, and he felt he should know her. Yet he had met no one but Brody and his cohorts. The girl, clutching something in her arms, turned and hurried away. He could not say why he felt uneasy, but he did. Best they not go back and finish their ales. Best they move to a new location. They should have their suppers then head for the ambush location. Since they were walking, they would need set out when the moon was high. Thankfully the sky was clearing. The rain seemed to be over.

Looking about the neat, but shabbily furnished room, Esmeralda sighed. Loughborough's Star and Ball Inn was no match for the Haycock Inn in Leicester where they had stayed the previous night. Despite intermittent drizzle, the trip from Toms's hunting lodge to the Haycock Inn had been accomplished without incident, and they had arrived in Leicester well before sunset. The D'Arcys, Toms, and Amaryllis had been able to enjoy their final evening together relaxing in the inn's parlor, and Esmeralda had enjoyed a restful night's sleep on a commodious cot with two feather mattresses and a soft down quilt.

Eyeing the lumpy mattress on the trundle bed the Star and Ball Inn was providing her, she had a feeling it would not offer her old bones much comfort. Sighing again, she directed Norwood where to put Selena's and her portmanteaus then bid him take Fate for his walk. The footman obliged, and with the dog in his arms and a bob of his head, he exited, leaving Esmeralda to unfasten her portmanteau and dig for her sturdy hog-bristle brush. Now that the sun appeared to be coming out again, she meant to give Selena's riding wear a good brush over. Having arrived at their night's lodging in a timely fashion, she would have the opportunity to get at least the worst of the mud off Selena's breeches and coat. Thankfully, bidding Toms and his outriders farewell had not overly delayed their departure. However, she could not but wish Toms had been able to accompany them all the way to Derby. Not only did the added escort make her feel safer, but his presence helped keep Selena entertained so she was not getting into mischief.

Having found the brush and set it aside, she was busy pulling out a gown and petticoats from Selena's portmanteau when she heard Bess's light step at the door. Turning to thank Bess for retrieving her wrap from the coach, she stopped her work when she saw Bess's face. "What is the matter, child? You look frightened."

Her blue eyes round, her body quivering, the girl said, "I saw him, Mistress Shadwell. I saw Farr. He was across the road with several mean-looking men."

The girl had stressed the word mean, and Esmeralda felt a quiver go up her own spine. Selena and Reginald were in her charge and should anything happen to either of them, she would never be able to face their parents. She had grown to care for Amaryllis and her siblings, and she wanted no evil to befall them, but had she known their presence would be putting the D'Arcys at risk, she would have been compelled to argue against aiding them. Not that it would have done her any good, but her conscience would smite her less.

"You are certain?" she asked Bess.

"Oh, yes, Mistress Shadwell. He has cut his hair and shaved, and his hat and clothes are different, but I would not mistake him anywhere. His eyes..." She paused and shivered. "The way he looked at me. And at Mother. 'Twas...'twas... well, it made me feel sullied."

Her mind swirling, her heart pumping, Esmeralda said, "We must find Master Reginald at once. Go tell the innkeeper to send someone to fetch him to me immediately."

"Yes, Mistress," Bess said and hurried from the room.

Esmeralda slowly resumed laying out Selena's clothing, but she could not shake the feeling of foreboding coming up from deep in her gut. It told her they should not continue on. They should send for Selena and Reginald's father. They would be safe if they stayed in the inn. If only Toms had been able to continue to escort them. After finishing with Selena's clothing, she started unpacking her own gown and toiletries. What was taking them so long? How many times had she looked at the door? When it finally did open, she was so grateful, she came close to swooning.

Selena entered first with Reginald on her heels. "Good heavens,

Esmeralda, you are white as a ghost," Selena said. "Whatever can be wrong? The innkeeper said you must need see Reggie immediately. I thought you must be ill and hurried here with him."

Esmeralda saw Bess waiting outside the door and beckoned her to come into the room. "Come, child. Come and tell them what you saw."

Bess slowly entered the room and, at Esmeralda's renewed urging, repeated what she had told Esmeralda. "Oh, indeed, Mister D'Arcy, I could not be mistaken," she said when Reginald questioned her description.

"You say you saw them across the road from here?"

"Yes, sir. In front of a house that I think might be an alehouse."

"So be it," Reginald said. "I will get Nye, Billings, Crouch, and the others, and we will have this out now."

"Master Reginald!" Esmeralda held out her hand to him. "What do you mean to do? You cannot mean to confront him. He is obviously dangerous."

"I do mean to confront him and turn him over to the Loughborough constable. Bess and Betty can both testify against him."

"I suppose you will not allow me to accompany you?" Selena said.

"Yee, gads, no!" Esmeralda cried, reaching out to grasp Selena's arm as Reginald shook his head and said, "Have no fear, Esmeralda. This is one time Selena will not get her way."

Selena frowned, but to Esmeralda's relief, she seemed to know her brother would not relent. All the same, Esmeralda intended to stick to Selena's side until Reginald returned. It was bad enough Reginald meant to take on Farr. Surely with the outriders and Nye and the rest of the coach staff, he would come to no harm. If only Toms had not needed to return to his manor. If only he and his outriders were still with them. Her heart fluttering in fear, she warily followed Selena downstairs to the private parlor where they would wait to learn the outcome of the confrontation.

※ ※ ※ ※

With his armed staff following in his wake, Reginald marched across the road to the alehouse. Touching his arm, Billings bade him wait and let him go in first. Knowing Billings was far better trained in armed confrontations, Reginald acquiesced. His pistol drawn, Billings, with Crouch backing him up, stepped into the alehouse's dark interior.

"What is this!" Reginald heard the alehouse keeper cry. "Do you mean to rob me in broad daylight? I have little enough for you to take."

"Nay," Billings said. "We are looking for some men that were here." He looked back out the door. "They are not here, Mister D'Arcy. Rooms empty but for the keeper here."

Reginald entered the alehouse and addressed the keeper. "I need information," he said. "There was a man here – mayhap going by the name of Farr. He had several other mean-looking men with him. Do you know where they went?"

Tilting his head to one side, the keeper said, "Mayhap I know something. Mayhap not."

Billings started to grab the keeper, saying, "Do you know something, you will tell us now or you will be wishing you had."

Reginald put a hand on his outrider's arm. "Hold, Billings. I think a six pence may revive his memory. Violence need not be necessary." Plopping a coin in the keeper's hand, he said, "Has your memory improved?"

The keeper nodded his head. "Aye, it has indeed. I cannot tell you was anyone named Farr. The one paying for the ales called himself Smith. I recognized a couple of the men he was with, and you are right, they are not just mean-looking, they are mean. Hated to see them come into my house, but then the one called Smith kept buying rounds, so I had no complaints. Truth is, they ne'er finished their last round. They got up to look at something, and ne'er returned."

"How many men were with this... Smith?" Billings asked.

"Six. One named Brody, another named Meir, I could not tell you anymore."

"Describe the one named Smith," Reginald said, and the keeper gave him the same description as Bess had. So the fiend was now going by the name of Smith. "Have you any idea where they might have gone? Did they mention anything or place?"

"Nay. I paid them little heed. Just wanted to keep out of their way."

Reginald put another coin in the keeper's hand. "Do they come back, or do you remember anything else about them, let me know. I am across the way at the Star and Ball."

The keeper nodded his head. "Aye. I will do that, sir."

"What now?" Billings asked when they stepped outside.

Looking up and down the road, Reginald considered his next option. "My guess is something spooked Farr or Smith or whatever his name is. He might now be hiding out, but then, he might have removed to another alehouse. I think you and Crouch should visit some of the ale-houses. Do you chance upon them, come back and get me. You should not try to take them on by yourselves. Too many of them."

"As you say, sir." Billings nudged Crouch. "Let us be off."

Turning to the postilion and coachman, Reginald said, "I want special watch kept on the coach tonight. 'Twill be up to the two of you until Billings and Crouch return. I will need Norwood and Nye to alternate guard duty at Amaryllis's door."

"Aye. No one will get near my coach again," Pit said.

"Good man." Reginald slapped his coachman on the back and headed back across the road. Selena met him at the door to the inn.

"What happened!" she demanded.

"Naught. He had already fled. Where is Bess?"

"Helping Betty ready Tabitha and Charlie for bed. They have had their supper."

Reginald turned to Norwood. "Fetch Bess and tell her I want to see her in the parlor. Then you take the first watch at their door. After Nye has eaten, he will relieve you so you can get your supper. You two can work out which one of you has which shift."

"Yes, sir," Norwood said, and hurried to do as bid.

Amaryllis came down the stairs as Norwood trotted up. "What is amiss?" she asked. "Bess was upset and whispering something to Betty, but she clammed up when I came near."

Selena linked her arm in Amaryllis's and said, "Come into the parlor, and when Bess joins us, we will tell you all. Much as I would prefer not to upset you, you must need know the whole of it."

Reginald sighed and followed after his sister and Amaryllis. He wished he could spare Amaryllis this added fear, but Selena was right, they could not keep this threat to her brother from her. She needed to be

216

part of whatever decision they made as to the boy's safety.

No sooner were they all seated than Bess arrived. Reginald bade her have a seat until they briefed Amaryllis. As he had feared, Amaryllis was visibly shaken, but she squared her jaw and asked, "What do we do now?"

"That is what we must decide," he answered and turned to Bess. "Do you think Farr recognized you? Might that be what scared him off?"

Bess shook her head. "I could not say, sir. I do think he saw me staring at him. But I cannot think he would recognize me. Not dressed as I am now." She ran her hands down the gown Selena had given her that had been altered to fit her smaller frame and figure. "Nor could he expect me to be here in Loughborough."

"She is right," Selena said. "He cannot know he has been recognized. He must have feared having a large group of men hanging about would make people suspicious. My guess is he has no reason to think we are aware of any nefarious plans. I am thinking he means to attack us somewhere between here and Derby."

"Ohhh," Amaryllis said, and Reginald reached over to take her hand. "Never fear…" He started to say, "my love", but caught himself. "Never fear," he repeated. "We are well-armed, and we know of his probable plans. Nothing will happen to Charlie. I give you my word."

"But what of you?" Esmeralda said. "What of Lady Selena and the rest of us? Someone could be hurt. Hurt badly. Look what has already happened to Handle."

"She is right," Amaryllis said, her lovely eyes wide with worry. "I could not bear for anyone else to be hurt on our account."

"I have thought of that," Reginald said, tilting his head and narrowing his eyes. "I have been considering what might be our best option."

"We should send for your father and wait here for him to arrive," Esmeralda said.

Frowning at their devoted servant, Reginald said, "Nay. I will not have Father thinking I cannot protect Selena or the rest of you. However, I do intend to send word to Godwin Crossly that we are a day away and that we suspect trouble. I will ask that he have the Derby constable alerted should we need aid. I will need Billings and Crouch with us, so I will ask the innkeeper if he can find a reliable man to take the message to Godwin. In no way do I think a band of rabble can be a match for Billings, Crouch, Nye, and Pit. And I am confident I am a true shot as well. So all of you may rest easy."

He looked at his sister. "Selena, I will want you to ride in the coach tomorrow."

Selena raised her chin. "You may want it all you want, Reggie, but I will not ride in the coach. You know full well, I am as good a shot as you."

"Lady Selena! You cannot mean to expose yourself to those ruffians," Esmeralda said.

"Dear Esmeralda, I know you worry about me, as foolishly does Reggie, but I will not be cooped up in that coach waiting for something to happen. When have either of you ever known me to be intimidated by anything or anyone?"

Reginald glared at his sister. His father would have his hide did anything, even some minor little thing, happen to Selena, but short of trussing her up and stuffing her into the coach, he could not see how he could get her to stay safe inside. He hoped he was not being foolhardy, but he could not allow his father to come rescue them. Not if he wanted to prove himself man enough to marry Amaryllis and start a family. His father had been no older than twenty-two when he had gone off to fight with King Charles and later had joined Charles in Europe. If his father could take on the Roundheads, he could take on a few cutthroats.

Chapter 27

Resting back on his haunches, Felton peered through the thick foliage at the farmer in his wobbly cart passing by his hiding place. The farmer, having naught but hay in his cart, did not appear in the least bit wary as had a couple of gentlemen who in passing kept their horses at a brisk trot while glancing from side to side. Looking over at his cohorts, he frowned. They were all stretched out in the underbrush napping. Not that he blamed them for catching a few winks. It had taken them a good portion of the night to reach their destination. But now, he alone was left to keep watch for the D'Arcy coach.

He was not sleepy, though. He was too buoyed by the prospect of finally achieving his goal. This time he would not fail. The place for their ambush could not be more perfect. They had cut a large tree to the point that it was ready to topple onto the road at the slightest push. Naught but a rope was currently keeping it from falling over. The downed tree would stop the coach, and the high sides of the road as well as the denseness of the woods would keep the coach from being able to turn around.

While his cohorts jumped D'Arcy and his staff, all he need do was rush the coach, jerk open the door, grab the boy and slit his throat. It could be over in moments. The boy need not suffer. Whether any of D'Arcy's men or even D'Arcy might be killed or injured could not concern him. He had endured numerous trials to earn the promised annuity and a life of leisure. He would not let anything spoil this perfect opportunity to win his prize. He had no money left. He would need his share of the bounty from the sale of the D'Arcy trappings to get back to Albertine so he could start collecting his annuity.

He had told none of his cohorts, not even Brody, about his need to kill the boy. No reason they should know. They but needed to provide him with the means of getting to the boy. That one or more of the men might be killed or injured in the fight mattered not to him. That their plan should succeed was all he cared about. He smiled. How could they fail? The plan was flawless. The surprise would be complete. By nightfall, he and his cohorts could be back in Loughborough celebrating their good fortune and reveling in their spoils.

☘ ☘ ☘ ☘

Selena drew up on her horse's reins. Brigantia obediently halted, but she stamped about and shook her head, jangling her halter. The outrider, Billings, had brought his horse to a halt at the top of a rise. As the road dropped, the woods on either side thickened.

"I am not liking the looks of it," Billings said when Reginald rode up beside him. The previous evening when Billings and Crouch had searched Loughborough taverns and alehouses, they had found no evidence Farr existed. No inn had him as a guest. A couple of alehouse keepers knew Brody. Described him as a big, broad-chested man. Not a man they would wish to cross, but they had no idea where he lived or where he might be found. Billings and Crouch had returned to Reginald no wiser than when they had started their search. And so they had set out that morning with no knowledge of what might await them.

"The road has been worn down," Billings pointed out. "The ruts are making a gully. I think we need make our way through there as quickly as we might. Have Pit set to with the horses. Get a steady gallop going down this rise. Nye and I will ride a little ahead, our guns out and cocked. Do we see anything amiss, we will give a shout, and Pit should get the horses into a full run. No matter what, he is not to stop."

Selena let Brigantia prance around in a circle while she waited for Reginald to give instructions to everyone. Reaching into her pocket, she fingered the small pistol. She had never shot anything other than targets before. Had never thought she would ever have to shoot a person. But if she need use the gun to protect young Charlie from his assailant, she would do so. She stared at the road ahead. Sheltered by trees, it looked muddy from the previous day's rain. She hoped the coach would not get stuck.

Her stomach did a little flip-flop when Billings signaled for them to start down the rise. She wished she had not eaten quite as much when they stopped in Kegworth for an early dinner, Reginald being fearful they would not find another inn as good farther up the road. Nervous from having been on constant watch all morning, she had stuffed her meal down without thinking. Now the beef steak pie lay like a lump in her stomach.

Riding between Reginald and the coach, she kept a firm hand on Brigantia's reins. She wanted complete control of the mare. Behind her, the thudding of the coach horses' hooves and the rattling of the coach as it bounced over ruts and road debris gave her a slight smile. Charlie and Tabitha would be enjoying themselves, but Esmeralda would feel battered and bruised. Poor dear. When they reached Godwin's, she would not let Esmeralda lift a finger. She would have Betty see to Esmeralda's needs. Bess could care for the children, and she had no doubt Godwin would have maids who could see to Amaryllis's and her needs.

A whoosh and a loud thunk startled her and had Brigantia rearing up to avoid running into the branches of a tree that crashed down across the road. Her gaze darting about, she glimpsed Pit sawing on the coach reins to bring the horses to a halt. The postilion, his fists knotted in the reins of the two lead horses, jerked the horses around enough to keep them from colliding with the downed tree. Reginald was not as lucky, his horse could not stop. Horse and rider went smashing into several branches. Sherard neighed in surprise and pain.

Selena hoped the horse was not badly injured, but she had no time to give additional thought to her brother or his horse. Men brandishing clubs and knives were emerging from behind bushes and trees. One man, a large club in his hand, grabbed at Brigantia's halter. "Up girl," Selena said, pulling back on the reins. Rearing up on her hind legs, Brigantia threw the man off balance. Avoiding the hooves, he steadied himself and turned to aim a blow at Selena, but she was quicker. She had her pistol out of her pocket in a trice. She aimed her shot at the man's chest, it being the largest target. The man yelped, released Brigantia's halter, and grabbed his chest with his left hand. Powerfully built, he seemed little more than annoyed by the shot. It seemed to have caused but minor harm. Again he raised his club, and again Selena yanked up on Brigantia's reins. The horse's right front hoof nicked the man on the shoulder causing him to drop his club. Snarling, he bent to retrieve it, and Brigantia came down on his back and head with her front hooves. A loud groan ensued and the man fell face down in the road. At the same instant an earsplitting blast reverberated through the air. Whipping around, Selena saw smoke wafting from Pit's blunder-buss. A man, still clutching an ax in one hand, lay on his back in the mud. Half his face and chest were blown away.

Selena's stomach lurched upward. Pulling her gaze away, she spotted a man in a cockade hat, advancing on the coach. Holding a large knife, he yanked open the coach door. Before she could scream a warning, a whirl of skirts flew out the open door to land on the man and knock him backwards. Selena recognized Betty as the man's assailant. Grappling with him, Betty was hitting, kicking, and scratching. A second and a third set of skirts flew out the door. Bess and Amaryllis joined Betty's attack. The man was no match for the three women. In a matter of moments they tripped him, got his knife away from him, and had him, pinned on the ground, yelling and cursing. At a high-pitched neigh from one of the coach horses, Selena twisted on her saddle. She was relieved to see Mills, their postilion, was keeping the terrified horses under control. The horses could easily hurt themselves by rearing up and coming down on each other or on the shaft between them. Glanc-ing beyond Mills, she caught sight of her brother, and her heart leapt into her throat. Reginald was off his horse and immersed in a fight with a man wielding a knife. With the coach and horses between her and Reginald, she could not get to him to try to help. Though how she might be able to help, she was not certain.

The sound of a shot had her swiveling around to look to the rear of the coach. She saw a man, his chest stained red, stretched out on the ground, and Crouch had his second pistol aimed at a small skinny man. Eyes wide with fright, the little man threw down his club and darted back into the woods. Crouch let him go and turned to aid Norwood. Involved in a fisticuff, Norwood was holding his own, but Crouch, swinging down off his horse, put an end to the fight, whacking the brigand's head with the handle of his pistol.

Whipping back to her brother's fight, she saw Billings clambering over the fallen tree. Her fear eased some. Billings would help Reggie.

At the same moment Billings jumped to the ground, Reginald landed a punishing left to his assailant's jaw. The blow knocked the man onto his back. Before the man could rise, Billings was on him. He flipped the man over on his stomach, jabbed a knee into his back, yanked a cord from his pocket, and had the man's hands bound behind him in an instant.

"Are you all right?" Selena called to her brother.

Shaking his left hand before rubbing it with his right, he said, "Aye, never had a chance to get my gun out. Fellow pounced on me almost before I was out of the saddle. What is happening on your side? I heard shots, now naught but a lot of hollering."

Looking about and taking stock, Selena said, "That would be the man I think to be Farr." She smiled broadly. "Betty, Bess, and Amaryllis have him pinned to the ground, and he can do naught but curse. But I do think the fracas is over and 'tis fairly won. One footpad has fled, the others, except for Farr, appear to be either unconscious, restrained, or dead."

Shock and concern showed on Reginald's face. "Amaryllis has Farr pinned on the ground? She is not hurt, I pray."

Selena laughed. "Nay. She is presently sitting on Farr's legs. Bess and Betty are kneeling on his arms, and despite all his struggles, he cannot shake them off."

Reginald shook his head and said, "Who would have thought it? Farr, repulsed and apprehended by the women." He then glanced toward his horse, and Selena's gaze followed his. Sherard's reins and saddle were tangled in the tree branches. The horse had stopped struggling, but he could not escape on his own. "Billings and I have got to free Sherard," Reginald said.

"Best you do." she agreed, laying a gentle hand on Brigantia's neck. Her mare was still nervously prancing, and the coach horses were still neighing and stomping, but at least the fight was over. Selena avoided looking at the man the coachman had shot, but glancing down at the man she had shot, and Brigantia had stomped, she noticed him stirring. Fearful he might try to rise, she called to Crouch. Involved in tying up the footpad he had knocked unconscious, Crouch told Norwood to give her a hand.

Pit, dismounting from his perch, halted Norwood. "You help the ladies with the one making the ruckus. I am sick to death of his blathering. I will see Lady Selena's varlet goes nowhere. The idea – attacking a lady, the Earl's daughter at that. Man should be horsewhipped."

Norwood, his coat sleeve torn, his left eye looking red and puffy, gave Pit a nod. "I will see to him, all right." Standing over the man Betty, Bess, and Amaryllis held flattened on the ground, he stuck his shoe toe next to the man's head and ordered him to stop his cursing or he would knock him senseless. The man, his eyes darting frantically from side to side before resting on Norwood, seemed to realize he had no escape. With a deep sigh, he obediently clamped his lips shut.

The following quiet was like a soothing balm. Brigantia stopped her prancing. The coach horses stopped their stamping and head bobbing. The postilion, at last able to steady the horses, slipped off the left lead horse. He waggled his hands and fingers and stretched his back and legs then began stroking the horses and talking calmly to them. Selena could not think anyone else could have done a more masterful job of keeping the horses from injuring themselves. He had earned the liberal wage her father paid him.

Pit used a strip of cloth torn off Selena's assailant's coat to bind the man's hands. He then dragged the man into a sitting position. The man looked to be in considerable pain. Blood dripped from his head, and a bright red stain was growing on his chest. Selena could almost feel sorry for him, but when she looked back at the man Norwood was trussing up, anger replaced her sympathy. These men had meant to kill Charlie. Could well have meant to kill all of them.

"Selena!" She turned at her brother's call. "'Tis quiet. Everyone all right?" he paused. "Amaryllis?"

Her brother could not conceal his concern for Amaryllis. Or his love. Answering with a smile, she said "I think all are fine, but I need to check on Esmeralda and the children."

"Do that. Then do you please see to Sherard. We have freed him, but he has got some nasty looking scrapes. I have got to go with Billings to the other side of the tree. Nye is trapped under several branches. He told Billings he is not badly injured. He wanted Billings to help us, so he might not have been truthful."

"Oh, good heavens, yes, go help Mister Nye. Poor man. I will see to things here." Rather Crouch will, she thought, pleased to have the competent outrider take charge. Crouch ordered the two dead men dragged over to the side of the road. Obeying his directions, Norwood and Pit deposited them face down under some bushes. Selena was glad to have them out of sight. The other three men were bound to trees near their fallen comrades. Grabbing the ax he had twisted from the dead man's hand, Norwood said, "I am off to see can I help free Mister Nye."

Dismounting, Selena joined Crouch and Pit. "Young Mistress Bess has identified this lout," Crouch said, referring to the man Norwood had tied up and dragged to his feet. "She says he is the man who stayed at her house and went with her father to work at Mister Toms's house."

"What are you to do with him?" Selena asked, eyeing the man who had caused them all so much trouble. The man who had been willing to kill a small child.

"We cannot take all these varlets to Derby with us, but we can take this one." Together, he and Pit forced the man known to them as Farr up onto the foot stand at the rear of the coach. Crouch secured Farr to the handhold before turning back to Selena. "The rest, we will leave tied to those trees and hope they will still be there when the constable from Loughborough arrives to find them." He chuckled. "Even should they escape, there is not a one of them will not feel the misery in the morning. They will be wishing they had never attacked the D'Arcy coach."

"Thank you, Crouch," Selena said. "If all is secure, might we let Mistress Shadwell and the children out of the coach?"

"Certainly, let them out," Crouch said. "I think we can safely say the young baronet is no longer in any peril. Once they are out, I will see can Pit, Mills, and I get this carriage backed up a bit. Safer for the horses. Make it easier to remove that tree, too. That will be a job in itself."

Selena handed Brigantia's reins to Pit who offered to tie the horse to a tree on the other side of the road. "She is a bit fracas after all this," Selena said. "Best be sure her lead is secure."

Assenting, Pit led the mare off, and Selena glanced at the tree blocking the road. It was indeed, quite large. How they would remove it, she could not guess, however, she had complete faith in her brother and their staff. Shaking her head to clear her thoughts, she peered in the open door of the coach. Amaryllis had climbed back inside and was cuddling her young brother in her arms. His head pressed against her shoulder, she rocked him back and forth. "No one will ever try to hurt you again, Charlie," she promised the boy.

Holding Fate on her lap, Tabitha sat on the coach floor petting the little dog. "Are all the bad men gone now?" she asked.

"They are all tied up and can no longer cause any harm. If you wish to stretch your legs and take Fate for a walk, you may do so. I will help you down."

"What of Charlie?" Tabitha asked, looking up at her brother.

"He may stretch his legs, also, once Amaryllis says 'tis all right." After handing Fate and Tabitha over to Bess, Selena looked up at Esmeralda. "How are you, dear friend? Will you ever be able to forgive me for involving you in this horrendous fray?"

Esmeralda, her cap askew, looked over at Amaryllis and Charlie, then looked back at Selena. "I have no need to forgive you. I look at that sweet little boy and know he is safe. I look at you and see you are safe. I know your brother to be uninjured and know the worst is now over. I will make no complaints."

Before Selena could answer Esmeralda, Betty stepped up behind Selena and said, "Mistress Shadwell, might I assist you to alight? I have spread a blanket over a log to the other side of the road, away from those gallous dastards. Be a good spot to wait while the men figure out how to get that tree off the road."

Esmeralda nodded and smiled. "Thank you, Betty. Yes, do please help me out. Mind, my legs may be a bit shaky."

Selena stepped back and Betty lowered the steps to the coach. A firm grip on Betty's arm, Esmeralda slowly descended. Mills hurried to help, and soon the three were circling the rear of the coach and making their way to the side of the road.

"If you are all right, I need see about Reggie's horse. He may have been injured when he ran into the tree branches. Reggie is seeing to Mister Nye. He was trapped under some tree branches," Selena told Amaryllis.

"Oh, poor man. Yes, we are fine. Charlie and I will join the others soon." She placed a hand on Charlie's head. "I am so relieved to know

Charlie is safe. Yet I feel so badly about all that has happened to you and your staff. I do hope Mister Nye is not badly injured."

"Everyone, including Mister Nye, will be all right, I feel certain. We are all relieved to know the danger is over. Now, I will see to Sherard." She left Amaryllis still rocking her brother. The two needed a few moments alone together, but Selena doubted not that Charlie would soon be wanting to join Tabitha and Fate in their play. Children were resilient. Today's trauma could well pass from his youthful memory. In the meantime, she had a horse to attend.

❊ ❊ ❊ ❊

"How do you, Nye?" Reginald asked his valet. "Had a bit of a scuffle with the tree, it seems." He tried to be light, but he feared he had not done a good job of keeping the concern from his voice. Both Nye and his horse were pinned down by two large tree branches. The horse, lying on his side, looked to be lying on Nye's leg. Broken branches and scuffed earth beneath the horse's hooves showed where the horse had made occasional attempts to rise. The animal, now breathing quietly, looked up with sorrowful brown eyes. Reginald hoped he would not have to shoot the creature. Even more, he hoped the horse had not crushed Nye's leg.

"Is the boy safe? Was anyone hurt?" Nye asked.

Squatting down to examine the branches more closely, Reginald shook his head. "Charlie is safe, and none but the cutthroats who attacked us suffered any major injury. Fools those poltroons were to take on mounted, armed men. At close range, it is hard not to hit your target."

Joining them, Norwood sank down beside Reginald and picked up the tale. "As might be expected, two men attacked Crouch. Knowing he would be armed and well-trained, they would think they need dispatch him first."

"Humph," Reginald said. "Culls underestimated his seasoned acumen, or overestimated their own adroitness. Three might have taken him down. Two, never. Not unless they also had guns, which they had not."

"The women's contributions should not be undervalued," Norwood said, putting a gentle hand on the frightened horse. "I saw Lady Selena shoot one assailant. And Betty, Bess, and Mistress Bowdon fairly burst from the coach and dispatched Farr or Smith or whatever his name is." While still soothing the horse, he added, "Crouch was tying Farr to the back of the coach when I left to come here. Guess I will have a companion, at least until we reach Derby. Not that I am anxious for his company."

Eyeing Norwood's other hand, Reginald asked, "What is that you have?"

Norwood held up the ax. "Took it out of the hand of the man who dared cross Pit. Pit's blunderbuss blew the man away."

"Guess they used that ax to cut this tree down," Reginald said. "Now we shall use it to free Nye." He looked again at the branches then back at Nye. "We will have to be careful where we land the blows, huh, old friend?"

Nye smiled up at him. "Aye, Master Reginald. Most careful."

"Riders coming," Billings said. "Riding hard."

Reginald stood up and stared down the road. What now? Surely they would not be beset by highwaymen. As the riders drew closer, Reginald let out the breath he had been holding and started to chuckle. He knew well the man in the lead. His uncle, Nathaniel D'Arcy, could never be mistaken. A large man, and a daring rider, he and his horse moved as one.

Stepping forward, Reginald shook his head as the group of riders drew up in front of him.

"Ho, boy," his uncle said, swinging down from his horse. "Looks like you have had a wee bit of trouble. You unscathed? Selena, all right?"

Reginald grasped his uncle's outstretched arm in greeting. "Aye, Uncle Nate, we are all fine. But I cannot believe you are here. How come you to be here?"

"Your sister's letters telling us where you were headed, and your letter telling us what you were about, and that you expected trouble brought us here. But enough about that for the time being. I see you have a man and a horse trapped under these branches." Glancing over his shoulder, he said, "Godwin, Milo, give your greetings to this young

228

rascal, then let us set to work and get this tree off this man."

Near as surprised to see his uncle's stepsons as he was to see his uncle, he clasped each in an embrace. They then introduced him to Godwin's wife's brother, David Stoke. "How fortuitous you have all come," Reginald said, again shaking his head in awe, but he swung around when he heard Selena's voice. She had climbed part way up the downed tree, and her head was poking over the bushy branches.

"Reggie is Mister Nye all right?" she questioned, but before he could answer, she spotted her uncle. "Ye, Gads!" she cried. "'Tis Uncle Nate! How come you to be here?"

Her uncle glanced over at his niece. "The better question, gel, is how come you to be here? You have your aunt distraught, and no doubt your mother and father as well."

Reginald could not imagine his level-headed Aunt Rowena being distraught and apparently neither could Selena for she laughed her tinkling laugh and said, "Oh, nay, Uncle Nate, I have written letters to all explaining our side trip to Derby. 'Twas a necessity."

"We will talk of that later, now we must see to this man and his horse." He beckoned to a couple of men Reginald took to be Milo's outriders for they wore Milo's livery. "Either of you men good with an ax?" he asked.

One man stepped forward. "Aye, Lord Rotherby. I have used an ax afore."

"Good." That his uncle would take command of the situation did not surprise or annoy Reginald. His Uncle Nate had led his gang of highwaymen all over England and had never been caught. He had years of experience in making quick decisions. "I suggest you cut these branches," his uncle said, pointing to the branches he had in mind. "Cut right next to the trunk, if you can wedge yourself in between those other branches and still manage to swing the ax."

"Aye, sir, I think I can," the man said, proceeding to work his way in amongst the branches. Once he was in place, Norwood handed him the ax.

Intently watching the man readying for his first swing, Reginald started when David Stoke joined him and asked, "Where might I find Mistress Bowdon and my wife's nephew and niece. I am thinking they are with you and are unharmed."

"Oh, aye," Reginald said. "They are safe." Turning, he saw Selena still peeking over the tree branches. "Selena," he snapped, "did you see to Sherard?"

"Aye, Reggie. He has some scrapes as you mentioned, and his fetlock is showing a slight swelling, but I led him about, and he is not limping. I think you should be able to ride him."

"Thank you. Now allow me to introduce Mister David Stoke. He is married to the children's aunt, and he wishes to see Amaryllis and the children to make sure they are well." He looked back at Stoke. "Mister Stoke, my sister, Lady Selena. Do forgive her clothing. She prefers to ride astride, and Father lets her."

Making no obvious note of Selena's attire, Stoke swept off his hat and bowed at the waist. "I am honored, Lady Selena."

Selena beamed. "Mister Stoke, Amaryllis will be so pleased to see you. You will have to excuse her appearance, though. She is a bit mussed from having fought the man who was trying to kill Charlie." She shook her head. "I simply cannot believe you, and my uncle, and my step-cousins are here. What a delightful happening." Beckoning him, she said, "C'mon, climb over this tree, and I will take you to them."

Stoke clambered through the branches and over the trunk to follow Selena. Reginald wished he was the one going to see Amaryllis. He was proud of her courage – that she would join Betty and Bess and fight Farr – at the same time, his stomach turned a flip when he thought that she might have been injured.

A whack and a crack brought his attention back to the outrider. A few well-placed hits, and the tree branch was severed from the trunk. With each blow of the ax, Nye's horse flicked his ears, rolled his eyes, swished his tail, and ineffectively kicked his legs, scraping them against the ground and the branch resting on him. Uncle Nate tried calming the horse, petting him, speaking gently to him, but by the time the branch was hoisted off Nye, the horse was wild-eyed.

Reginald breathed a sigh of relief when he and Norwood pulled Nye free, and he saw Nye's leg had not been crushed under the horse. Nye's leg and foot had been wedged tightly against the horse and the saddle, and a smaller branch concealing his leg had put enough pressure on the leg that not even Nye had known for certain his condition.

Helping Nye to his feet, Reginald kept a firm grasp on his valet. Nye was wobbly at first, his foot having gone to sleep, and he was bruised and scraped on numerous parts of his body, but he appeared to have no broken bones. Norwood helped Nye over to a nearby stump he could sit on until the tree could be removed, and Reginald looked down at the frightened horse. Each time the ax fell on the branch pinning the horse down, the horse started screaming and thrashing about. Uncle Nate's attempts at calming the poor creature were to no avail.

"I fear he will do real injury to himself," Uncle Nate said, concern obvious in his voice.

"I had best send for Selena." Screwing his mouth to one side, Reginald shook his head. "Are we ever to get this tree out of our way, we have to get the horse up."

"Why send for Selena?" his uncle asked.

"She has a way with animals," Reginald answered. "Can anyone calm the poor beast, she can." He turned to Billings. "Do fetch my sister, please."

"Yes, Master Reginald," Billings said and hurried to climb over the tree.

"Now that you mention it," Uncle Nate said, scratching the back of his head under his hat. "I remember Selena's way with animals. It does bring back the memories." He looked at Milo. "Do you remember the time she was allowed to go on her first fox hunt? 'Twas at Walling House at one of the family gatherings. I know you were there."

Milo began chuckling. "Aye. I remember how the fox led us on a merry chase and circled back around to where Selena had stopped." Squinting his eyes and tilting his head, he added, "I cannot remember why she stopped where she did. 'Twas near an oak tree right before a rather high fence. But she was so at home on a horse. I cannot think she was scared to jump."

"Yes, curious, but I think she was no more than sixteen," Uncle Nate said. "Mayhap she was afraid to try that fence.

"She was seventeen and she was not scared," Reginald said, his tone disgusted. "She stopped because she saw a bird had been injured. Had a hurt wing. I remember because she kept that bird for a month. It was always chirping and flapping about her room. Made a pet out of it she did, but for once Father stood firm and made her release it once its wing was healed. I swear though, that bird never left the nearby trees. It would come down and sit on Selena's shoulder. That went on for a couple of years, then one day, it found a mate. After that its appearances were more rare. It still remains around the grounds. Bet it is missing her now."

"Well 'tis the fox I remember," Milo said. "The hounds were baying, and we were all trailing after them, and there sat Selena, under the tree with that fox in her arms. Poor dogs had no idea what to do. They circled her and howled piteously, but none neared her. They seemed to know they were not going to get a chance at their prey."

"And there was not a one of us willing to take that fox away from the gel," Uncle Nate said. "So we gathered up the dogs and went home empty handed." He looked at Reginald. "Your father stayed with her until she felt it safe to release the fox. According to Ranulf, that fox trotted off with its fluffy tail in the air and with naught but one backward glance."

"Yes, but he let her keep the damn bird."

"Reggie, do I hear you still complaining about Rusty?"

Reginald whipped around to find his sister had joined them. "Ah, never mind that, Selena. We need you to calm Nye's horse while we cut away the branch."

"Oh, of course, poor fellow," she said, dropping down beside the horse and laying her small hand on the horse's muzzle. "How is Mister Nye?" she asked, while gently stroking the horse's soft nose.

"Bruised and sore, and his clothes are torn, but he will be all right."

"Thank goodness. Before I forget, two horsemen just rode up. They have offered to help remove the tree."

"Splendid," Uncle Nate said. "We can use all the help we can get."

"Here comes another who may help," Milo said. "Looks to be a farmer."

"Surprising not more people have happened on us," Reginald said. "I would think this to be a relatively busy road."

"So it often is," Godwin said. "I have had to travel it oft enough with

232

legal business taking me here and there. I have no doubt we will have more helpers 'ere long."

"By the by," Selena said, "Mills, Pit, and Crouch got the coach backed away from the tree, and the horses have been unhitched and allowed to rest until we are again ready to travel. Crouch wants to know do you wish him to return to Loughborough and fetch the constable, seeing as the two newly arrived horsemen can help with the tree removal."

"Aye, good thought," Reginald said. "Billings, tell Crouch to go for the Loughborough constable. And tell those two horsemen, we will appreciate their help." Glancing up at Milo's outrider, the ax balanced on his shoulder, he said, "Let us try again."

Selena had her hands on either side of the horse's head and was bending in close to the horse, their noses almost touching. Reginald thought he heard her crooning a soft song to the horse. With each whack, the horse's withers shivered, but the horse did not thrash about. A last loud crack, and the work was complete. Reginald, Norwood, Milo, and Godwin, were able to lift the branch off the horse. Leaves and thin branches brushed against the horse and Selena, but the horse stayed down until all was clear.

"All right, fellow," Selena said, "let us see can you stand." Rising to her knees, her hands still on the horse's head, she turned his head forward. Following after Selena, the horse struggled onto its front knees. Slowly Selena rose to her feet. The horse wobbled and thrashed a bit, but with Selena's encouragement, he got his back feet under him, and stood.

"Huzzah!" Uncle Nate said. "You are a wonder, Selena. But think not that all is forgiven."

Not looking at her uncle, her attention still on the horse, Selena smiled. Reginald knew that smile all too well. Selena expected no consequences, and he guessed she would be right. After all, they had prevented the murder of a little boy. Who could scold her for that?

Chapter 28

Settling back against the coach cushions, Amaryllis let her thoughts ebb and flow with the swaying of the coach. Charlie was safe. Her dear friends were uninjured. And Reginald had announced to one and all, that he and she were betrothed. He had little choice but to make the announcement after sweeping her into his arms and kissing her with a passion that left her breathless. He apologized to her for not making a more formal announcement, but he said he was so proud of her, he could no longer contain himself. She felt equally proud of him. He had been so brave, so resourceful, and had shown such care and concern for his staff and his horses.

At Reginald's announcement, Selena had laughed and given Amaryllis a hug. "Dear friend, I knew you two were in love. I simply cannot understand why you waited so long to tell us. Now, at last I am to have a sister. I could not be more pleased."

"Indeed," Esmeralda said, "Master Reginald has made a fine choice for a wife, and so I shall report to Lord and Lady Rygate."

"How could you not say so?" Reginald asked, putting a possessive arm around Amaryllis.

"Well, from what I can see," Lord Rotherby said with a genial smile, "you will make a lovely addition to our family, Mistress Bowdon. Even though neither this rapscallion nor his hoyden sister have bothered to present you."

Reginald made a quick introduction, and Selena said with a giggle, "How could we introduce you, Uncle Nate, when Reggie was so busy kissing her?"

Amaryllis found herself blushing, but she managed a smile and a curtsy. Introductions were then made to the Crosslys. The two brothers looked nothing alike. Sir Milo, tall and slender with shapely hands and narrow feet encased in expensive riding boots, had dark brown hair and brown eyes framed in dark lashes. He looked the part of a wealthy baronet. Godwin Crossly, married to David Stoke's sister, Mary, was shorter, a tad stocky, and had thick golden blond hair and vivid blue eyes. Both had bright grins, and they heartily welcomed her into the family. Amaryllis liked both men, and appreciated their cordial words, but she was most grateful Lord Rotherby seemed pleased about the betrothal. If he approved of her, that should help win over Reginald's parents. What they would think of his sudden engagement, she could not hazard.

She liked Reginald's tall, powerfully built uncle. With his dark hair and blue-green eyes, strong chin, and straight nose, Lord Rotherby could easily pass for Reginald's father, so similar were their features. That Reginald's uncle, his step-cousins, and the children's uncle had come racing to their rescue, she found admirable, though they arrived too late to prevent the attack. If not for Betty and Bess, Charlie could well have been murdered.

Spying Farr with knife in hand advancing on the coach, Betty had declared, "He will not have the chance to hit me again." Amaryllis knew not what Betty intended, but the instant Farr snatched open the coach door, Betty leapt out at him. Bess thrust Fate into Tabitha's arms and followed after Betty. Seeing the two servant women struggling with Farr, Amaryllis drew upon her courage and sprang from the coach to join them. Reaching down, she had grabbed Farr's leg, yanked on it with all her might then delighted in seeing him tumble to the ground. In trying to save himself, he lost his grip on his knife, and it flew from his hand. No sooner did he hit the ground than Betty and Bess brought all their weight down on his shoulders. He bucked and twisted trying to free himself. To help restrain him, Amaryllis plopped herself down on his legs. She had wished she was heavier. He had her bouncing up and down and all around, but she determined he would not shake her from her position. The language that spewed from his mouth was more foul than anything she had ever heard. Her ears aflame, she was sorry she could not stuff a dirty stocking in his mouth.

With her attention directed on Farr, she had not really known how the other members of the D'Arcy party faired. She saw Selena still sat her horse, and a man lay unconscious near the stamping horse's feet, but she had no idea where Reginald might be. She heard gun shots, and prayed with all her heart that the shots had not been aimed at Reginald. Then the fray ended. The attackers were vanquished. Peace reigned. With Farr safely restrained by Norwood, she scurried back into the coach to comfort her siblings and allay their fears. Cuddling Charlie on her lap, she looked out the coach window to see Reginald, hale and hardy, clambering over the fallen tree. Relief flooded through her. All was well with the people she loved.

She had no idea how long she sat rocking Charlie after Esmeralda and Tabitha left the coach, but eventually, she calmed enough for them to join Bess, Betty, Esmeralda, and Tabitha on a blanket Betty had spread out under the shade of some trees. The children's uncle had briefly joined them before going back to help with the removal of the tree from the road. She had met David Stoke but once before. Neatly dressed from head to toe though dusty from his ride, he was of medium height and weight and had kindly brown eyes. His concern for the children had been apparent, and they, though at first shy with him, warmed to him when he complimented them on their bravery, Esmeralda having told him neither had cried out or shown any great fear.

Two horsemen and a couple of farmers traveling the road helped with the tree removal. Clearing the tree far enough off the road that none of the branches would block the passage of larger vehicles had not been easy, but with so many men working, it had been accomplished in a minimum of time. The horsemen and farmers then went on their way.

Upon learning of Mister Nye's injuries, Esmeralda insisted he ride inside the coach not up on the seat beside the coachman. Bess had quickly volunteered to ride beside Pit. Tying her cap under her chin to secure it over her unruly curls, she proclaimed, "This will be quite the adventure. My brother, Robby, will be so jealous when he learns of this."

Leaving Sir Milo's two outriders to guard the villains until the Loughborough constable arrived, the journey at last resumed.

Watching Betty worry over Mister Nye, Amaryllis wondered if Betty might be forming an attachment to Reginald's valet. He was somewhat older than Betty, but Betty was a sensible young woman, mature for her age. Amaryllis meant to keep her on as the children's nurse did their grandfather agree to it. And did Mistress Sermon release Betty from her contract. They owed much to Betty. And to Bess. Amaryllis would keep Bess on as her personal maid. The girl was young and would need training, but she, too, was bright and quick-witted. Amaryllis could not think she could ask for more loyal servants. She meant to see them rewarded financially for their selfless bravery.

Looking down, Amaryllis smiled at her sleeping sister. Tabitha's head rested in Amaryllis's lap, her feet in Esmeralda's. Amaryllis lightly fingered her sister's soft curls. Good the children should sleep. It would be late before they reached Godwin Crossly's home. Charlie had found a place amongst the feet on the coach floor and had curled up with Fate in his arms. The children had become so attached to the dog, and the dog to them, though the little fellow did perk up whenever Selena came near. Selena was, after all, Fate's savior. Selena had assured Amaryllis that she intended to give Fate to the children, and Amaryllis knew the children would be thrilled.

"Never meant to keep Fate could I find him a good home," Selena had said. "I know not what to expect when I reach Whimbrel. I may have little time to care for a little dog. Best Fate stay with Tabitha and Charlie."

Stoke told Amaryllis that his wife had written to the children's grandfather about the situation. Stoke expected Sir Cyril Yardley to arrive at Godwin Crossly's home within a day or two. As the children's primary guardian, he would be the one to decide what should happen next, where the children should live, and what would be needed to keep them safe from their Aunt Elva. Might Charlie's aunt hire another villain to try to kill him?

Amaryllis hoped Tabitha and Charlie would be allowed to live with her and Reginald once she and Reginald were married. Reginald insisted he wanted the children in their home. "I cannot but think Ardenstrath will be cold and lonely do we not have the children about," he said. "And I cannot think you will be happy do you not have Tabitha and Charlie with you."

He was right. As much as she loved Reginald, she would not be whole did she not have her siblings with her. They had been in her care too long for her to think of giving them up. She hoped the children would not miss Churlwood. Reginald had not made his manor house sound particularly appealing, but then, she resolved, they would make what changes might be necessary to make it bright and cheerful. A lovely place to raise children – her siblings and the children she and Reginald would eventually have. With that thought she blushed.

She could scarcely wait until she and Reginald were wed. She knew little about what was expected of a wife in the privacy of the bed-chamber, but the feelings Reginald sent raging through her body told her she would enjoy the discovery. Reginald's kisses left her craving more, longing to have an emptiness sated. The desire for her that she read in his eyes, assured her his passion matched her own. He told her he meant to have no long betrothal. He meant they should be married as soon as he could obtain a special license from the Bishop in Derby. Considering Amaryllis was yet in mourning, the wedding would be small and quiet.

"That suits me," he said. "Fact is, I prefer a simple wedding. Besides, I have no intention of waiting for your time of mourning to end before I may take you for my bride. Nay, I would ne'er survive such a wait."

Nor would she, she thought. She looked down at the little dog cradled in her brother's arms. Funny how Fate had brought them together. Who would have guessed a little dog could do so much.

❀ ❀ ❀ ❀

Standing on the small foot platform at the back of the coach, his hands and feet bound so securely he could not change his position in any manner, Felton wished he had never seen Amaryllis Bowdon in Albertine, had never seen her climb into the D'Arcy coach. He wished he had never gone to see Mistress Elva Bowdon or listened to her offer to pay him for killing the young baronet. It had seemed like such a simple thing to do, but three times, he botched it. Now, he knew he faced the hangman's gallows. The attack on the D'Arcy coach alone was a hanging offense. Throw in his murder attempts, and his plight was hopeless.

Hopeless unless he could bargain his way out. He had no doubt that Brody, did he survive his injuries, would attempt to place all the blame on him. And to think the failure of their plans were all due to Brody not following his instructions. Instead of joining Meir and Webb in attacking the outrider, Brody had gone after the girl. Had they taken out the outrider first, subduing the others would have been easy. Then, too, who would have known the girl would have a gun and know how to use it? And who would have thought, how could he have known, that instead of cowering in the coach, the three women would jump out of it and attack him?

Yes, all had gone awry, but he might yet be able to save his neck. Could he but convince the D'Arcys and Mistress Bowdon that he was but following Elva Bowdon's orders, he might win a reprieve. Mayhap he would face naught but transport to the colonies. Better to face ten years servitude in the unknown than to twist and kick at the end of a rope. How unfair was his life. How unfair his fate.

※ ※ ※ ※

Riding beside his uncle, Reginald occasionally entered into conversation with him, but he had trouble keeping his mind focused on any one topic. He appreciated his uncle's praise as to how well he had handled the attack, and he accepted a gentle reprimand that, instead of putting his sister and the others at risk, he should have stayed in Loughborough until help arrived, but he knew, had he to do it over again, he would do the same thing. Had he waited in Loughborough, they might well not have Farr, was that his name, in custody. A larger force could well have foiled Farr's plans. 'Twas not until Toms's extra riders were no longer with them that Farr had made his move.

Better to have Farr in custody than to be wondering where he might strike next. He had hopes they would be able to learn from Farr why he had tried to kill Charlie. Was he being paid by the boy's aunt and uncle? Was that the case, the boy could still be in danger. Could be in danger for the rest of his life. He felt certain they would be able to get Farr to talk – even did they have to offer him a bargain.

His thoughts turned back to Amaryllis as they had over and over again since they had resumed their trek to Derbyshire. What a remarkable young woman she was. Gently reared, yet, without a thought to her own safety, she had sprung to the defense of her brother. Her courage equaled that of his Aunt Rowena who had wrested her daughter, Cecily, from the clutches of the lascivious Puritan who would take the fourteen-year-old Cecily as his wife.

When the tree had finally been cleared from the road, and he had at last been able to join Amaryllis, she had looked so adorable with her hair mussed, her gown crumpled and torn, and a smudge of dirt on her cheek, he had been unable to resist sweeping her into his arms and kissing her with a fervor he had too long held in check.

That Selena was delighted with their betrothal was a given. That his uncle approved of his bride-to-be was a boon. Uncle Nate's approbation, Reginald hoped, would do much to ease his parents' concern about his sudden marriage. That Amaryllis had a good portion to bring to the marriage should also help appease his parents, though he knew his mother would be grieved she was unable to attend the wedding ceremony. He had no doubt that when they met Amaryllis, his parents would be delighted with her. Who would not be? She was an angel.

He would have to send word to the steward at Ardenstrath that he would need to prepare for a new mistress to the estate. Did he need to retain additional help, he should do so. The house should be cleaned and aired from top to bottom, and the gardens and grounds should be made presentable.

Reginald looked forward to having several months alone with Amaryllis while they adjusted to married life. His need for her was so great, he could scarce wait until he could call her his wife and take her to his bed. He hoped to be at least partially satiated, and not a randy goat, when he eventually took her to meet his parents.

Thinking of his parents brought his thoughts around to Selena. Was it not for her and her soft heart where animals were concerned, he would not now know the greatest happiness of his life. He had near cursed her for the delay she had caused them when she had insisted on rescuing Fate. But had Selena not delayed them, he would never have met Amaryllis. Would never know the grandest love any man could ever know. He wished he knew some way to thank Selena. Could he save her from the fate their parents had imposed on her, he would, but he knew no way to stop the inevitable. Selena would have to go to Whimbrel and learn to be a lady. He was not at all sure he wanted her to become a lady. Despite her eccentricities, he liked her just as she was.

Glancing over his shoulder, he saw Selena rode between Milo and Godwin. The three seemed involved in a lively conversation. No doubt the conversation revolved around dogs or horses or hunting. Nice Selena would have a few days with the Crosslys before she would be hustled off to Whimbrel and her internment.

His glance swept from Selena to Bess, perched on the coach seat beside Pit. He meant to reward Bess and Betty for their aid in subduing Farr. He liked both young women and hoped to keep them on in his employ once he and Amaryllis were married. That Bess had generously given up her seat in the coach to Nye raised her even higher in his eyes. He could not help but feel guilty that because he had chosen not to wait in Loughborough for help to come from his father or his uncle and cousins, Nye had been injured, come close to being killed. He knew Nye would not blame him. He was too devoted, but in some way, Reginald meant to make it up to his friend and valet. Mayhap, when the Ardenstrath steward retired, he would make Nye steward.

"Pay heed, Reggie, you are wool gathering," his uncle said, bringing Reginald back to the present. "There is an inn in the village ahead. I think we must stop to rest the horses and have a wee bite, does anything look palatable. Our next stop will be the constable in Derby, then Godwin's to deliver Mistress Bowdon and her siblings to Mistress Stoke, and finally Milo's that we may put an end to this long day. I grow old for this kind of hard-riding."

Though knowing his uncle to be somewhere in his mid-fifties, Reginald still had trouble believing his uncle might be wearied by age. Yes, he could be weary, as Reginald was also weary, but his uncle was yet too robust a man to be subject to the aches and pains of age. No matter, a respite would be welcome. Surely Tabitha and Charlie were getting restive by this time. A good romp with Selena was what they needed. His sister, as usual, looked as fresh as when they had started out in the morning. She would have no trouble leading them on a merry chase, and with Farr tied to the back of the coach, they need have no fear for their safety.

"Aye. I could do with a rest myself. Moving that tree has my back and arms sore. An ale and a bite of bread and beef will suffice me. Also, I want to check Sherard's leg. Want to make certain the swelling has not worsened."

"So be it," his uncle said, drawing up that he might inform the rest of their party of the upcoming stop.

Reginald road on ahead that he might alert the innkeeper to their arrival. He knew the last part of their journey would be traveled under the light of the moon. They would not reach their final destinations till late in the evening, but reach it they would, with all safe and sound. Fate had been good to him. Very good.

Chapter 29

Snuggling under the soft down quilt, Amaryllis sighed contentedly. The room the Crosslys put her in could not be more pleasant nor could the four-poster bed with its light linen curtains, more comfortable. She no longer had to fear for Charlie's life. He was safe, and he was young enough that hopefully all memories of his brush with death would fade with time. He and Tabitha had been put to bed in the Crosslys' nursery with Betty attending them. They were sharing the nursery with the Crosslys' three-year-old daughter, Maitena. Upon their very late arrival at the Crossly home, Glenwood House, they had found the children's grandfather, Sir Cyril Yardley, awaiting them. Having been notified by his daughter, Juliet, of the danger Charlie was in, he had ridden with his older son, Ansel, at breakneck speed to reach the Crosslys', only to learn a party put together to meet up with the D'Arcy coach had already departed. Their horses exhausted, and their own weariness apparent, they surrendered to Sir Cyril's daughter's insistence that they rest and wait with her for the party to return.

Farr, or Felton, as they learned was his true name, was locked in the Derby gaol. Reginald told her Felton had begged them to let him make a deal. He would tell all he knew. Tell all was he given a reprieve. Reginald had agreed to return on the morrow to hear his confession, but he made him no promises. Let the man squirm through the night. He deserved far worse.

That Reginald and Selena had gone on to Sir Milo's Crossly Oaks Manor was a tad daunting. Used to being greeted by Reginald in the morning, Amaryllis feared she would be disconcerted by his absence. She had become dependent upon his presence. How sorely she would miss his bright smile and the loving glow in his eyes. She knew he would join her as soon as he could, but she also knew he could not be rude to his host, much as he longed to be with her.

She and the children had been too exhausted to give much more than warm greetings to Sir Cyril, but he had not pressed them for more. "Come morning, when you are rested, we will talk," he told Amaryllis. "I cannot begin to thank you enough for saving my grandson. And I know I owe much to D'Arcy. But off to bed with you. Your eyes are barely staying open."

Mary Crossly escorted her up to her room. At the doorway she embraced her. "Do you need anything, send your serving girl down. I had a fire lit to take the chill off the room but left the window open a tad that you may enjoy the fresh air. Myself, I do hate a stuffy room."

"I am sure all is perfect," Amaryllis answered Mary, while admiring the flowered wallpaper above the wainscoting. A china washbowl and pitcher set on the cherrywood toiletry stand. A gilded looking-glass hung above the stand and soft, white towels hung on a dainty rack attached to the stand. Bess had Amaryllis's night shift laid out on the bed and stood waiting to ready her for bed.

"Well, then, good night," Mistress Crossly said and gently closed the door behind her.

With Bess's help, Amaryllis was soon in bed. Bess, pulled out the trundle bed tumbled into it and was quickly lost in an exhausted sleep. Amaryllis could hear the girl's soft breathing. Bess had a right to be tired after the day they had all endured. But their trials were now over. Peace would again reign over their lives. With that thought, Amaryllis drifted into a weary sleep.

❀　❀　❀　❀

Selena tucked her feet under her and leaned closer to Fonda Whitaker Crossly. They were having a late-night cozy chat on Selena's bed. Selena had adored Milo's wife from the first time she met her. Though Fonda was fourteen years Selena's senior, Selena recognized in her, a kindred spirit. "You cannot say you have actually seen his ghost?" Selena hissed.

Fonda laughed. "Nay, I never see the Baron. 'Tis more like I feel his presence."

They had been discussing the age of the hall when Fonda mentioned a chill she sometimes got in what was once the chapel of the oldest part of the house. That section of the house had once been part of a castle. "In a bid to bring his barons under his control after the terrible civil war between King Stephen and Empress Matilda," Fonda continued with the history of the house, "Henry II had this castle razed. Well, at least most of it. All the outer walls. Only the solar, the chapel, and a portion of the hall below them were left standing. Baron Burell fought to keep his castle, but in the ensuing battle, he was killed. Legend has it, he died in the chapel."

Selena loved listening to Fonda's soft mesmerizing voice, 'twas near like a purr. Fonda could not be considered beautiful nor even pretty. Her nose was too short, her mouth too small, her chin sadly lacking, and her non-descript brown hair, brows, and lashes could elicit no acclaim, but when she spoke, her voice always drew everyone's attention. Milo claimed he had fallen in love with her at her first utterance.

"The chapel being next to the solar, our bedchamber," Fonda continued, "we turned it into my sitting room. There I do my sewing or reading. On inclement days, I play with the children." She lowered her voice. "'But 'tis when I am alone that I feel his presence."

"You are certain 'tis the baron?"

"It could not be the Baronet, Sir Lindell. From what Milo has told me of his father, the man was too plagued by too much drink and other infirmities to be haunting the old chapel. He died peacefully in his bed. His heart stopped. Why would he now go haunting the chapel?"

Ever since she was but a child of nine or ten, and an aged maid had told her ghosts could foretell the future, Selena had hoped to see a ghost. Her home, Rygate Park, was too new, the maid told her, to house any ghost, but the old cemetery behind the village church would have plenty of ghosts. What a scolding she and Reggie had received when they were found traipsing about the cemetery on a dark, moonless night. The maid had been dismissed, and she and Reggie had both had to solemnly promise they would never go out alone at night again. But even as she grew older and accepted that ghosts were not real, she could not escape a niggling hope that the nay-sayers were wrong. Cocking her head, she asked, "I wonder has Aunt Rowena ever felt Baron Burell's presence. Has she ever said?"

"I asked her once after I first felt that chill in the room. She said, no, but then Milo's mother is too practical to pay heed to a chill in the air. To her, it would be naught but a draft coming from the chimney. The solar was her husband's and her bedchamber, but the chapel was still a chapel. No doors connected the rooms, and the chapel had no hearth as it now has."

"Yes, I suppose Aunt Rowena would have no time for ghosts. Yet, 'tis not hard to picture her climbing down the ivy outside your bedchamber window to chase after that nasty Puritan making off with Cecily," Selena said, imagining her aunt in her younger days.

"She was an intrepid soul. Especially where the well-being of her children was concerned. Those years when she was flitting about the country with your uncle's highwaymen, she always managed secret visits with Milo and Godwin. She could never have managed those visits without dear Liverna and Milo's Uncle Artus. They took incredible risks so Rowena could spend time with her sons. Now, 'tis I who cannot manage without Liverna. We have a younger nursemaid who helps Liverna, and a governess for Elisel, but Liverna is my anchor."

Liverna had been Rowena's nurse, then maid, and had come with her to Crossly Oaks when, at fifteen, Rowena married the fifty-year-old Sir Lindell Crossly. When Rowena fled the hall to rescue her daughter, Cecily, from a forced marriage, Liverna remained and continued to care for Milo and Godwin. She was presently the head nurse in Fonda's nursery. Indeed, Selena had to wonder how Fonda would manage without the aged nurse to keep her brood under control. Fonda had but two rules for her children. They must brush their teeth both morning and evening, and they must never be deliberately disrespectful to adults. With such lenient dictums, Selena guessed the household would be in a turmoil if not for Liverna.

That they might greet Selena and Reginald, Fonda had allowed her nine-year-old daughter, Elisel, and five-year-old son, Wilbur, to stay up, despite the late hour. Only her new baby, Dorisande, had been put to bed. The newborn would have no interest in the late-arriving guests. Elisel remembered Selena from the last D'Arcy family gathering that they had every four years at Uncle Kenrick's estate in Oxfordshire. Elisel would have been six that summer, Wilbur but two. He could have no memory of his step-cousins, but it mattered not to the little round-faced boy, he greeted Selena and Reginald as though he had known them all his youthful life.

"Will you be telling us a story?" Wilbur asked. "Elisel says you tell good stories."

"Yes," Elisel said. "Have you rescued another fox? Or more birds?"

Squatting down to the children's level, Selena said, "No foxes or birds recently, but I did rescue a wee dog. And such a brave little fellow he is. Would you like to hear about him?"

"Yes, yes," both children cried.

"Very well. One story and you must give me your word you will press for no more. I am that weary, and I must crawl into bed ere I drop."

"But you will give us another story tomorrow, will you not?"

Selena smiled at the little girl who was a feminine version of her handsome father. "Yes, Elisel, I promise, I will give you another story tomorrow."

"You heard her," Fonda said. "Go brush your teeth and get into bed. Selena and I will be up as soon as I give her a glass of sherry to ease her into sleep."

True to their words, after Selena told Elisel and Wilbur about Fate and the little dog's fearsome defense of Charlie, the children applauded the story but had not protested when Fonda led Selena away to her room. Fonda's own maid was there to help Selena ready for bed, Esmeralda having been sent off to bed in a room of her own once she had been given a light refreshment. Selena meant for Esmeralda to have several days of rest. Her loyal servant had endured much yet had made no complaints.

Once Selena was in her night shift and her hair had been combed out, Fonda returned that the two of them might enjoy a private commune. "Quiet time around here can be rare," Fonda said, directing the conversation away from the house, ghosts, and her mother-in-law. "Milo is very gregarious, so we are ever hosting friends and neighbors. Not that I object," she said with a smile, "but I would have speech with you without interference. I must know all about your adventure, and the young baronet you have rescued."

Between sips of a second glass of sherry, Selena gave Fonda a brief description of their meeting with Amaryllis and her siblings, their perilous trek, and their defeat of the would-be assailants. Fonda was thrilled to learn Reginald was to take a bride, and said she would begin plans for the ceremony on the morrow.

"That will please Reggie," Selena said. "My brother is sadly lovesick. I think does he not soon wed Amaryllis, he could well go mad. He has not the patience of my brother, Giles, who has been courting his future bride for near a year."

"Reggie is like my Milo. We had not known each other a fortnight, and Milo was asking could he speak to my father. I said indeed he might, and thought the sooner the better. Milo wanted to be married by special license, but Mother insisted we post the banns for three weeks. She said she wanted to give me time to get to know Milo better, but I needed no extra time. I was totally astounded that a man as handsome as Milo could be in love with me, and I had no intention of questioning the matter. The three weeks, though, did give Rowena and Nate, and Milo's siblings time to journey to London to be there for the wedding."

"I cannot think why you would have questioned Milo's love for you," Selena said. "Indeed, I cannot think how he could not love you."

Fonda smiled. "You are kind, dear Selena. How I do enjoy your company. But I fear I take after my mother in looks. She was never a great beauty, but she is ever so clever. Her father, a woolen merchant, was known not only for his business acumen, but also for his witticism. Mother must have inherited his cleverness and ingenuity. Certainly my father loved her nimble wit, and I suppose Milo must love mine. So he says, anyway."

"Well, I know I love your wit and your humor and your easy freedom. Could I but somehow capture your ability to be a lady, yet still enjoy your freedom, I think I would not mind quite so much that I must be turned into a lady."

Laughing, Fonda gave Selena a hug. "You will manage it. I know you will. Remember, Rowena traveled about England with a band of highwaymen for years. Like you, she sometimes dressed in male clothing, yet no one could ever doubt she is a lady. Otherwise, your mother would not be sending you to her. I have no doubt Rowena will be understanding of your needs."

"I hope you may be right."

"I know I am. Now, your eyes are drooping. I have kept you from your sleep long enough. To bed with you, and I shall tuck you in."

Selena obeyed and as Fonda took her candle and started for the door, Selena said, "You must not expect me to be up early tomorrow. Mornings and I seldom deal well with each other."

"Never think you need rise early on our account. I am seldom up before eight myself. Now good-night. Sweet dreams."

Selena hoped she would have sweet dreams. Of late, all her dreams had been depressing. She had been traipsing about in gowns. Brigantia had laughed at her when she had tried to mount her in a riding costume. Reginald had laughed at her when she tried to flutter her fan to attract a group of men. Of course, she knew her horse could not laugh, and she knew Reginald would not be at Aunt Rowena's to be laughing at her. All the same, the dreams made her despair of ever becoming a lady. Well, at least her trip to Whimbrel would be postponed until after Reginald and Amaryllis were wed. She was happy with any reprieve she could get. With that thought, she drifted into sleep.

Reginald could not believe his good fortune. Milo was good friends with the bishop in Derby, and Milo had assured Reginald he would have no trouble getting a special license. They could get it on the morrow when they returned to Derby to question Felton. Reginald's Uncle Nathaniel had also assured Reginald that he approved of Amaryllis, and would write to Reginald's parents assuring them they had naught to worry about in Reginald's sudden choice of a wife. He also said he saw no reason Reggie and Amaryllis could not be married as soon as the situation with Felton was cleared up.

Tossing on his bed, trying to lay his excitement to rest, Reginald thought he could hardly wait for the morrow when he would see Amaryllis and tell her the good news. He hoped she would not be overwhelmed by his family. True, the Crosslys were but step-cousins, but they had been a part of the D'Arcy family for as long as he could remember. Amaryllis would have naught but her young siblings at hand.

But then, she would not want her father's brother's family at hand, and she had no other close family. Well, soon, his family would be her family.

Against his will, he could not fight off thoughts of his wedding night. He knew he needed sleep, needed to be able to rise early in the morning, and needed to have his wits about him. But a vision of Amaryllis kept appearing before him. How lovely she would be with her golden hair sweeping down her back and over her shoulders. He envisioned her in a frilly silken shift with little bows down the front that he would take pleasure in untying. He would then slip the shift down over her shoulders until her creamy, white breasts were exposed. And then....

No! He thrashed about. Good God! He was never going to get to sleep. Better to concentrate on that villain, Felton. He knew Felton would hope to be transported to the colonies to serve a term of indenture rather than hang. No doubt he would tell them everything they needed to bring charges against the children's aunt. That is, could they prove Felton was telling the truth. But then, why else would Felton attempt to kill the boy was he not being paid to do so?

Surely they would be able to prove the aunt was guilty. They had to prove it, or Charlie might never be safe. His breathing slowing, Reginald reviewed the day's events. He could not but regret the injury Nye suffered, but after a light repast, he had seen Nye settled in a comfortable bed. Both Nye and Esmeralda were to be pampered for the next few days. And so they deserved it. Pit, Norwood, Mills, Billings, as well as Couch, when he returned with news from Loughborough, would also receive a good rest, and Reginald would write his father asking him to provide the staff with a monetary remuneration for their loyalty and bravery.

His mind devoted to his various chores, he at last drifted into a deep sleep.

Chapter 30

In but three days, Amaryllis had grown completely comfortable with the Crosslys, the Stokes, and the Yardleys. She found them to be warm and friendly and accepting of her and her siblings. Tabitha and Charlie had quickly taken to Mary Crossly's three-year-old daughter, Maitena, and to Lady Crossly's son, Wilbur, and daughter, Elisel. By the end of the first day, Amaryllis was on a first-name basis with Mary Crossly and Juliet Stoke. Both women had been eager to start planning Amaryllis's wedding. They knew, as Amaryllis was still in mourning, despite her lack of mourning clothing, that the ceremony and celebration could not be elaborate, but they promised Amaryllis they meant her wedding to be memorable.

The Crossly estates bordering on each other, and the houses not more than three miles apart, the two families were ever jaunting back and forth between their homes. Seated on a velvet settee beside Selena in the well-appointed parlor at Crossly Oaks, Amaryllis expressed her envy of the Crosslys that they had such a happy family relationship.

"We mean our children to be as close as are Milo and Godwin," Lady Crossly said with a smile at Mary, who nodded in agreement. "I cannot but think 'twas providence Godwin's grandmother left Glenwood House to him. We do feel blessed our children will grow up as close as any siblings. Mary's Emil and my Dorisande were born but weeks apart, and already, when we put them down on a blanket together, they have such fun cooing at each other."

Amaryllis caught a sad smile flash across Juliet's face. She suspected the children's aunt longed for her own baby. Juliet and David Stoke had been married five years and still had no children. And Juliet was so good with the children. Not in the same way as Selena. Selena had such a near child-like attitude that children were drawn to her. Juliet was simply so sweet and loving. With her dark hair and slightly slanted hazel eyes under perfectly arched brows, she was far prettier than her sister, Beatrice, Tabitha and Charlie's mother, but in some ways she reminded Amaryllis of Beatrice. She was not shy like Beatrice had been, but she had a quiet eloquence to her – unlike her brother, Ansel, who had boisterously slapped Reginald on the back upon learning of his betrothal and upcoming wedding.

A year younger than Reginald, Ansel was the image of his father, strong chin, straight nose, firm mouth, and dark hair. But Ansel had not his sister's or Sir Cyril's dignity. He did, however, have a wide, infectious grin, and his dark eyes sparkled with joviality. A merry soul, he was intent on keeping the ladies entertained while their men were absent.

The absent men were on their way to Churlwood. The previous day, Felton had agreed to give evidence against Elva Bowdon. In exchange, Reginald and Sir Cyril would request leniency in sentencing for Felton at his trial. Felton, in the custody of the Derby deputy constable, was accompanying them. Amaryllis knew the men meant to ride hard. They planned but two stops, one in Leicester at the Haycock Inn, and the other at Richard Toms's house. Reginald had sent Billings on ahead to alert the inn. He was then to ride on to Toms's where he would await them.

Besides confronting Elva Bowdon, as Tabitha and Charlie's primary legal guardian, Sir Cyril meant to remove Irwin Bowdon and his family from Churlwood. He would appoint a new steward to manage the estate until Charlie came of age. He was joined on his quest by Reginald, Lord Rotherby, David Stoke, Sir Milo, Crouch, and Sir Milo's two outriders, who with Crouch, had returned the evening before from Loughborough. Crouch had reported the Loughborough constable had taken the three surviving assailants into custody. A trial date would be set when the quarter session was called. Reginald assured Amaryllis the three would be found guilty and would most likely hang. She could not feel sorry for the footpads. They had meant to kill Charlie. And if hanged, they would not be a threat to other innocent travelers.

"As we are taking no personal servants with us," Reginald had joked, "we will be fending for ourselves, and most likely none too well. At least at the Haycock Inn and Toms's, we can count on a good meal, good beds, and good care for the horses."

Reginald carried two letters for Amaryllis with him, one to Mistress Sermon, and one to Bess's mother. Amaryllis was telling Mistress Sermon that she would like to keep Betty on as the children's nurse, would that not discommode the kind-hearted lady. And she was asking Bess's mother if she might keep Bess on as her personal maid. Yes, the girl would have to be trained, but she was a fast learner. Amaryllis prayed both requests would be granted. Did Mistress Sermon need a personal maid to take Betty's place, Amaryllis could recommend the maid she had used when at Churlwood. As Mistress Sermon lived in Watford, it would not take the maid far from her family.

"You are entirely too lost in your own thoughts, Mistress Bowdon," Ansel Yardley said from his stance before the hearth. A smile stretched wide across his face. "I would know what so occupies your lovely head. Thoughts of that rogue, Reginald, I will warrant."

"Nay," Selena said, answering for Amaryllis, "she, like me, is wondering when we might expect Godwin that we might have our supper. My stomach is rumbling."

Having an appointment with a solicitor that, for an important client's sake, he dared not miss, Godwin had not accompanied the others to Churlwood. Stuck in Derby for the day, he had his dinner there, but he had promised he would join them for supper.

"Mayhap that is him arriving now," Juliet said.

"Nay," Lady Crossly said, rising. "That is way too much commotion. Come let us see what is causing all the fuss." As she headed for the door, a maid rushed in and bobbed a curtsey. "Lady Crossly, three coaches have pulled up before the house. One coach is quite grand."

Amaryllis's heart plummeted. A grand coach could mean but one thing. She had been told Reginald's Aunt Rowena had decided to come to collect Selena, and that she should be arriving any day. Amaryllis had been dreading meeting the Countess. She knew not what to expect. What if when Lady Rotherby learned of Amaryllis's betrothal to Reginald, she failed to approve of her? After all, Amaryllis thought, she was naught but a commoner, and Reginald was an Earl's son.

She was surprised when Selena gripped her hand. "Come meet my formidable aunt. The one who is to make a lady of me."

Selena's words failed to stave off Amaryllis's panic despite the smile Selena wore. All the same, she let Selena lead her from the parlor. As they followed the others through the great hall, she wondered if she might excuse herself to go see to the children. But no, that would make no sense. The children had four nurses watching over them. She could do naught but hope to make a reasonable impression on the Countess. She glanced down at the gown she wore. It was another of Selena's. A pretty gray skirt and bodice with pink petticoats. Selena had said it was too sweet a gown for her. Would the Countess think Amaryllis shameful because she was not wearing mourning for her father? Should she have tried to borrow a darker gown from Mary Crossly, if Mary had one?

Too late. She had no more time to think about what she should or should not have done, she was about to be presented to the regal looking Lady Rotherby. The Countess's dark hair, what showed of it under the fashionable hat she wore, was streaked with gray, but few lines or wrinkles creased her face. Releasing Lady Crossly from an embrace, the Countess stretched out her arms to Selena. Dropping Amaryllis's hand, Selena laughed her tinkling laugh and gave her aunt a bountiful hug.

"Do look at me, dear Aunt," Selena said, stepping back. "Am I not the picture of propriety?" Selena wore the sapphire-blue gown over cream-colored petticoats that seemed to be her favorite. Her unadorned hair, as usual, when not tied at the nape of her neck, was in a neat bun atop her head.

"You look charming, my dear," the Countess said, her large brown eyes looking Selena up and down. A smile softened her face. "Now. A messenger from my husband intercepted us on our way here. Thinking I should be informed of the latest developments, your uncle informed me that Reginald is betrothed. So, before you greet Cecily, introduce me to his lovely bride-to-be."

A small, slender, woman with pale blond hair and vibrant blue eyes emerged from the coach. An attractive woman, she hugged Mary Crossly then looked expectantly at Selena, but Selena, obeying her aunt, turned to Amaryllis. At Lady Rotherby's announcement that she knew of Reginald's betrothal, Amaryllis blanched, but Selena held her

254

hand out to her. "Come, dear friend. Come and meet the Countess of Rotherby."

Her heart hammering in her chest, Amaryllis took Selena's hand, and Selena said, "Aunt Rowena, may I present Mistress Amaryllis Bowdon." Amaryllis curtseyed as Selena added, "Amaryllis – my aunt, Lady Rotherby."

Before Lady Rotherby could do anything more than acknowledge the introduction, Mary Crossly put an arm around Amaryllis's shoulders and said, "Mother Rowena, we have much to tell you about how brave Amaryllis has been and how much we have already come to love her. Godwin will tell you the same." She glanced to her left, and Amaryllis's gaze followed hers. Godwin having ridden up and turned his horse over to a stable hand, heard his name mentioned and quickly joined his wife.

Giving his mother a kiss on the cheek, Godwin said, "I see you have met the soon-to-be, newest member to our family."

"So it would seem," the Countess said, a smile twitching her shapely lips. Her direct gaze met Amaryllis's. "I understand from my husband's message that he and my nephew are off on some errand that will keep them away for several days. That is good, it will give us time to get acquainted. Now, let me introduce you to my daughter, Mistress Cecily Bardwith."

Mistress Bardwith stepped forward, a warm smile touching her lips. Introductions were made, but all Amaryllis could concentrate on were Lady Rotherby's words. 'They were to get acquainted.' Oh, dear Lord, she silently prayed, do let the Countess like me.

The drive in front of the house was chaos, but Lady Crossly's house steward seemed to be getting it under control. Children, maids, and nurses poured from the coaches. Postilions and footmen jockeyed with the horses and the various parcels and bags. A dove-like woman, introduced as Lady Rotherby's cousin and companion, Mistress Carola Mead, greeted Amaryllis in a twittering voice. Lady Rotherby's daughter's three children, an older girl, Brilliana, Amaryllis guessed the girl to be in her teen years, a boy, Teagan, she thought must not yet be out of grammar school, and a girl, Ampora, who could not be a lot older than Tabitha, were also introduced. The older girl, who looked a lot like her mother but was already taller, eyed Amaryllis curiously, but the other two children dashed off to greet their cousins who had come down from the nursery.

Tabitha and Charlie at first clung to Betty's hands, but after a few moments Tabitha hesitantly joined Ampora and Elisel, and the three were soon chatting away. Charlie held back until Maitena took his hand, and the two, ignoring the older children, sat down to play with Fate. The little dog's tail was all a-wag, but his ears twitched, and his eyes darted about. Lots to make a small dog nervous. He had to be careful not to get stomped on.

Soon Lady Crossly was shepherding her guests inside. "Husted will see all the baggage gets sorted and to the correct rooms. He will also see the maids get to the correct rooms and will see your staff gets their supper. I cannot imagine how I would go on without him." She looked back around at the younger children and their nurses. "Oh, Liverna, do you please see the children and their nurses back to the nursery. The children will be needing their supper."

"Yes, Lady Crossly," Liverna answered, and the other nurses joined her in herding up the children. The boy Teagan looked longingly after the adults, but finally with a frown and the five-year-old Wilbur at his heels, he followed the others inside. Lady Crossly put and arm around Brilliana. "You, my dear, must take supper with us. How old are you now?"

The girl smiled a smile that lit up her whole face, "I am fifteen, Aunt Fonda."

"Well, indeed, much too old to be sharing the nursery. I will see you have your own room. No more nursery for you. Why, soon you will be putting your hair up."

"You must not put any such ideas into her head, Fonda," Brilliana's mother said. "To my thinking, she is growing up too fast. However, you are right, she is too old for the nursery. Fact is, she has her own maid now. But you need not give her a separate bedchamber. She can share a bed with Carola."

"Oh, that is splendid. Now I will not need to move Reggie's valet into Reggie's room. Poor man was sadly injured when their coach was assaulted by footpads. But enough of that for now. We will let Selena and Mistress Bowdon tell all in the parlor after supper."

The general chit-chat flowed around Amaryllis, and she tried to keep a bright smile on her face, but her stomach was in a knot. How she wished Reginald was with her. She was not used to such grand personage. She had found Reginald's uncle easygoing and unpretentious, but Lady Rotherby seemed every inch a Countess, a grand lady. Amaryllis prayed when they sat down to supper, she would not spill anything, or use the newfangled fork in the wrong way.

At least she had a slight reprieve. The new arrivals needed time to refresh themselves before sitting down to supper, and she would have time to compose herself. Lady Crossly and her staff were busy adding place settings to the table. The poor cook would somehow have to put together enough food to feed the increased number of guests. Amaryllis knew her own dear Cook would manage to put a plentiful meal on the table, but she would be certain to complain about the ordeal the following day.

Joining Amaryllis as they returned to the parlor, Selena said, "Had they arrived but a little later, we would already have had our supper. Oh, well, I suppose my stomach will have to rumble awhile longer. Now, come sit by me, and I will tell you more about Aunt Rowena that you may not fear her. She will love you. I promise you."

Amaryllis wished she could be as certain of the Countess as was Selena, but she had no time to reflect on Selena's assurances as Ansel interrupted, stating, "Such stories as my father has told me of Lady Rotherby. She rode with them, you may know, when they were highwaymen robbing the Puritans to send aid to the King."

Her mouth open, Amaryllis stared at Ansel. What had he said? She had learned that Sir Cyril and Lord Rotherby were old friends, that Sir Cyril had ridden with Lord Rotherby when after the battle at Worcester and King Charles II's defeat, they had chosen to remain outside the law rather than surrender to the Puritans. But what could he mean about Lady Rotherby riding with them? Was he joking with her?

Coming into the room, Godwin asked, "What are you telling Mistress Bowdon about my mother, Ansel?"

Ansel's wide grin spread across his face. "I have told her little at this point, Godwin. Naught but that she rode with my father and Lord

Rotherby. But I do have a number of stories I could recite. Some quite thrilling. Stories of my Aunt Arcadia are exciting, as well."

Godwin chuckled. "My mother, and no doubt your aunt, would as soon have those stories laid to rest. They are now both respectable ladies."

Ansel snorted. "Lady Rotherby may be respectable, but Aunt Arcadia is as headstrong as ever, or so Father says. Father says she keeps Uncle Deverette on his toes. I know my cousin, Silvester, dares not cross her."

"Well, I have not met your aunt, but I have heard stories about her. My mother adores her. I do think they may correspond, but when they last saw each other, I could not hazard."

"'Tis great fun to have this opportunity to meet Lady Rotherby and to again see Lord Rotherby," Ansel said. "I am certain it has been at least ten years since last my father and Lord Rotherby met. 'Twas when Lord Rotherby was going to visit his older brother on the Wirral Peninsula. He passed by our home on the way and stayed several days with us. If I recall correctly, he and Father had a grand time reminiscing. I loved to sit and listen to their stories."

Amaryllis's gaze darted back and forth between the stately barrister and the exuberant youth. Overwhelmed by all she was hearing, she looked at Selena. Giving her hand a squeeze, Selena said, "Hear the pride in their voices? You cannot say Godwin fails to admire his mother or Ansel his aunt. I do hope he will tell some stories about his aunt. She sounds like someone I would love to know."

Hearing Selena, Ansel laughed. "Aye, Selena." As was normal with Selena and Reginald, they immediately insisted they be on a first name basis with Sir Cyril's son, and he eagerly complied. "You would love my Aunt Arcadia. Informality is the norm in her home. Not that they never have any stately dinners. Uncle Deverette, being the third Baronet of Britteridge Hall, he must at times host local or visiting gentry and even nobles. But Aunt Arcadia says she gets far more enjoyment hosting the local farmers and tenants at their various festivals and feasts. But then, I cannot say we Yardleys are particularly formal either."

"I fear Mary and I must often be more formal than we might choose due to my offices in Derby," Godwin said. "I must host clients, barris-

258

ters, members of the town council, even judges. Mary never complains, but I know at times it must get tiring."

"It never gets tiring, dear husband," Mary said, following Lady Crossly into the room. "And you cannot say we dispense more hospitality than do Milo and Fonda. I do say, both Fonda and I are ever pleased to entertain, be it friends, family, or acquaintances. We have enjoyed readying the table for Fonda's expanded number of guests. 'Twill be a merry supper, and no doubt a lively evening."

"Indeed," Selena agreed, "and here come Aunt Rowena, Cecily, Brilliana, and Mistress Mead, all at once. So now, please God, may we go into supper. I am starved."

Chuckling, Lady Crossly said, "Yes, everyone to the table."

Foreboding in her heart, Amaryllis followed the others into the great hall where a long table had been set, and servants waited to serve Lady Crossly's guests.

Chapter 31

Elva Bowdon sat at her desk running the feather of her quill pen up and down the slant of her nose. Close to a fortnight had passed, and she had heard nothing from Felton. How hard could it be to kill a little boy. She decided he had but taken the horse and saddle she loaned him, and the traveling funds she had given him, and absconded with them. She would no doubt never see him again. He must know she would be fearful of pressing charges against him. He would confess what she had hired him to do. She could deny his claims, but some would be suspicious. Then did the young baronet meet with an accident, they might begin to believe Felton. Might even ostracize her. That would not be good for Averil's or Dorian's future.

Yet she had been so certain Felton wanted that promised annuity. How his eyes had gleamed at the thought of never having to work again. Perhaps he had not trusted her, had not believed she would uphold her end of the bargain? She had not made up her mind whether she would keep her word to him or not. But now, she was getting desperate enough, that did he suddenly return with news of the boy's death, she would not only arrange the annuity, she might well give him a bonus.

Vacillating between anger and desperation, she had remembered her cousin, Offa Ledeen. Always living beyond his means, always coming to her with his hand out, he could well accomplish what Felton had failed to do. She had decided to send Offa to Derby with the arrest warrant for Amaryllis, and the writ to return the children to Churlwood. By now, Amaryllis would have arrived with the children at Glenwood House where the aunt was visiting. The estate could not be hard to find. Especially with help from the Derby constable. It could work.

The very day Amaryllis had run off with the children, when Irwin returned from his fruitless chase after the stage to Aylesbury, she had insisted he take her to Albertine to accuse Amaryllis of abducting the children. Irwin had complained. He was tired. He had ridden after that stage all for naught. They could wait till the morrow. Mayhap Amaryllis would return with the children, but she had known better, though she told him nothing of her meeting with Felton.

The Albertine constable had been leery of lodging any charges against Amaryllis, but he had promised to do some investigating. The following day, he returned to Churlwood with the information Elva had already learned from Felton.

"We cannot be certain Mistress Norton was actually Mistress Bowdon," the constable hedged. "But she and the children do match your description. According to the ostler at the inn, they boarded a coach owned by the D'Arcys and left with them on the road bound to Leicester. The D'Arcys are the children of Lord Rygate of Surrey. I cannot believe they abducted Mistress Bowdon and the children. The ostler says they boarded the coach of their own free will. The innkeeper's wife says Mistress Norton or Bowdon, as the case may be, dined with the D'Arcys the previous night. She believed them to be old friends who had accidentally met up at the inn."

"My guess is the D'Arcys had no idea she was abducting the children," Elva said. "There is no telling what lie she might have told the innocent D'Arcys." She wanted no trouble with powerful nobles and would not try to place any blame on them. "The problem is, the children are missing and my husband and I are responsible for them. I must insist you issue an arrest warrant for Mistress Amaryllis Bowdon."

The constable had hemmed and hawed, but eventually had agreed to ask the local magistrate for the warrant. After all, the children were missing. With her cousin Offa's agreement to go to Derby with the warrant and the writ to retrieve Charlie, Elva's hopes had again been raised. Surely the Derby Justice of the Peace would honor the legal documents.

Delving into her dwindling hoard of coins, she had given her cousin sufficient funds to travel to Derby and to return with the boy. Was he successful, she had promised him the same annuity she had promised Felton. She had no doubt her cousin knew she needed Charlie dead, though she had not expressed it in exact terms. She had suggested that should some accident befall the boy on his way back to Churlwood, he could not be held responsible. Whether he would insure an accident happened, she could not be sure, but it mattered not. Without Amaryllis around, she could do the job herself. No more near misses.

That was four days past. Now, she could do naught but wait. Wait and wonder whether all her scheming would come to fruition. If not, if Amaryllis got the children to their grandfather, if he believed Amaryllis's tales of mistreatment of the children, he could well decide to turn her, Irwin, and their family out of Churlwood. Sir Cyril had been content to let them move into Churlwood to be guardians of the children so Tabitha and Charlie might continue to live in their own home. But did he turn out to be a doting grandfather, all her plans would be for naught. Averil would not inherit Churlwood as he so rightly should.

She could wish Averil's temperament more like hers. Dorian was like her, but Averil was like his father, honest and trusting. Were they turned out of Churlwood, forced to return to their meager home in Langley, and Irwin forced to return to his law practice, what would happen to Averil? The boy had no skills, he had naught to inherit but their Langley home. He was handsome enough, but not enough to attract some rich heiress. He would most likely be forced to take work as a clerk. That would never do for her firstborn.

Dorian could expect little better, actually less, for he would not inherit the house. He had a temperament that would make him willing to do whatever might be necessary to secure a better living, but he was lazy. His marks in school were low. He had cultivated no friends among the upper classes. Fact was, he had few friends at all. He was slovenly in his attire and selfish, but he was bright. He knew they needed to get rid of Charlie. When she had suggested he climb the ladder leaning against the tree, and that he should heed whether Charlie might follow him and watch did the child fall, he had known she was telling him to force Charlie up the ladder and then make him fall. That the fall had done no serious injury to the boy had been unfortunate.

The plan had been so perfect. Knowing full well that her present high wages and future retirement annuity were dependent upon who was the baronet, Elva's maid had done her part. She had removed the children's young nurse, Molly, from the garden with Elva's fake summons, and had taken Tabitha away that she might not report what transpired. All had gone according to plan, but the plan had failed.

Getting rid of Molly had been Elva's next goal. Easy enough to have the cat scratch Charlie and to blame Molly's lack of supervision for the injury. Finding the right nurse to take Molly's place had not been as easy as she had thought it would be, but from the moment Nurse Palmer first spoke in her hard, clipped tone, Elva knew she had found an ally. Here was a person forced to earn her living, but obviously hating her occupation. Palmer had no love of children, but to keep the job, she would follow Elva's instructions to the letter.

Had Amaryllis not interfered, the slow poisoning of the young baronet would have succeeded. But Amaryllis had to insist Cook prepare every morsel Charlie ate, then Amaryllis would be the one to carry the food up to the nursery. She would sit with him until he had eaten his fill. The boy quickly regained his health, but Elva could see by the way Amaryllis started watching over him that Amaryllis was suspicious of her. She had never dreamed, though, that Amaryllis might spirit the children away.

Then there was Cook. Elva had no doubt Cook had drugged Palmer. Given her something to make her oversleep. Could Elva dismiss the obnoxious woman, she would, but that was the one thing Irwin put his foot down about. He liked his meals. And Elva had to admit, Cook's meals were always excellent. Elva would have liked to get rid of the entire Churlwood staff and hire her own staff who would be loyal to her, not Amaryllis, but she had not dared do that. She could not reasonably have found fault with the whole household. Some might have complained to Sir Cyril, and he might have come to investigate the situation. That she had not wanted.

Well, at least she had heard no word from him at this point. That must mean Amaryllis had not yet been able to talk to him. Offa or Felton might yet succeed. She could but pray. In the meantime, she must resume her letter to Sir Cyril. Mayhap she could throw off his suspicion did she tell him of the children's disappearance, express her concern and worry, and her complete lack of understanding as to what should have caused Amaryllis to run off with the children.

A tap at the door brought her head up. The footman, Dill, opened the study door and said, "Mistress Bowdon, Sir Cyril Yardley awaits you in the parlor."

Elva's heart dropped. "Sir Cyril? Here?"

"Yes, Mistress Bowdon, and I go now to inform Mister Bowdon."

"Well, first tell Sir Cyril I will be with him directly."

"Yes, Mistress Bowdon," Dill said and silently closed the door.

Elva rose slowly and smoothed her skirt. She put a hand to her head and made certain her cap was on straight. As usual, Dill's face had been but a mask, but she noted his eyes sparkled. They were all against her. She knew that. She raised her chin. She would act as though she had done nothing wrong. She picked up the letter she had been writing to Sir Cyril. She would tell him she had been hesitant about writing him, hoping Amaryllis would return with the children, but at last she had decided she must inform him of Amaryllis's abduction of the young baronet and his sister. She would then show him the letter she had started.

※　※　※　※

Reginald looked around the spacious Churlwood parlor. The furnishings were sparse, but well-suited to the airy room with its white marble hearth and large windows. He was impressed with the brick house and the well-kept grounds and looked forward to seeing more of the manor. This was Charlie and Tabitha's home, and he and Amaryllis meant the children should spend a certain amount of each year at the manor. Sir Cyril had already agreed that once Reginald and Amaryllis had some time to themselves at Ardenstrath, the children could come to live with them. In the meantime, Sir Cyril would take Tabitha and Charlie back to his estate in Cheshire. It would be a treat for him to have his only grandchildren spend a few months with him.

Tired and sore from three days in the saddle, Reginald still felt exhilarated. He could not wait to see Elva Bowdon's face. He, Sir Cyril, and Felton, his hands bound behind him, stood to the forefront. Uncle Nathaniel, David Stoke, Milo, the Derby deputy constable, the Albertine constable, and Richard Toms, who was with them because he wanted to be able to report all that transpired to his aunt, stood in a semi-circle behind them.

The door opened. Elva Bowdon entered, a smile of greeting on her face, but the smile froze. Her eyes widened and appeared to near pop out of her head when her gaze rested on Felton. Somehow, she composed herself, and in too high a voice asked, "Well, now, what is this, Sir Cyril? I was not told I had so many guests."

"Do you not recognize this man?" Sir Cyril said, pushing Felton, still in his torn and bloodied clothing, a little forward.

Swallowing hard, she said, "Why no. Should I?"

"Well, he knows you. He is going to testify that you hired him to kill my grandson."

"What utter nonsense. I have never seen this man before. And why would I want to kill the young baronet?" Confidence returning, her lips curved in a disgusted sneer, and her voice dropped back into a normal range.

"That be not true," Felton said anxiously. He would receive no reprieve did he not prove Elva Bowdon's duplicity. "You ask that fellow what opened the door. He will tell you I was here. Was him let me in to this very room to see Mistress Bowdon."

"We will be questioning him and others of the Churlwood staff," Sir Cyril said. "I will be questioning the staff about the accidents my grandson suffered. 'Twas the threats on his life that made his sister feel she had to get him to safety."

Elva Bowdon raised her chin. "Threats on Charlie's life! Again, nonsense. So he had a couple of accidents. Those things do happen. And by the by, that is why I terminated his young nurse and hired Nurse Palmer. A woman of experience."

Reginald had to give Elva Bowdon credit. She was doing a masterful job of defending herself. Too good a job.

Leaning a little forward, she peered at Felton. "Mayhap, does this man go by the name of Felton, I do know him, though dressed as he is, he is near unrecognizable. Yes, he bought a horse from me. And a saddle. And he yet owes me the final payment on them."

"Nay, she tells not the truth," Felton cried, his voice rising over her protests. "She gave me the horse and saddle and coins to pay my way so I could follow after the D'Arcys and kill the young baronet. She promised me an annuity so I would ne'er haf to work again in my life did I kill the boy."

Elva Bowdon was shaking her head in denial when her husband entered the room. "Elva what is this?" He looked about at all the men in the room, then his gaze rested on Sir Cyril. Reaching out a hand in greeting, he said, "Sir Cyril, what luck you have come. Elva was saying she must write you. The strangest thing, Amaryllis has run away with Sir Charles and Mistress Tabitha."

As if it were planned, Mistress Bowdon held up a piece of paper. "Why yes, my husband is correct. Here is the letter I was writing to you when I was told of your arrival. Mayhap we should have told you sooner of the abduction, but I had hopes Amaryllis would come to her senses and would bring the children home. I hoped not to worry you, Sir Cyril."

It all sounded so plausible, but Reginald knew every word was a lie, and his temper was rising as Mistress Bowdon accused Amaryllis of abducting the children. If not for his uncle's hand on his shoulder, he would have stepped forward and shaken the woman.

Sir Cyril did not bother to take Irwin Bowdon's hand or the paper, but the Albertine constable took the letter. On their way through Albertine, they had collected the constable, fully expecting he would be taking Elva Bowdon into custody. But the constable was looking terribly uncomfortable, and at this point he seemed to be having trouble believing Felton. Indeed, it would be hard to believe the child's aunt would pay someone to kill the boy.

"Sir Cyril," the footman said from the doorway. "I have the staff gathered in the hall."

"Good, Dill," Sir Cyril said. "Now we will get some answers."

"Will someone please tell me what this is all about?" begged Irwin Bowdon.

"We believe your wife paid this man, Felton, to have Sir Charles killed that you and then your son would inherit the baronetcy," Sir Cyril said, pushing past Bowdon and marching out of the parlor and into the high-ceiling hall. Tapestries graced the white walls, and chairs lined two side walls, otherwise the room was empty but for a multi-candle chandelier. Raising his voice that the assembled servants might hear, Sir Cyril added, "I am asking charges be brought against your wife,

Mister Bowdon, and she will stand trial. Anyone who fails to cooperate will stand trial on a charge of accessory."

Reginald saw the servants eye one another then turn their eyes on two women. By the looks of the two, hard faces, cold eyes, he would guess they were Mistress Bowdon's personal maid, and the children's nurse.

"But this cannot be, this cannot be," sputtered Irwin Bowdon, following after Sir Cyril. "Elva try to kill young Charlie? Why she has been out of her head with worry. The very day the children disappeared, she had Averil and me ride after the stage to Aylesbury to see if Amaryllis might be taking them to you, Sir Cyril. She worried about the children being on the stage. Charlie being so young. She said we must bring Charlie home, but we should let Amaryllis and Tabitha go on." He looked at his wife. "Is that not right, Elva?" He then looked to the Albertine constable. "You must remember, we came to you that same day to tell you of the abduction and of our fear for the children. Do you not recall that?"

"Hush, Irwin, you have said enough," his wife said, putting a hand on his shoulder.

Confusion in his eyes, he looked at her, but then brightened when a young gentleman entered the hall. "Oh, look, here is Averil. He will tell Sir Cyril what I say is true."

"What is this Father, Mother?" the smartly dressed young man asked. "I saw all the horses out front. And why are all the servants in here? There was no one in the stable to see to my horse."

Reginald could almost feel sorry for the young man. Averil's confused eyes searched the crowd. At the sight of Felton, his nostrils flared in distaste, but he turned his gaze back to his father. "Please, Father, what is amiss?"

"Sir Cyril, for some unknown reason, thinks your mother hired that man." He pointed to Felton. "Hired him to kill Charlie. I have been telling them how addlepated that is. I told them how upset your mother was at Charlie's disappearance. How she insisted we ride after the stage in hopes of finding Charlie and bringing him home."

Averil looked at Sir Cyril for the first time. "Sir Cyril, I am sorry I failed to recognize you in this crowd. What Father tells you is true.

Mother said did Amaryllis reach you and tell you lies about her treatment of Charlie that you might turn us out. She was most anxious to have Charlie safe back here so you could come and see how well he did. Why Mother has had naught but concern for Charlie. When I saw Dorian boost Charlie up on a limb of the apple tree and then push him off, why you should have seen how upset Mother was when I told her what I had seen. I know she must have given Dorian a thorough scolding."

"That is enough, Averil," Elva Bowdon said, her hands twitching nervously at her side.

"You saw that happen?" Reginald could not help but ask.

Averil glanced at Reginald momentarily before looking back at Sir Cyril. "'Twas not long before Dorian went back to school."

Sir Cyril sucked in a deep breath and blew it out through his nose. He then fixed his gaze on a tall, thin-lipped woman. Better dressed than the other servants, she had to be Elva Bowdon's personal maid. "You are Mistress Bowdon's maidservant?" Sir Cyril asked, and the woman nodded. "You gave the young nurse, Molly, a fake message and then shepherded Tabitha inside, leaving Charlie alone with Dorian. What have you to say for your actions?"

The tall woman blanched but raised her chin. "Mistress Bowdon told me to give Molly a message to meet her in the study. She told me I should then clean up Mistress Tabitha who had been playing on the ground with her brother. As Dorian had come out, I saw no reason not to leave Sir Charles in his care. This is the first I heard of Dorian pushing the child from the tree."

"You thought a fourteen-year-old boy a good caretaker for a two-year-old child?"

"I had my orders to obey," the maid answered defiantly.

"I am most confused by all this," Irwin Bowdon said. "You are trying to make this sound like my wife was deliberately trying to harm Charlie. But you are wrong. Wrong I say. Elva may not have been the most gentle aunt. I did think her treatment of the children at times harsh, but she would never try to harm them." He looked at his wife, looked at Sir Cyril, and then at all the other people in the room, including the servants.

Sir Cyril shook his head and said, "I would speak with the head stableman."

A man looking to be in his late thirties with tousled, cropped hair and a brimmed cap tightly clutched in his hand stepped forward. "I be the head stableman," he said.

"Have you ever seen this man before?" Sir Cyril pointed to Felton.

"Aye, Sir Cyril. The Mistress come out to the stable with him 'bout a fortnight ago. She said he had bought the dun horse and a saddle and bridle. She said I was to fix him up. Surprised me. I knew Felton. He worked here at Churlwood for a bit, but the baronet, Sir Abner, dismissed him. I had to wonder where Felton got the money to be a-buying the dun. The dun being Mistress Bowdon's own horse.

"I asked her what saddle and bridle he was buying, seeing as the only ones not belonging to the manor was Master Dorian's. She said he was buying Master Dorian's, then she swept about and left me to see to her dictates. Well, I knew Felton to be a ne'er-do-well. While I readied the dun, I asked him how he came by the money for the horse and gear. He chuckled and said he had his ways and said he would be coming into plenty more ere long. Enough so's he would ne'er have to work again. We said no more till I helped him mount, and he rode off."

"You see. 'Tis as I said," Felton cried. "I had no money. Ye can ask anyone in Albertine. Ask the constable here. Where would I have the money to buy a horse and saddle? And was I not being paid to do so, why would I want to kill the baronet?"

The Albertine constable started nodding his head. "Aye. Felton lives in a hovel not fit for swine. He would ne'er have the money to buy a horse."

"Have you heard enough, then?" Sir Cyril asked. "Will you be taking Mistress Bowdon into custody?"

Elva Bowdon took a step back. "I am telling you, he had the money!" she snapped. "I sold him my horse because I hate to ride. I sold him Dorian's saddle and bridle because Dorian was due new ones. Why would any of you believe that villain over me? He is lying in hope of saving his own neck at the expense of mine. How could you think I would try to harm Charlie?"

"Mother is right," Averil broke in. "She would ne'er think to harm

Charlie. Why, when he was so sick. Had the diarrhea and was throwing up, Mother was so concerned. She had a special medicine she..."

"Averil, quiet!" Mistress Bowdon gasped.

Sir Cyril, put a hand on Mistress Bowdon's shoulder to still her. "Nay, Averil, continue," he said "You were telling us of your mother's concern."

Averil looked from his mother to Sir Cyril and back to his mother who was shaking her head. He looked even more confused.

"Go ahead, Averil," his father said. "We must disprove these lies."

"As you say, Father." He looked again at Sir Cyril. "When Charlie was so sick, Mother would slip tiny grains of a white powder into his morning porridge."

"You saw her do this?" Sir Cyril asked in amazement, and Reginald saw his hand on Elva Bowdon's shoulder tighten when she started to protest.

"Oh, yes, Sir Cyril," Averil said, his voice earnest. "I had come in from a ride, and I took off my boots because they were muddied. Left them by the door to be cleaned," he added as if the information was of some importance to his tale. "Being in but my stockings, I think Mother must not have heard me come up the back stairs. She had set a tray with two bowls on it down on the table where we keep extra candles. She dropped the grainy powder into the porridge in one bowl and stirred it up. She started when I asked her what she did, but then said 'twas medicine she hoped would make Charlie well. It worked, too, for within a week, he started getting better."

Reginald could but stare in wonder when Averil concluded his tale and raised his chin. Could he not know he was signing his mother's death warrant.

"Nay!" spoke up a heavy-set woman with hefty forearms and a large apron covering her gown. Reginald had no trouble recognizing her as the cook. "Sir Charles started getting better when Mistress Amaryllis and I started monitoring every bite he put in his mouth," Cook said. "We let no one else touch his food. You ask my staff here." She pushed forward two young girls, also in aprons. The girls were both nodding their heads in assent. "'Tis after that poisoning of the little baronet that Mistress Amaryllis knew she had to get Sir Charles away from Mistress Bowdon to the safety of his aunt and then his grandfather," Cook concluded.

"'Tis a lie," Averil shouted. "'Twas medicine, I tell you. She kept it in a little blue pouch. She can show you the pouch, I have no doubt. After she mixed the medicine into the porridge, she gave the porridge to Nurse Palmer to take up to Charlie in the nursery."

"No! You cannot put the blame on me," Nurse Palmer cried. "I knew the boy was sick, but you cannot say I knew he was being poisoned. I was but following instructions. Make sure he eats it all, she would say. Then he would get sick. But how could I know 'twas poison?"

Reginald had heard enough. They had Elva Bowdon now. "I would guess do we search her room," he suggested, "we will find that pouch. What say you, Sir Cyril?"

His face thoughtful, Sir Cyril nodded. "Aye, an excellent idea."

"Nay!" Elva Bowdon broke away from Sir Cyril's grip. Eyes narrowed, her mouth drawn up in a snarl, she hissed, "You will not search my room! None of you will dare go in my room."

"Elva, what is this?" beseeched her husband. "Why do you act so? Do you but have the pouch, you can prove your innocence."

Grabbing a poker from the hearth, she held it out in front of her swinging it a little while backing toward the grand staircase. "All of you stay back. Lies! It is all lies, I tell you."

"Mother." Averil reached out to her. She swung the poker at him, the end catching on his sleeve and ripping it. "Mother!" he exclaimed, grabbing his arm and looking down at his coat.

"Elva? What can you be doing? Put down that poker before you hurt someone!" Bowdon pleaded, but she only swung the poker more threateningly.

"Does she get to her room and lock her door, she can destroy the evidence before we can break the door down," Reginald said in Sir Cyril's ear.

"Aye," Sir Cyril said. "We must stop her. You go to her left, I will take her right. But be careful. She could do you some injury with that poker. Lord knows I would like to shoot the vixen, but we dare not. Should we not find the evidence, we could be hard put proving our accusations, and the scandal could be hard on everyone."

The Albertine constable joined them as they worked their way up the highly polished stairs after their quarry. "Mistress Bowdon," the constable said, "you are making yourself look guilty by this action. Are you innocent, 'tis easy enough to prove."

Elva Bowdon said nothing, but her eyes darted from Sir Cyril, to the constable, to Reginald. She moved from the railing to the center of the staircase to keep them from being able to flank her. Her husband continued to beg her to put down the poker, but she gave no indication she heard him. Her whole being was concentrated on keeping her pursuers at bay.

Reginald glanced down into the hall. His uncle had advanced to the foot of the stairs, as had Stoke, but Milo and Toms remained with the Derby deputy constable and Felton. Good thinking. With all the attention directed on Elva Bowdon, Felton might try to make an escape. The Churlwood staff had all turned to watch the drama being played out on the staircase, but none of them tried to interfere. They all stood wide-eyed and frozen in place.

Reginald moved closer. Might he trip her? Seeing his movement, she jabbed at him with the poker. He stepped back. At the same time, she took a quick step up to the stair behind her. Her shoe heel caught in the hem of her skirt. In trying to regain her balance and disentangle her foot, she flailed her arms wildly. Reginald saw it all as if it were happening in a dream. The poker went flying straight at the Albertine constable. The constable dodged it, but in so doing, he lost his footing, stumbled backwards, and was unable to reach out to halt Elva Bowdon's fall. She toppled head over heels down the center of the staircase, and landed on the poker. Her head landed on the bottom step.

Chapter 32

"Mother!" Averil cried.

"Elva!" Bowdon cried, dropping to his knees beside Mistress Bowdon.

Reginald moved warily down the steps. Elva Bowdon's neck was at a crooked angle, her left leg was tucked under her in an unnatural state, and a trickle of blood appeared at her mouth.

"Mother, Mother," Averil wept. Kneeling beside her, he brought his gaze up to search his father's face. "Can you not help her, Father?"

"Let me through," the cook said. "Let me have a look at her."

Bowdon moved enough to let the heavy-set woman squiggle in next to him. Cook tsked, then said, "See can we get that poker out from under her."

Reginald helped to gently raise Mistress Bowdon enough that Cook was able to slip the poker out, but when Mistress Bowdon was let back down, she let out a lamentable groan.

"'Tis her ribs are broke," Cook said. "Mayhap her back. That blood at her mouth means she has got some sort of internal injury. For certain her neck and her left leg are broke." She looked up at Bowdon. "I think do we try to move the Mistress, we will but cause her more pain. Mayhap a blanket for her and a pillow to prop her neck a bit. I suppose you should send for the surgeon in Albertine, but I am thinking 'twill do little good."

Bowdon rose and said, "Smith go directly for the surgeon. Take the fastest horse."

"Yes, Mister Bowdon," a slender young man answered and bounded from the hall.

"I will get a blanket and pillow," Nurse Palmer said and started up the stairs.

Reginald caught her wrist. "We will be going with you," he said, nodding to Sir Cyril. "You can take us to Mistress Bowdon's room."

The nurse reddened but nodded and said, "This way, sir."

Sir Cyril called to Milo and Stoke to accompany them, and the four of them tromped up the stairs behind Nurse Palmer. Opening the door to Mistress Bowdon's bedchamber, Nurse Palmer started to enter, but Sir Cyril stopped her. "Nay, Nurse Palmer. You find a blanket and pillow from some other room. Until we are finished searching this room, you will not enter it."

The woman swallowed hard, nodded her head, and turned to a room across the corridor.

Reginald entered the room first. He wondered if it had once been Amaryllis's mother's room. Lacy yellow curtains framed the window that looked out at a rose garden. A white baluster bed with yellow canopy and matching quilt graced one wall, a white armoire trimmed with tiny yellow flowers, the opposite. A yellow and pink flowered paper covering the walls above a cherry-wood wainscoting gave a bright cheerfulness to the room.

"'Tis important we find that pouch, so make a careful search," Sir Cyril said, and they each took a section of the room. The search did not take long.

"Look here," Milo said, holding up a small blue silk pouch he had pulled from the bottom of a chest at the foot of the bed. "This could be it."

Taking the bag, Sir Cyril cautiously opened it. Peering inside the pouch, he wet his finger and poked it inside. When he withdrew his finger, a grainy white powder clung to it. He placed the tip of his tongue to his finger. He shrugged. "It has no taste, except perhaps 'tis a tad sweet. It will have to be tested, but I have little doubt 'tis arsenic."

Reginald pitied the mice who would be fed some of the contents from the pouch. Did the mice die, the powder would be determined to be arsenic or mayhap some other lethal poison, but poison all the same. They would have proof Elva Bowdon had been attempting to kill Charlie.

When they returned to the hall with their prize, Reginald saw most of the servants had been sent back to their stations. Only the cook, the house steward, Nurse Palmer, Elva Bowdon's personal maid, and the head footman, Dill, remained. A blanket had been placed over Mistress Bowdon and a pillow cushioned her head, but her breath came in ragged snatches.

"Cook says the ribs must have punctured her lungs. She may not last much longer," the Albertine constable said, taking the pouch from Sir Cyril and peeking inside it. "Be this the pouch you saw, Mister Averil?" he asked, holding the pouch out for viewing.

Averil rose. "Yes, yes, that is it. Now you will see 'twas but medicine in it."

"I fear we may not," the constable said, tucking the pouch into his pocket. "I will need take it back to Albertine. Have the apothecary test it."

"I will be going with you," Sir Cyril said. "And best we get Felton locked up in your jail for the night. As the crimes he committed took place in Leicestershire, we will be taking him back to Leicester to stand trial."

The constable nodded. "Aye, but first we will need his statement concerning Mistress Bowdon. Do the pouch contents prove to be poison, and does she live, she will have to stand trial." He looked down at Elva Bowdon and shook his head. "I am doubting she lives, though."

Sir Cyril looked at Reginald. "You will stay here till the end?"

Reginald nodded. "Aye."

Sir Cyril nodded and looked to the house steward. "You and Dill see rooms are made up for us. We will not be expecting a large supper, but see the table is set." He glanced at Averil then back at the steward. "Whether the Bowdons choose to join us, I could not hazard. They may choose to eat in their rooms, do they choose to eat at all." He lowered his voice. "I am not expecting Mistress Bowdon to last much longer."

He started to leave but turned back to the steward. "I will want to go over the house accounts with you on the morrow. Be certain they are ready."

"Yes, Sir Cyril," the steward answered.

"And where is the Manor steward? Why is he not here?"

"He grows old, Sir Cyril. He has been the manor steward since before Sir Abner became the baronet. He started with Sir Abner's father. He has hoped for his retirement for a couple of years, but then with Sir Abner's death, he felt he must stay on until a new steward could be found, and he could train him, introduce him to the ways of the manor." The house steward glanced at Bowdon and lowered his voice. "He was leery of letting Bowdon choose the next manor steward. He had hopes you would do so next time you visited. Anyway, he is presently laid up with a cold. You can find him abed in his cottage, I have no doubt."

"Thank you. Send him word I will be calling on him on the morrow."

"Yes, sir."

Sir Cyril turned and beckoned to his son-in-law. "David, do you ride with me. Sir Milo, we will take one of your outriders in case we need to send any message back to you."

"Aye," Milo answered as Stoke joined his father-in-law and the constable.

When they left, Averil dropped back down beside his mother. His eyes tortured, he said, "Dear Mother, why did you act so? They have the pouch with the medicine and can now prove you innocent. Why did you not want them in your room?" That he still believed his mother innocent, amazed Reginald.

Her voice low and raspy, Elva Bowdon said, "I did it all...," she wheezed, her breath rattling in her throat. "All for you, my beloved," she at last managed. Her hand groped for his, and he caught it and clutched it to his heart. A semblance of a smile touched her lips. "Mayhap Offa may yet save all for you."

Bowdon reached for her other hand. "We have a surgeon coming, Elva. Have faith."

She never turned to look at her husband, but her last sentence sent a chill creeping up Reginald's spine. "Who is Offa?" he demanded. When no one answered him, he grabbed Bowdon by his coat front. "Who is Offa?"

Forced to rise a little, Bowdon looked up. "Offa Ledeen. He is Elva's cousin. He was here the first of the week. Always asking for money. A ne'er-do-well," he said, and shaking off Reginald's hold, he sank back down beside his wife.

Reginald looked at his uncle. "I have to get back to Amaryllis. I fear there may yet be another threat on Charlie's life. I told Sir Cyril I would stay, but I must leave immediately."

"I am going with you," his uncle said. "But remember, boy, your Aunt Rowena is there by now. She is not apt to let anything happen to young Charlie."

"He is right, Reginald," Milo said. "Fonda, too, is not like to let strangers near the boy. All the same, best we alert everyone to the chance of trouble." He looked at his step-father. "But 'tis better I should go with Reginald, Nate. I know you are yet hale and hearty, but this has been a fast, hard ride here. Best you rest. Besides, Sir Cyril may well need your help. There will be much to do to straighten things out here."

His mouth in a thin line, Reginald's uncle slowly nodded. "Aye, Milo is right. I could well slow you down. You will take your other outrider, Milo?"

"Nay," Milo said. "Reggie has his two, you may have need for mine."

"I am going with you," Toms said. "We can change horses at Mere Manse, and again in Leicester. I know a good stable there."

"I thank you both," Reginald said.

"I will get you gents some food packed up," Cook said. "You have had no refreshment since you arrived. You are to have a bite before you leave ere you faint off your horses and be of no benefit to Sir Charles."

Reginald could see the sense to what Cook said. They did need to eat.

"Sir," Dill said, looking at Milo, then at Reginald. "Sir Cyril told your outriders to take your horses to the stable. Said to have them walked, rubbed down, and fed. Should I tell them now you will be needing those horses?"

"Aye, and tell them not to over feed or water the horses as the poor things must again take to the road. Oh, and do tell the outriders, Billings and Crouch, to come to the kitchen to get a bite to eat ere we leave," Reginald said. "We will be grabbing a bite there ourselves."

"This way, gentlemen," Cook said, and with a glance over her shoulder, added. "I will send one of the maids with some ale for you, Lord Rotherby. You and Mister Pim," she nodded to the house steward, "may have a bit of a wait ere we see the end."

Before following after the cook, Reginald took one last look at the grouping on the floor. Bowdon on one side of his wife, Averil, tears in their eyes, on the other, each one clutching one of Elva Bowdon's hands. A sorrowful scene, but it provoked no empathy in Reginald's heart. To the end, the woman showed no remorse. She had to know she was dying, yet even so, she still hoped Charlie would be killed that her own son would inherit the baronetcy. She was evil. With a snort of disgust, he fell in behind Toms and Milo. He had to get back to Amaryllis and Charlie.

Chapter 33

Amaryllis laughed and gave Charlie a hug when he stopped to show her the pretty pebbles he had collected. The little boy then went running off after Maitena. The two had become fast friends. They had no interest in the five older children who were engaged in a giggling game of Blind Man's Bluff. Amaryllis thought Brilliana watched the game wistfully, no doubt torn between a longing to join in the fun, and a desire to appear grown up.

The grassy meadow behind the Glenwood House was the perfect place for a picnic. The tiniest brook trickled through the meadow, and butterflies fluttered around the daisies dotting the field. Bees buzzed merrily by and birds sang in the nearby trees. The sun beat down, but awnings Mary's servants had erected gave shade to those who wanted it.

After enjoying a feast of roast capons, venison pasties, pickled beets and cucumbers, carrot pudding, lemon pudding, boiled spinach sallet, fluffy white bread and creamy butter, black bread and cheddar cheese, and dessert of little sugar cakes and Marchpane, all accompanied with a choice of wine, a light ale, or ginger beer, Amaryllis, her stomach and taster satiated, had chosen to sit on a blanket and enjoy the sunshine.

Juliet and Brilliana had chosen to join her. Lady Rotherby, nay, she must remember the extraordinary woman had said, as Amaryllis was marrying Reginald, she must call her Aunt Rowena, was seated on a folding chair under the striped awning. A blanket had been spread and cushions scattered for Mary, Mistress Mead, and Mistress Bardwith, rather Cecily. When giving Amaryllis a welcoming hug, Cecily had insisted Amaryllis call her by her given name. Lady Crossly also insisted she be called Fonda. "Our family is not often apt to stand on formality," Fonda said. "Did you not know it before, you will soon learn that you are marrying into a very large, close, and loving family. As you and Reggie will be living at Ardenstrath, we will no doubt be regular visitors back and forth. Ardenstrath being less than a day's ride away."

Mary's and Fonda's nursemaids were under another awning with the babies, Emil and Dorisande, on a blanket. Neither baby was yet crawling, but they were doing some scooting and rolling, and a lot of baby chuckling when the nurses tickled them or played peek-a-boo. Betty, after bringing Maitena and Charlie back from the brook, joined the other two nursemaids, but her eyes never left Charlie. Amaryllis prayed Mistress Sermon would release Betty from her contract that she might remain as Tabitha and Charlie's nursemaid. Betty had such a love of children, and Tabitha and Charlie had grown very attached to her.

"Now, I wonder if they might make a match?" Juliet said, and Amaryllis brought her attention back to Charlie and Tabitha's aunt.

"I beg pardon," Amaryllis said, "I was enjoying watching the children play and paying little heed to anything else.

"Oh, yes, childish laughter is so heartening," Juliet said with a wistful smile. She then added, "I said I was wondering whether Selena and my brother, Ansel, might make a match. But I think I will have to say no. Selena needs a man. Ansel is yet a boy."

"I but hope she may find someone who will appreciate all her wonderful qualities. I have never known a more loving, giving, kind-hearted person," Amaryllis said, her gaze resting on the pair wandering along the brook toward the trees. Fate tried to follow Selena, but the little dog's savior gave him a pat then shooed him back, and of course, the dog obeyed her. How the little fellow darted about with his one leg strapped to the wooden brace was amusing to watch.

"Well, I have only just met Selena," Juliet said, "but I do find her intriguing. Ansel is fascinated by her. He says he never knew a woman who knew more about horses and dogs than he knows. He still has trouble believing she dresses in breeches and rides astride like a man when traveling. He says she reminds him of our Aunt Arcadia."

"That is something Grandmother is supposed to put a stop to, am I not mistaken," Brilliana said. "However, both Grandmother and my mother wore breeches and rode astride in their younger days." Her eyes sparkled as she looked at Amaryllis and said, "You have so much to learn about this family you are marrying into." Shaking her head, she giggled. "Such stories."

"I know but a few of them," Juliet said, "but, as Ansel says, our Aunt Arcadia was once known to pretend to be a boy. Still, 'tis always amusing when Godwin takes off on one of his tales. His and Sir Milo's clandestine meetings with their mother are both humorous and thrilling. David and I do so enjoy our visits here at Glenwood."

"'Tis never dull with this family," Brilliana agreed.

Amaryllis was learning quickly that Brilliana's statement was an absolute fact. She had been terrified at the prospect of meeting Reginald's aunt, and had instead found the lady was as kind and loving as Selena and Reginald. After the late supper at Fonda's the previous evening, Lady Rotherby had announced she intended to take Amaryllis up to Fonda's sitting room and have a chat that they might get acquainted. Amaryllis had near fainted of fright, but laughing at her, Selena said, "Dear Amaryllis, look not so fearful. You will love Aunt Rowena, and she you.

"But do let me know do you see the ghost of poor Baron Burell," Selena added with a giggle as Lady Rotherby took Amaryllis's arm in hers.

Lady Rotherby looked back at Selena and then at her daughter-in-law. "Oh dear, Fonda, have you been telling your tales to Selena?"

Fonda chuckled. "I have. We had a lovely chat the night she arrived."

"Yes," Selena said, "but I have yet to experience Baron Burell's presence."

"And you are not apt to," Selena's aunt said in a disgusted tone. "Come Amaryllis. You must pay no heed to their foolishness. There are no ghosts in Fonda's sitting room."

At the time, Amaryllis had no fear of ghosts. 'Twas Lady Rotherby she feared. How groundless that fear had been. Once Lady Rotherby had them both comfortably seated on the floral brocaded sofa in Fonda's cozy sitting room, she patted Amaryllis's hand. "Before I ask you to tell me anything about yourself, I first want to tell you about me."

Shocked, Amaryllis could do naught but stare, then nod.

"Let me say, I was surprised to receive the message from my husband telling me of Reggie's betrothal. I have known the boy near since he was born. He has his own dear place in my heart. I want naught but his happiness, so I was pleased my husband praised you so highly." She waited as her words sunk in on Amaryllis.

"His lordship praised me?" Amaryllis finally managed to murmur.

"He did indeed. He said in his opinion, Reggie could not find a more fitting wife."

"He said that?"

Lady Rotherby chuckled. "He did. Now, at this point, we know little of your family, only what Reggie has told his uncle. And we know nothing of what portion you might be bringing to the marriage."

"Oh, I have a good…" She started to tell Lady Rotherby about her dowry, but the lady put her hand to Amaryllis's mouth.

"Nay. Such does not matter. Does Reggie love you. We are satisfied. We can talk of any settlement latter. My aim now is to make you feel welcome and comfortable in our family. I will start by telling you that my husband, like Reggie, is a second son. Nate is a first-generation earl. He was gifted his title and land by King Charles for services he rendered the King during the King's years in exile. True, the first D'Arcy came over with the Conqueror, but he was only a knight. No great lord. Over many generations, the D'Arcys prospered, and hopefully will continue to do so. However, you must not think the D'Arcys believe themselves so grand they can only marry into other noble families. Was that true, Nate and I would not now be married."

A knock at the door gave Amaryllis time to digest what Lady Rotherby said, but she was not certain what she was implying.

A youthful maid bearing a tray with two goblets on it entered at Lady Rotherby's bidding. "Lady Crossly bid me bring you some wine," the girl said.

Lady Rotherby took both goblets, asked the girl to thank Lady Crossly, and as the girl curtsied and left the room, Lady Rotherby handed a goblet to Amaryllis.

"Now where was I?" she said. "Oh, yes, I was about to tell you about me." She paused, took a sip of wine then said, "On my mother's side, my great grandfather was a peasant, most likely a younger son, who made his way to Derby. We know not from where. He never chose to say – that we know of, anyway. But he prospered. Married well, and he and his wife had my grandfather. Grandfather had a keen mind and was an astute businessman, a wool merchant to be exact. He too married well. Grandmother was the only surviving child of a sokeman who had also prospered. His freehold was substantial. Fact is, Godwin's estate is that freehold I speak of."

Amaryllis nodded. "Oh, yes, I do think this afternoon Mary said something about Godwin's grandmother leaving him the estate."

"Yes. 'Twas her dowry left to her by her mother. My mother married Thierry Plaisance, Esquire. He, like the D'Arcys, was descended from a knight. A knight who came over with Henry II when he became King. Unlike the D'Arcys, the Plaisance family holdings remained stagnant. Elkton Hall, which belongs to my brother will someday belong to Milo as my brother is childless, and the manor is not entailed. So my brother may will the manor as he sees fit. Elkton Hall is all the Plaisance family ever owned. They lost acreage during the plague in the thirteen hundreds, and the famine in the late fifteen hundreds. Now, what is left of the estate is either leased out or is but grazing land for sheep. So what I am telling you is that my family has no great ancestry. 'Tis quite humble. Yet, I and my children are completely accepted by the D'Arcys.

"And so you and your siblings will be. So do you have any fears that you are marrying into some richly noble family who may look down their noses at the daughter of a baronet, forget those fears. You are marrying into a loving family, an accepting family, albeit a family with some rather eccentric members. Selena being a prime example."

Amaryllis knew not what to say. She had never expected Lady Rotherby to be so kind. Or so understanding. Then when the lady insisted she call her Aunt Rowena, as she would soon be Amaryllis's aunt in truth, Amaryllis could do naught but repeatedly thank the gracious lady for taking the time to make her feel even more at ease with the members of the family she was marrying into.

"And wait until you meet Lady Rygate. She will love you," Lady Rotherby assured her. "Reggie's mother is the dearest, loveliest woman I have ever known. So sad she cannot be here for Reggie's and your wedding, but that cannot be. Still, Reggie will soon take you meet her and his father, Nate's younger brother, Ranulf. He will love you, too, and will understand why Reggie could not wait to make you his wife."

Amaryllis blushed at Lady Rotherby's last words. She knew she was as eager to wed as was Reggie. She but hoped she would not disappoint Reggie. She had a feeling did she have any questions regarding what to expect on her wedding night, her new aunt would be most willing to give her advice and ease her anxieties.

"Do you think of your wedding?" Juliet asked, bringing Amaryllis back to the present. "You are blushing."

Juliet's comment and Brilliana's giggle made Amaryllis blush even hotter. "I fear I do. I love Reggie so deeply. I hope I may be a good wife for him."

Juliet patted her hand. "You will be."

❦ ❦ ❦ ❦

Offa Ledeen sat his horse and stared at the party situated on the lush green meadow. A low stone fence, high enough to keep the sheep grazing in the distance from wandering, lined the narrow lane leading to Glenwood House. Trees on the opposite side of the lane shaded him and his companion and made them less visible to the group he intently studied. With the exception of one young man, who was strolling toward the woods with one of the women, the group consisted of women and children. He saw no male servants near to hand. Could he truly be this lucky?

His plan had been to arrive at Glenwood House with his arrest warrant for Amaryllis and his writ to claim the child, Sir Charles. He assumed he would meet with some opposition, but he expected the household to be intimidated by the official documents. He would then take the boy with him, and his companion would take Amaryllis to the constable in Derby. His companion was expecting to reap a large reward for capturing Amaryllis, but unbeknownst to the man, the constable had already refused to cooperate or to honor the documents.

When first arriving in Derby, Offa had sought out the constable. The man had been quite belligerent. Had even threatened to arrest Offa. "Are you a fool?" the constable had asked. "Those writs are of no consequence here." His eyes narrowed, he leaned forward and peered at Offa. "Be you in league with that villain, Felton?"

Confused, Offa had replied, "I have no knowledge of anyone named

Felton."

The constable straightened and nodded. "Let me tell you, my assistant, along with Sir Cyril, Sir Milo, and Mister D'Arcy, is taking Felton back to the young baronet's home that Felton may identify the person who paid him to kill the child." The constable again peered at Offa. "Are you aware of the plan to kill the child?"

"Kill Sir Charles! Nay! Never! I was but sent to bring him home safely. 'Twas believed Mistress Bowdon abducted him. But you say that is not the case, eh?"

The constable rocked back on his heels. "According to Mister D'Arcy and Sir Cyril, the boy's guardian, the boy's sister saved him by bringing him here to safety. Now you take that writ and that warrant and go back to Albertine and tell your magistrate to be more careful, know his facts the next time afore he goes about issuing such documents."

"I will do that," Offa said nodding, glad to be escaping the wary constable. He gave some thought to searching out the Derby Justice of the Peace, but decided that would probably not help him. Man was most likely in league with the constable. Who Felton was, Offa had no idea, but the fact that Felton was being blamed for wanting to kill the young baronet made it simpler for Offa. If on the way back to Churlwood, the boy had an accident, Offa could lay the blame on someone connected with this Felton.

Without the Derby constable's assistance, his job was made more difficult. Still he had the legal documents. But he would need help. Luck had been with him. In the public room of his inn, he found the perfect man to back him up. A tall, burly man with huge arms and a neck the size of his head was only too eager to earn the reward Offa assured him was being offered for the arrest of Mistress Bowdon. The man even had his own pistol. Offa would have to rent a horse for him, but Elva had been generous with the funds she had given him.

He told his burly companion he had no need of the reward, himself. He but wanted to get the boy and take him safely home. And so, with directions from the helpful innkeeper, they had set off for Glenwood House, Offa's companion anticipating a reward that did not exist, Offa anticipating an annuity that would keep him out of debtor's prison.

"What do we wait here for?" his companion asked.

Offa rolled his eyes but answered patiently. "I look to see if mayhap our prey are there in the meadow. They appear to have had a picnic. I see no servants about. Naught but women who will no doubt be easily frightened. I think this is much more to our plan than to go on to the house. We will leave our horses here," he said, wondering how far they could make it across the meadow before they would be noticed. Did they keep pleasant looks on their faces, mayhap no alarm would be sounded. No one would start screaming. He had no wish to have to shoot anyone, but did he have to, he would. After all, he had the documents giving him the legal right to take whatever actions might be necessary to achieve their goal.

Chapter 34

"Now who do you suppose those two men are?" Brilliana said. She was looking out across the field to the lane that led to the house.

Amaryllis whipped about. She had been wary for so long, she could not help being suspicious. A giant of a man strode along beside a smaller man in modish dress.

"Mayhap 'tis someone seeking Godwin," Juliet said, and she called to her sister-in-law. "Mary, two men cross the meadow. Might they be looking for your husband?"

Mary slipped out from under the awning, and shielding her eyes with her hand, said, "I cannot recognize them. And I cannot think why they might seek Godwin here."

"I wonder might they have news from my husband or Sir Cyril," Fonda said, joining Mary.

Amaryllis rose to her knees. As the two men drew closer, something about the smaller man looked familiar, yet she could not think who he might be or why she might know him. All the same, something inside her told her to beware. The closer the men came, the more leery she became. The bees still buzzed, the birds still chirped, the laughter of the children still floated on the air, but a cold chill crept up her spine.

"Good afternoon, ladies," the smaller man said, stepping in front of the burly giant and sweeping off his cocked hat. Though dressed in the latest fashion, Amaryllis could see the fabrics were not of the best quality, and his wig looked more like it was made of goat or horse hair rather than human hair. He was attempting to give the appearance of a man of some consequence, but to her eyes he failed. She guessed he was not impressing Mary or Fonda either for both women but stared at him, no smiles cracking their faces.

"What do you here?" Mary asked. "If you seek my husband, you will find him in Derby."

"Nay," the man said, reaching into his pocket and pulling out some papers. "I seek Mistress Amaryllis Bowdon, and I see she is right here."

The moment the man looked into her eyes, Amaryllis recognized him. Offa Ledeen. Aunt Elva's cousin. But why would he be seeking her? And what were the papers he held? And who was the giant accompanying him? She rose to her feet.

"Offa Ledeen. I recognize you now. What is it you wish with me?"

Inclining his head slightly, he said, "I have here a warrant for your arrest, and a writ to take Sir Charles back to his home."

"You will do no such thing," Fonda said before the whole meaning of what Ledeen said sunk in on Amaryllis.

With a silky smile, Ledeen slipped a small gun from his pocket. "I feared I might meet with some resistance, so I came prepared. You, Mistress Bowdon, will go with my companion here, and I will take charge of Sir Charles." Looking over his shoulder, he told the giant, who had also drawn a pistol from his pocket to keep the ladies covered. "We would hate to have to shoot anyone, but these warrants give us the right to do what is necessary to fulfill them."

"You will not be taking Mistress Bowdon or Sir Charles anywhere," an imperious voice stated. Amaryllis knew its owner without turning around. "I am Lady Rotherby," her future aunt said, "and do you harm one hair on the head of anyone here, I will see you both hang."

The giant and Ledeen looked cowed for a moment, but Ledeen, drawing up his chin and straightening his shoulders, said, "Lady Rotherby, I am a sworn deputy from Albertine, and I am but carrying out the orders of the Albertine magistrate. I have no wish to harm anyone, but do you think I will not, you are sadly mistaken."

Amaryllis saw a determination in his eyes that surprised her. From her limited acquaintance with him, she would not have suspected him capable of standing up to Lady Rotherby. Aunt Elva must have promised him a sizable sum that he was willing to take on a lady of the nobility. However, his determination meant naught to her, she would never let him take Charlie, no matter his threats to shoot.

"You will not take my brother anywhere," she said, heat rising to her face. "Do you mean to shoot, then you had best do so for I am not budging."

"Yes," Fonda said, stepping forward and gently edging Brilliana aside, away from the madman and his gun. "You had best shoot then prepare to hang."

Ledeen looked bewildered. He could not have expected such staunch resistance. Mary and Cecily also stepped forward, but at the same instant, Charlie, with Maitena at his heels, came running up, exclaiming, "Ryllis, Ryllis, I catch fly, I catch fly."

Opening his hands to show his sister his prize, he squealed when the small blue butterfly escaped. Turning to chase after his treasure, he ran right into Ledeen's arms. Ledeen scooped up the child, turned, and started running across the meadow.

Amaryllis shrieked and started to run after them, but the giant caught her by the wrist. "No, you go with me," he growled.

Her eyes on Ledeen, Amaryllis tugged and twisted her arm in an attempt to free herself. Looking to her friends in desperation she saw Lady Rotherby slam the giant in the stomach with her chair. He grunted then yelped when the tiny Cecily grabbed his arm and sank her teeth into it. In trying to shake Cecily off, he released Amaryllis. At the same time, Fonda and Mary grabbed his other arm. The gun he held went off, but Amaryllis was free and with no other thought in her head than to rescue her brother, she yanked up her skirt and raced after Ledeen.

❉ ❉ ❉ ❉

The instant she heard a shot resound, Selena whipped about and started running back toward the picnic area. She could not imagine what had happened, but she did not need to know. She but knew something untoward had happened and her friends and family might be in need. Hiking up her skirt, she cursed it as it interfered with her stride. Ansel had been slower to respond, but he swept past her in an instant. How she envied the freedom men had.

Drawing closer, she saw a melee ensuing outside the striped awning. Ye gads! Her Aunt Rowena was scuffling with an oversized man. Cecily, Fonda, and Mary were also involved in the tussle. But beyond them, a desperate race caught her eyes. She could make out the top of Charlie's head poking over the shoulder of a man dashing toward the rock fence bordering the lane. Amaryllis, Juliet, and Brilliana trailed after him. Little Maitena, her chubby legs pumping, her arms waving, followed at a distance.

Looking beyond the fence, Selena could make out two horses concealed in the shade of the trees lining the lane. Did the man carrying Charlie reach the fence and then his horse, he could be gone with Charlie, and they would have little way of catching him.

Ansel jumped into the struggle with the large man, but Selena continued following the others across the field. The shot must have been heard at the stables for she could see several stablemen and a couple of footmen headed for the fracas. They were too distant to be of immediate help. The man with Charlie was lengthening his distance. She could understand why. He had not to contend with skirts or stays that hindered each panted breath drawn.

Then from the direction of the tent that had been set up for the ladies' convenience, a figure in a plain dark blue gown and white apron streaked across the field. Selena recognized Betty. A smaller figure with a crutch attached to his leg raced beside her. Dog and nursemaid were gaining on the abductor. The dog shot ahead. He ran right in between the man's legs. The man stumbled, tried to regain his balance, but unable to find his footing, he tossed Charlie aside, and fell on his stomach.

The fall was bound to have knocked the wind from his lungs, all the same, he rolled quickly up into a sitting position and drew a small pistol from his pocket. He had no time to aim, though. Betty reached him and landed a hard kick to his hand. The gun dropped to the ground and before the man could retrieve it, Betty aimed another kick to his face. He dodged the kick, but his movement landed him on his side. Betty's next kick landed in his groin. Howling, and ignoring Fate's tugging at his wig, he curled into a fetal position. The little dog, prevailing in his quest, pranced about with the wig in his mouth as Amaryllis raced past the downed man to scoop Charlie up in her arms.

Selena arrived but moments behind Juliet and Brilliana. Grabbing the pistol off the ground, she aimed it at the groaning man. "I have recently shot one man who tried to harm Charlie. You would be a fool to think I would not shoot you."

Looking up out of ravaged eyes, the man continued his moaning, but his gaze went from Selena to Betty to Brilliana, then rested on Amaryllis and Juliet, both with their arms around Charlie. A shrill squeal drew his gaze to Maitena. The little girl stopped in front of him, shook her small finger at him, and said, "Bad man. You are a bad man." She then scurried over to check on Charlie.

Tabitha was next on the scene, and behind her came two footmen. Seeing Selena with a gun pointed at the writhing man, one footman asked, "What is toward here, Lady Selena?"

"This man attempted to abduct Sir Charles. Beyond that, I know little, but I intend to learn more. In the meantime, if you would drag him up, I do think he and his partner will have some explaining to do."

"That is Mister Ledeen," Tabitha said. "He is Aunt Elva's cousin. He is not nice. He always tells us to go away and not bother him."

"I see," Selena said, keeping the gun pointed at Ledeen as the two footmen each took an arm and yanked Ledeen to his feet. The children's aunt had sent yet another villain after Charlie. That woman would have to be stopped.

"What shall we do with him?" the footman asked.

"Take him back across the field where I see they have his partner restrained. We will ask Mistress Crossly what she wants done with them. They are trespassing on her estate."

With the footmen near dragging Ledeen across the meadow, Selena turned to Amaryllis. Her friend had relinquished Charlie into his Aunt Juliet's arms and had wrapped her arms around Betty. "How can I ever thank you for again being so brave and for saving my brother?"

Blushing Betty said, "Had I been near to hand, the scoundrel would ne'er have laid a hand on Sir Charles. I had taken Mistress Tabitha to the convenience tent when I heard the commotion and then the shot." She ruffled Tabitha's hair. "Poor dear, Fate and I left her to tend herself. And Fate did his part. I think I would have caught that wretch at the fence, but 'twas better he fell." She looked over at Charlie. "Long as Sir Charles is not injured."

"He seems fine," Juliet said.

Giggling, Brilliana said, "Look at Fate. He is having quite the time with that nasty wig."

The dog had given up prancing about with his prize. Stretched out, his bandaged leg sticking off to his side, he was thoroughly enjoying gnawing on the wig.

"Well, let him keep it for now. He earned it." Selena reached down to scratch Fate behind the ears, and for a moment the dog stopped his chewing to gaze up with loving eyes at her. "What a dear little fellow you are," she said before straightening. "Shall we go see what Mary, and Aunt Rowena have decided to do with the two culprits."

Everyone agreed, and they began a slow march back across the meadow. The beautiful day had almost come to a tragic end. But Charlie was safe. No one had been injured. And they would have much to talk about when the men returned.

※　※　※　※

Godwin paced angrily back and forth across the parlor floor. "The nerve of the man! To come to my home! Assault my wife, my guests, my mother, even! Endanger my children. By God, he should be pilloried then drawn and quartered."

Amaryllis could understand her host's anger. She felt much the same way. She was still so shaken by the day's events, she could scarcely sit quietly in her chair. She had been loath to leave Charlie once she had him tucked safely into bed, but knowing Betty was with him eased her worries. "Now, Mistress Bowdon, you go relax," Betty insisted, urging Amaryllis toward the door. "I will be here with Sir Charles all night. He and Mistress Tabitha will be fine."

And so Amaryllis had gone down to supper, only to find she could eat little of anything. Fortunately, no one had tried to force her to eat. The meal had been rather quiet after all the excitement. Everyone was waiting for Godwin to return from Derby. Once Ledeen and his henchman had been tied up in the barn, one of the stablemen had ridden to Derby to fetch Godwin and the constable. With their arrival, the culprits had been carted off to jail. Godwin had gone back to Derby to learn what he could about who had planned the abduction attempt.

Having just returned, and not even taking the time to change his clothes or have his supper, he launched into his tirade. "Seems Baker,

Ledeen's henchman, was taken in by Ledeen. The writs Ledeen has are real enough. But the constable had already told Ledeen those warrants were not legal in this county due to Felton's attempts to murder Charlie, his admission he was being paid to commit the murder, and the fact he was being taken back to Albertine to confront the person paying him. However, the constable never said 'twas Elva Bowdon who had paid Felton, so Ledeen, still believing the writs were legal, ignored the constable and decided to serve the writs himself. He told poor Baker there was a reward for Amaryllis." Godwin looked over at Amaryllis and shook his head. "The man had no idea he was being culled. As no one was injured when his pistol went off, I have asked the assault charges be dropped against him. But not the trespassing charges. That is, do you give your approval, Amaryllis."

She rubbed her arm. Sore and bruised, it was the same wrist that had been injured when the coach had turned over. But if the man had not known the writs were not legal, he should not be punished. She looked around the room. "Lady Rotherby, and Mary, and Cecily, and Fonda are the ones who struggled with the giant. Do they agree the abduction charges against him could be dropped, then I am comfortable with the decision."

"I think we can agree to that," Lady Rotherby said, "But my dear, you must call me Aunt Rowena. You and Charlie and Tabitha are family now. The wedding is but a formality."

Amaryllis managed a smile. "Yes, Aunt Rowena. I will try to remember."

Nodding, Godwin continued, "As for Ledeen. He seems to have been promised the same inducement as Mistress Bowdon offered Felton. Ledeen knew nothing of Felton. He was not asked to kill Charlie, just to return him to Churlwood. He says he did have the feeling that should an accident befall Charlie on the way, his cousin would not be disappointed. He, too, is willing to testify against the woman to get a lesser sentence. The fact that the writs were legitimately issued by the Albertine Justice of the Peace may save him from abduction charges, but not from trespassing or assault."

Frowning, Selena said, "I but hope when Reggie returns, he can tell us that Mistress Bowdon has been put in jail, and that she can never again pay someone to harm Charlie."

Amaryllis smiled wistfully at Selena. "I know I will not feel safe about Charlie until I know Aunt Elva has been arrested."

"I have no doubt ...," Godwin started to say, but was interrupted when a footman entered.

"Mister Crossly, sir, a number of riders have arrived. I do think 'tis Sir Milo and Mister D'Arcy."

Amaryllis's hand went to her heart. Reggie back! So soon!

Selena, Mary, and Fonda hastily rose and followed Godwin into the hall. A general chatter from the others remaining in the room floated over and around Amaryllis, but she paid it no heed. Reggie had returned. How she needed to feel his strong arms around her. He would return her life to its stable foundation. He would make sure no one ever threatened Charlie again. The stomp of boots sounded in the hall. Her heart skittering about, Amaryllis stood. Then a dusty, but ever so handsome Reggie appeared in the doorway. All she could do was run to him.

Chapter 35

Taking Amaryllis in his arms, Reginald held her tight against his chest. Her hair smelled clean and sweet. God how good she felt. He had tried to hold her at arm's length, warning her of the dust and sweat that covered him from head to toe, but she had ignored his cautioning and had flung herself into his arms.

"Oh, how glad I am to see you," she said when at last he released her enough that she could peer up at him. "Never did I think to see you this soon."

He frowned. How was he to tell her their trouble was not over. "I am back early, my love, because I bring news. We must yet be wary."

"What is this you say, nephew?" his aunt demanded. She had risen at his entrance, but had waited for Amaryllis to greet him before joining them.

He shook his head. "I fear Mistress Bowdon may have sent another lout to make an attempt on Charlie's life. Milo and Toms and I hurried back that we might prepare for him."

Gasping, Amaryllis's hand went to her throat.

Hoping to reassure her, Reginald said, "Am I not mistaken, 'tis a cousin of Mistress Bowdon. Knowing who he is, we should be able to apprehend him before he can try anything."

"Oh," Amaryllis said with an obvious sigh of relief. A small smile touched her lips. "I feared Aunt Elva had hired a third cutthroat."

"A third cutthroat?" Reginald shook his head in confusion.

"Humph," Aunt Rowena sniffed. "We have already dealt quite sufficiently with Mister Offa Ledeen, Elva Bowdon's cousin. He is currently residing in the Derby gaol."

"Indeed he is," Godwin said, entering from the hall. "And I intend to see he remains there. Milo has told me Mistress Bowdon is most likely dead by now. We will need no additional testimony against her. I want

295

Ledeen to pay for what he did, though."

"Aunt Elva, dead?" Amaryllis breathily asked.

"That is what Milo says," Selena said.

"Yes, we do think she must be dead by now, but what is all this about Mistress Bowdon's cousin? Someone tell me what is going on," Reginald insisted, looking from Godwin to his aunt and back to Amaryllis.

"We have much to tell," Mary interrupted, "and the hour grows late. But you men have yet to have your supper. Hurry and wash and shake off the dust while I have the table set for you, then we will gather round, and as you have your supper, we will tell our tale. Then you must tell us yours." She took Reginald's arm. "Release Amaryllis, you have gotten her all dusty. Go with Godwin and clean up. Make yourself presentable. You will have time later to steal a kiss." Smiling, she pushed Reginald toward the door. "Take your Mister Toms with you. Poor man. He must think this a mad house. No decent introductions, naught but confusion and chaos."

"Come along, Toms," Reginald said, slapping his friend on the shoulder. "I am as befuddled as you must be. We have a house full as you can see. I will introduce you to the rest of the family after we have cleaned up. Let us follow Godwin."

With the help of Godwin's valet and two footmen, Reginald, Toms, Milo, and Godwin were made presentable and were soon tromping back down to the hall to find one end of the table spread with various delectables. The women, seated at the other end, had goblets of wine and a plate of biscuits in front of them. Ansel, it seemed, had decided to enjoy a second supper, and had joined the men at their end of the table.

Before sitting down to delve ravenously into his supper, Reginald introduced Toms, then asked about the outriders. Selena, as would be her usual, had seen to the outriders' care. "Billings and Crouch, as well as Mister Toms's men are presently in the kitchen gobbling down a meal not unlike what is being served to you. I asked Mary's cook to be sure they had plenty of ale, and I told them when they had finished eating, they should go on to Milo's and go to bed. Fonda assured me they have plenty of room above the stable to house Mister Toms's men."

"We do indeed," Fonda agreed. "And I sent word to Husted, my house steward," she added with a smile to Toms, "to move Reggie's valet into

Reggie's room, and make his room ready for you. Mister Nye is much improved, Reggie, you will be happy to know."

"He should be improved the way Esmeralda has been pampering him," Selena said. "I do think without the children to mind, and little to do for me, she is bored. However, no doubt tonight she will be waiting up for me to hear firsthand all that has transpired here today."

Reginald, too, was eager to hear what had transpired, and so he said as he sat down. The women took turns telling about the event as they had witnessed it. His eyes widening, Reginald stopped with a wedge of mincemeat pie halfway to his mouth as he listened to the women's account of Ledeen's attempt to abduct Charlie. That his sister, that his Aunt Rowena, would exhibit such pugnacious behavior in their efforts to save Charlie did not to surprise him, nor, that Amaryllis would do all she could to save her brother. But that Mary and Fonda and Cecily and even Brilliana and Juliet had taken part in the subduing and subjugation of the would-be abductors he found all too amusing. He held his laughter in check, though, for he knew that to Amaryllis, the entire event had been all too terrifying. That again they had Fate to thank for his part in the drama left Reginald in some awe. He could scarce believe how much he owed that little cur he would have left by the roadside.

And Betty! What a blessing she was. When he had a chance to be alone with Amaryllis, he would give her the letter from Mistress Sermon assuring Amaryllis she was happy to relinquish Betty's contract. He also had a letter from Bess's mother happily agreeing to let Bess continue as Amaryllis's personal maid.

"'Twas but lucky no one was injured when Baker's gun went off," Ansel was saying, bringing Reginald's thoughts back to the men's end of the table. "Wait until you see Baker. He is huge. Neck as big as his head. Yet, when I arrived on the scene, he was near to being overwhelmed by the ladies." He looked down the table at the women, all of them had smiles on their faces. Chuckling, he shook his head. "I went behind Baker, got down on my knees, the ladies gave him a push, and down he went. Head crashing to the ground, pistol flying, feet up in the air, and before I could get back on my feet, Lady Rotherby slugged him over the head with the ale pitcher. It being a heavy crock pitcher, Baker could do naught but lie on the ground and groan until the stablemen arrived. Despite his size, he offered no resistance when they hauled him to his feet, bound his hands, and carted him off to the barn."

"I must say the children all behaved well," Fonda said. "I think they were at first completely stunned, but none of them cried or screamed. They gathered around Teagan, him being the eldest, and found courage from his stoic posture. Naturally, after all the excitement, they protested when told they must have their suppers then off to bed, but they acquiesced and are hopefully all now sleeping peacefully."

"What of Charlie?" Reginald asked. "Think you he will have nightmares?"

Speaking before Amaryllis could, Selena shook her head and said, "My guess is he will not. Little fellow has been through so much, but he is such a resilient little moppet. And he has Tabitha and Maitena and Betty right there with him. However," she looked over at Amaryllis, "I would not be surprised does his older sister have some nightmares. I have offered to stay with her tonight, but she assures me she will be fine now she knows her aunt can no longer make any attempts on Charlie's life. Which brings us around to you, Reggie. Do tell us all that happened at Churlwood. How is it that Elva Bowdon was near to death when you rode away."

Reginald, with comments interspersed by Milo and Toms, recounted the events, starting with their arrival at Churlwood. He also added how impressed he was with the manor. His audience asked few questions as he revealed all the minute details to them. When the tale was completed, he saw Amaryllis's eyes glistening with unshed tears. He could not believe those tears were for Elva Bowdon, but she soon made her sentiments clear.

"I have not been this at ease since that woman moved into Churlwood," Amaryllis said. "I tried to like her, tried not to believe she could be so evil, but Tabitha knew from the start that she meant to harm Charlie. Had I listened to Tabitha, I might have saved Charlie some of his other injuries at Elva's hands. I cannot be sad if she is dead. I hope she is dead. I cannot wait until Sir Cyril rids Churlwood of Uncle Irwin and his sons. I hope never to see them again."

Looking around the table as she made her speech, she let her gaze rest on Reginald. "I cannot but think how very lucky I am to have been befriended by the D'Arcys." She looked at Selena. "You will always be my dearest friend. Never will I be able to thank you enough for all you have done for me and for Charlie and Tabitha."

"Nay," Selena said, "'tis you and Charlie and Tabitha have brought joy into our lives. And the greatest of joys into Reggie's life. Could any man be more in love?"

"Well," Milo said with a saucy look at his wife, "I admit to being slightly enchanted by Fonda. At the moment, I may not be as puppy-eyed as Reggie, but there was a time."

"Aye," Godwin agreed, looking at Mary. "I cannot imagine any other woman in my life."

Selena's laughter tinkled out over the hall. "I stand rebuked. Your love for your wives is yet all-consuming. But you must admit, new love is ever so sweet and bright. Can I someday find such a love, I will welcome the travails Aunt Rowena plans to put me through."

The table joined in Selena's laughter, and Reginald's gaze caught Amaryllis's. He had no doubt his love for her would be as boundless as his cousins' love for their wives. He and Amaryllis were fated to be together, and God how he longed for their wedding day.

☙ ☙ ☙ ☙

Reginald had but a few moments alone with Amaryllis in the parlor before he had to leave for Milo's. He admitted to being bone-weary, yet once he had Amaryllis in his arms, tasted her tender lips, he had no wish to be parted from her. She was thrilled to receive the letters from Mistress Sermon and Bess's mother. "We must in some way thank Mistress Sermon," she said, looking up at Reginald with her heavenly eyes.

He kissed the tip of her nose. "She is a grand lady. Her wish is for Betty to have work that makes her happy. She says when she returns to Watford, she will interview your former maid. She has already posted a letter telling the maid of her intention. So rest easy there. And as for Bess's mother, Toms has promised when she is no longer serving as maid to his aunt, he will endeavor to find her a position suitable to her skills. His aunt is most pleased with Goody Burke and intends to write her a glowing recommendation."

Amaryllis clasped her hands together. "How wonderful. Selena will be pleased. She was much impressed with the woman as I recall."

Loving the glow his news brought to Amaryllis's face, Reginald added, "Toms is also impressed with young Robby Burke. Says he is a bright boy who catches on quick. He is giving him work in his stables. He says, does the boy do well there, as he matures, he will give him more responsibility. He realizes there are times the boy will need to work his few acres, his father being worthless, but he thinks the boy has as good a future as his sister, Bess."

"Oh, Reggie, I cannot wait to tell Bess the good news about her family. She is such a dear and is trying so hard to learn all she must do to become a good lady's maid."

"And if anyone can teach her, you can," Reginald said with another kiss to his love's adorable nose.

"Reggie," Milo hollered from the hall, "let us go. You may spend all day tomorrow with Mistress Bowdon. Come. Your friend, Toms, is ready for his bed. What kind of host are you making me out to be. My wife, my mother, my sister, and my niece, as well as your sister have already set out for Crossly Oaks, let us escort them."

"I am coming," Reginald called before scooping Amaryllis into his arms. His lips claimed hers with a kiss that he wished never had to end. But it did. Forcing himself to release Amaryllis, he held her at arm's length. "My dear one, I can hardly wait until the morrow. But as Milo says, we may spend the entire day together. We will plan our wedding. What say you?"

"I say your cousins' wives have already been planning our wedding," she answered with her sweet laugh. "But go now. Mister Toms must be treated as royally as he treated us. I know you will see all is well for him. And tomorrow, I will tell you the things Fonda and Mary have been planning. I love you," she added.

"I love you," Reginald said and releasing her, turned and left. He dared not look back. He feared if he did he would not be able to leave her. But soon, he would not have to leave her.

Chapter 36

Amaryllis could not hide her surprise when the Bowdon coach and four drew up in front of Glenwood House, and her footman, Dill, hopped off his perch at the rear of the coach and opened the coach door to two of Churlwood's housemaids. The older of the emerging two maids, after first bobbing a curtsey, said, "Oh, Mistress Amaryllis, I cannot tell you how grand it is to see you again. To know that you and Sir Charles and Mistress Tabitha are safe and well. And to think you are to be married." She grabbed the hand of the younger maid. "Lotty and I are thrilled that we have been chosen to come to work for you in your new home."

"Yes, well, oh my, yes," Amaryllis said in confusion. Her coach, several of her servants – what an unexpected delight. "It is so wonderful to see you, Sarah," she managed. "You, too, Lotty, and you, Dill." She looked up at her coachman who was grinning down at her. "And you, Milburn."

"Best we unload the things Sir Cyril said you would most be needing," Sarah said. "He said most of your belongings could stay packed until you arrived at your new home." Turning to the footman, she added, "Come, Dill, help us with these parcels and portmanteaus."

As the three servants busied themselves in the coach, Sir Cyril, Lord Rotherby, and David Stoke, having dismounted and handed their horses' reins over to two of Godwin Crossly's stablemen, joined Amaryllis on the front steps. Stoke hastily greeted his wife, who with Mary and Amaryllis, had bustled from the house upon hearing the rumble of coach wheels on the drive. They had been expecting the Rotherby and Crossly coaches. They had plans to go into Derby. Amaryllis guessed those plans would now be postponed.

Sir Cyril took Amaryllis's hands in his. "You look astounded, my dear. I cannot think why. You could not think I would return without bringing you your comforts from home, could you?" With a chuckle, he bent forward and kissed her cheek.

Still wordless, she could do little more than shake her head and look over his shoulder at the various items her servants were unloading from the coach. The top of the coach was also loaded with numerous crates, boxes, and trunks.

"We asked your former maid, and the children's former nurse, Molly, to help select the various items you might most be needing," Sir Cyril said. "The gel, Molly, was given time off from her new position to help choose the items for the children. She did say I should tell you that thanks to your glowing recommendation, she secured a most favorable position with a family in Albertine. Your maid insisted you would be wanting your mourning weeds, though I must admit I hate seeing young women shrouded in black. Especially one who is soon to be wed. All the same, you will find such gowns among the parcels being unloaded, as well as shoes, and hair ribbons, and hats. Besides clothing for the children, Molly packed some of their favorite toys."

"Oh, Father," Juliet said, giving her father a hug. "How grand of you to think to bring Amaryllis's and the children's things to them."

"'Twas your husband's idea to bring the personal items. Nate, suggested we bring the coach and a couple of the Churlwood servants, him knowing his nephew's Ardenstrath to be understaffed, and that Reggie had no coach. Could hardly have Mistress Amaryllis traveling to her new home sitting on a pillion behind her husband. Nay, would not do."

Stepping forward, Mary said, "I applaud the lot of you, but here is Delbert and a couple of our maids. They will help Amaryllis's servants carry the parcels and portmanteaus up to her room and to the nursery. Now, I can see no reason we should all be standing around on these steps. Let us go inside, and I will have some ale poured. No doubt you are all thirsty."

Lord Rotherby agreed to being thirsty, but said, "Let me first see the coachman and outriders get taken care of and that the coach can fit into your coach house with all its traps on top. Like Cyril says, no need to unload things not needed until they set up housekeeping."

"Nonsense, Father Nate," Mary said. "Look, my head stableman has returned. He is perfectly capable of seeing to the coach, the horses, and the outriders. Do come inside. We are expecting Fonda, and your wife, and the others from Crossly Oaks anytime now. We were to go into Derby for the afternoon. We had a fitting for Amaryllis for her wedding gown, but I can send word that we will come tomorrow instead. We intended to amuse ourselves with a little shopping. But nothing of any major importance. 'Tis far more exciting to have you home safe and sound. We know you will have much to tell us, but best it wait until the others arrive or you will be repeating yourselves. While you have refreshments, we will tell you our news."

Amaryllis let herself be herded inside with the others. The kindnesses she was receiving at the hands of her many future in-laws, as well as her siblings' grandfather, were overwhelming. How pleased Reggie would be when he learned they were to have a coach. It was not something either of them had talked about, but now with the coach here, she realized what a necessity it was. She could not say she would have relished traveling by pillion whenever she and Reggie wanted to go anywhere.

By the time the men washed up and were seated in the parlor with mugs of ale in their hands, Selena, Fonda, Lady Rotherby, Cecily, and Brilliana arrived. The Rotherbys embraced with a passion that Amaryllis found endearing, but Brilliana giggled and teased her grandparents. "One would think you had been separated for years not a mere two weeks."

"Seemed like a year to me," Lord Rotherby said, tweaking his granddaughter's chin. "Wait until you fall in love. Does it not seem like you are lost, adrift when not with your love, then you have not found the right mate. And you must keep looking."

Amaryllis knew exactly what he meant. That was how she felt when she and Reggie were apart. She missed him and knew he would be sorry to be absent for his uncle's return. He had decided to visit Ardenstrath to see that all was being made ready for their arrival after their wedding. She had been relieved Ansel Yardley and Sir Milo had chosen to go with him.

"I have not seen the place in so many years," Reggie had said. "I have little idea of what to expect. I do think there is a housekeeper rather than a house steward. Helps keep the expenses down with none of the family living there. The estate steward knows we are coming, but I still prefer to check that my instructions are being carried out." So that very morning, he kissed her goodbye, and with Billings and Crouch accompanying them, they set out for Ardenstrath, not to return until the following evening.

"Yes, we did receive word from Ansel that Elva Bowdon's cousin had been successfully dealt with," Sir Cyril said in answer to a question Selena put to him. "And though I am sure at the time, it was terrifying for all of you, I must admit, I find it amusing how you ladies foiled his plot. Or I should say, Elva Bowdon's plot."

He shook his head. "'Twas a sad way she died, but no doubt better than swinging from a gibbet. Better for her family, too." He looked at Amaryllis, "And for you and your siblings, my dear. There is enough scandal being bandied about without you having to go to court. The magistrate agreed 'twas best all-around did we let the matter go down as an accident. Of course, servants talk, and word got out of what really happened. But it will be forgotten, what with Irwin Bowdon and his sons gone, and Churlwood closed up until you and the children stop there after a visit to London to meet Reggie's parents.

"No reason to go back before then. Pim is a competent house steward, and I left him a minimal staff, including that fabulous cook, to keep things up. And I hired a man I feel will make a fine estate steward to replace your father's aging steward. Set the old steward up with his annuity, and he is glad to turn over the responsibility to a younger chap. However, I have arranged for your father's solicitors to go over the books with the new steward every quarter."

"Thank you, Sir Cyril," Amaryllis said, her hands clasped to her chest. "You have done so much. I cannot think how I can thank you enough."

"Nonsense. I am my grandson's guardian. I could do no less. And I may say, I talked with your solicitors about your upcoming marriage. As you are of age, they have acknowledged your decision to wed and are arranging to have your funds made available to you. Quite a nice portion you have coming to you. I can see no reason Reggie's parents should not be most pleased with his choice of a bride."

"They would be pleased had she not a penny to her name," Lady

Rotherby said. "Amaryllis is a delight, and anyone can see why Reggie adores her."

Blushing Amaryllis said, "Thank you, Aunt Rowena, you are most kind."

"'Tis naught but the truth," Selena chimed in. "You are far better than Reggie deserves, but he cherishes you so I know he will do his best by you. But Sir Cyril," she said, looking at the baronet, "tell us how the Bowdons took their dismissal from Churlwood."

"To tell you the truth, I think Bowdon was pleased to be leaving. The house could have nothing but sad memories for him and his son. They took Elva Bowdon's body back to Langley, that she could be buried in a local cemetery. We decided not to pursue any charges against the nurse, or the maid, or young Dorian. 'Twould be hard to prove they had known Mistress Bowdon meant to kill Charlie. 'Tis best not have the children involved in what would become a scandal."

"I think you made a wise decision, Sir Cyril," Lady Rotherby said. "But what have you done with that villain, Felton?"

"As his attempts on Charlie's life took place in Leicestershire, we took him to Leicester. He is in jail there, along with his cohorts who were involved in the attack on the D'Arcy coach. They will await the next Court of Assize. Reggie could well be called to attend the trial, but we left letters with the magistrate asking for leniency for Felton, as per our agreement. Felton did his part in convincing the Albertine constable of Mistress Bowdon's guilt. That is what forced her hand. Then, she knew she could not let the poison be found in her room. She had no choice but to try to reach it first and destroy it."

"Enough of this morbidity. Let us turn to lighter subjects," Lord Rotherby said. "I am much impressed with that fellow Toms. We stopped at his home on our way south to Churlwood, then again on our way home. Both the man and his aunt could not be more hospitable."

"Aye," Selena said. "We were sorry to see Mister Toms leave. He stayed but two days with us before he said he must return to Mere Manse."

"We have assured him he will always be welcome does he ever come this way again," Fonda said. "I found him most entertaining."

Selena looked at Amaryllis and smiled, and to Amaryllis's relief, made no mention of the rude manner in which Toms had initially addressed her. Selena but said they had first made his acquaintance at the same inn where they met Amaryllis and her siblings. "And a lucky meeting it was. Staying at Mere Manse while our coach wheel was repaired was a boon to us all."

"Well, 'tis Toms's aunt, Mistress Sermon, I find admirable," Sir Cyril said. "Was I not a happily married man, I would be courting that woman. She may be no great beauty, but she has mettle. Reminds me of my sister, Arcadia. Oohoo, what a pair they would make."

"I have the same opinion of her, Sir Cyril," Selena said. "I found her gracious, amusing, and not afraid to speak her mind. But most importantly, she has a kind heart. Not only in her hospitality to us, but in the way she let Betty accompany us to help with Tabitha and Charlie. And the way she gave Goody Burke a chance to prove herself, and was not disdainful of her present circumstances. Mistress Sermon is a true lady."

"Who is this Goody Burke?" Lord Rotherby asked.

"The woman who is currently acting as personal maid to Mistress Sermon," Selena answered. "But that is a whole other story. Goody Burke is Amaryllis's new maid's mother."

"Ah, yes," Lord Rotherby said. "The young chit who helped disarm and subdue Felton when he attacked your coach. Must have a good rearing. Now, to change the subject again." He looked at Amaryllis. "I want to know how the wedding plans are coming along."

Not giving Amaryllis a chance to answer, Fonda slid forward on her chair, and in her beguiling purr, said, "We have been but waiting for your return, Father Nate. As it must be but a family wedding, Amaryllis still being in mourning, we have decided to have it in our hall. Reggie has arranged for the special license, and our vicar is ready to perform the ceremony whenever we have all ready."

"Amaryllis was to have her final fitting on her wedding gown today," Mary said. "Her wedding being a blessed occasion, she agreed that despite her mourning, she would wear purple trimmed with lavender rather than black. The gown will be beautiful as will the bride."

"I would be honored, Mistress Amaryllis," Sir Cyril said, "did you allow me to give you away. I know this day would have meant so much to your father."

Amaryllis smiled brightly at the kindly man who had done so much for her. "I am the one who will be honored, Sir Cyril. Yes, gladly I accept your offer."

"Oh, Father," Juliet chirruped, "how grand."

"Yes, 'tis perfect," Lady Rotherby said. "And you men will be pleased to know Fonda and Mary are planning a superb breakfast feast. Milo has even ordered champagne. This wedding may be reserved to naught but our family, but we intend it shall be memorable."

"And it will be," Fonda said, the dulcet timbre of her voice giving her words a sensuous quality. "Milo and I have determined they are to have our bedchamber for their first honeymoon night. We will have it made up like a bower with flowers and lace. That they leave the following morning to go to Ardenstrath makes it all the more important they have a lovely start to their life together." Her eyes took on a dreamy look. "I can still so perfectly recall my wedding and my wedding night. My fondest wish was fulfilled that day. The only days that come close to matching the magic of that day are the days my children were born."

"Oh," Brilliana said, clasping her hands together. "'Tis so romantic."

Her grandfather chuckled and started to comment, but voices in the hall drew his attention. The door opened and Mary's steward, Delbert, announced, "Viscount ..." He never got the viscount's name out, for the youth, pushing past the steward into the parlor, said, "Gad zooks, Delbert, you need not announce me in my own brother's house."

"Ewen, what a lovely surprise," Lady Rotherby said, rising to embrace the dust-covered young man who had burst into the room. There could be no doubt he was Lady Rotherby's son. He looked just like her, Amaryllis thought, same dark hair and dark eyes, a generous mouth, and thin straight nose. He was a handsome youth, especially with the wide grin he was wearing.

"You could not think I would miss my cousin's wedding, surely." He looked around the room. "Where is the dunderhead?"

Selena had sprung to her feet when her cousin entered, and laughing, was next to embrace him. "Oh, Ewen! You will not be calling him a dunderhead once you meet his bride. Come, let me introduce you."

Taking her cousin's hand, she led him over to Amaryllis. "Dear one, allow me to introduce you to Ewen, Viscount Sutherlin. He is ever full of mischief, but we cannot help but love him anyway." She turned to the Viscount. "Ewen, may I present Mistress Amaryllis Bowdon, my newest and dearest friend."

Viscount Sutherlin did naught but stare, and Amaryllis blushed under his intense gaze. Catching himself when his father said, "For heaven's sake boy, make your bow." Shaking his head, he said, "My apologies, Mistress Bowdon." Taking her hand, he bowed over it. "Indeed, I will say Selena is right. Reggie is no dunderhead. He is the luckiest man I know."

Amaryllis blushed even more at his words, and Selena batted his wrist. "Release her, you dolt. You look like you are trying to eat her up."

"Oh, would that I could. How did Reggie ever find you, and have you a sister?" he asked finally releasing her hand and straightening.

Selena's merry laugh made him turn to her. "She has a lovely sister," Selena said, "but I fear she is but six years old. Unless you plan to wait for her to grow up, you are out of luck."

He looked back at Amaryllis. "Does she look like you, she will be worth the wait."

Brilliana started giggling. "Oh, Uncle Ewen, 'tis a good thing Reggie is not here. I cannot believe he would take kindly to your ogling Amaryllis."

"The girl is right," Lord Rotherby said. "Come here and meet an old and dear friend of mine. Rode with me in my marauding days."

Ewen whipped about. "One of your highwaymen?"

"Aye." From his chair between Lady Rotherby and Sir Cyril, Lord Rotherby beckoned to his son. With hand extended toward his friend, he said, "Cyril, my son. A scapegrace he is at times, but his mother dotes on him, so I put up with him."

Lady Rotherby chuckled. "I would say 'twas more the other way around."

Giving his wife a smile and a nod, he said, "Mayhap she is right. Anyway, Ewen, this is Sir Cyril Yardley. You will have heard me and your mother speak of him many times."

"Oh, aye, indeed, 'tis an honor, sir. Father often said he would not still be alive if not for you. He said you were always at hand when he most needed you."

"'Tis no more than what I have said about him," Sir Cyril said. "Indeed, he and your mother saved me from certain hanging. Broke me out of that jail that I landed in through no one's fault but my own."

"Wanting time with your wife is a better excuse than any I can think of," Lady Rotherby said. "And you cannot forget the parts your sisters played in your escape."

Sir Cyril shook his head and chuckled. "Nay, Sidonie was ever true, but Arcadia had her own motives. Once she set her eyes on Dev, he never had a chance, poor soul."

A wistful look spread across Lady Rotherby's face. "Arcadia and I exchange letters, but how I would dearly love to see her and Sir Deverette again. Would love to see their children. Seems the only time Nate and I travel anywhere, is here to see my sons or to Surrey to see his brother, Ranulf. We have not been to Cheshire in years. Why, the last time we saw Nate's sister or his older brother was … oh, when was that?"

"Most likely at the last family gathering at Walling House three years ago," Selena said. "How I love those reunions. I can scarce wait until next year's gathering."

"Ah ha!" Lord Rotherby said. "I have a splendid idea. Now that Amaryllis and her siblings are to be part of the family, I think 'twould be only right that Cyril and Arcadia bring their families as well." He looked from Sir Cyril to Juliet and David Stoke. "Our gatherings are always crowded affairs, but I have no doubt we can find room for more. What say you?"

"Do say yes," Mary said. "You cannot imagine the fun we have. And Walling House is quite large, then there is the gate house, and the steward's house, and several accommodating inns in nearby Wallingford. I have been to but one reunion, but I did so enjoy myself."

Juliet looked at her husband. He in turn looked at Sir Cyril. "Myself," Sir Cyril said, "I cannot think of anything I would enjoy more. We will plan on it."

"Splendid," Lord Rotherby said, slapping his knee.

Amaryllis could almost feel the excitement crackling in the room.

She was amazed by this family she was marrying into. Her stepmother, Beatrice, had never mentioned that her father had been a highwayman, albeit one who fought for the King. But then, Beatrice had not a lively soul. She had been a shy, sweet, and loving woman, but not one to make a fuss about things. She might even have been embarrassed by her father's past. That was certainly not how the D'Arcys viewed it. They seemed proud of their daring exploits.

Dragging her thoughts back to the conversations whirling around the room, she saw a maid enter with a mug of ale for Ewen. She had a feeling with his arrival on the scene, her wedding would no longer be the quiet ceremony she had envisioned.

Chapter 37

Nervously twisting his hands together, Reginald stood at one end of the Crossly Oaks's hall and looked toward the staircase. Soon Amaryllis would appear. Sir Cyril awaited her at the bottom of the steps. When she descended, Sir Cyril would take her arm and lead her to the altar Milo's servants had constructed. Fonda and Mary had set floral arrangements all around the hall and hung garlands of satin and lace from the rafters and down the stair banister. Extra tables had been set up in the hall to accommodate all the family members, including the children. The nurses would have the babies present at least for the ceremony. Servants would also attend the ceremony before retiring to their duties. His and Amaryllis's servants, though, would be given the day off and would be served a fruitcake with marzipan frosting after a hearty breakfast in the servants' hall.

The genial vicar gave Reginald a smile. No doubt the man could see how nervous he was. He was not nervous because he was entering a whole new chapter in his life. He was nervous because he wanted nothing to go wrong. He wanted everything to be perfect for Amaryllis. He wished his father and mother could have attended, but at least he had his aunt and uncle and his sister and cousins in attendance. He had not known who to ask to be his witness, but with his cousin Ewen's arrival, he had his attendant. Selena, of course, was Amaryllis's witness.

On the morrow, when they set out for Ardenstrath, he hoped Amaryllis would not feel bereft without Tabitha and Charlie by her side. Sir Cyril had said he would very much like to have the children with him for the summer. Amaryllis had reluctantly agreed her siblings should have the opportunity to get to know their grandfather and grandmother. Reginald thought it a splendid idea. It would give him and Amaryllis the summer to settle into their new life together. And it would give him time to redo the nursery. It was in sad disrepair, not having been

311

used for generations. He was pleased with how Ardenstrath had been cleaned from top to bottom. The housekeeper had brought in extra help from the village to ready the house for him and his bride. But it was still an ancient house with none of the modern conveniences. And, as he had remembered, it was dark. The windows were small, some not even glazed. Though the housekeeper had strived to have it aired out, it and the furnishings smelled musty. Better he and Amaryllis had the summer to make changes and brighten up the house before the children came to live with them.

He felt a tad guilty, taking Amaryllis from her lovely home. Clean, spacious, well-furnished, and modern, Churlwood was all Ardenstrath was not. Well, it would be his job to make his estate profitable and comfortable. If Toms could do it, he could do it. Mere Manse, though not near as old as Ardenstrath, had not the beauty and charm of Churl- wood, but it afforded all the comforts anyone could ask for. He meant Ardenstrath to one day be the same.

He could not begin to thank Sir Cyril for giving him and Amaryllis the use of the Churlwood coach and four until such time as Charlie came of age. By that time, he expected to have his own coach. He was also pleased five of Amaryllis's servants had chosen to come with Am- aryllis to her new home. She would be more comfortable having her own staff about. That the coachman, along with a Churlwood grooms- man, would have charge of his stables was another blessing. Arden- strath had but one very old stableman, and Reginald had made note that he would have to hire someone to help with the old man's duties. That dilemma was now solved.

The footman, Dill, could serve their table, and the two maids, he hoped would work well with the Ardenstrath housekeeper. She seemed a competent woman, but the maids and Dill were used to working un- der a house steward. Could be troublesome did they resent taking in- structions from a woman, albeit one of dignified stature and refined speech and manner.

A hush fell over the hall, and he looked up. Amaryllis stood at the top of the staircase. She looked more beautiful than he had ever seen her. She glowed. Her gown of a rich purple hue, trimmed in a silvery lavender, accented the creaminess of her skin. A wreath of purple and pink flowers adorned her golden hair that floated about her shoulders. Her smile radiant, she started down the staircase. Fonda and Mary, and Betty and Bess, waited at the top. They had dressed the bride, and would wait until Amaryllis was met at the bottom of the steps by Selena and Sir Cyril before hastily descending and taking their places, Fonda and Mary on seats next to their husbands, Betty and Bess with the other servants.

As soon as Amaryllis stepped off the final stair, Selena embraced her and gave her a kiss on the cheek, then grinning broadly, she started walking toward Reginald. Amaryllis looked to Sir Cyril. He took her arm, and they walked slowly and regally to the altar. The ceremony was simple. The vicar read from the Book of Common Prayer. Reginald and Amaryllis made their vows and pledged their love, they and their witnesses signed the register, and it was over. Amaryllis Bowdon was now Amaryllis D'Arcy, his wife. Had he ever known such happiness?

※　※　※　※

Amaryllis wanted to store every moment of this wondrous day in her memory. From the moment she awakened until the moment she would eventually close her eyes to sleep. She wanted nothing to escape her notice. Nothing to someday disappear in a fog. She decided she would start a diary once she and Reggie settled into their home together. Until she could put the events down on paper, she would have to daily relive this day of her wedding in her mind. The breakfast had been so very grand, and she had eaten with a ravenous appetite. She had relished the bubbly champagne, loving how it tickled her palate. She cherished all the hugs and kisses she received from her new family members, all the congratulatory declarations from the servants, and most importantly the joy she saw on Tabitha's and Charlie's faces. Her beloved siblings adored Reggie and were ever so happy she had married him.

They were a bit uncertain about going away from her with their grandfather for the summer, but knowing they would have Fate with them eased their wariness. And they had developed a true fondness for their Aunt Juliet. That they would be riding to their grandfather's home with their aunt in her coach gave them added comfort. They had never been away from their sister for any lengthy period. Fact was, Charlie would be unable to remember any time Amaryllis had not been near to hand. Still, he was determined to be stoic and told her in his piping little voice that he would be very brave, like she always told him to be.

After the breakfast feast, the party moved out to the gardens. Fonda would have liked to have dancing, but honoring Amaryllis's mourning period, she settled for various lawn games. The children ran and whooped, the adults played at bowls or took walks in the various gardens. After a time, the nurses took the children in for a small dinner and their naps. The adults settled on blankets and cushions under cherry trees, and the servants brought out wine, dates, nuts, and pieces of cake.

When all were settled with their nibbles, Fonda picked up her lute and began to play softly. "Who will sing with me?" she asked.

"Play something that we all might sing," her husband said. "Something light and airy."

"So shall it be," she agreed and began a popular ballad about a traveling cloak and its many adventures. Her next song was a ribald drinking song that she said Sir Milo had taught her. The men all seemed to know it and sang out in full-voiced good cheer. "Now one for the ladies," Fonda said in her silky voice. After strumming a few notes, she sang softly of a maiden awaiting the return of her true love. Other men courted her, but she would have none of them. She would wed none but her own true love. Selena joined in on the chorus, her clear voice blending with Fonda's honeyed tones. When the song ended, Amaryllis saw that Lady Rotherby had tears in her eyes. She wondered if her new aunt was thinking of how long she had had to wait before she had been able to marry her true love.

Fonda played a few more songs, then put down the lute, saying, "'Tis time for story-telling. Father Nate, let us have one of your stories. Then we must have one from Sir Cyril." Looking at Sir Cyril, she added, "You must tell us a tale from your highwayman days. I tell you now, Juliet has never made mention of your exploits. But now we must hear one since you and Father Nate have renewed your friendship."

Sir Cyril chuckled. "Nate's and my friendship needed no renewing because it has never ceased. We have corresponded often over the

314

years, but having done so much traveling during our years on the road, I am afraid, I have not been good about visiting. And, my wife gets sick riding in a coach, so we have seldom gone far from home. The farthest, I would say, has been to visit my sister, Arcadia, not a day's journey. As to my daughter saying naught of my adventurous life, that would be her mother's doing. Tamar thinks 'tis best people forget that past. She thought 'twas best for the children so they were not teased about their father's roguery, even though the King pardoned us and gave us a nice reward."

"Of course, whenever we visit Aunt Arcadia, or she us, there is no hiding Father's past," Ansel said. "Aunt Arcadia is proud of her impishness, and I do think wishes she had played a bigger role in all their devilish deeds. She loves to brag on Uncle Deverette."

"I believe Mother, too, is very proud of Father's aid to King Charles," Juliet admonished her brother. "She just prefers not to brag of exploits that some consider were breaking the law."

"And, so we were breaking the Puritans' law," broke in Lord Rotherby, "but I could not feel that the Puritans, who broke the law by beheading King Charles I, were a legitimate government. So their laws were not legitimate. Therefore we were not truly breaking the law. And that is how Charles II saw it, and why we were all, not only pardoned, but rewarded.

"Now I shall tell my tale, but this one will not be about my roguish days. I will instead tell you a tale of my youth. Then Cyril shall have his turn."

Seated beside Reggie with her hand in his, Amaryllis sighed happily. When she had set out from Churlwood, fear in her heart, she had never dreamed she would end up marrying the man of her dreams. How fate had changed her life.

※　※　※　※

Looking over at Amaryllis and her brother, Selena thought she had never seen a more perfect couple. She wondered if she would ever know the kind of love that her brother had found, that her cousins, her aunts and uncles, and her parents knew. If learning to be a lady would help her find such a love, mayhap it would be worth it. Yet, something in her heart told her she would be giving up a piece of herself if she became the lady her mother wanted her to be.

On the morrow, she would leave with her aunt for Whimbrel Hall – well, after a short one day stop-over in Derby to visit Aunt Rowena's brother who had but recently returned from a visit to his wife's parents' home in Southern York. Aunt Rowena had agreed to let Selena ride Brigantia to Whimbrel, but she had to reclaim her riding costume from Amaryllis and ride sidesaddle like a lady if she was going to ride. Selena believed her aunt was letting her ride, albeit sidesaddle, because her coach was already crowded with Cecily and her children. Cecily's coach was needed to accommodate the maids that had accompanied them to Derbyshire.

Aunt Rowena's smaller coach, with Mistress Mead and a young maid as its passengers, was setting off to northern Cheshire to retrieve Aunt Rowena's younger daughter, Flavia. Selena's cousin had been fostered with their Aunt Phillida in Cheshire, but Aunt Rowena wanted her daughter home to be companion to Selena and to help with Selena's education. The coach would travel in tandem with the Stoke's coach and Sir Cyril for most of the trip, all the same, Uncle Nate was sending his two outriders and his son, Ewen, with them so his daughter would have appropriate escorts for her journey home. Ewen seemed not to mind the assignment. He and Ansel Yardley, having determined they had much in common, had begun a fast friendship. Ewen invited Ansel to return with him to Whimbrel after he collected his sister, and Ansel readily accepted. Sir Cyril and Uncle Nate seemed pleased their sons had become friends. Did the two boys' friendship continue to develop, it would keep their fathers in closer contact.

Thinking about all the departures on the morrow brought a sharp pang to Selena's heart. She would not only be saying goodbye to her brother and Amaryllis, the children, and little Fate, she would be saying goodbye to Esmeralda. There was no reason her dear maid and companion needed to go on to Whimbrel. Selena was now in the care of her aunt. Esmeralda could go home. She would stop at Toms's Mere Manse and retrieve Handle. Selena hoped Handle's leg was healing as well as Fate's had healed. Esmeralda's journey would be made more pleasant as Uncle Nate had decided to accompany the coach. He would be stopping at the homes of friends, which meant Esmeralda would not have to stay in various inns on her way home. Selena knew how Esmeralda distrusted inns. Uncle Nate thought he had best visit Selena's and Reginald's father to reassure him about Amaryllis. Besides, it would give him the chance to see his sister, Phillida, who had recently arrived in London.

Billings, Crouch, Norwood, Pit, and Mills were leaving with Esmeralda. They would all be going back to their home, back to Rygate Park, her home. How she envied them.

Soon the Crosslys would have their homes back. She wondered if it would be a relief to settle into their normal lives again, or if they would miss all the bustle. She had thoroughly enjoyed her visit with them, but she was a bit disappointed she had never seen the ghost of Baron Burell, or even sensed his presence.

Aunt Rowena shook her head at such talk. So did Milo. Both were ever practical. Down deep, Selena, too, knew Fonda's insistence that Baron Burell's ghost haunted her sitting room was but a fantasy, yet she had harbored a secret hope, that did he truly exist, he would make his ghostly presence known to her. She had, according to her father, an uncanny affinity with animals. Might she also have such an affinity with a ghost? She would have liked to ask him to predict her fate as she had been told ghosts could do. Would she find happiness and love, or would she end her life a spinster, unable to conform to the mores of society? Well, no matter, the ghost failed to appear, and on the morrow, she would say goodbye to Crossly Oaks and its reclusive ghost and face her unknown future.

Glancing again at her brother and Amaryllis, Selena could not help but wonder, would she ever love and be loved. She hoped so.

Chapter 38

Propped up against a multitude of fluffy pillows in the large four-poster bed in Sir Milo and Fonda's elegant bedchamber, Amaryllis waited breathlessly for her husband to arrive. After a scrumptious supper that Amaryllis had barely been able to touch, so nervous had she become at the prospect of finally being alone with her new husband, the female members of her new family had escorted her up to the bedchamber. Bess and Fonda's personal maid had been awaiting her, Bess with a smile on her youthful face stretching from ear to ear.

The frilly gown and robe that Fonda had helped Amaryllis choose for her wedding night was laid out on the bed. Amaryllis had expected the women to leave once they reached the room, but they had all stayed. They lit candles, sprinkled rose petals around the room, on the floor, the bed, the dressing table, any and every surface. Floral arrangements and floral garlands bedecked the room, and wine in crystal goblets set on a table beside the bed. When the maids had Amaryllis readied for bed, her hair combed and arranged about her shoulders, they left the room, and Amaryllis's new family put her to bed. For a moment they all stood back and studied her.

"Yes," Fonda purred, "she is absolutely the most beautiful bride I have ever seen." She looked at Selena. "Your brother is a very lucky young man."

Smiling, Selena nodded. "Oh, he is indeed. And he knows it."

Amaryllis blushed at their praise, but Lady Rotherby said, "Enough, her bridegroom awaits her. Selena go signal your brother he may join his wife." Selena obeyed, and Lady Rotherby took Amaryllis's hand. "Be not fearful dear. Reggie's and your love will make this the most beautiful and memorable event in your life."

"Yes, Aunt Rowena." Amaryllis was grateful Lady Rotherby had taken her aside the previous day to give her a brief description of what she should expect and experience. "'Tis more painful for some women than for others, but the pain will be brief, and once the maidenhead is broken, you will not again experience any pain. With the love that you and Reggie bear one another, I am certain you will know naught but the bliss that accompanies such love."

The sound of footsteps made the women turn to the door. Pushing it open, Selena entered. She was followed by her brother. Standing in the doorway, he stared at Amaryllis. She felt herself blushing even more fiercely, especially as Reggie's uncle gave him a push that sent him stumbling into the room. His relations followed after him.

"What!" Ewen said. "Are we not to be treated to retrieving the bride's garters."

Turning on his cousin, Reggie snapped, "You are not. That is one custom I will not abide. In fact, I demand the lot of you leave. I need none of you to help put me to bed with my wife. I can manage quite nicely on my own. Nay, I have not even the need of Nye's services. Out, out!"

Laughing and slapping Reggie on the back, the men left. His female relations left more slowly, each stopping to give him a kiss on the cheek. After Lady Rotherby, Selena was the last to leave. She blew a kiss to Amaryllis, kissed her brother, and closed the door on her way out.

❉ ❉ ❉ ❉

For a moment, still lost in his wife's beauty, Reginald stood rooted to the floor, then as Amaryllis smiled tentatively at him, he shook himself and hurried to her side. "I cannot think how you manage it, my dear, but every time I see you, you are more beautiful." He bent and softly kissed her lips, her, oh, so sweet lips. Straightening, he said, "Give me but a few moments, and I will join you."

Nodding, she again smiled sweetly, and he started for the closet. Then he halted and looked about the room. A multitude of brightly burning candles in tripods and single ornate holders sat on every flat surface in the room. The bedchamber was ablaze. That would not do. Spotting a candle snuffer on the mantle above the dimly glowing hearth fire, he grabbed it, and turning to Amaryllis, said, "Would you mind do I extinguish these candles? I think do we leave one tripod lit, and with the glow from the fire, we will have sufficient light. What say you?"

"I think that will suit me fine, Reggie," Amaryllis answered.

Setting to work, Reginald soon had the candles snuffed, and the room took on a subdued glow. "Much better," he said, putting the snuffer back on the mantle. "I will be quick," he assured his wife, who looked even more lovely, could that be possible, in the soft flickering light.

When he returned to the bedchamber wearing naught but the silken robe he had bought for their wedding night, he found Amaryllis had removed her frilly robe and draped it over a chair. The satiny pink chemise exposed her bare arms, lovely neck, and the upper portions of her breasts. His breath caught in his lungs. She was all he had ever longed for, all he had ever envisioned, she was perfection.

And she was an innocent. Wanting to do nothing to frighten her, he stopped at the side table and picked up the crystal wine goblets. Handing her one, he raised his in a toast. "To our life together. May we ever know the love and happiness we share this day."

Her eyes glowed. "Oh, yes, Reggie. What a lovely toast. To us." She lightly clinked her glass to his and took a sip. He started to drain his glass, but thought better of it. He had had sufficient wine for one night. He had no desire to have his brain foggy. He wanted to devote his full attention to his wife. Setting the wine goblets back on the side table, he turned his back to slip out of his robe. His desire for Amaryllis already in evidence, he decided he would slip under the quilt with Amaryllis before he exposed her to his obvious need for her. He intended to pleasure her before he sought his own release.

Taking Amaryllis in his arms, he lightly kissed her, and she responded with the fervor that never failed to arouse him, not that he needed to be any more aroused than he already was. Pulling her gently against him, his throbbing member pressed against her stomach, he ran his hands up and down her back, then down and around her hips before moving to her breasts. The feel of her body beneath her satiny gown was near driving him mad, but he needed to feel her skin against his.

She seemed to have the same desire, for she whispered, "Might we take a moment to remove my nightdress? I want to feel all of you against me."

"By all means." He somehow managed to drag his voice up out of his throat, and he watched, mesmerized, as with one swift movement, Amaryllis sat up, pulled the gown off over her head, tossed it to the floor, and sank back down next to him. In the dim light he could see her beautifully rounded breasts, creamy white. She was killing him, gently, yes, but killing him nonetheless.

After giving her breasts the attention they deserved, he expanded his effort to bring her to her fulfillment. The soft little moans she made as his fingers found their target soon intensified. Her hands on his shoulders tightened their hold, then to his delight, she began shuddering. Muffling her climatic cry with his lips, he held her close, closer, until she at last relaxed in his arms. Pulling away from her but a fraction, he looked down at her to see a wonder in her eyes.

"I had no idea it would be like this. Is it always like this?"

He smiled. "I will do all in my power to make it so for you, my love. But I fear now as I find my release, I will cause you some pain. But it will only be this one time."

She reached down and touched his engorged member. Her hand closing around him nearly made him explode, and yelping, he pulled away from her. "God, Amaryllis, you will be my undoing."

She stiffened at his response, and her face showed her hurt and surprise. "I am sorry," she whispered, a little crack in her voice.

Immediately contrite, he said, "Nay, my love. You did naught to be sorry about. 'Tis my need for you is so great, your touch near sent me over the edge. Please, smile again for me. 'Tis I who am sorry I spoiled this moment for you."

To his joy, she did smile, and again reached for him. "I am ready for you, my husband. Come, let us unite as one."

He needed no additional encouragement. Positioning himself over her, he claimed her as his wife, his love. He broke through her barrier with minimal effort, and heart pounding, found his release more rapidly than he could have wished, though, mayhap 'twas best so as to cause the least pain to Amaryllis.

Rolling off her, but pulling her into his embrace, he said, "I hope 'twas not too bad for you, my dear wife."

Snuggling next to him, Amaryllis said, "'Twas not near as bad as

I expected. But then, Aunt Rowena did tell me 'twas worse for some women than others. I guess I must be one of the lucky ones. Still, 'tis nice to know it is but a one-time pain."

Kissing her brow, he said, "Aye, I could not well enjoy our lovemaking did I repeatedly hurt you. I love you so much, my bride."

"And I you, dear husband. Now, I wonder, should we put out the candles. I can see from here the wicks are in sore need of trimming."

"I shall put them out, but I will add another log to the fire. I like having a little light in the room. Do I wake later, I want to be able to see your lovely face as you sleep."

His wife giggled at his words, and he again kissed her brow before rising to snuff out the candles. Being in the buff, he was very careful when he placed the log on the fire and stirred up the sparks to get the log to catch flame. He was glad Fonda had a log fire laid for them rather than a coal fire. He liked the crackle of a wood fire, not to mention the soft glow a wood fire cast that could never be obtained with a coal fire. The bedchamber chimney had a good draw, so the room was not smoky. Fonda had thought of everything.

Filling a chill on his skin, he hurried back to bed, and slid in under the quilt beside Amaryllis. Again he pulled her into his arms. Her head cradled on his shoulder, she sighed. "What heavenly bliss we have found," she said. "I wish the whole world could be this happy."

"We are fortunate indeed, but now, I think we must see if we can sleep. Tomorrow we leave for Ardenstrath, and it is near a full day's journey."

Snuggling a little closer, Amaryllis sighed again. "Mayhap we need not go to sleep this moment." She ran her hand down his chest to his stomach then lower, and as if by magic, he was instantly hard. "This being our wedding night, mayhap we should not let it slip away from us so quickly. What say you, Reggie?"

He answered her with a groan as his lips claimed hers, and she sighed into their kiss.

❁　❁　❁　❁

Amaryllis thrilled to her husband's touch. Her desire for him, even before their first kiss had kept her awake at night, but never had she dreamed lovemaking could be so intensely pleasurable. Seeing his firm, bare buttocks as he bent to stir the logs in the fire had inflamed her. Sleep was the furthest thing from her mind. She wanted to again experience that heavenly flight he had taken her on. She loved the feel of his hard muscles pressed against her. His thighs, his chest, his stomach, his arms aroused a passion in her she had not known she possessed.

When he entered her the second time, she not only felt no pain, she experienced a whole new sensation. A longing to draw him deeper inside. Soon she found herself moving in sync with him, but this time his thrusts were unhurried, each one seemed designed to stimulate her senses. As his thrusts quickened, she let out a little squeak and again took flight as they both flew heavenward together.

Pulse racing, breath coming in pants, they clung to each other as they descended back to earth. She could feel his heart beating in rhythm with hers. Their breaths mingled and slowed. "My God, Amaryllis," he said, "I have never known such resplendent gratification in my life. You are indeed the angel I first took you for. How else could I have glimpsed paradise?"

"I am in equal thrall," she answered him, punctuating her words with a kiss to his chin.

"I must be getting heavy," he said and rolled off her before she could protest that she liked the feel of his weight on her. Pulling her into his arms, he kissed her, a long, lingering kiss. Oh, how his kisses sent anticipation racing through her body. "Hmmm," he said, ending the kiss. "I must stop this, or in truth, we will never get to sleep."

"Did I not worry about you falling asleep on your horse and so falling off, I would say who needs sleep. But I will be riding comfortably in the coach. I can even nap. I suppose you would not consider riding in the coach with me."

"Nay, sweet one. There would not be room for me. You will have Bess, and your two maids from Churlwood riding with you. Even did they squeeze together onto one seat, was I sitting next to you, in such close contact with you, and then be expected to keep my hands to myself, to be circumspect and never kiss you ... Nay, 'twould never work."

She sighed. "Yes, I can see you are right. I would feel the same. It would be torture to ride beside you all day and not be able to kiss you, to hold you in my arms. So sleep it is, and a sweet sleep it will be. I know I will dream about the wondrous day and stupendous night."

"At least tomorrow night, we will be sleeping in our own bed, in our own home. And best of all, after our journey, we will have every excuse to retire early."

Smiling, she snuggled closer to her husband. "Yes, an early retirement sounds exactly like what I will need. Goodnight my love."

"Goodnight sweet wife. Sweetest of dreams."

Her head pillowed on Reggie's shoulder, her hand resting on his chest, she listened to his regular breathing. Soon he was asleep, his breath coming out in occasional little puffs. She would soon drift into sleep, but first, she went over the details of her wedding day. She must remember it all, especially the rapturous moments she had experienced. Nothing must be forgotten. Nothing.

Chapter 39

Amaryllis thought she had never seen such commotion as the hustle and bustle in front of Crossly Oaks. Servants loading various trunks, parcels, and baggage into and on top of the coaches jostled one another as they scurried around between the seven coaches drawn up in the circular drive. Riding horses, made nervous by all the flurry, neighed and pranced, kicking up wisps of dirt. The coach horses, held in check by groomsmen, did little more than bob their heads as distracted maids counted portmanteaus and food hampers.

Other than Godwin and Mary's coach, which would simply take them back to Glenwood House once goodbyes were made, the coaches would be setting off in four different directions. She and Reggie would head north, Selena, her aunt and cousins would go east, Esmeralda, accompanied by Lord Rotherby, would go south, and Mistress Mead, Juliet and her husband, and Sir Cyril, would go west. Tabitha and Charlie accompanying Sir Cyril.

Saying goodbye to her young siblings after all they had been through brought tears to Amaryllis's eyes, but she blinked them away. Did they see her cry, they might get upset and be too fearful to leave her. Even now, instead of playing one last time with their new friends, they clung to her skirts. Juliet stood nearby. She had Fate on a leash, and the little black-and-white dog stayed close by her feet. The dear little fellow. He seemed confused and perhaps a bit worried someone might step on him as they raced here and there.

So many goodbyes had been made, everyone promising to write, promising they would visit. Sir Cyril and Reggie made plans to meet at Churlwood in mid-autumn. Sir Cyril would bring the children there. The visit to Churlwood would give him the opportunity to check on how the new steward was performing his duties. "Not that your father's able solicitors will not be looking in on him," Sir Cyril said. "All the same, best the steward and the household staff know Charlie's interests are being monitored."

After a short stay at Churlwood, she, Reggie, and the children would travel on to Rygate that Amaryllis could meet Reggie's parents. "Did we not have much that needs doing at Ardenstrath to get the house up and running and make it a suitable home for Tabitha and Charlie," Reggie said, "I could wish we could go sooner to meet my parents, but that is not to be, and Uncle Nate has said he will put my father's mind at rest."

Amaryllis was glad of the delay. Lady Rotherby had assured her she would love Reggie's parents, and they her, all the same, after meeting so many of Reggie's family, she was happy to have a bit of a respite before meeting more, especially his parents.

"Well, now, Tabitha and Charlie," Selena said, joining them, and squatting down on her haunches to be on the children's level. She was wearing a form-fitting riding costume rather than the breeches she preferred, but the gown in no way stopped her from behaving as though she was dressed in men's attire. "What a wondrous adventure you are going to have!" she exclaimed, excitement in her voice. "How I wish I was going with you instead of to Whimbrel Hall. You do promise me you will take good care of Fate."

"Oh, yes," Tabitha said, at last releasing her hold on Amaryllis's skirt to turn to Selena. "We will take very good care of him." She looked up at her aunt. "Aunt Juliet says when we get to her house, she knows a very nice surgeon who will look at Fate's leg and see if his brace can come off. I know he will be happy to have it off."

"You are right. He will be able to run and jump and have so much fun with you and Charlie." Selena cocked her head and looked at Charlie. "But he will need lots of love."

"Oh," the little boy said, he too now releasing his hold on Amaryllis to join Selena. "I already give him lots of love."

"I do, too," Tabitha said, not to be outdone by her brother.

"That is wonderful. Now you must remind your grandfather that he must write me and tell me how Fate is doing. You will not want me to worry."

"No," Tabitha said. "We will make sure Grandfather writes."

"Good, now here comes Betty," Selena said, encircling an arm around each child and drawing them to her that she could give each a kiss on the cheek. "Is it not delightful she is going with you. Not only will she be nursemaid to Charlie, but until you have a governess, Tabitha, Betty can work with you on your letters and numbers. How lucky you both are."

Selena made their visit with their grandfather sound so natural and such fun. Amaryllis wished she had been able to be as persuasive with her siblings. Selena had turned their mournful little faces to cheery ones.

Amaryllis noted Betty had been saying goodbye to Bess and to Esmeralda, but she had also spent time talking to Bernard Nye. Reggie's valet seemed completely healed from the injuries he received when the tree fell on him, and he would again be riding at Reggie's side when they set off for Ardenstrath. Having watched Betty and Nye together on other occasions, Amaryllis suspected the two had formed an attachment. She approved of it. Nye was so stable and Betty so bright and gregarious. She believed they would be well-suited to one another.

Sir Cyril joined them at the same time Betty arrived. "Ah, my gel," he addressed Amaryllis, "you must finish your goodbyes. We have a long ride ahead ere we reach our evening's destination. I wish not to be traveling after dark."

Amaryllis nodded, and Betty said, "I am ready, Sir Cyril. I have checked and double-checked the children's luggage. We have games, and clothes, and some tasty biscuits do we get hungry afore we stop for the lovely picnic Mary's cook packed for us."

His dark eyes merry, he looked down at Tabitha and Charlie. "And how about you two? Are you ready to go give your grandmother the greatest thrill of her life?"

"Of course they are," Selena answered for them when their little faces started to pucker with uncertainty. "They know how excited their grandmother will be to get to see them again. Poor dear. Amaryllis says she has not seen them since Charlie was a wee new born baby." Standing, she added, "Do give your sister a big hug and kiss while I bid my little Fate farewell. I would not release him to anyone's care but the two of you."

Amaryllis went down on her knees, not bothering that she was spoiling her gown, to gather her siblings into her arms. Again fighting tears, she hugged them close then pulled away to look at the two of them. "As Selena says, you will have great fun with your grandfather and grandmother, but promise me you will not let them spoil you inordinately."

Both, their lower lips trembling, shook their heads.

"No, Ryllis, we will not get spoiled. But you will come to Churlwood to get us, will you not?" Tabitha asked.

"Oh, darlings, of course I will. How could you think otherwise? Reggie and I will have Ardenstrath all ready for you when you move in with us. Now, come, I will help you into the coach." With Selena, Betty, Juliet and Juliet's maid following them, Amaryllis led the children to the coach at the head of the line of coaches. The children were to sit beside their aunt, Betty and the maid would sit opposite.

After all were in the coach, Selena placed Fate on his blanket on the flooring. "There you go little friend," she said. Perking up his ears and wagging his tail as he always did whenever Selena paid him any attention, the dog licked her hand. "I will miss you, but I know you will be well cared for." She looked up at the coach occupants. "Goodbye to all of you. Safe journey, and I hope I shall see all of you again before the year is out."

Working to keep her voice under control, Amaryllis echoed Selena. Just when she thought her heart would break at the parting, Reggie was at her side, his arm possessively around her waist. He issued a hearty goodbye, and promised Tabitha and Charlie he would take good care of their sister, and that he would have rooms all ready for them come fall.

"We must be going," Sir Cyril said, stepping forward to close the coach door. He then motioned to the coachman to drive on. The Stoke coach was followed by the smaller Rotherby coach carrying Mistress Mead and a young maid, and the coach was followed by the two Rotherby outriders. Sir Cyril gave both Amaryllis and Selena hugs, beckoned to a groomsman to bring him his horse, and with a wave to Lord and Lady Rotherby, he mounted and set out after the coaches. His son-in-law, David Stoke, trailed by his valet, joined him. Glancing over his shoulder, Sir Cyril called, "Ansel, Ewen, let us go."

Looking at Amaryllis in a way that caused her to blush, Ewen chuck-

328

led and slapped Reggie on the back. "Lucky man you are, cousin," he said before giving Selena a hug and a promise that he would be seeing her in month or so. He expected it to take him some time to get his sister home. "Roads to the west being what they are, and Flavia not liking to travel and needing a rest every couple of hours." Then he and Ansel mounted their horses and galloped off after Sir Cyril.

"Fear not, my love," Reggie said. "Tabitha and Charlie will be fine. They have a loving aunt to console them and a loving grandfather to give them treats. Now, come make your goodbye to my uncle and aunt."

Glad to have something to occupy her so she would not burst into tears, Amaryllis let Reggie lead her over to his aunt and uncle. Esmeralda was already in the D'Arcy coach. She would be riding alone until they stopped at Toms's to pick up the injured footman, Handle. Amaryllis would ever be grateful to Esmeralda for her help with Tabitha and Charlie. She hated saying goodbye to all the D'Arcy staff. They had been so courteous to her and had all fought so bravely to protect Charlie. She owed them much, and once she received her dowry, she meant they should be substantially rewarded.

But saying goodbye to Selena was the hardest. "My dear friend, never, never can I thank you enough for seeing our need and rescuing us. Please, try not to let them change you too much. Reggie and I and Tabitha and Charlie and little Fate, we love you as you are."

Selena laughed her tinkling laugh. "How I wish you had been about when Mother made me promise I would learn to be a lady. But now I must mount up. Uncle Nate is to ride with us as far as Derby that he may give his regards to Aunt Rowena's brother before he continues on his way. I will write as soon as we reach Whimbrel."

Amaryllis hugged her, clung to her a moment, then released her that her brother could give her a hug. Mister Nye gave Selena a mount up as Reggie gave hugs to his aunt and uncle and cousins. Amaryllis hugged Cecily and Brilliana and again thanked them for their help at thwarting Ledeen and saving Charlie. Then before she could blink the tears from her eyes, the D'Arcy coach and the Rotherby coach were pulling away from the house. Selena waved, then leaned over to say something to her uncle. He laughed, and together they sprinted off, passing up the coaches and racing up the road.

"Well, none left but us now," Reggie said. "Let us make our goodbyes and be on the road. If we are to retire early this evening, we must arrive in time for supper." He gave her a look that set her pulse to racing. Yes, best they get started.

Goodbyes and thanks were made to Mary and Fonda and their husbands. Promises to visit as soon as they had Ardenstrath in order were made. Bess and the Churlwood maids climbed into the coach, and after more hugs and promises, Reggie handed Amaryllis up. Once seated, her skirts arranged comfortably, she smiled at her husband, and he closed the door. As the coach pulled away, she leaned out the window to wave to both Crossly couples standing on the steps.

Finally she leaned back against the cushioned seat. She enjoyed being back in the Churlwood coach. It might not have glass windows, and it might not be as well sprung as the D'Arcy coach, but it was familiar, and that was somehow comforting. She liked that she could look out the window and see Reggie. She was glad they could easily reach Ardenstrath before nightfall for they had no outriders, and but one footman. Not that she was worried. They would be traveling a major, and busy, highway according to Godwin. In recent years, he had heard of no attacks on the road from Derby to Nottingham, and Ardenstrath was but a few miles out from Nottingham.

She was again wearing a mourning gown. Reggie said he thought she looked lovely even in black. "Naught can hide your beauty," he said with a kiss to her nose, but donning the dark outfit after wearing Selena's colorful apparel had been a bit daunting. Well, she owed her father this form of respect. She had loved him dearly, and he had left her well-provided for. Her yearly stipend would enable them to make whatever changes they deemed necessary to ensure their comfort at Ardenstrath.

Sighing, she closed her eyes. She wanted to relive her wedding day. And her wedding night. And she wanted to envision the coming night. They would be settling into their marriage bed. Their children would someday be born in that very bed. Her life, that had seemed so dreary after the loss of her father, now seemed so wondrous. What surprises it might hold, she could not fathom, but with Reggie at her side, she had no fear of the future. As Fate had brought them together, so they would forever be bound in an endless love.

The End

Look for my Next Novel!

Excerpt from

And The Ground Trembled

Chapter One

London, England 1681

Elizabeth D'Arcy could not remember when she had last been so excited. Her stomach fluttered and her pulse danced a jig. She had been presented to Queen Catherine the previous morning, and this afternoon she would be attending a ball where King Charles was certain to be in attendance. She had heard many tales of his attraction to pretty women, and her Aunt Phillida had warned her not to flirt with him should she catch his eye. Even so, she had hopes the monarch would ask her to dance. She wanted to tell him how as a child she had thrilled to tales of his heroism and his daring escape from the treacherous roundheads. She thanked God he had survived to return to England as the rightful heir to the throne.

She had heard too many horror stories of the joyless life under the Commonwealth and Cromwell's rule to ever want to experience life without their merry monarch. She had been born in sixty-one, the year after the Restoration, but two of her brothers and several cousins had been born during the years of the harsh Puritan constraints. Her father and uncles, strong supporters of the King, had been amply rewarded for their devotion to King Charles.

"Elizabeth, you dawdle. 'Twill not do to be late. I have no wish to offend the King."

"Yes, Aunt Phillida." Elizabeth tried to stand still as her serving girl, taking great care not to muss her hair, helped Elizabeth slip the skirt of her gown over her head. Elizabeth's dark hair, pulled starkly back from her face, cascaded about her shoulders in a mass of finger-size ringlets, but tiny curls clustering about her forehead softened the severity of the coiffure. While her maid attached the skirt to the gown's bodice, Elizabeth licked a finger and ran it over her eyebrows. She had plucked them so they formed perfect arches over her blue-green eyes. Lastly, she bit her lips and pinched her cheeks to heighten their color. She wanted to use red ochre to redden her lips and kohl to darken her eyelids, but her aunt had forbidden the use of such embellishments.

"Your own youthful beauty enhances you more than any fake ornamentation. However, you are welcome to wear some of my rose water. I think in the crowd, we will need it."

Elizabeth glanced into the parlor at her aunt. She was instructing her maid to have their beds turned down and fires in the hearths upon their return. With another furtive look, Elizabeth pulled the puffed sleeves of her gold silk bodice lower on her shoulders. Tucking her red gauze pelisse about her shoulders, she hoped her aunt would not notice she was displaying more of her bosom than she might deem appropriate.

Getting anything past her aunt's watchful eyes was never easy, all the same, she loved her aunt almost as much as she loved her mother. She should. She had been fostered with her and Uncle Berold since she was ten. She understood the practice of sending adolescents to relatives to be educated. Parents were seldom strict enough with their own beloved children. Her mother and father were seldom able to deny her anything, especially after the deaths of her two older sisters. She had learned that early in her life – long before she had been sent to Aunt Phillida's.

The practice was growing less common. Her younger brother, Garrett, had not been sent from home. Her parents hired a tutor for him until he turned twelve. They then engaged a seaman to train him to sail so one day he might captain his own ship. Her brother loved the sea, and as he would inherit no properties, seafaring would provide him with an honorable mode of support.

Elizabeth wished a girl's education could be more like a boy's, except for having to learn Greek and Latin. But learning about the world, its history and geography – that she had always thought she would enjoy. Then to go on the Grand Tour and travel around Europe. How thrilling! But no. Girls were trained in the social graces and how to manage a household.

Elizabeth feared she had not been the most responsible student. She loved the dancing, archery, riding, and especially the music – she could play the lute quite well, and all said her singing was lovely – but oh how she had hated the needlework, the nursing, and the household chores, in particular butter churning and making soap. Aunt Phillida insisted she must know how to do all these chores, including bed making and serving at the table, in order to properly train and supervise her servants when one day she would be the lady of her own household.

At least she had had the comradeship of her cousin. Flavia, two years her junior, had often conspired with her to escape the drudgery of their tasks. They would hide out with Flavia's brother, Ewen, and go fishing or hunting. Ewen taught them to swim, though he received a bottom tanning from Uncle Berold when they were discovered. Ewen was Elizabeth's age, and she guessed he would have preferred the company of other boys had any been fostered with them, but sadly for him, he had but his sister and his cousin to offer him companionship.

She would enjoy having her cousins with her now. What great fun they could have. But Flavia was headed home for a visit with her parents. And for the past four years, Ewen had been at Oxford. His father wanted him properly educated to assume management of the three manors he would one day inherit.

Elizabeth knew she had been brought to King Charles' court to find a husband, but what she wanted was adventure. And love. She wanted to find a man she could love as her Aunt Phillida loved Uncle Berold and as her mother loved her father. Of course, she wanted to be loved in return. Her father, the Earl of Tyneford, had sent three suitors to court her at Harp's Ridge Hall, Uncle Berold's primary residence, but she had not been taken with any of the three. The first, a boy two years her junior with a pimply face and dirty hair, had been shy and rather sweet, but he had certainly not set her heart to cart wheeling even if he was in some way she could not remember, related to the King.

The second suitor, heir to two Earldoms, had been in his mid-twenties and in appearance, she had found him fair to look upon, though he was a tad on the stocky side. However, she had discovered he had a cruel streak. She had seen him slap a serving girl and use his whip on one of the stable boys. When she told Uncle Berold about his behavior, young Lord Macon had been hastily, if politely, asked to leave.

Her third suitor, the Viscount Abercar, she had actually liked. She even allowed him to kiss her, but no trumpets blared, no goose bumps clamored up her arms, she had felt no flush of exhilaration. After the kiss, she looked up into the Viscount's genial blue eyes. "Lord Abercar, felt you the ground shake?"

Smiling at her, he shook his head. "No, I felt no such tremor."

She frowned. "Nor did I." She thought him quite handsome for an older man. Surely he was in at least his mid-thirties, but he looked to be fit, no paunchy stomach or spindly legs. She had no idea what his hair might be like for he wore a wig. He could have had his head shorn. He had a strong chin and delightful crinkles about his eyes when he smiled. And she knew him to be a fine horseman. They had been out riding several times. But she could in no way believe herself to be in love with him, or he in love with her.

"Does it matter?" He brought her attention back to the kiss. "I mean, that the ground failed to shake?"

"I know you will think me silly, but yes, it matters to me."

He took her hand in his. "My dear, sweet Lady Elizabeth, I do believe we would deal well together, and that we could build a happy enough life for ourselves. Yet I cannot fault you for wanting the ground to shake. In my youth I had such hopes myself."

She thought he looked sad. He had looked past her, almost as if he was seeing someone else. She wondered if he had once loved someone and then lost her. His eyes came back to hers and his bright smile returned. "I shall tell my grandfather that you are most charming, but that we failed to suit. He will be disappointed, as he was a great friend of your father's father, and he hoped to unite our families. However, he has survived many other disappointments, he will survive this. Now, I should go find your uncle and tell him I plan to depart on the morrow.

So Abercar had departed. And here she was in London, on her way to the King's ball. Matching her stride to her aunt's, she glanced out of the corner of her eye at the beloved woman's profile. Elizabeth thought her Aunt Phillida, though in her mid-fifties, was still a handsome woman. Her dark hair tinged with strands of gray, parted down the middle and pulled starkly back from her high forehead, was not softened by curls as was Elizabeth's, but her clean straight jaw line and high cheek bones combined with a slim straight nose and curvaceous mouth gave her a regal, yet winsome appearance.

"Step lively child," Aunt Phillida said as they hurried out a side door and down the covered passageway that connected the residence where their lodgings were located with Whitehall Palace. They were staying at her Uncle Ranulf's apartment suite. It consisted of a parlor, a dining chamber, and three bedchambers with adjoining servants' closets, but meals had to be ordered from a central kitchen on the ground floor that served all the apartments in the building. Her uncle, a favorite of the King's from their days together in exile, made frequent command visits to London, so he kept his own rooms close by the palace. Soon immersed in a throng of people hurrying into the already crowded Banqueting Hall, Elizabeth and her aunt locked arms that they would not be separated. People of varying social rank and title, all dressed in their most resplendent attire, all hoping to be noticed by the King or at least by one of his minions, pressed in through the wide doorway.

"Close your mouth, Elizabeth, you look all agog," Aunt Phillida hissed, and Elizabeth dutifully snapped her mouth shut, a flush creeping up her face. She did not want to be thought a bumpkin, yet she had never imagined such splendor nor such a host of people. She could not help but be impressed with the beautiful tapestries and the carved and inlaid paneling, the lifelike statues on tall marble pedestals, and the velvet draperies patterned with silver and gold threads. But the ceiling murals and huge hanging candelabras near took her breath away. And the gowns on the women – vibrant in incredible hues of greens and blues, oranges and reds such as she had never before seen. The fabrics were as astounding, bombazine blends of silk and wool, elaborately designed damask, deep-piled velvets, brocades, satins, fine cambric linen, and gossamer lawn linen. She was in awe.

Aunt Phillida took her elbow and directed her to a less crowded area. "How anyone is going to find room to dance is what I am wondering," Aunt Phillida said with a shake of her head. "I had forgotten how much I dislike court life, or I would have never allowed your father to press me into bringing you here."

Elizabeth knew her aunt had acquiesced because Elizabeth's mother was too infirm to accompany her daughter to London. Years of consumption had sapped her strength. Thoughts of her mother momentarily dampened Elizabeth's spirits, but she pushed the thoughts aside. Her mother would be pleased did she find a husband, and that she intended to do.

"Why you could not have found a husband close to home as my Vivien did, is beyond my understanding," Aunt Phillida said, and Elizabeth smiled, and giving her aunt's arm a squeeze, said, "Vivien, and Timandra, too, are fortunate to have found wonderful and loving husbands. I will count myself fortunate do I but find a man I can love as my cousins love their husbands. Of course that man must love me as their husbands love them. I could ask for nothing more."

Aunt Phillida returned her smile and patted her hand. "You will find such a man. I but hope you find him quickly. We have been here little more than a week, and I am ready to return to Harp's Ridge." She brought her scented lace hanky up and fluttered it under her nose. "I do believe some of these people have not bathed all winter. I cannot understand why His Majesty fails to command his subjects to bathe regularly."

Elizabeth shared her aunt's disgust with the odor of unwashed bodies in the too compact space, but it seemed a minor annoyance in comparison to the excitement that filled the air. She watched the people bowing and nodding to friends and acquaintances while she looked around in the hope of spotting the only person of her age she had thus far met. She and her aunt had been so busy with fabric selections, fittings, and sightseeing that she had had little time for socializing except with a couple of Aunt Phillida's friends who were once ladies in waiting to the queen.

Elizabeth was not surprised when she finally caught sight of her new friend backed up against a wall and almost disappearing into the drapery. Annis Blanchard was small, exquisite, and timid. Elizabeth first met Annis when she had come across her crying in a doorway of a dark secluded corridor. The girl had eluded her guardian in her need to seek solace away from prying eyes. Elizabeth, returning with her maidservant from a fitting, had heard the heart-wrenching sobs. Sending her serving girl back to their rooms, she tried to console the youthful maiden whom she at first mistook for a child, so small was she.

"Are you lost," she asked. Certainly since her arrival in London, Elizabeth had already turned down several wrong passageways in the maze of buildings that surrounded Whitehall Palace. She could understand how getting lost could be terrifying to a youth. But the girl shook her head and cried harder. "Well, all the same, I must insist you come back to my rooms with me. 'Tis not safe for you to remain here in this lonely corridor." She took the girl's arm and urged her toward her lodgings. Only when the girl looked up from the handkerchief she had had pressed to her face had Elizabeth realized she was a young woman near her own age.

Once back in the parlor, Elizabeth, after asking her maidservant to bring them some wine, convinced her aggrieved guest to sit beside her on the only modern piece of furniture in her uncle's lodgings, a blue tufted couch. Every other piece of furniture from beds to dining table dated back to the Restoration and was of heavy, durable oak. Having coaxed out her guest's name, Elizabeth learned between sobs and hiccups that Annis was being forced into a marriage she could not endure.

Elizabeth was indignant. "Why do you not refuse to marry the fiend?"

Annis pushed back a lock of her golden hair and turned her lovely tear-stained face up to look at Elizabeth. Her vibrant blue eyes were still brimming with tears and her moist golden lashes sparkled in the candle light. "I cannot refuse to marry him," she answered, her bow-shaped mouth curving downward as a teardrop slid off the side of her dainty little nose. "King Charles himself has given his approval of the jointure."

As they sipped their wine, Annis calmed enough to relate her tale. Her parents had died when she was but a year old. She had been raised by her grandfather. Now he too had died. Ever a loyal supporter of the

King, her grandfather had lost a portion of his landholdings during Cromwell's reign. Though those holdings had not been restored to him when King Charles returned to the throne, her grandfather had borne the King no ill will. However, he had never forgiven the man, who by trickery, had taken his land. It was that man Annis was now expected to marry. A man near old enough to be her grandfather. In marrying Annis, her grandfather's sworn enemy would take control of the remainder of her grandfather's wealth and landholdings.

Incensed, Elizabeth assured her new friend she would help her find a way out of her terrible dilemma. What she would do, she had yet to determine, but she did not believe any woman should be forced into an unwanted marriage. After all, this was the seventeenth century. They were no longer living in a barbaric society. She had asked her Aunt Phillida's advice, but her aunt had told her she must not meddle in court intrigues, especially if the King was involved. So she was on her own to think of a solution. And she would, she knew she would.

Biography

Celia Martin is a former Social Studies/English teacher. Her love of history dates back to her earliest memories when she sat enthralled as her grandparents recounted tales of their past. As a child, she delighted in the make-believe games that she played with her siblings and friends, but as she grew up and had to put aside the games, she found she could not set aside her imagination. So, Celia took up writing stories for her own entertainment.

She is an avid reader. She loves getting lost in a romance, but also enjoys good mysteries, exciting adventure stories, and fact-loaded historical documentaries. When her husband retired and they moved from California to the glorious Kitsap Peninsula in the state of Washington, she was able to begin a full-fledged writing career. And has never been happier.

When not engaged in writing, Celia enjoys travel, keeping fit, and listening to a variety of different music styles.

Visit my web site at:
cmartinbooks.kitsappublishing.com

CPSIA information can be obtained
at www.ICGtesting.com
Printed in the USA
FSHW012011100620
71105FS